A BOSSY ROOMMATE

JOLIE DAY

A Bossy Roommate © Copyright 2024 Jolie Day

Copyright notice: All rights reserved under the International and Pan-American Copyright Conventions. No part of this book may be reproduced or transmitted in any form or by any means, electronic or mechanical, including photocopying, recording, or by any information storage and retrieval system, without permission in writing from the publisher, except in the case of brief quotation embodied in critical reviews and certain other noncommercial uses permitted by copyright law.

This is a work of fiction. Names, places, characters and incidents are either the product of the author's imagination or are used fictitiously, and any resemblance to any actual persons, living or dead, organizations, events or locales is entirely coincidental. The author acknowledges the trademarked status and trademark owners of various products referenced in this work of fiction. The publication/use of these trademarks is not authorized, associated with, or sponsored by the trademark owners.

Warning: This story contains mature themes and language.

A Bossy Roommate; Jolie Day

info@joliedayauthor.com

Cover Design: ARP Book Covers

ISBN: 9798344709833

For all the girls seeking a man who breaks their bed, not their heart—this one's for you.

1
CARTER

I open my eyes to near darkness.

My mind shuffles through the haze, taking in unfamiliar surroundings as I attempt to figure out my location. Motel room. Sketchy area.

I glance over at the nightstand to check the time.

4:56 a.m.

Way too early to be awake for most. But for me, it's all part of my routine. Wake up early, work out, have my protein shake, jerk off in the shower, spend five minutes enjoying my morning coffee, then off to work.

Today's going to be a little different.

I run my hand down my face, feeling naked tits against my arm. Brief flashes of smooth skin, eager lips, and warm thighs cloud my mind. I look over to find yesterday's conquest fast asleep.

I met her at the most unexpected place.

It was precisely 9:41 p.m. when I stopped to get gas in Wakefield, Bronx.

The cool blast of air-conditioning hit me when I pushed open the door to the small, somewhat dingy-looking place. It was a welcome relief from the humid summer night outside. I strode inside, black helmet in hand, my boots clanging against the floor. The rich scent of ice cream reached my nostrils, but there was nothing about it that piqued my interest.

"Black coffee, please," I said, my voice a little hoarse from the long drive after meeting a potential client outside of town.

Without so much as a tired nod, the elderly barista stopped cleaning the counter to fill a mug with steaming hot coffee and slid it to me. As I took in my surroundings, I noticed that all the chairs had been stacked except for two at a small table in the corner. It seemed like the place was going to close soon. I headed over and took the empty seat.

Just when I pulled out my phone and started scrolling through my emails, the bell above the door chimed.

Glancing up, I noticed a young woman walking in. Her thin orange sundress fluttered around her legs. Long ebony hair was pulled up into a knot. She looked around the counter, her eyes wide with excitement. It was almost cute.

She asked the barista if they had cupcakes (they didn't), and while he was cleaning, she cross-examined him with a million questions about each of their remaining ice cream flavors. His curt answers didn't seem to bother her. Instead, she kept smacking her lips as if trying to taste the flavors before even ordering. Finally, she chose a triple scoop of something that had a brighter color than the flickering neon sign outside. I shook my head, refocusing on my phone, wondering how anyone could pick something with that much artificial food coloring.

Next thing I knew, she was making her way over to me, her heels click-clacking loudly, her cone threatening to topple over with each step.

"Excuse me," I heard her say happily. "This seat taken?" With one quick glance, I took in her features. Red toenails, legs for days, wide hips, bouncy tits. Her lips were painted a nude color, while her green eyes stood out against a brownish eyeliner, drawing my gaze toward them.

"Go ahead," I grumbled. "I'm about to leave."

Instinctively, I scooted away to avoid any accidental collisions with the cone, already irritated by her humming and the sweet smell of her ice cream. Why would anyone need that much sugar in their system?

"Do you come here often, on your bike?" Sitting down, she pointed to my black helmet, droplets of melting ice cream dribbling onto the table.

I leaned even further away. "Not really. Just passing through."

"Yeah, my first time in the Big Apple too. Just arrived, staying in a small but adorable motel nearby. My new apartment is about one hour across town, but it won't be available until tomorrow afternoon. That's why I'm staying here for the night." She crossed her legs and raised an eyebrow. "Black coffee, huh?"

I nodded, taking a sip. She was still looking at me when I put the cup back down on the table. "Yeah, not into the sweet stuff," I answered, my gaze trained on my phone.

"Well, I guess that means you're not sweet enough for me."

When I glanced back up, there was a smirk, a playful glint in her eyes.

Meeting my gaze, she moved the melting ice cream cone to her mouth. I anticipated that she would indulge in a—boringly clichéd—ice-licking motion while savoring her triple scoop.

Instead, she folded her lips over her teeth and slowly bit into her ice cream. Then she sucked it in with a loud *slurp*.

I found the sound incredibly irritating.

"*Fenfitivefeeth*, *ouch, ouch*," she mumbled. She scrunched up her face, wiggled her head, then closed her eyes, and finally swallowed. "Oooh my gosh...ohh, this is amaaazing," she moaned softly.

"It is?" I asked, thinking the sugar rush was going to hit her hard.

She opened her eyes. "You should try some."

"No, thanks, I'm good with my coffee."

She persisted, holding the cone out toward me.

I shook my head. "Really, I'm good."

"Let me guess. You never indulge, you never do anything forbidden, anything fun. You prefer to stay strong and focused, not wired on sugar."

She waved the cone, still offering me a bite. "Last chance. What? You worried it'll kill you?"

That was when the cone toppled over and dropped directly into my coffee, splattering the ice cream and the contents of my cup all over the table. A few small droplets landed on my dress shirt, but the dark gray fabric concealed any mishap. Luckily, I'd left the coordinating tie with lighter patterns I'd been wearing all day in my motorcycle case. My blue jeans got a few splashes—however, they were barely noticeable.

The young woman snort-laughed, catching me off guard, and then she grabbed a napkin. It was a full-bodied sound. She found it funny? What the fuck? "Oh, no, I'm so sorry! But bullseye!" She kept laughing and dabbing at the almost non-existent wet spots on my shirt. Something odd rippled through my chest.

"That'll teach you." She continued dabbing my pec. "Next time, just take a lick."

She didn't seem to take life too seriously. I didn't budge, letting her do her thing, watching her. What was a girl like her even doing here? She was still dabbing at my chest as I observed her green eyes, her hand proceeding to my arms, back to my pecs, wiping down my six pack, from there to my belly button, continuing to my belt, going lower toward my—

"*Whoops.*" She seemed to come to her senses and quickly moved her action away from my body to mop up the actual spill on the table.

Her cheeks were pinker. She released a giggle-snort.

I kept watching her.

"Well, that was a...sticky situation." She shrugged her shoulders, which were almost bare except for the thin straps of her dress, leaned over to put the drenched napkins to the side, and sat back down. "I'm pretty sure this means we're officially dating now." She crossed her legs, forcing the hem of her dress to ride up, revealing her smooth, creamy thigh and narrowing her eyes at me expectantly.

"Oh, are we?" I asked, sliding my phone into my pocket.

"Yep. When am I going to meet your family?"

"First, let me get you another one," I offered, about to raise my hand to the barista for a refill of her almost-empty cone (that she'd been holding on to during the whole thing. Obviously, she had priorities).

"No, thank you! I'm good. Maybe I should stick to coffee." She bit into her waffle cone and took a tentative slurp of the remains, savoring the flavor.

I glanced at my watch. "It's almost ten. This place is closing. I know a bar not too far from here."

"A bar? Are you asking me out for a drink? Just like that?" She grinned, looking up at me with those big bright eyes. "Well...that depends," she challenged, not giving me time to answer, taking another bite of her cone.

"On?"

"Depends on what you expect to happen if I agree."

I leaned closer. "No expectations. Only a guarantee."

"Which is?"

"That you're in for one hell of a ride."

A flush came across her cheeks, and her eyes grew huge at my suggestive invite. She swallowed. Her gaze was almost frozen on me, her grip loosening on what little was left of her waffle cone.

This was the moment I knew. There was no doubt in my mind that we were going to end up naked and sweating in the sheets.

"I could use a good ride." Those piercing green eyes pulled me in as she pushed the last bit of cone into her mouth.

A tidal wave of desire ricocheted through my being, straight down to my dick. "I bet you could."

"Not sure if it'll be fun though," she challenged, wiping her hands with a napkin.

"I'm a fun time."

She snort-laughed. "Is that so? Despite the non-existence of sweetness in your life?"

"Haven't had any complaints so far."

"Well, *Mr. Fun Time*, how about you buy me that drink, and we'll see where the evening takes us?"

We ended up sitting in a bar six blocks down. We drank, we talked, we danced, and about an hour later, I took her hand and escorted her outside to where my bike waited. Passing her my helmet and leather jacket, I settled into my seat. She hopped on the back without hesitation, her hot body pressed against me.

"*Finally*," she said when she wrapped her arms around my waist. "But when you said 'ride,' I had something else entirely in mind."

I revved the engine. "Don't worry, we'll get there."

Soon enough, I had her against my chest—naked and beautiful and wet—her curvy hips grinding against mine, her pert nipples against my pecs, her moans growing deliciously more desperate in my ear while we moved to the soft music playing from the motel room's small TV. The room was her suggestion—it was one she had rented. It was a sketchy place to say the least, with several lights out in the parking lot, but she seemed incredibly chill and optimistic about the whole thing.

I was too focused on the firecracker of a woman to care where we ended up, as long as there was a bed involved.

I GLANCE AT THE NIGHTSTAND.

4:59 a.m.

Seems like our marathon session has knocked her out good.

Her long hair fans out beneath her head like a halo. In the lowest of early-morning lights, I can make out more of her facial features. Soft cheekbones, delicate jawline, plump lips smeared with lipstick.

Still curled on her side and facing me, she barely moves, except for her soft breathing. The blanket has slipped to the bottom of the bed, allowing me to see the bare and tantalizing dip of her hips. Carefully, I grab the blanket and cover her sleeping body, my gaze following the movement of the bedspread along her naked curves. When I softly brush a loose strand of hair from her face, a sweet gasp escapes her lips.

The sound rings in my ears. Every whimper and moan plays on an endless rotation in my mind.

It was a memorable night, and when I made sure she was thoroughly satisfied, she passed out within seconds.

She'll still feel my cock inside her today, I'm sure about that.

Last night, I planned to sneak out after she fell asleep, but the bed was too inviting—despite the suspicious noises it started to make after one more round. I banked on the mixture of exhaustion and an active night to keep her sleeping long enough for me to make my escape in the morning.

Yeah, she's attractive. But our night together can't be more than a one-time thing.

It's easier that way. I don't have time for relationships. Anytime I've tried in the past, they haven't ended well. I prefer one-night stands. Fewer complications that way.

Quietly, I slide out of the uncomfortable bed.

A loud squeak cuts through the quiet, and my gaze darts to her.

There's not even a hint of movement from the young woman. With practiced silence, I slip into my clothes, one item at a time, casually checking on my bedmate.

Nothing. Just a little snore.

Good.

Dressed, I check the time: 5:05 a.m. I know I have to get out fast if I want to make it back home in time to start my morning routine. At the door of the motel room, helmet already in hand, I pause and look back at the bed. Her face is peaceful, and her chest steadily rises and falls with each breath.

"Thanks for the night," I whisper, before I slip out of the door, quietly closing it behind me.

2

EDEN
MONDAY MORNING

His clothes are gone. His helmet is gone. All that he left is the manly scent on his pillow.

Leather.

Musk.

A zesty hint of orange.

I shouldn't be surprised. I should have known the jerk wouldn't be here when I woke up. There was nothing about last night that made me think it was anything other than a one-time thing.

No kiss. Not even a peck.

It was just raw, filthy hot sex.

Still, I'm pissed to find the spot next to me empty. What a dick! He couldn't even stick around to say goodbye?

It's not like I was going to suggest we get breakfast and eat cupcakes or anything.

I've just arrived in New York City, all set to start a fresh chapter. I know I'm not the first girl to be left at the altar. But discovering your ex-fiancé wiped out your joint bank accounts? That's a new low, even by my standards. A girl can only take so much.

I'm over Rob. My ex.

Yet I can still see the church ladies exchanging whispers as they watched me standing there alone in my white dress, their gazes filled with pitying glances and outright stares. *Rude.* After what seemed like a gazillion years of waiting, I finally made my grand exit, sprinting like my gown had burst into flames, unable to face another living soul. Little did they know, in that very moment, a dream shattered within me.

I could have done without a grand wedding. Or an over-the-top cake. Or a gown straight out of a fairy tale. What had devastated and sent me spiraling into a deep abyss had been something else entirely. I believed Rob and I would grow old together. "'Til the end of all days" wasn't just a cliché to me—no, I really believed in it. Marrying the man who loved me unconditionally (and vice versa)—that's what I always dreamed of.

See? Now you know why I need a change. When I was offered an apartment to stay in, rent free, for six months, I jumped at the chance.

And onto *him*.

Carter Donovan.

That's what he introduced himself to me as.

In my defense—he was darkly handsome, and said all the words I desperately needed to hear. Honestly, it took *very* little convincing for me to invite him into my bed. I mean, really, why not go for it? If anyone deserved a night of crazy hot sex, it was me—or so I thought.

Now, gazing at the vacant bedside, all I wish is for the ground to open up and swallow me whole.

I haven't had sex like that in *months*. Actually, I don't think I've ever had sex like that. His hands, his mouth, his dirty words...just thinking about it is sparking a delightful flutter between my thighs.

It was on a whim that I met him, my one-night stand. Carter.

I had finished a nearly six-hour drive from my childhood home in Ellsworth, a small city in Maine, to NYC. It was dark by the time I arrived, but I still marveled at the city lights. With my apartment not ready until later today, I opted to spend the night in a cheap motel. Little did I know, my night was about to take a sweeter turn.

His presence? Breathtaking. Commanding. He owned the room without even trying. Broad-shouldered, dressed in a blend of rugged charm and sophistication, with black biker boots that screamed "I've seen some things." And that dark hair? Tousled just right, framing an unforgettable jawline—a jawline that clearly maintained a twelve o'clock shadow, regardless of how recently he had shaved. But what truly captivated me? His eyes, hidden behind long lashes, finally lifting from his phone.

I glance at the clock.

It's almost ten minutes before six. The last thing I want is to be late on my first day, and I need to get ready. I want to start my first day at work refreshed and motivated.

"At least I don't have to do the walk of shame," I say aloud, sitting up in the squeaky bed. "There's always a silver lining."

I refuse to dwell on some jerk ditching me.

Last night was a whirlwind of fun, a temporary escape from reality. Judging by the soreness between my legs, I'll definitely be thinking about it for a while—ouch!

What I won't think about is *him*. Today marks a new beginning.

It's all about moving forward and leaving the past where it belongs: in the rearview mirror. The thrill of finally being here, of finally having the chance to experience the Big Apple, is as strong as it was when I first made my decision. I'd always wanted to go to New York City, but Rob never shared my enthusiasm. Despite my numerous attempts, he consistently brushed off any plans I proposed for us. So, since he isn't in my life anymore, this is the perfect time to do what I've always dreamed of.

My sister, fifteen years my senior, thinks I'm crazy (which, to be fair, might have some merit), and refused to help me financially, not that I've asked her. I still have some pride. Also, it's not as though she has the financial capability, even if she had entertained the thought (which she did not).

"You have a job and life here," she said when I told her of my plans. "I don't see how running away to New York is going to change anything."

"I'm not running away," I insisted, easing her concerns by offering to help find a temporary replacement. "Just wait six months. I'll be back before you know it."

A Bossy Roommate

Having to go back to living with my sister in my childhood room after everything that had happened had been the worst part of the entire experience, worse than being left penniless. Following our parents' passing, my sister and her husband had moved into the small family home.

She held a deep dislike for Rob and had been vehemently against our relationship, and even more so, our marriage. I'd been too much in love to see what she had. Too blinded by love. I was so ready to be Rob's wife, to start a family with the man I loved. Until the rug had been pulled out from underneath me.

Seven years of my life—wasted on someone who never wanted the happily ever after with me. But amid the wreckage, thankfully, I made at least one smart decision. Before heading to NYC, I'd emailed an attorney for a free consultation. If she decides to take my case, it could mean a chance to reclaim at least some of my money. But deep down, I don't have high hopes. Until her reply, I'm determined to erase the damn scammer from my mind.

I'm not going to let him ruin my day.

And I'm not going to let my one-night stand ruin it either.

"I'm swearing off men for good." I get out of bed and stretch. "No more men. *Period*," I say, forcing myself to ignore the wobbliness in my muscles—muscles that had had the best workout last night. "Okay, not for good, of course, that's too dramatic. But for a very, *very, very* long time. Six months minimum!"

Six months. The time I plan to be in NYC before returning home.

This city, teeming with countless individuals, offers the perfect environment to sharpen my instincts, to become better at reading people. The fact that I misjudged Rob to such an extent has dealt a serious blow to my confidence. But I refuse to let it dampen my optimism. Six months away from home presents the perfect window for me to rebuild my self-esteem, regain my confidence, and return home prepared to join forces with my older sister.

I'm grateful that at least two kind souls in their seventies, Kate and her husband, Lewis, family friends of my late parents, reached out to me to offer support. They had been some of the first to RSVP to our wedding. After everything happened, I wasn't expecting to hear from anybody, so when they called and told me they felt at a loss for words over Rob's actions, it was a comforting surprise.

Despite his true nature, Rob is widely adored by people (save for my sister), but Kate and Lewis were compassionate enough to examine the situation more closely, especially in the aftermath of what occurred.

Lewis used his contacts in NYC to get me a job interview via phone with Legacy Builders, a prestigious construction firm in Manhattan that needed an administrative assistant. I hadn't been able to get out of my PJs for days, but thanks to Zoom, I was hired by HR anyway. But the real stroke of luck was when Lewis and Kate offered their already-furnished apartment for me to stay rent free, so long as I took care of the place. Apparently, the current resident, an older lady, had unexpectedly decided to move out on the tenth. And, as even more luck would have it, Kate and her husband weren't able to find anyone suitable to move in until my time there was over.

"You'd be doing us a favor. We'd rather it not sit empty," Kate said when they took me out to lunch to present the offer, and I insisted that I couldn't possibly say yes. "It's the least we can do. If you want it, it's yours."

"I don't know what to say." I was close to tears, emotional over their generosity. "I don't really have much…"

"We know," Lewis said. "Don't worry about rent. You need help until you get back on your feet, and we're more than happy to provide it."

He forced the spare key to the apartment into my hands.

And just like that, the stage for my comeback was set.

The motel I'm staying at is the only one within my budget. While it may not boast luxury, it offers comfort, affordability…and a truly unique experience.

"It's my time." I repeat the words I said to my sister as I squeeze toothpaste onto my brush. "I'm a bad bitch, and I'm going to show everyone—including myself—how a bad bitch bounces back after a bad breakup."

And I believe it with my whole heart.

"You do that." My sister had sighed in disbelief and pulled me into an unhappy hug.

It takes a while for the water to heat up in the shower, and even then, it's lukewarm. I don't mind. I find it refreshing, and it helps wash away any lingering headache. (Too much sugar yesterday.)

Selecting my favorite pencil skirt with an elegant light-blue button-up blouse, I get dressed. While my brown hair is still wet, I twist it and pin it up into a sleek bun.

Instinctively, I go to grab my necklace from my jewelry bag before I remember I don't have it anymore. Rob gave it to me on our first anniversary. After the whole altar-dumping-and-bank-account-clearing event, I took it straight to the pawnshop. That, and my engagement ring. The money I got from it had paid for my road trip. It feels weird not to have it after wearing it nearly every day for such a long time.

I leave my neck bare and put on a little foundation, a little mascara, and nude lipstick.

With my head held high and pride in every step, I execute my absolute *best* walk from the motel—far from any hint of a walk of shame. Confidence is key.

After throwing my stuff into Kiki's trunk (my beloved blue 2012 Kia Rio), I climb in and wince when my eyes land on the gas gauge—just over a quarter of a tank left. Hopefully I won't get stuck in morning traffic too long. I still need to find my way there, and in the evening, all the way to my new kick-ass NYC apartment.

After that, I'll figure something out.

With rock music blaring and me singing along to Destiny's Child's "Survivor," I plug my new work address into the GPS and peel out of my parking spot. The sun is warm, and the sky is the brightest blue I've seen in a while. No need to plead with Kiki's temperamental windshield wipers like I did the day before when an unexpected shower forced me to pull over and wait patiently until it passed.

Everything looks great. Sure, the traffic is terrible, and there are some daredevil drivers out here, but it gives me a chance to familiarize myself with the road and nearby businesses.

Unscathed by any obstacles, I reach the office building.

3

EDEN

*A*fter parking my Kiki in the large parking garage, I grab my purse. With excitement and first-day jitters, I get out of my car and follow the other people headed inside. The garage elevator takes us to the main lobby, and when I step out, the sight renders me speechless.

The atrium is *huge*. I've never seen an entry like this outside of a museum or church. With lofty ceilings and floor-to-ceiling windows along one side, I'm blown away by the stunning view. So much so that I have to remind myself to keep walking and stop acknowledging the constant soreness between my legs. An imposing receptionist desk dominates the center of the room, manned by a woman with a tight low bun of honey hair who looks like she means business.

When I approach, she offers me a bright smile. "Good morning. How can I help you?"

"Hi, I'm Eden Ryan. It's my first day, and I'm supposed to meet Gretchen…" The last name of the woman I'm supposed to ask for suddenly slips my mind. "Er…sorry, I forgot her last name. She's the head administrative assistant."

Noticing me flounder, the elegant receptionist chuckles, peering at me over the rim of her glasses. "I got you."

"Oh, okay, thank you."

"Why don't you have a seat over there, and I'll call Gretchen." She gestures to the left. "Welcome to Legacy Builders."

"Thank you," I say graciously. "I'm excited to be here."

I take a seat on one of the empty chairs, eyes wide as I observe the hustle and bustle around me. Even with it being early in the morning, the place is buzzing—just like the city around us. Any lingering nervousness is buried beneath my excitement. This is exactly what I've been looking for: the kind of fast-paced challenge I've been dreaming about. I'm sitting for less than a minute before a woman about ten years older than me, dressed in a form-fitting pantsuit, approaches me. Her makeup is flawless, and her blonde hair is pulled into a twisted knot like mine. The round red frames of her glasses complement the welcoming and approachable nature of her face and match her bright hair color perfectly.

"Eden?" she asks.

I smile and stand, extending my hand in greeting. "Yes, that's me. You must be Gretchen."

Gretchen shakes my hand. "I am. I'll be handling your training for the next week. I'm the administrative assistant to Mr. Huxley, the Executive Branch Manager-slash-CFO, as well as the supervisor to the other admin assistants."

"Wow, impressive." Her boss holds significant decision-making power here in NYC, positioned just below the CEO in the hierarchy.

"Thanks, I like to think so too." She chuckles and motions for me to follow her past the receptionist. "I've been here a long time. Stick with me and I'll show you the ropes."

I like her already. She has a cool confidence about her and a warmth that instantly puts me at ease. "Great. I have experience in the position, but this is definitely a bigger business than I'm used to." I don't get into any detail about how my admin experience stems from working for my sister's small mom-and-pop operation.

"Legacy Builders is one of the most prestigious construction firms in the city," Gretchen explains while we walk. "My boss, Mr. Huxley, is one of the senior partners. He's the only one who works out of the New York office. The CEO sits in Connecticut, and the others run the offices in Massachusetts and Vermont." Gretchen leads me to another set of elevators, and we step on as soon as the doors open. "So, is this your first time in New York?" she asks while the elevator climbs.

"Yes, it is. I just got in late last night."

"Well, I know it can be overwhelming. I've been here for years, and it still can be daunting at times. If you need anything, work related or otherwise, I'm right here."

"Thank you, I appreciate it."

The elevator stops at the 12th floor, and I follow Gretchen through a set of glass double doors. "In my interview with Human Resources I was told I was going to be the assistant to Mr. Bancroft," I explain. "I take it he's not one of the partners?"

"No, Mr. Bancroft isn't a partner yet. But he honestly should be. He's smart, and as our COO, he plays a key role in the company's strategic direction and handles most of the major jobs that come through." She leans in close and whispers, "Not to mention he's quite easy on the eyes."

I laugh softly. "At least that'll be something pleasing to look at."

She gives me a "Girl, you have *no* idea" smile.

We'll be best friends, I can already feel it.

Gretchen shows me the important office spaces, like the break room and bathroom. She also explains that Legacy owns the building from the 8th to the 12th floor and that I will rarely, if ever, have to visit any other floor than the one we're on.

"Simple enough to follow," she says.

"And zero danger of getting lost—hopefully," I joke, and her laughter joins with mine.

"That's the other assistants. I'll introduce you later." Gretchen waves back to two women as we pass through conference rooms and the sales floor. "You'll soon notice we assistants always stick together. If something comes up, we try to cover each other's shifts to keep things running smoothly. But otherwise, we exclusively work for the managers we're assigned to. This will be your desk..."

We step through a modern glass door. It's sleek and framed with brushed steel.

The sign reads:

Carter Bancroft
Chief Operating Officer

Huh, Carter?

Just like the first name of my one-night stand.

Except his last name was Donovan. Weird and also a twisted little joke from the universe. I hope that name isn't going to haunt me from now on like the memories of his touch will.

The glass door leads into a small lobby separate from everything else. In the middle of the room is a large mahogany half-moon desk. It doesn't face the open doorway, but rather a closed wooden door and three modern and comfortable-looking chairs.

"Whoa," I say when we approach. "This is the biggest desk I've ever worked at. And I get this space to myself?"

Gretchen nods with a smile. "It's great, isn't it? Please sit down. It gives you some semblance of privacy, which you'll need when managing Mr. Bancroft's appointments and meetings. His office is right through these doors." Gretchen points to the big, closed mahogany double doors across from us, then leans in and lowers her voice. "He likes things done in a very specific way, so you need to be on your toes...believe it or not, he's still using a small black book to keep track of his appointments, just like in the old ages. Luckily, the board stepped in and compelled him to embrace the efficiency of our new cutting-edge system...but I'll let him tell you himself."

"When will I get to meet him?" I sit down at the desk, sinking back into the high, comfortable office chair. There's a brand-new computer with two wide-screen monitors and a sleek black phone.

Gretchen adjusts her glasses and checks her tablet for the time. "Mr. Bancroft is in a staff meeting with the other managers right now, but they should be wrapping up soon. So, anyway, here is a folder with your login for the computer and the applications."

She spends the next few minutes walking me through the basics and showing me where to pull up the training videos I need to review. Being well versed in computers, familiarizing myself with all the programs I have to access is a breeze. Once she's satisfied I have retained everything, she gives me a warm smile.

"You're going to do great," she says. "Honestly, once you get the hang of things and know what he expects from you, it's fairly straightforward."

"Thanks for showing me the ropes."

"My pleasure. If you need help"—she points out the glass door to another one right across the hall—"I'm right through there. You can always wave me over. Or try the new in-house instant messenger, and I'll pop by."

"Ahem."

I hear a man clear his throat behind Gretchen.

She turns around. "Oh! Good morning, Mr. Bancroft. I was just getting your new assistant acquainted with our system."

The man steps around Gretchen.

I get up.

When I see the face of the well-groomed man, I nearly pass out.

Tall.

Six foot two.

Dark hair.

It's *him*. It's my one-night stand from last night! *Carter.*

Except, he told me his last name was Donovan, *not* Bancroft.

Shit, holy shit. I blink, twice, trying to keep my expression neutral and hide the utter surprise I feel, or worse, trying not to laugh at the coincidence.

My eyes connect with his.

Those whiskey-brown eyes that had looked at me with heat when he'd thrust into me last night are now hardened and cold.

He steps up to the desk and extends his hand. "Carter Bancroft," he says formally.

He glowers at me, his eyes never leaving my face.

I nod, wiping my sweaty hand on my skirt before I shake his. I can't believe this is happening. I can't *believe* I know what he—my new boss—looks like naked. What his thick dick looks like fully erect. Exactly how girthy, and long, and perfectly *filling* it is.

"Nice to meet you, Mr. *Bancroft*," I say, forcing myself not to add "again" at the end of the sentence. What I can't stop myself from, is emphasizing his last name. I have to remind him that he blatantly lied to me, and I know it.

The second our hands touch, more flashbacks from the previous night rush through my head. His fingers intertwined with mine as he hovered above me, pressing my hands into the bed. His jaw pressed against my cheek while he whispered those dirty, dirty words into my ear. His tongue playing with my clit, brushing over it, edging me to the brink of insanity. His hard cock filling me completely, utterly, *perfectly*—now *that* feeling is burned into my memory forever—and honestly, I'm still feeling him inside me physically, *right now*—and I have the hardest time not thinking about how jaw-dropping his thrusts felt.

Nor can I stop thinking about how that sinful dirty mouth of his fell open when he came.

I know what my boss's coming face looks like, I realize.

How his eyes intensified.

How they bore into me.

How he growled when he came, with a double "ahh." "*Ahh-ahhh.*"

How his cock pulsed.

How he thrust three more times.

Eden, think about something else, I scold myself. *Don't think about the fact that less than twelve hours ago, he made you come harder than any man has before, and as a sign of appreciation, you then rode your new boss's cock like a mechanical bull before he flipped you over and made you come again.*

"Remind me of your name again," he says.

Come again? Bitch. He did not.

Ouch. Gotta say, that one stings.

He isn't playing. That line definitely takes the wind out of my sails (and my mind off the mechanical bull). "Eden Ryan," I answer, trying to sound unaffected and professional. "I'm looking forward to working with you."

"*For* me," he corrects, glowering at me.

It takes me a blink to process what he just said.

Good lord, what a *bosshole*.

Do I really want to work *for* him?

This can only go downhill from here. But I need the job. Desperately. In fact, judging by his cold expression, I have to wonder if he even *wants* me to work for him. It seems more like he's contemplating when exactly to break it to me that I won't be working with him *nor* for him.

He turns his intense gaze on Gretchen. "Anything else? I'd like to speak with my new assistant."

Gretchen shifts her gaze between the two of us, almost as if she senses something is off. But she's smart enough not to point it out. "I am done, sir," she immediately retracts. "I'll be at my desk should either of you need anything."

I don't even get a chance to thank her before she hurries out of the room. As soon as the glass door closes behind her, Carter turns that stern gaze on me.

There's a beat of silence.

"Well," I say, trying to break the awkward taciturnity, but choosing my next words wisely. "This is...unexpected."

"Let's talk in my office. Now."

Without waiting for me to say anything else, he steps away and storms into his office. I follow him, in a less-than-stormy way. In fact, I follow him in a paralyzing "shit's gonna go down" way. I have no idea how he's going to react to this new development. This bitch needs the job and can't stand the thought of getting fired before she has even started. Though, I don't think he technically can fire me when I haven't done anything wrong *on the job*. Or can he?

A drop of nervous sweat runs down my spine. I watch him make his way behind his desk, all grumpy and stern, obviously getting ready to fire me.

"Shut the door," he orders, in that same impossible growl he used when telling me to behave, and that I looked so pretty while taking every inch of his cock.

I do as he demands.

As soon as the door clicks shut and I turn back around, I launch into a speech. "Before you say anything else, I swear I can convince you not to fire me. For one thing, you need an assistant, and I'm the perfect candidate for the job. I'm loyal, smart, driven, and desper...dependable, which is why HR hired me on the spot. Second, yesterday, you weren't technically my boss yet, so I don't think it really breaks any kind of ethical or company code. Third—"

"Eden," Carter growls sharply, holding up his hand to cut me off. "Stop talking. Sit."

I clamp my hands together while I sink onto the chair across from his desk. I thought my desk was huge. His is almost twice as big, and when he sits behind it, power and control radiate off him. It makes me think of how in charge he is all the time, just like last night, when he'd told me I was going to sleep with him before I'd even had a chance to process, and how later in the bar, he told me he was going to fuck me until I came *and* passed out from coming so hard before I had a chance to process that either.

Honestly, still processing that. Not going to think about how he then held true to his word.

My new boss watches me like a hawk before he speaks again, his voice more stern and deep than before. "Obviously, it goes without saying that I didn't realize who you were when we met last night."

Obviously, it goes without saying...?

"Obviously," I say, echoing the word back at him, annoyed at his choice of statement. "Given you told me your last name was Donovan... and you couldn't even remember my name."

He has the decency to wince, but it's slight, and I wouldn't have caught it if I wasn't staring intently at his annoyingly handsome face, and those annoyingly full lips that had been wrapped around my clit half the night.

"That wasn't a lie," he says simply. "Bancroft is my last name. Donovan is my middle name."

"Noted. So, what happens now?"

"What happens now is, you go back to your desk and go through your training. We move forward as if nothing has changed." He rests his folded hands on the desk. "We also keep what happened between us to ourselves. I don't want people to get the wrong idea."

"You and me both," I agree.

"No gossip in my department. Clear?"

"Trust me, it's hard enough being the new girl without people thinking I did *that* with my boss to get the job. It's best we forget it ever happened. It won't happen again."

"I'm glad we're on the same page," he says, turning to face his computer. "You're dismissed."

"Of course, Mr. Bancroft."

On shaky legs, relieved I survived and wasn't fired, I leave his office. Once out, I close the mahogany door behind me and lean against it for a moment.

Oh. My. God. What have I gotten myself into?

4
EDEN

I wish desperately for the rest of the day to go smoothly.

I don't have such luck.

After my world was thoroughly rocked by the fact that my hot, handsome, perfect one-night stand is now my stern, grouchy boss, I sit at my desk for at least two hours, trying to get through the training that's only one hour long. It's hard to focus, especially when I know *he* is in the other room. I slept with my new boss. All night. And now I have to pretend like I didn't, and everything is all hunky-dory.

Eventually, I get through the training videos, and am about to message Gretchen to ask her what I should focus on next, when Carter steps out of his office.

"When you're done with the training, there are some appointments I need you to enter into my calendar," he orders, placing a small black book in front of me. "The company has a new calendar and instant messenger system. Make yourself familiar with it. My appointments need to be synced with the calendar and the correct information, then color-coded. After you do that, you'll need to send a confirmation email for the meeting itineraries I've saved on my private drive. This must happen for each one. Whatever is on the calendar is what I will go by. If there are conflicts or change requests, you handle them yourself. If there are any urgent matters that require my attention, handle them to the best of your ability and only notify me if you cannot resolve them on your own. Never interrupt me unless it's absolutely necessary. Understood?"

His whole attitude rubs me the wrong way. Judging by his demeanor, you'd think he never got his cock sucked, let alone got laid. I don't know if he's being a jerk because we slept together or if that's just the way he works, but I'm taken aback. I've barely been here half the day, and he's already barking orders at me.

"I understand." I give him a curt nod. "I do have a question about some logistics. I know I'm only here six months and won't be taking any time off, but if something comes up—"

He cuts me off as he did earlier. "Not my problem. You'll need to find someone to cover your shift and leave me out of it."

"Noted," I say.

"Good. I'll be gone for the next hour. When I get back, we'll sit down in my office and go over day-to-day expectations. After that, you can have lunch."

Without another word, he walks out of the office.

A few seconds later, Gretchen pokes her head in. "How'd it go?" she asks.

"What a...!" I don't say it out loud, but she knows the word I have in mind: "dick."

Smothering her laugh, Gretchen steps into the lobby and approaches my desk. "He can be a handful," she whispers. "He knows what he wants and how he wants things done. You'll get used to it."

I want to explain that my evaluation includes more than our brief interactions this morning, but I don't. I agree with Carter that we need to keep what happened secret, and I'm trying very hard not to let it color my judgment of him.

"Did he give you an assignment already?" Gretchen wants to know.

"Yes. He wants me to update his calendar." I pick up the old-fashioned black book and open it to today. It's a peculiar quirk that a man like him would use an antique book to jot down his (confidential) appointments. "He also said I had to send confirmations to everyone."

"Okay, cool, no problem. I'll help."

Thank God for Gretchen. She walks me through the process, which is fairly straightforward. Once I get the hang of it, it's easy. She has to go back to her office, which leaves me to work in silence. It's too quiet. I think about listening to some music by Green Day, but I don't know if that would be appropriate, and I decide to hold off until I have a chance to ask Gretchen. It's Gretchen I'll ask, not Bosszilla. Bosszilla would definitely say no.

Bosszilla returns soon after. An older, sturdy gentleman accompanies him, and they're deep in conversation. I look up from my work to greet them, but neither gives me the time of day. They walk past as if I don't exist, disappearing into Carter's office. I know he said he wanted to meet with me, but I figure that will have to wait until he's done.

I've started to receive messages regarding his upcoming appointments as well as requests to reschedule time with him, which gives me something to work on while I wait. Around twenty minutes later, the door opens and Carter appears, showing the older man out.

"You'll see, Bancroft," the man says with that condescending tone older people tend to use when speaking to someone younger than them. "It'll be for the best. I've been in this business a long time. I know what is best for the company."

"I've also been in this business a long time, Huxley," Carter says with an edge to his voice I hadn't yet heard in that capacity and instantly recognize as annoyance. "Don't mistake my age for lack of experience."

Huxley waves him off and looks at me. "Oh, you must be Bancroft's new assistant," he says, all smiles—ignoring the hard look Carter gives him—and approaches my desk. "How do you do, young lady? My name is Saul Huxley, and I'm the senior partner in charge of this branch."

Oh, I recognize his name. He's Gretchen's boss. I stand to reach across and shake his hand. "Eden Ryan. It's nice to meet you, Mr. Huxley," I say with a smile.

"Now what is a bright, pretty young thing like you doing working for Bancroft?"

Oh. *Eww*. I get the feeling that he meant what he said as a compliment, but given that it's not 1950 and this is a workplace, I definitely don't take it that way. Also, if looks could kill, Carter's gaze would catapult him six feet under.

"I'm excited to have the chance to work at Legacy Builders," I say with a professional tone, but quickly turn my attention to Carter and hand him back his little black book. "I've entered all your upcoming meetings and sent confirmations."

"Quick and smart as a whip!" Saul Huxley praises, his gaze following the book as Carter tucks it away. "Don't let this assistant get away, Bancroft."

"Don't you have a meeting to get to?" Carter asks him.

Not six feet under. *Sixty* feet under.

"Too right you are! Have a good first day, Eden." Mr. Huxley shakes my hand again before he pulls away. "Bancroft, I'll talk to you later."

I watch him leave, and once he is out of earshot, I face Carter. "He seems like a character."

Carter ignores my comment. "Grab a notepad and come into my office."

Ever heard of the word "please?" I grab a pad and pen from one of the desk drawers I examined earlier and follow him. Once inside, I close the door.

"Besides keeping track of and scheduling my appointments, there are other things I'll need you to stay on top of," he says, moving to sit behind his desk. "People will always try to get around my schedule and force a meeting. I'm not seeing anybody who doesn't have an appointment. I don't care how important they say it is. No appointment, no meeting. Got it?"

I sit down and open my mouth to respond, but he keeps going, completely ignoring the fact that I was going to speak.

"Next, make yourself familiar with the pre-approved list of names and phone numbers, which are allowed to be transferred to my personal line," he continues. "If they aren't on the list, then you're to take a message. I'll need their first and last name, phone number, company, and title. Keep the message brief. I don't have time to read long blocks of text. No sales calls. Ever. I don't have the patience for them."

"What if they want to leave a voice mail?"

"Have you not been listening? Only those on the list."

My eyebrows shoot up, and I purse my lips to keep from talking back. *Bosshole.*

"You'll do well to memorize it," he adds.

Honestly, who the hell does he think he is spouting directions like this? I get that I'm his assistant, but that doesn't mean he can be so rude. What happened to the man I slept with? Sure, he hadn't exactly been a ray of sunshine when I approached him in the ice cream shop or later in my motel bed either, but *this*? This is unacceptable. "While we're speaking, I have some stipulations of my own." I speak up before he can continue.

It's his turn to hoick up his eyebrows. "I'm listening."

"Well...this is a two-way street, Mr. Bancroft. If we're going to work together and work together *well*, we should both respect each other's boundaries."

Carter studies me intensely as he leans back in his chair, steepling his fingers. "Go on."

Emboldened by his response, but also cautious of the fact that he's my boss and I need to tread carefully, I continue. "'Please' goes a long way, sir," I say. "Yes, I'm your assistant, and I'm here to help you with what you need, but I would hope you would show me enough respect to speak to me as if I'm a human being. I was hired because HR thought I could handle this position, and I know I can. Also, you don't need to worry about me not understanding your directions. I'm a quick learner."

"I have no doubt." Carter folds his hands. "However, I don't always have time for pleasantries. You've seen my calendar. Every minute of my workday is accounted for, and I will be coming and going frequently. Get used to me not having the time to say please and thank you."

"You don't have a second to treat me like a human being?"

A tense silence fills the room.

At once, I know I've overstepped. Me and my big mouth. But it's out there, and I can't take it back. Besides, him saying he doesn't have time to be polite is BS. I don't care how busy someone is, there should always be time to thank the people who help you.

"This is your first day so I'm going to let that comment slide," Carter rumbles. "In the future, Eden, I don't appreciate being talked back to. I'm your boss, you're my assistant. I don't appreciate being questioned, and in the future, I won't be lenient about it. Are we clear?"

"Crystal," I say. "I'm sorry I spoke out of turn."

Things are tense after that. He goes over other office tasks before he dismisses me for lunch.

5

EDEN

I desperately need a break. When I get back to my desk, I receive an instant message from Gretchen.

GRETCHEN:
Are you ready for lunch? Been waiting for you.

Thank goodness.

ME:
Absolutely! Let's go.

I grab my purse and meet her in the hall. She's wearing a sympathetic expression behind her red-framed glasses. I don't even have to say anything for her to know what's going through my mind.

"He is a lot," she says once we're out of earshot of my office. "But, again, he's a total hottie."

"Yeah, well, looks can only get you so far."

"He doesn't give a very good first impression, but you'll get used to him."

This is the second time she's mentioned "getting used to him." People like Carter speak the way they want and do what they want because no one tells them otherwise. I'm not about to be that person. Also, she has no idea that I have a vastly different first impression of him than she did.

"I can handle it," I say. "Besides, I'm only here for six months. I've worked for stricter people much longer." Me talking about my sister like that is a clear sign of frustration, not because I don't love her. I love her dearly. When I'd started working at the firm she'd taken over from Dad, she had been strict, even difficult at times—it was as if she'd been preparing me for this crazy venture my whole life without knowing it—but she had at least taught me the importance of words like "please" and "thank you."

Gretchen gives me a sympathetic look and slides her arm around mine. "Come on. There's a little café about five minutes from here that me and the girls like to go to. My treat since it's your first day."

Gretchen has just become my new best friend. We take a brief walk to a small café where the other two assistants have already saved us a table. They wave us over when we come in.

"Eden, this is Jaylin and Lexi. Ladies, I'd like you to meet Eden," Gretchen introduces us as we join their table. "She's Mr. Bancroft's assistant for the next six months." Gretchen clarifies that Jaylin and Lexi serve as assistants to the two vice presidents here in NYC at Legacy Builders. Jaylin assists the VP of Human Resources, while Lexi supports the VP of Marketing.

Both women say hi and we shake hands. Jaylin is a spunky, plus or minus forty-year-old African American woman, with her hair slicked back from her face into a natural elegant ponytail. She's enjoying a large Cool Wrap with a tall glass of iced tea. Lexi is just shy of thirty with a thin face, classic rectangular glasses, high cheekbones and straight brown hair that falls midway down her back. In front of her is a veggie salad with a bottle of seltzer water.

Gretchen turns to me. "What can I get you?"

I eye Jaylin's plate. "That Cool Wrap looks good."

Jaylin gives me a thumbs-up. "It's today's lunch special. It even has avocado."

"Oh, yeah, definitely that. Thank you, Gretchen. Oh, and an ice water."

Gretchen smiles. "Coming right up." She looks at the other women. "Don't spill the tea until I'm back."

"Welcome, Eden." Lexi gives me a cheeky smile as soon as Gretchen wanders off. "Happy to have you join our little group. Too bad Gwen couldn't be here."

"Gwen is our friendly front desk manager you met this morning," Jaylin explains.

"Maybe she'll join us later. She's always too busy with who knows what. We don't typically eat out for lunch, but we figured we'd make your first day a special one."

"Thanks, I'm excited to be here." Something about both women immediately puts me at ease. I'm not one to be anxious, but being in a new city surrounded by new people is enough to rattle anyone. And yet, the ladies give off nothing but positive, chill vibes. They seem genuinely happy to have me here.

"So, Mr. Bancroft, huh?" Jaylin asks in a cool, smooth voice, leaning forward. She waggles her eyebrows. "What do you think?"

Oh, we're in way too public a place for me to tell these women exactly what I think of Mr. Bancroft. Also, I don't want to risk unleashing a juicy tidbit that could morph into a wild rumor, eventually reaching my boss's ears and ending up in a hilarious "let's fire her" rendition. So, instead, I answer, "He's certainly something."

"That's one way to put it." Lexi grins. "We all had to fill in over the last couple of weeks, and he's very...*demanding*."

"That's putting it lightly," Jaylin says and sips her iced tea. She leans in and whispers, "Bosshole." She returns to her former position. "Not my words, girls. That's what his former assistant called him."

Lexi laughs. "As in boss asshole," she explains to me, and I make an "ah-ha" expression, as if I'm not familiar with the term and calling him a "Bosshole" would never have crossed my mind.

"It definitely has a ring to it," I agree.

"But a hot bosshole." Lexi makes swoon-eyes at us, then adjusts her glasses. "Like, stupidly hot. Panty-wetting hot. I swear, the first time I met him, I lost my train of thought, and then I had to go change my underwear."

We laugh. She's not wrong. *Been there, done that.* Last night I, too, had lost my train of thought when I'd seen that man sitting in the corner of the ice cream shop. He stood out like a sore thumb amid the comfortable place with his black helmet, tattooed arms, that sad black coffee in front of him, and that intense gaze of his when our eyes met. The whole panty-wetting thing came later. Like two seconds later. The image of him underneath me with those intense eyes, guiding me with his rough controlling hands and his controlling cock, groaning and watching me ride him, circling and teasing my clit with his thumb as I did, start flashing in front of me.

Luckily, Gretchen joins the table with our drinks, distracting me from taking any trips to forbidden territory.

"Food should be out in a minute," Gretchen announces, handing me my ice water. "What are we talking about?"

I quickly grab the glass and take a huge sip of the cold drink. Aaah. Better. Much better. "Thank you. We are talking about—"

"The hotness of Eden's boss," Lexi jumps in before I can finish my sentence.

"And about wet panties," Jaylin adds.

"Oh, *that.*" Gretchen nods as if it's a topic they've discussed (and possibly experienced) in real life a million times.

All innocently, with my halo shining brighter than the brightest star, I say, "I see that everyone feels the same way about him."

"He pulls off the 'dress shirt and tie but with cool jeans' look perfectly." Lexi lets out a wistful sigh, her slender shoulder rising and falling in a dreamy swoon. "But on special occasions, you know, for important presentations, board meetings and such, you'll see him in his tailored three-piece suit. So hot. It's a company rule. Rumor has it, he hides tattoos under his suit. I doubt it." She fans herself with her hand. "Well, a girl can dream at least. Too bad we'll never know the truth. Gossip is really, *really* bad around here. People talk, and talk, and talk, it's crazy."

"Yeah, *crazy*," Jaylin teases, eyeing her.

"Why he's single, we'll never know." Gretchen adjusts a blonde strand of hair and clips it back. "After all, he's one of NYC's top five most eligible billionaire bachelors. I've been working here a long time and have seen countless women throw themselves at him. But he simply doesn't take notice."

Jaylin swallows, dabbing the corners of her mouth with her paper napkin. "I think it speaks of his professionalism to keep his private life a mystery. Besides, a boss checking out his employees or, for that matter, ogling any women in front of his workers—*so creepy*. He's simply focused on his career. Becoming partner."

"I, for my part, think he simply has impossibly high standards," Lexi says.

Gretchen nods in agreement. "Sky-high standards, true, but his sense of humor? MIA."

Ignoring the two women, Jaylin faces me. "The good thing is, you won't have to worry about him getting too touchy-feely with you."

Right.

"Okay, well, aside from him, what else can you tell me about Legacy?" I ask, eager to change the subject.

One of the servers brings over my and Gretchen's food while we talk about the company, and the lunch gets better from there. It's nice to be with new people who don't know I was a small-town gal, who *accidentally* managed to sleep with one of NYC's most eligible billionaires, despite his impossibly high standards. With a confidence boost of one trillion-gazillion, I enjoy my break with my new friends. It's exactly the kind of pick-me-up I need to help me get through the rest of the day.

AFTER WE RETURN to the company, I go back to my desk where I find a slew of emails from Carter, outlining tasks he wants me to tackle before the end of the day. He's tied up with meetings for the rest of the afternoon, which is a godsend. I'm happy to throw myself into my work, especially without having to train my traitorous mind to stop looking and thinking about him.

Five o'clock rolls around, and I'm ready to call it a day. Overall, I'm glad about the way the assignments worked out. The tasks themselves came naturally to me and being able to jump right in without delay felt good. I'm ready to get to my new place and have a nice quiet evening getting settled.

After saying goodnight to my new coworkers, I retrieve Kiki from the parking garage. The old lady now sports a shiny new parking sticker, courtesy of HR. Singing to the music and plugging in my apartment's address on my phone's GPS, I'm finally on my way to my new home, but not before stopping at a bakery to buy a box of cupcakes called "Raspberry Euphoria Delights" (delectable cupcakes adorned with a velvety buttercream frosting, delicately handcrafted using a luscious raspberry puree) and stuffing it in one of my bags. I'm already anticipating the delight of indulging in my cherished celebratory treat, a personal reward I never fail to bestow upon myself for reaching significant milestones.

THE BUILDING I pull up to is *enormous*. Down in the garage level, I can immediately tell by the other cars in the lot that it's much fancier than I expected. Every car around my spot is sleek and expensive. Amid the shiny Ferrari fellas, my little Kiki will be gasping in disbelief all night. I even catch sight of a couple of big motorcycles carefully tucked away under tarps. Between no rent, manageable bills, and the nice chunk of money I'll be making at Legacy, I'll be able to get my life together in no time.

I grab my bags and two rolling suitcases, grateful to be the only one in the elevator because it means no one will see me as the silly bag lady struggling to carry all her belongings in one trip.

Ping.

The elevator doors open on my level, the 6th. It's nice and quiet when I step out. It also smells good. The hallway is spacious, and there are only two apartments. One on the left, number fourteen, and one on the right, number fifteen. Fifteen, that one's mine. The thought of having only one neighbor to deal with is exciting. Back in Maine, my tiny old apartment shared paper-thin walls with neighbors all around me. Between having active kids, playing their TV loudly (at least I hoped the screaming was TV), and shouting at their barking dogs all the time, my hopes are high that my new neighbor will be the quiet, pleasant kind.

As I struggle to find my keys, my bag bumps against the door.

It suddenly opens.

"Oh!" The unexpected sight of two light-brown eyes staring at me scares the crap out of me, and I end up jumping in surprise and almost dropping the stuff I'm still carrying.

"Gosh, I'm so sorry to startle you," says the old woman in a British accent, opening the door fully. She wears a comfortable-looking cashmere sweater and clean slacks. With a well-put-together appearance, her eyes sparkle with curiosity. "Can I help you at all?" Her accent is a little slice of uniqueness that makes her even more endearing. I wonder if she lived in England for some time or if she grew up in a family with British heritage.

"Oh, I'm sorry, I must have the wrong apartment," I say, my hands too full to reach my phone to double-check. "I'm looking for apartment fifteen."

"This is the one, love!"

My stomach drops. "Oh, are you the...?"

"That's right, I reside in this very place. Hattie Hutton is the name I go by. And who might you be?"

I stand there for a second, holding the bags that contain my life. "I'm Eden, Eden Ryan, and I was supposed to be staying here for the next six months."

Hattie's eyes light up. "Oh, wonderful! Good old Lewis mentioned there would be a young lady keeping the place cozy until they found someone to rent it full time."

Relief washes over me. "Yup, that's me."

"It's lovely to meet you. I'm sure you'll find the place quite delightful.

The views are absolutely gorgeous, and it's a pretty peaceful place to live. As long as you're not bothered by the chilly man next door, that is."

"Chilly man next door?"

"Yes, over in flat fourteen." She gestures to the apartment to the left. "Ooh, an unbelievably sour soul. Not a friendly bone in his body. Detests animals. Never spares a moment for a friendly chat. Never smiles, you know."

Oh, he sounds awful. So much for having a pleasant neighbor. "I'm sorry to hear that…"

"It would be wisest to avoid him," she adds.

"Well…no problem. I don't plan on doing much socializing anyway. Are you just collecting a few things before heading out?"

"Oh, no, dear, I shall be here for the next two weeks."

My stomach drops through the floor and falls all the way down into the garage. "But…Lewis told me you would be out by the tenth."

Hattie huffs and puts her hands on her hips. "Gosh, that man! Bless his heart, he means no harm, but he's forever muddling up dates. It's the twenty-fourth, dear. I'll be off on the twenty-fourth, at *ten* in the morning. Precisely when the movers arrive."

Shit. Now what the hell am I supposed to do? Even if it had been her fault, not even in my wildest dreams would I try to kick a sweet old lady out of her apartment so I could use it. Worse, I don't have enough money to put toward a motel room.

"Oh…okay." My arms are shaking and it *finally* occurs to me to put my bags down. "I…have no idea what I'm going to do."

"Fret not, my dear," Hattie says. "You're very welcome to stay here with me."

"Oh, really?" How kind! Oh, my God. Of course I'll take her offer. It's incredibly sweet, and the fact she would open her home to a complete stranger at the drop of a hat tells me all I need to know about her.

Besides, spending time with a sweet older lady will be good. I miss my sister, and having a motherly figure around sounds comforting.

She opens her door farther and steps aside, waving me in.

All of a sudden, my nose starts to twitch, and my throat becomes itchy. This can only mean one thing. I look down at the floor to see three fat orange tabby cats winding their way around Hattie's legs.

Immediately, I turn away to sneeze. It happens again, and a third time before I force myself to take a few steps away from her.

"I don't think that's a good idea," I say, sniffling. I've been allergic to cats since I was small, and just seeing the three animals makes my body start to break out in hives.

"Are you feeling quite all right?" Hattie asks with concern. She tries to step forward, but I put my hand out to gently stop her.

"Cat hair," I say while sniffling. "I'm highly allergic to cat hair…"

"Oh goodness, I do apologize." Hattie nudges the cats with her foot and closes the door a bit. "You three, shoo, off you go! Back inside, go on, back inside."

This is such a mess. I'm broke and homeless, standing in the middle of the hallway of an expensive NYC apartment with my allergies trying to kill me. What am I supposed to do? I don't relish the thought of spending the next two weeks in my car, but by the looks of things, that's exactly where I'm going to end up.

Ping.

The sound of the elevator doors opening comes from behind me, and I turn around to find myself facing the person I least expected to see.

Carter. Did he follow me?

"You?" I ask, wiping my watering eyes with the back of my hand. "What are you doing here?"

For the third time in less than twenty-four hours, this man has appeared in my life out of nowhere. *Grrreat*. This is exactly what I need right now, for my new boss that I slept with to see me surrounded by numerous big bags, homeless, hopeless, with a red face and nose.

"Oh, Mr. Bancroft, how fortunate that you're back." Hattie waves. "It appears there's been a bit of a mix-up."

Carter's eyes bore into mine, their intensity as strong as they were last night, just before he unbuckled his belt. I have no idea what is headed my way.

6

CARTER

Mrs. Hutton stands in the doorway of her place, wearing the red slacks and oversize sweater she always wears. Next to her stands Eden, taking up most of the hallway with a ridiculous number of bags. And why is she crying?

"Oh! You two are acquainted?" Hattie asks, catching on to the familiarity.

Eden nods.

"What is the problem?" I ask her.

Even though I posed the question to Eden, Mrs. Hutton answers. "There's been a bit of a muddle, you see, and dear Eden here arrived a fortnight ahead of schedule," she explains. "I would be absolutely delighted to offer her accommodation, but it looks like she's rather allergic to Mitsy, Myrtle, and little Ruth."

And probably the other twenty cats you have in there, I think.

Eden sneezes again. "It's fine, I'll figure something out..." She opens her purse and rummages through it, looking for something.

I take my handkerchief out of my pocket and hand it to her.

"No problem. I'll make a few calls," I say as she wipes her face, pulling my phone out of my pocket, ready to book her into a nearby hotel.

"No, that's not necessary." Eden seems determined to figure out the predicament on her own. She's also trying her damnedest not to look me in the eye. "I'll just..." She trails off, and I know she has no other options.

Last night she told me she was new in town, and I gathered by the motel room that she doesn't have much money. Otherwise, she'd already be headed back there.

"Why doesn't she just lodge with you?" I hear Mrs. Hutton ask.

Eden's eyes widen, portraying the perfect deer in the headlights look. I'm just as surprised as she is, and we both turn to look at Hattie Hutton. What the hell is that woman thinking? Yeah, we know each other, but that doesn't automatically make us friends, even less roommates.

"No, no, that's not a good idea, seriously," Eden protests, and she lowers the handkerchief.

"I don't think—" I begin.

"Mr. Carter Donovan Bancroft!" Mrs. Hutton throws out in a scolding tone that I swear every old spinster has mastered. "Are you truly suggesting that an innocent young lady should haul all her belongings downstairs and sort out this mess, when you possess a perfectly suitable spare room? After all, she's hardly a stranger. The two of you are evidently acquainted."

All the objections I have prepared die when I notice the outraged way the old woman is looking at me. Damn it if she doesn't remind me of my aunt. *For fuck's sake.* I look at Eden, who has finally stopped sneezing. Her eyes are red like Mrs. Hutton's slacks, and so is the tip of her nose. I realize it's because of allergies, but it also looks like she's been crying—or at least is close to tears. I make a split-second decision I know I'll regret later.

"Sure, you can stay with me." I give a curt nod toward my door.

Usually, I'm not rash, but something in Eden seems to not only bring this side of me to life, but also seems to provoke it.

Eden's eyes widen even more. "Oh, no, I couldn't do that."

I cock an eyebrow. "Do you have a better option?"

She stares at me, eyes large as saucers, and it's like I can see her mind trying to think of something else, another way to get out of this mess.

"That's what I thought," I say, not waiting for her response. "It's no big deal. It's only for two weeks."

Mrs. Hutton smiles brightly. "What a considerate young gentleman," she says as if she hadn't just conned me into agreeing with her. "There you are, Eden. Predicament resolved." From inside her apartment, I can hear a cat meowing. "Oh, I must go. Little Ruth needs her blanket. It was a pleasure to make your acquaintance, my dear. We shall chat again before too long." A bit more reserved, she says, "Mr. Bancroft."

With that, she closes the door, leaving me and Eden standing there.

"Are you sure about this?" she asks, clearly nervous.

"I'm sure. Let's talk inside." Eden bends to pick up her bags, and I incline closer at the same time to help her. "Here, let me."

I lean down to grab the heavier bags, and as we shuffle around, our hands accidentally touch. A shot of electricity moves from her body to mine as it did last night. The proximity causes her scent to invade my nostrils, and the smell of citrus washes over me.

We pause, breathing in the same air for half a second before I step back.

When she looks at me, I can see her eyes freeze for a second, before she turns away to grab the rest of her belongings.

Yeah, it's best we ignore whatever the hell that was.

I open my apartment and gesture for her to enter. Together, we carry her stuff inside, and I'm cursing in my head the entire time. This is not what I expected or hoped my evening would look like, but my elderly neighbor has left me with no other choice. How the hell was I supposed to turn down her suggestion without looking like a complete asshole? There was no way, and I can tell Eden is exhausted. As for the hotel, I can always offer her that out tomorrow morning.

"Thank you," she says in a small voice.

"Don't mention it. Seriously, don't. We don't need the office knowing we're living together, even if it's only temporary."

The expression on her face tells me she and I are on the same page —we won't be making any of this public. I won't treat her differently to any other new assistant. Just because we slept together, and she now temporarily lives in my apartment doesn't mean our dynamic will change. Not in the least.

I have to admit she did a good job today. She completed everything I gave her, and it was done correctly. That was more than any of my previous assistants could handle.

"Where's the spare room?" she asks.

"This way." I lead her to a guest suite down the hall. It's next door to my bedroom, has a private bathroom connected to the hallway, and a balcony. "You can stay in here," I say, walking inside and putting her bags on top of the chair next to the bed. "Keep everything neat, and we won't have a problem."

"Don't worry, I'm not even going to unpack everything," she says with a heavy sigh. "Wouldn't make sense if I'm moving again in two weeks anyway."

"I'll text Lewis and tell him to have Mrs. Hutton's apartment deep cleaned. That way your allergies won't get the better of you when you move in."

She looks at me, surprise etched across her features. Lewis was a good friend of my late father and one of the last few decent human beings left on this planet. He'll try to accommodate and properly hand over the apartment. Even if he protests for whatever reason—he likely doesn't know that old Mrs. Hutton is farming a cat population in his apartment, and as annoying as the thought is, I won't rat her out—I'll simply tell him to bill me.

"I appreciate it. And you'll get your handkerchief back, I swear. I just want to wash it first."

I rub the back of my neck, unsure of where to go from here. It's a unique and awkward situation I haven't found myself in before. "Are you hungry?"

"Starving."

"I'll order us something."

Leaving her in the guest suite, I walk past a loft area I've turned into a master suite with an additional adjoining bathroom. The living room is a large open concept with windows all along one wall, and in the center, a comfortable sofa faces a fully functional fireplace. No flat-screen TV mounted above it like you typically see. I despise mundane time-wasting activities.

The kitchen opens into the living room, and the interior designer had put a table and chairs in the middle of the two as a makeshift dining area. With Eden's guest suite down the hall, next to a small laundry room, we will at least have some semblance of privacy between us. I only really go down that hall when I go to my bedroom or home gym.

The main reason I'd moved into this apartment, aside from the spectacular view, was the clever allocation of the rooms. It's my home, my solitude, the one place I can go where no one will bother me. Who needs the interruptions? And yet, now I have a visitor.

Luckily, it's only for a limited time.

My stomach growls, and I pull my phone out of my pocket. Just as I unlock the screen, my phone rings. My aunt's name and photo appear on the screen.

"Hello, Auntie," I answer.

"Carter, my darling nephew!" Her French accent is loud and clear. "It's great to hear your voice."

Eleanor Toussaint is my only living relative. At sixty-six, she has taken to calling me every couple of days to check in and keep tabs on me. Not that I mind. I love my aunt dearly, and with her living in France, visits in person aren't too frequent. Especially lately. She's been talking about having health issues when she isn't hounding me about getting married—her favorite topic.

Thankfully, I've been able to keep her at bay with a little white lie.

"How is married life treating you, *mon chéri*?" she asks.

"It's great, Aunt Eleanor. Things are going well."

"I am so glad. I cannot wait to meet her."

Yeah. I'd lied to her and told her I got married. It'd all started with a misunderstanding I hadn't cleared up. Truth is, I don't relish the deception, but after years of her asking and nagging, I figured it was the easiest way to get her off my back. It has worked perfectly well over the last few months.

As always, I expertly pivot the situation away from the idea of her meeting my imaginary wife. "How are you feeling?"

Aunt Eleanor sighs. "Not well, I'm afraid. My doctors have me on a strict medication regimen."

"I'm sorry to hear that. Is there anything I can do?"

"There isn't. On the plus side, they cleared me for flying. I am coming to visit you this weekend."

My stomach churns, and my heart rate kicks up. "Come again?"

"I said, I'm coming to New York this weekend. I need to visit my favorite nephew and meet the woman who finally got him to settle down."

"Auntie, I'm your only nephew." I resort to the well-used line to buy myself more time.

Think.

Think.

"All the more reason to visit!"

"Are you sure that's a good idea?" I try. "I don't want you to risk your health on my behalf."

"I've already made up my mind, *mon chéri*," she says with her stubborn voice that I've heard all too many times throughout my life. "The ticket is reserved, and I'm already packing."

"How long will you be staying for?"

"Oh, just the weekend. I wanted to bring you my wedding gift in person. By the way, what's the name of my new niece-in-law? It occurred to me that I never asked, forgetful old bat that I am. I want to make sure I add her name to the congratulations card."

Fuck. *Fuck.*

Quick, Carter, think *faster.*

Eden comes down the hall, and our eyes meet across the room.

"Her name is Eden." I answer my aunt's tricky question, a brilliant idea forming in my mind.

"Eden? What a beautiful name! Oh, this visit is going to be so fun! I cannot wait to meet her. Now, I must go and finish making last-minute arrangements. I will see you in a few days, *mon chéri*. Love you!"

She hangs up before I can respond.

Eden gives me a quizzical look when I lower my phone.

"Who was that? Why did you say my name a second ago?" she asks. "And what's with the funny look?"

My mind races with solutions to the situation I've found myself in. In hindsight, Eden's predicament might turn out to be a blessing in disguise. She's already planning on staying with me for two full weeks. I'm sure I can convince her to go along with this charade for two days.

"First, I have a proposition for you," I say, slipping the phone back into my pocket.

"Does it have to do with what to order for dinner? Because I'll eat anything right now. I'm hungry as can be."

"I need you to marry me."

Her eyes widen. For a brief moment, I see something like hurt flashing behind her eyes. Then, as if nothing happened, she snort-laughs out loud. Clearly, she doesn't believe me. "Come again?"

"It's a personal matter. One that I'm going to need your help with. I need you to be my wife."

The amusement is gone from her face as quickly as it appeared. "Wait, you're serious? Your wife? Where is this coming from? Last time I checked, you didn't even want to acknowledge that we had sex. Now you're suddenly asking me to marry you?"

"Here, sit down. Let me explain."

I motion for her to join me on the couch. We sit facing each other, Eden staring at me like I've suddenly grown an extra head. Which is fair, considering what I've just thrown her way.

"I'm all ears…?"

"I was just talking to my aunt," I explain as patiently as I can. "She's in her sixties and not doing well health-wise. She wants to visit me this weekend so she can meet my new wife."

"But you don't have a wife. Wait, do you have a wife? Shit! Did I have sex with a married man? Sweet Jesus, Carter! *Great*, just perfect. I slept with my married boss. This gets better and better! I swear to God—does your wife know?"

She keeps babbling on and on, asking if I have kids, and all I can think to do is put my hand over her mouth, so I do. "Quiet for like, two seconds, okay? I'm not done explaining."

She huffs and knocks my hand away. "Fine, keep going."

"Aunt Eleanor is my only living relative and I'm hers. My uncle passed away years ago and she doesn't have any children. She lives in France where she moved after she remarried. We talk regularly. She was always hounding me about settling down and getting married. Recently, with her health failing and her second husband passing away, she's really amped up the nagging, so to get her off my back, I told her I eloped. It was meant as a joke. She was ecstatic and the nagging finally stopped."

"You invented a wife to get your aunt off your back?"

"No. It was a joke. One that I never cleared up. Hey, she's a formidable woman. And it sounded like a good idea at the time."

"Except now she wants to visit."

"Exactly. That's where you come in."

Eden studies me for a moment, her green eyes not as wide but still as piercing. "Couldn't we just pretend to be married?" she asks. "Why do we have to actually go through with the nuptials?"

"We don't. We won't go through with the legal part. We'll *pretend* to be married—"

"Oh."

"—but my aunt is smart. She's going to want to see photos. Us in wedding outfits. Ring. The whole shebang."

Her face grows expressionless for a second as I list what's required. "Isn't she going to ask for the marriage certificate?"

"What? Nobody wants to see that."

"Sure? What if she does?"

"I'm not worried about that. Her eyesight isn't great."

"Still, this is *insane*." Eden shakes her head, getting to her feet.

"Nope. I'm not going to fake marry you so you can continue lying to your elderly aunt."

"Eden, if I tell her the truth, it'll devastate her," I explain. "Her health has been steadily declining over the last few months. If me being married makes her happy and puts her at ease, then so be it."

"Why the hell should I help you? This morning you wanted nothing to do with me. Must I remind you that you snuck out of my motel room without even leaving a note?"

Damn. She has me there.

"This isn't about us," I argue. "But a favor for a favor is only fair."

"Are you saying that my staying here obligates me to fake marry you?" Eden's eyes flare with outrage. "Absolutely not, Carter! I'm not going to let you lord this over me. I'll sleep in my flipping car if I have to."

She starts to march away, but I stand up and block her path. "Don't be ridiculous. Sleeping in your car in New York is dangerous. Also, the marriage thing will only be for the weekend. Afterward, everything will go back to the way it's supposed to be." I pinch the bridge of my nose, trying to hold a headache at bay. "If you do this for me, I'll make it worth your while. I'll order dinner for us the entire time you stay here, and... wait," I say, fishing for my phone.

"And breakfast."

I look up. Her demand takes me aback for a second. That's it? Is she really going to accept the deal in exchange for dinner and...*breakfast*? Her bargaining skills clearly need work. Unless I've missed something. She's either a negotiating rookie, business-*un*-savvy beyond hope, or really desperate. "Come again?"

"Breakfast and dinner," Eden corrects. "The only reason I'm staying here is because I can't afford a motel. I also don't have money for food and gas. Feed me in addition to giving me shelter, and we have a deal."

This has to be the easiest deal of my lifetime.

"Done. The kitchen will be fully stocked throughout your stay." When she looks at me like I've saved her life, I decide this isn't the right moment to be a complete asshole. I unlock my phone and enter a number into the display. "And you get a big bonus if everything goes well." I turn the phone to her.

"Oh. My. God." Not only does her jaw drop, but her eyes grow to the size of dinner plates. Clearly, her poker face needs work too.

"With that, I will lay down some ground rules, and some requirements." Not just because of her, but also because of my tendency to do things in her presence that I wouldn't normally do.

Immediately, she shakes her head. "I'm not having sex with you! Nopeee, sir. No sexual favors. That ship has sailed."

My eyebrows fly up so fast they're in danger of disappearing in my hairline. (So much for a poker face.) "Who's talking about sexual favors?"

"Well, all those zeros just now...they suggest, you know—"

I shake my head in frustration. "This isn't about sex. In fact, not even close. First off, you need to have dinner with my aunt and me. Don't leave me alone with her, for the love of God."

"Didn't you say you love her?"

"I do. More than life. I can only imagine her next mission is going to be me having children and that is a conversation I am adamant about avoiding."

Eden chuckles. "The big bad wolf is scared of his elderly aunt. This is too good."

"Aunt Eleanor is a tough, smart woman," I say, ignoring her smartass comment. "Knowing her, she'll want all the details about the wedding and how we met. I've already shared my side of the story with her, so you need to follow along with what I've said to keep things consistent. You have to sell it. She has to really think that we're married and in love. She'll leave for France a happy woman."

"You're certainly going to a lot of trouble to impress your aunt."

"She's the most important person in my life, and she's adamant that me being married will make me happy. It's ridiculous, but I don't see the harm in letting her think that's the case."

"Got it."

"Secondly, we need to keep our 'marriage' a secret at work. Obviously none of this can be mentioned to anybody in the office."

"All of that sounds doable."

"I'm not done. Thirdly, no falling in love." The last thing I need is romantic complications or worse, a fake bride who wants to become a real bride.

For a second, her jaw tenses, but then she snort-laughs aloud. "Easy. I would *never* fall in love with you. In fact, you're the last person on this planet I would fall in love with."

I narrow my eyes at her, curious as to what she means.

"Bosses are taboo. Everybody knows that. I'm not risking my new job."

Well, that makes sense. "Good. Make sure it stays that way."

She pulls the pin out of her hair, letting long shiny brown locks flow down her back. I have the mental image of her doing something similar the night before, right before she walked toward me. "So dinner with your aunt, no improvising, and make her think I'm the devoted, loving wife," she lists back at me, running her hand through her soft hair. "Keep our 'marriage' a secret at work. Play the devoted wife, but no falling in love. Got it."

"Good. Then we're done here." I glance at the time. This has already taken way too long.

"Wait. If you have ground rules, then I have some of my own as well."

I cross my arms and lean against the wall. "And they are?"

"If I have to sell this thing, then you do too," she says, pointing an accusatory finger at me. "I'm more than happy to act like the doting wife, but marriage is a two-way street. You have to be the doting husband, right? We're newlyweds and need to act like it. I deserve to be fawned over."

"What makes you think I won't?"

"You really don't want me to answer that."

"I know what I want and how I like things done, and I'm not ashamed of that."

"Which works in the business world and is what makes you a good businessman. But would make you a terrible husband."

"I resent that remark," I tell her, irritated. "When I commit to something, I go all in, not just giving one hundred percent, but excelling."

"What does that have to do with marriage? It's not a competition, Carter. You can't approach marriage like you do a business deal."

I hold my hand up, gesturing between the two of us. "And yet..."

Eden scoffs and waves me off. "This doesn't count. It's not a real marriage, remember? Anyway, I'm not done listing my stipulations."

"Do continue."

"Where do I sleep?"

"You're staying in the guest suite unless told otherwise. Once my aunt arrives, we share my room."

"Wait." She frowns. "I was serious before—we're *not* having sex."

"Are you talking about sex again, woman?"

"I am. And I'm telling you that I've sworn off sex and men while I'm in New York."

"Obviously that went over so well last night."

"The rule was put into place when I woke up alone in my motel room."

All right, that hits a nerve. I'm not a monster. Part of me feels bad for ditching her, but in my defense, I didn't expect to ever see her again. "There are two beds in my room. Happy? Anything else?"

Eden seems satisfied with my reply but still ponders for a moment. "Nothing that comes to mind," she concludes. "But my ground rules are subject to change."

At that, I smirk. "Meaning if you get hot and bothered, you're free to try to seduce me?"

"No, meaning if you do something inappropriate, I'm out. Gone. *Hasta la vista*, baby." Eden extends her hand. "Deal?"

Not breaking eye contact, we shake on our arrangement. She's not going anywhere.

"Good. Glad we're on the same page."

"We can make all the arrangements quietly." I fish my phone out of my pocket again. "I'll have my lawyer draw up a contract and an NDA."

"How romantic."

"Thursday," I tell her, ignoring her comment. "We're flying out to Vegas on Thursday. I've got a meeting in Phoenix that demands my presence, and right after that, we're jetting off to Vegas to capture the wedding shots. Phoenix and Vegas are practically a stone's throw away, so it makes sense to combine the trips. Start planning and reschedule any meetings accordingly. Allocate a time on Friday for us to meet up to get our stories straight before my aunt arrives on Saturday. Let's get it over and done with."

"You're such a sweet talker," Eden says sarcastically.

"I don't sweet-talk. I simply know how to communicate effectively. It saves time and gets results."

"Effective communication is one thing, but have you mastered the art of passive-aggressive remarks yet? That's where the real magic happens." When I give her a look, she adds, "Anyway, this is going to be an interesting weekend."

I agree. The weekend is certainly going to be one of a kind—and not in a good way.

"We're done here." I shove my phone into my pocket, heading to my room. "I've gotta get some sleep. I have an early day tomorrow."

"I already regret my decision," she says playfully. "Ask me to marry you, then immediately go pass out? Don't you want to celebrate? Eat something...sweet?"

Pausing, I turn to look at her. "Didn't you swear off sex?"

7
EDEN

"Who's talking about sex?"

"You just implied it." His voice is a low rumble.

"Hello? I wasn't asking to have sex with you. I was talking about cupcakes."

He doesn't think eating cupcakes is a good idea. Instead, he gives me a hard look. I can't help but suck in a deep breath as he walks past me. His manly cologne invades my nostrils, and I feel dizzy. A zesty musk. I have a weakness for citrus notes and earthy scents. As of late.

"Good night, Eden."

He walks away, leaving me there with my head spinning. I take a deep breath to put myself together. Little does he know that I was left at the altar and that my secret dream of "forever" has gone up in flames. Even if Carter did know, he wouldn't care. With another deep sigh, I go into the guest suite and change into the first nightwear I find: my favorite nightgown. Creamy white, a low V-neckline with intricate lace accents and beautiful detailing: it flatters my fuller bust. I've had it for years and it's grown thin after so many trips through the washing machine. But wearing it brings me comfort when I crawl into an unfamiliar bed in an unfamiliar place.

Speaking of comfort. The bed is heavenly, and the pillows feel like clouds. After a long, super-weird day, all I want to do is get some sleep. Unfortunately, my brain has other ideas. After a good ten minutes of lying here, I'm still wide awake.

After I spend the better part of an hour tossing and turning, I lie there in a huff.

Great.

What the hell am I supposed to do now?

Cupcakes. I think about the box of "Raspberry Euphoria Delights" and my stomach grumbles. Might as well celebrate alone.

I grab my white robe and slip it on before tiptoeing back to the kitchen. A quick search of the cabinets yields a plate to put my cupcakes on. I even find a small box of candles tucked away in the back. However, I can't find a lighter.

Back in my guest room, I scrounge around my bag for matches. Voilà! Smiling, I step out on the small narrow walk-out balcony and place the box on one of the flowerpots. I put one of the candles in the cupcake and light the wick. I watch the flame as I shake out the match, putting it down on the box. "Hurray for my new job, my new apartment, and my soon-to-be husband." I say the last part sarcastically, before blowing out the candle.

How did my life implode? How did I wind up as a fiancée in a stranger's apartment, eating a cupcake alone in the middle of the night?

Well. It could be worse.

The guy could be ugly. Poor. Not tattooed. With a small dick.

I lean against the railing, enjoying my sugary treat. And I smell smoke. I whip back around to see that I didn't put the match out properly and it has set the cardboard box on fire. Flames have started to consume the rest of the cupcakes.

Shrieking in terror, I drop my cupcake. "Oh shit, oh shit, oh shit!"

I turn to put out the fire. Unfortunately, I can't exactly pick up the flaming box of buttercream cupcakes with my bare hands. The flames grow and are about to spread to the soft blue curtains that are waving out from the open French doors.

"Ohhh...no! Oh, my God..."

The next thing I know, out of nowhere, a naked man with bed hair bursts onto my balcony.

"Stand back!" he yells and pushes me inside.

There's the sound of a fire extinguisher, and a puff of white douses the balcony. I watch in amazement as the fire goes out, replaced by a mess of white foam, melted wax, and charred cupcake wrappers. Coughing and waving away the smoke and foam, Carter steps back into my guest suite, holding the red fire extinguisher...in front of his you-know-what. Like a nut case, the first thing I think is, *he sleeps naked*. I'm too distracted by his body, his tattoos, and his deep "V" to even really acknowledge the life-saving fire extinguisher he produced out of nowhere and how practical it was to stop cupcake fires. And also, unfortunately, how functional it is to hide certain things from certain over-curious onlookers ("gawkers"). But wait...*ha!*...is that his tip peeking out from under it?

Just when I catch myself staring ("creeper"), I realize how funny and ridiculous the whole situation is and immediately launch into a fit of giggles. "I'm sorry! I'm so sorry!"

He moves his angry gaze to me. "What the fuck, Eden?"

At first, I think he's about to unleash some Hulk-like rage on me for trying to stare a hole into the fire extinguisher, but then I realize he's referring to the accidental debacle I set off. "It was the match. I guess I didn't put the match out all the way. I was just trying to have some fun with my cupcake."

"Fun with your cupcake?" Carter sighs heavily, the extinguisher firmly in his grip. He shakes his head, exhaling in a sharp huff. "Another rule added to the list," he says sternly. "Do not set my apartment on fire."

It takes all my willpower to keep my eyes on his, and not slide my gaze back down over his muscular pecs, to his defined six pack, and to other..."aspects" that are definitely peeking out from behind the fire extinguisher—not that I'm interested in them. After all, I know what he's working with. Like, precisely. I clearly remember what it felt like to touch, to lick, to taste his...

You can lower that thing—I've already seen you naked, I think, still reeling from the adrenaline pumping through my blood, and the humor of the situation, and the onslaught of graphic images.

Something about how his right hand holds the hose makes me think of how he would hold something else.

"What did you just say?" His eyes connect with mine.

OMG. Did I really say that out loud? *You can lower that thing—I've already seen you naked?* Don't ask me what just happened. It must have just slipped out. "Hmm? What? Never mind."

"No. What did you just say?" he insists.

"You can really work that thing. Thanks for saving the day," I say. "I mean, you really are a hero with that fire extinguisher."

He grunts, and the scowl on his face deepens. Since when is an attempt to trivialize a funny situation inappropriate?

"I'll clean this up," I offer.

"We'll deal with it in the morning. Get some sleep."

He turns (without revealing any aspects) and heads next door without another word. But I know I have just experienced a memorable moment—my burned cupcakes and a naked fire extinguisher-wielding bosszilla—one that will be quite a story to recall later. It sure was a euphoric delight of a different kind!

Also, I honestly have no choice but to take a "quick" glance at that firm naked ass of his as he walks out—unabashedly so. Two words: nice buns. They send heat rolling through my body. I almost laugh at knowing what my boss's ass looks like. Firm, slightly hairy (the good way, not the full-on hairy monkey way). His legs are hairy too—*swooooooon*. The light is definitely better here than in my dimly lit motel room—which is always a plus.

I lick a bit of frosting off my finger.

It's a good thing he left though. I don't think I could handle another *fiery drill* today. Internally scolding myself for being oh so hopeless, I turn my back to look at the mess I'm responsible for. Instead of leaving it as he told me, I get to work cleaning for no other reason than to work off the sexual frustration that has started to develop.

8

CARTER

5:00 A.M.

I wake up to the sound of my alarm—and someone singing. It takes my sleep-addled brain a good five seconds to remember I'm no longer alone in my apartment. Right. Eden. My new assistant. My temporary roommate and fake fiancée. The one who almost set my apartment on fire last night.

It's been the most peculiar twenty-four hours I've had in a long time.

I ease myself out of bed, taking a moment to wake up. And listen. The singing is soft and comes from the direction of the kitchen. After a while, I hear it travel through the living room and down the hall. It stops once the guest suite bathroom opens and closes. It starts again as soon as the shower turns on, annoyingly loud. "Walking on Sunshine," of all songs. It feels strange having another person in the apartment with me. I haven't lived with anyone in a long time and that's on purpose. I like my space and rarely enjoy it being invaded. Even when my aunt comes to visit, I start to get antsy for my solitude—especially once she starts playing matchmaker with every Jane, Alice, and Sarah she knows.

I'm not going to let the week throw me off.

Despite the new addition in my life, I'm determined to go about my daily routine. After a series of stretches, I throw on a pair of shorts and a T-shirt and head to my gym.

It has everything I need: free weights, a treadmill, an elliptical, and a punching bag. On one of the walls is a flat screen which I turn on to catch the local business report. While I watch, I hop on the treadmill and start running at a steady sprint. I enjoy running. It helps me center myself, to focus. Nothing beats the burning of my muscles first thing in the morning, followed by a cold shower.

"Whoa! I didn't know you had a gym!"

Eden's upbeat voice forces my eyes away from the TV. She stands in the doorway in nothing but a robe as she rubs her wet hair with a towel. I look away to avoid staring at the way water clings to her partially exposed chest.

"You're welcome to use any of the equipment," I offer. "Just not first thing in the morning. It's my time."

She grins. "What, you can't share?"

"It's not about sharing, it's about my routine being messed up. I have a strict workout regimen, and I loathe deviations. Why are you awake this early anyway? You don't have to be in for another two hours."

"Couldn't sleep," she says, resting the towel around her neck. "Also, I really wanted to apologize again about last night."

"What the hell were you doing with matches?"

"I put a candle in the cupcake as a mini celebration. After all, I did just get engaged, even though it's a sham."

The mental image of her alone on the balcony blowing out a candle strikes a chord with me. I try to ignore the feeling and return my focus to the news. "I'll be done running in ten minutes. Breakfast should be here in twenty. I leave for work in forty."

"You have breakfast *delivered*?"

The question is about as unexpected as finding a penguin in the desert. "Of course."

"Well, that's one stylish way to kickstart the day. Also, are you sure you don't want me to come in earlier? It doesn't make sense for me to hang around here doing nothing when there's stuff that can be done at work."

"If you want to. Obviously, we can't drive in together."

"About that, I don't really have gas in my car."

I remember her telling me yesterday about not having enough money to buy gas. I'd thought it was an exaggeration in order to work out a better deal for herself. I hadn't believed she *actually* didn't have enough to cover all of her basic needs. I stop the treadmill. It slows enough for me to step off, and when I do, I turn to give her my full attention. "I will pay for your gas."

Eden sighs, fiddling with the towel around her neck. "No, no, please. I don't want that."

"Then how are you going to get into work?"

She gives me a nonchalant shrug. "I'll catch the train. Or better, I'll walk. I love walking, that's how I stay fit. It's not that far."

"It's at least a forty-five-minute walk, and that doesn't count waiting for traffic to stop."

"Easy-peasy. I'll have plenty of time to get there before my day starts."

Her optimism is on the verge of naivety. She has no idea what the city is like, and I doubt she's prepared for the city's unpredictable weather, nor to join the mass of impatient born-and-bred New Yorkers who flood the streets every morning.

"Okay, here's what we'll do then. I'll add you to my Uber account," I say, pulling my phone out of my pocket. "You can use that until your first paycheck."

"Carter, it's really not a big deal. I'll just walk."

"What about when it rains? Or when it gets really hot? Or when you're late?"

"Then I'm going to use the train."

"No, you'll use my Uber. At least that way I know you'll make it to work on time."

"Way to do something nice while simultaneously making it sound bad."

"Eden, don't argue with me. Just take the Uber."

"Okay then." Her shoulder drops, and she gives me a genuine smile. "Thank you."

Once she gives me her info, I follow the app's prompts to add her name and phone number to my profile. After a quick second on my phone, I put it back in my pocket. "There, you should receive the invitation. I've got to get ready."

I SHOWER AND DRESS. By the time I finish fastening my cufflinks, there's a knock on the front door.

"I got it!" Eden calls brightly.

I hear her open the door, and a few seconds of exchanged pleasantries with the delivery man. A moment later, he leaves, and the unmistakable British accent of Mrs. Hutton floats through the front door of my apartment.

"Good morning, Eden, dear. You look very lovely today!"

"Thank you, Hattie. Would you like to come in?"

Don't invite her in, I think as I leave my room. It's not that I dislike my neighbor, it's that she's chatty, and pulling away from a conversation takes more time than I have available. When I reach the hallway, Eden is standing there with the bags of food. Hattie is still in the hall.

"Good morning, Mrs. Hutton," I greet her. "Eden, we better hurry. We've got to get to work."

Thankfully, Eden is smart enough to take the hint. So is our elderly neighbor. "Oh gosh, of course. You two enjoy your breakfast before it gets cold."

I take the bags from Eden and turn to carry them to the table around the corner. Mrs. Hutton stops Eden from leaving. Under her breath, thinking I won't hear, I hear her whisper, "Such a handsome young man. Stern and grumpy, I know, but handsome nonetheless. Anyway, the reason I popped in, dear, was just to make sure you made it through the night safe."

"Perfectly safe, Hattie," I hear Eden whisper back, brushing over the fact she almost set the whole apartment building on fire. "Thank you for asking, that's very thoughtful of you."

"I must tell you, I heard some rather peculiar noises. High-pitched shrieks and sudden whooshing sounds." I imagine Mrs. Hutton opening her eyes dramatically as she always does when she discovers a neighborhood scandal unfolding right before her very eyes. "You must have heard it as well, love?"

"Oh...I wish I had. Sounds quite the spectacle!" I hear Eden snort-laugh.

"It may well have been Myrtle causing a ruckus. She has a habit of hunting mice when sleep eludes her, and then she *kindly* stashes her trophies under my bed."

Eden laughs and says her goodbyes before closing the door. "That woman is a trip," she says, joining me at the table. "She's officially the sweetest and funniest person I've met in the city so far. Actually, probably the sweetest and funniest person I've ever met."

Wait 'til you meet my aunt.

"You must have lived a very sheltered life." I've barely picked up my fork to scarf down my egg-white veggie omelet with cheese and grilled whole-wheat toast before my phone rings. Knowing only one person who calls me this early, I answer it immediately.

"What do you want, Bradley?" I ask, spearing a piece of omelet onto my fork.

"Is that any way to talk to your best friend?" he asks.

"It is when he interrupts my breakfast."

I've known Bradley Everhart all my life. He and I had started working at Legacy around the same time. After several years, he was transferred to the Connecticut office where he continues to thrive under the CEO, Nathan Bernie. Just like me, he's not on the board yet. We're in the same boat, both in senior executive positions, overseeing the day-to-day operations, waiting for the older generation to retire and pass the torch.

"I'll be there in person for the meeting today," he says. "Don't make any plans. I'm taking you out to lunch."

"Why, what did you do?"

"Always so suspicious."

"I've only known you for too long."

"And yet it's still not long enough, right? But you're dead on. I've heard some *whispers* that I think you'll be interested in."

I know precisely what Bradley is trying to convey. "Whispers" is code for him having information about the partners that he doesn't want to discuss out in the open. Bradley knows I hate gossip, and he knows better than to bring it up to me unless there's substance to it.

My interest piqued, I say, "Works for me. I'll have my assistant make lunch reservations at Giuseppe's."

"Ohhh, you finally got a new assistant? How is she?"

I glance across the table at Eden who is busy eating her breakfast and scrolling on her phone. "We'll talk later."

"See ya, bro."

I end the call and put my phone down. Eden glances up at me. "Everything okay?"

"It's fine."

"But has anyone told you that you work too much?"

My eyebrows shoot up. "Old news."

Eden shrugs, focusing back on her food. "Old news? It's timeless. It's just my observation being around you for the last thirty-plus hours. You're on your phone with work all the time."

"Just because we're technically engaged doesn't mean you get to play the nagging wife."

"*Fake* engaged. And just because you're my supervisor doesn't mean you can play the grumpy boss when we're not at work."

"Another ground rule," I say, picking up my ringing phone again. "I don't want to hear a peep about how many hours I work. Speaking of which, make sure the partners are clued in that I won't be reachable this weekend due to family business. Keep my schedule open Saturday and Sunday. If there's something on my agenda, reschedule it."

Eden only nods in response. I quickly finish my food while I answer several more phone calls. I'm out the door at my usual time, heading into the office before everyone else. I like getting there early. Usually, that's my only time to get work done without being constantly interrupted. Though now I have an assistant, I expect things to run more smoothly.

Legacy Builders is a large firm and growing larger by the day. We've recently acquired several smaller firms throughout the city and our reach continues to expand. I've overseen at least a dozen mergers and takeovers, one of them particularly huge, with several more in negotiations. We're on the verge of becoming one of the leading construction firms in the state.

I know we can do that and more.

I have a five-year plan to expand Legacy through several states across the country. But Huxley won't let me pull the trigger. His reasons to "not rush anything" and "act cautiously" make no sense. The economy is thriving, we have the resources and skilled labor. Expanding is the logical next step. Problem is, with Huxley's seat at the partners' table, I can only do so much. I'm not too worried though. I know his time at the company is limited.

∼

AN HOUR LATER, I'm focused on preparing for my morning meetings when I hear the glass door to the office's lobby open and Eden turn on her computer. Twenty-five minutes later, I stand up from my desk and leave my office to talk to her face to face.

"Good morning, Mr. Bancroft," she says cheerfully as if we hadn't had breakfast together earlier. Good. I appreciate her sticking to her role. "I've been through all your messages, and the important ones should be in your inbox."

"I saw. Listen, I'm expecting a visit from Bradley Everhart this morning. He's not on the schedule, but you can send him in when he gets here."

"Bradley Everhart, a COO, just like you, but of the Connecticut branch," Eden says promptly, already familiar with the basics. "Got it. Is there anything you need me to do to prepare for his arrival?"

"Can you make reservations—"

"To Giuseppe's?" Eden suggests. "I took the liberty of checking out the best restaurants on my Uber ride in."

Hmm. I guessed there was something positive that would come out of sharing a space with my assistant. Still, I can't help but feel suspicious of Eden's peppy behavior.

She stares back at me. "Why are you looking at me like that?"

"I'm trying to figure you out."

"Come again?"

"I said, I'm trying to figure you out."

"There's nothing to figure out, Mr. Bancroft. I'm here for a change and a fresh start. Nothing else. Also, if memory serves, I already told you all that last night, and...the night before."

Her cheeks flush at the mention of our night together and I have to focus on her. Her flush makes me think about her naked in that dark motel room, with that redness spreading across those full tits while I kissed my way down her stomach.

Heat simmers between us.

It only lasts a second before Eden pulls back and clears her throat.

"Anything else I can do for you, sir?"

"Just your job."

ONCE BACK AT MY DESK, I get back to work. Sometime later I hear the door open, and Bradley's booming voice as he says, "Well, hello there. Who might you be?"

Rolling my eyes affectionately, I go back out to greet him. Bradley is leaning against Eden's desk, giving her what he calls his "panty-dropping" smile. Eden smiles back and extends her hand to shake his.

"Mr. Everhart, I presume?" she asks.

"Aw, I'm flattered. You know my name, but I don't know yours."

"Eden Ryan. I'm Mr. Bancroft's new assistant."

"*Welcome.*" Bradley turns to look at me, giving me a "you lucky son of a bitch" gaze.

Eden raises an eyebrow and before she can say anything, I save her from my best friend's shameless flirting. "Come in. We don't have that much time before the meeting."

I gesture for Bradley to follow me into my office. I give Eden a reassuring expression, one that tells her Bradley has a solid character, *usually*. Understanding my hint, her demeanor softens. I want her to feel safe and not creeped out, and I can tell that my approval puts her at ease.

Bradley is one of the guys you can count on no matter what. He's smart, caring, and she'll soon understand that he was just messing with *me*. Even though Eden's stay is limited, it's important that she feels comfortable in our company.

Bradley gives Eden a small wave before he closes the door behind us. Once we're alone, he lets out a low whistle. "Pheeew. *Dude.* Good for you. What's her deal?"

"You don't want to go there, Bradley." I take my seat again and motion for him to join me. "What are you doing in town?"

"Ohhh no, no, no, we're not changing the subject that quickly." Bradley sits across from me. "Your new assistant. Tell me where you found her." He waggles his eyebrows.

"Stop being creepy. She's only here for six months, not to mention she's getting married this Thursday."

"Fuck, that sucks. Lucky son of a gun." Bradley stares at me for a second, eyes suddenly narrowing in playful distrust. "You said that fast. Did you ask her out already and get turned down? I've never known you to learn *anything* about your assistants' personal lives, not even after months of working together."

I sigh heavily and rub my temples. "It's complicated."

"Booo. Shitty fiancé?"

"I'm her fiancé."

Bradley's eyes go wide as his mouth falls open. "I'm sorry, Carr, I think I misheard you. Did you just say that you're the lucky SOB she's going to marry this Thursday?"

"It's a long story but yes."

"She's pregnant."

"No."

"But you slept with her?"

I give him *that* look.

"Okay, now you're *really* going to have to tell me what's going on."

I give him a quick version of what had gone down. How she and I had had a one-night stand two nights ago and how she needed a place to stay. When I get to the part with my aunt and me needing a fake wife, Bradley shakes his head.

"Rookie move, bro." He chuckles. "You should've invented a wife who travels. That way you wouldn't be in this mess."

"It'll be fine. It's just for the weekend."

"The marriage will be. But she's still staying with you for two weeks. You gonna show her *your* Big Apple?"

"We agreed to no sex. Not when she's working for me." While Bradley enjoys his popularity among our female staff—not as much as he enjoys getting a rise out of me by asking stupid questions or making absurd remarks—he and I both live by the "no sex with employees" rule.

"Yeah, sure, employees are taboo. But, the curves on her, sheeesh. She's only here for a brief time. Dude, she'll be wearing your ring—that's your free pass. You can bang your fake wifey, can't you? Why not have some fun while you can?"

"Shut the fuck up. I'm done talking about Eden. Are you going to stop stalling and tell me why you're here in person?"

"All right." Bradley leans back in his seat. "You're not gonna like it."

"Shoot."

"I caught the tail end of my boss chatting with Huxley. He's planning to veto any changes you suggest at the sales meeting today."

"I know." I huff in annoyance. "Any time I make changes to sales policy and procedure, Huxley tries to go behind my back and attempts to undermine me. You'd think so long as it improves numbers it wouldn't matter."

"You know it's not about numbers with him."

Saul Huxley is a giant pain in my ass. He's been with the company since its inception, and because of that, he thinks he knows best. It also means he has a lot of connections and is well respected. At one point I let myself be misled by all the hoopla as well. But the longer we work together, the more I'm starting to see him for who he really is—a shrewd, self-centered businessman who will deny change unless he's the one presenting it. Ever since I started trying to expand Legacy, he's made it his life's mission to turn down every single proposal I present. Even if it has nothing to do with expansion.

It only makes me more determined. I've never failed at anything in my life, and I don't intend to start now.

"You could've just called," I say. "You didn't need to come in person and tell me what I already suspected. Huxley can fight all he wants. We're moving forward with the change that was implemented at the Connecticut office."

"First off, I figured it wouldn't hurt for you to have backup from someone who has firsthand knowledge that your ideas work, including the newest policy you set up. Secondly, I've got a meeting lined up for later. But those aren't the sole motives behind my presence." Bradley's eyes sparkle and he sits up, a clear indication he has an ace up his sleeve. "There's been talk that a few of our clients are going to be leaving us for Ecclestone Construction."

"That kind of talk happens all the time," I say, waving my hand dismissively. "Every few months people get it in their heads that Legacy and Ecclestone are fighting for clients. We don't have to fight them—our reputation speaks for itself. There's never been any evidence behind the rumors."

"Except this time, it's different."

I shake my head in disbelief. "How so?"

"One of my sales associates had their most recent prospective client swiped out from under him at the last moment by Ecclestone, undercutting us with scary accuracy. Only someone with insider information would have known what the exact quote was we provided."

Goddammit. I mull over what Bradley said. Damn office gossip. Ecclestone, in particular, seems to be everyone's favorite villain, living up to his name as a dishonest and immoral player on the chessboard, feeding the rumor mill nonstop. Things went quiet for a while around Ecclestone's CEO after some major scandal that I didn't pay much attention to. But apparently, shortly before shit hit the fan, Edmund Ecclestone signed the firm over to his nephew. I'm not "in the know" of what happened then. I have an aversion to gossip. However, if what Bradley is saying is true, I probably need to start paying attention.

That being said, one instance is hardly a reason to panic.

"We'll keep an eye on it and make sure it's not a recurring issue," I tell him. "Is there anything else?"

"Just that the other partners are growing tired of Huxley's... hesitancy."

I perk up. First good thing I've heard all day. "How so?"

"I believe Bernie's exact words were, 'Saul, give up this crusade on Bancroft. Get on board with the changes or suggest some of your own.'"

Leave it to Bradley to bury the lead. That *is* something new. Nathan Bernie, the CEO of the company who operates from Connecticut (and thus the person Bradley directly reports to), and the other partners have always backed Huxley's decisions. They always present a united front. But it seems that front is cracking. I know if I keep persisting something is going to give.

Mood improved, I smack the table. "That's what I like to hear."

Bradley grins, offering me his fist. "I thought you'd appreciate that. We're not the only ones who are getting tired of Huxley. He's clinging to a past that doesn't exist anymore. The other partners are all in their seventies and ready for retirement. Soon, he's not going to have any choice."

"Any idea when Bernie will be heading out the door?"

Bradley shakes his head with a sigh. "Nah. Not any time soon."

I check the time. "All right, let's go to the conference room. It's time for the meeting."

I walk out of the office, pausing by Eden's desk along the way. "Eden, reschedule my two o'clock with Mr. Miller. I want it scheduled for one o'clock tomorrow afternoon. Switch Mr. Banks into that empty two o'clock spot. Then I need you to get the copy of the Parker file out of the filing cabinet and go through it from front to back. There's a checklist on the inside cover. I need you to compare it to what's in the file and let me know if anything is missing. We were waiting on several items. Compile the list, then reach out to Parker for any missing items. Study the Grangers' profile. But first, get familiar with the Harbor View Developments account ASAP. We'll be meeting with them in two days and that only gives us today and Wednesday to finalize the slideshow we've been working on for weeks. Confirm the time and date while you're at it. You got all that?"

Eden had been scribbling furiously as I listed orders. When I'm done, she looks up and smiles. "Got it. Have a good meeting."

In the conference room, everything is set and ready to go. Saul Huxley is already there, sitting at the head of the table in the seat I usually claim.

Without batting an eye, I take the seat on the other end. "Morning, Huxley," I say as Bradley takes the seat nearest mine. "Where is everybody?"

"Morning." Huxley barely even looks at me as he ignores my question. Instead, he keeps his gaze on his phone, typing away. "Everhart, good to see you. I'm surprised Bernie sent you in his place."

"Bernie sends his regards." Bradley adjusts his jacket, unfazed by Huxley's aloofness. "I'm head of sales, and he trusts me to report back to him with relevant information."

"Does he now? Well, I was always more hands-on than he was." Huxley puts his phone down, and with his gaze trained on me, he folds his hands, resting them on the shiny top of the wooden conference table. "Since we're all here, we can get started."

I raise my eyebrow, noting the empty seats. "I'm sure the other sales staff would be happy to be here for this, given it pertains to them."

"I informed them that their attendance isn't necessary. You need to run these policies by me before bringing them to the team," Huxley says, waving his hand dismissively. "*I'll* decide if it's something we'll be moving forward to implement."

Typical Huxley. No matter how many times we've gone back and forth about changes, he'll always come back to me at the last minute as if we haven't discussed anything. It's his way of trying to trip me up, trying to find a hole in my logic or something I haven't thought of. Every time, he's proven wrong.

"If you insist," I say simply, not backing down.

I spend the next fifteen minutes outlining the new procedures. Bradley has already proven their effectiveness by testing them with his staff. Since then, they've received a near five-percent increase in sales conversation over the last ninety days. It doesn't sound like much, but it adds up to huge amounts. I'm confident that my team will be able to do even better, considering I hand-picked them myself and know what they're capable of.

When I'm done talking, Huxley drums his fingers on the table. "Ninety days hardly seems like a long enough time to prove you'll be effective in the long run," he argues dismissively. "I say we wait another ninety days just to be on the safe side."

"We measure all reports by the ninety-day mark, and it's been well-established that it's the right indication of our progress."

"Our normal day-to-day progress, yes. But not when it comes to new trends."

"I thought you might say that." I pick up the remote on the table and point it at the screen on the wall. A new report appears, revealing significantly more growth. "Which is why Bradley and his team implemented the change in procedure thirty days before the original launch date. The team has already been prepped and ready to go, so it doesn't make sense to delay."

Huxley remains silent. I notice him clenching his jaw.

"With the additional thirty days, that brings our increased sales to fifteen percent. More than enough of a margin of growth to indicate progress." Fifteen percent isn't more than enough, it's spectacular. He knows that.

Huxley tears his eyes away from me to look at Bradley. "And the transition process?" he asks in a sharp voice.

"Manageable and smooth," Bradley says without missing a beat. "Carter has done the training in person and the both of us worked with staff to ensure they were more than prepared."

I can virtually see the gears turning in Huxley's head as he tries to think of another angle. But I'm no stranger to his tactics and haven't given him an inch.

"I don't see the reason to change at all," he finally concludes. "The way we do things now has proven to work in the past. No reason to fix what isn't broken."

"I don't believe in the whole 'we've always done it this way' mentality," I tell him. "If we're blinded by what we know works, we're missing a wider audience. Things aren't the same as they were twenty years ago—hell, they're not the same as they were five years ago. We can either adapt or fade into obscurity."

Needless to say, the rest of the meeting goes about as well as the beginning. Eventually, Huxley has no choice but to call the rest of the sales team in to be debriefed. As I speak to them and reveal the timeline for implementing the new procedures, Huxley throws his two cents in here and there. I address all concerns without issues, unwilling to show my subordinates exactly how pissed off I'm getting at our boss.

By the time it's all over, I want to lock myself in my office for some peace and quiet. I don't get a chance to touch base with Bradley after. He has to step out to attend another meeting in the city. We'll meet up later at lunch.

A Bossy Roommate

. . .

When I get back to the office, Eden looks up from her computer with a smile. Which promptly fades when she sees my face. "Everything okay?"

"Fine," I say, not having the time for pleasantries. "Did you make those changes I asked for?"

"Yes, sure did. I switched Mr. Miller to tomorrow at one and called Mr. Parker to schedule him for two o'clock this afternoon."

"Mr. Banks."

"Pardon?"

"I told you to call Mr. *Banks* for today. Mr. Parker is the one whose file you were supposed to be organizing."

Eden's face falls. "I'm so sorry," she says, looking at her notes. "I must have gotten the names mixed up."

I try not to let anger take center stage. "Listen, I don't have time to hold your hand. If you can't keep a simple set of instructions straight, then maybe this isn't the job for you. Get on the phone, call Mr. Parker's office, and tell them that you made a mistake. Fix this now, Eden."

She nods, her face pale. "Yes, sir."

I march off to my office. Between Huxley trying to undermine me and Eden screwing up my schedule, I'm properly annoyed. It doesn't help that Aunt Eleanor will be arriving in four days, and on top of everything, I have to prep Eden for her visit and let her know exactly what she needs to say or do when around my aunt. It's vital that she retains the information I give her.

I throw myself into my work, blocking everything else out until lunchtime rolls around. I get a text from Bradley, letting me know he's on his way to Giuseppe's. I welcome the break.

Eden smiles when I leave my office, though it doesn't quite reach her eyes. "I fixed the issue with the schedule," she says promptly. "Mr. Banks will be here for two o'clock."

"Good. Don't let it happen again. Also, how are the preparations for Thursday going?"

"Thursday eleven o'clock with Harbor View Developments in

Phoenix is confirmed, and 'everything else' is set." She puts a special emphasis on "everything else."

Good. One less headache. Our Las Vegas pit stop will be perfectly masked by a meeting our potential client had planned months ago.

Eden flips a page, saying, "Friday after work would be best to sit down and go over the details for the weekend."

"Fine, we'll do it after work. I'm going out to lunch. Did you take a look at that Parker file?"

"I'm working on it right now."

"See that it's done before I get back. What about the Harbor View Developments account?"

"I'm working on it next."

"Get up to speed on that ASAP. There's a list with brochures and reports I need you to collect in the archive room for our meeting. Ask Jaylin for help if you can't find anything. She was involved when we reorganized the room."

∽

I LEAVE her to her work and drive to meet Bradley. We arrive at the same time, and the hostess leads us to our reserved table. They have my favorite table ready for us. Bradley and I order our usual, and once the waiter leaves to put in our order, Bradley gives me a sympathetic smile.

"God," he says, "I've never met anyone who fights so hard against change than Huxley. It's ridiculous."

"Welcome to my life. I can handle Huxley."

"Speaking of handling," Bradley says with a grin. "Now that we're not in the office, I need more details on that *wifey* roommate of yours. Tell me about the night you spent together. How good was it?"

Annoyance with Huxley aside, I think about the one-night stand. It was definitely memorable. I meet his gaze. "None of your business."

"Let me guess—you snuck out while she was sleeping?"

"That's what happened," I answer, my irritation returning.

Bradley chuckles. "Bet that was a shock walking into work to find your one-night stand there. So why aren't you two going to knock boots while she's staying with you?"

"I already told you why."

"Yeah, but how does *she* feel about the whole thing?"

"She's sworn off men for the next six months."

A broad, ear-to-ear smile adorns Bradley's lips, stretching across his face with exuberant delight. "Ohohoo...wow, *dude*. Were you really that bad that you turned her away from men in general?"

"Shut up. She was plenty satisfied when I was done with her."

"You sure? Maybe she was faking it."

"Maybe."

"Maybe I could teach you a thing or two."

I roll my eyes at his joke.

He leans in and lowers his voice. "You know that the louder a woman is in bed, the more she's faking it. She is desperate to get it over with. The louder the screams, the worse your performance is. She wants you to finally bust. Women think that we think that the louder they are, the more they're enjoying themselves. The opposite is true."

"Who told you that?"

"Dude. Life taught me that."

The waiter brings us our drinks, which we immediately pick up. Bradley lifts his in a toast. "In all seriousness, do you really think you can resist plowing her again?" he asks, tapping his glass to mine. "I mean if she wasn't your assistant and hadn't sworn off the opposite sex."

I picture Eden beneath me.

The way her back had arched when I'd tasted her in the motel room. How her legs parted instinctively for me, how her hips begged for my tongue, and how her whole body shuddered when she came undone, grabbing fistfuls of the sheets, beautiful, desperate moans filling the room. Her eyes were hooded, her nipples perky, top teeth digging into her bottom lip when I'd pushed in. She softly moaned my name as she clutched onto my shoulders, just before I caught a speck of heartache in her pupils, one she'd been effectively concealing behind a façade of confidence all night. She held onto me, onto my shoulders, her arms circling me tightly, fingernails digging into me, fully enveloped in the close embrace I offered her as I slowly filled her.

The way her body had wrapped around mine in the dark still made my heart stutter.

I'd feathered my lips across hers, locked eyes with her and pulled out and thrust back into her, pulsing deeper and deeper, fucking the sadness out of her. As long as she was with me, there would be no past to revisit.

There would only be us.

Her eyes had smiled at me when I'd fucked her. I'll never forget those green eyes and that look.

She'd given me a similar look last night when I'd put the fire out on her balcony.

"Of course I can resist her," I tell him. "It's not going to happen, so there's no use thinking about it."

Bradley chuckles, taking a sip of his drink. "Famous last words. Buddy, she's living with you now. Fake marriage scheme or not, sharing a space with someone you've had sex with and are physically attracted to can only go one way."

"You act like I have no self-control. Have you met me?"

"You are the most controlled person I've ever met in my entire life, true. However, a man has needs. Don't tell me you're not jerking off to her."

That almost gets a rise out of me.

It's no surprise that Bradley thinks I wouldn't be able to handle living with Eden without trying to guide her to my bed. The reason we're such good buddies is that we share the same philosophy. Our focus lies on relationship building. Having their best interest in mind, listening to *them*, caring. Everyone wants something. Knowing what other people want is the key to success in partnerships, deals, and negotiations. By understanding their objectives and desires, we figure out how to establish arrangements that are advantageous for all parties involved, resulting in win-win situations, and ultimately stronger relationships. The stronger the relationship, the stronger the team, the stronger we are as a company.

In this case, however, the one thing *I* want from Eden most is neither a relationship nor sex.

It's her cooperation to deal with my aunt.

"My needs are just fine, thank you," I tell Bradley, ready to end the subject. "Speaking of needs, whatever happened to that real estate agent from London you were trying to hook up with?"

At the mention of his own sex life, Bradley's eyes light up. "Oh, man, dude, you're in for a story. So, we met up with Jane last week..."

9

EDEN

I'm glad to see Carter leave for lunch. His verbal lashing earlier wasn't pleasant, to say the least. I feel bad about messing up his schedule, but there was nothing I could do other than fix it. Thankfully, I was able to quickly clear up the misunderstanding, and the client's assistant couldn't have been more pleasant. Considering it's only my second day, I'd say I'm doing a decent job, mix-up aside. Still, between staying with Carter and working with him, I need a break from his presence.

After he leaves, I decide I'll take my lunch too.

I grab my purse and the container of breakfast leftovers I brought. When I poke my head into Gretchen's office, she's typing away at her computer.

"Hey! Do you want to take your break?" I ask.

She looks up and smiles. "Yes, for the love of God. I haven't moved from this spot since I got in."

"Busy day?"

"Always." She logs off her computer and grabs her stuff.

Together, we go down to the break room. The other girls aren't there so we grab a table for the two of us. After heating up my food, I sink into my seat with a heavy sigh.

"Speaking of busy days," Gretchen says, taking the lid off her salad. "How's everything going today?"

"Well, for the most part, it's been fine. However, I did make a mistake with scheduling, which Mr. Bancroft was less than thrilled about. Thankfully I was able to fix it."

"That man is really particular about his schedule."

"I'll say. He was pretty pissed off. But I'm trying not to dwell on it."

Gretchen studies me for a moment as we start to eat. I'm not sure, but I get the sense that there's something on her mind. After we've each taken a few bites, her gaze shifts upward. "Hey, can I ask you something?" she asks in a low voice.

"Sure..."

"I can't help but get the sense that there's something between you and Mr. Bancroft."

My guard goes up, and I try to keep my face passive and my food from dropping off of my fork. "What do you mean?"

"It's hard to explain. I guess, there was a familiarity there that I wasn't expecting."

I contemplate what to say. Carter's adamant that no one in the company knows what happened between us. I don't owe Gretchen any explanation, nor do I want to give her one flat out. The only problem is, if the chemistry between me and Carter is this noticeable, not saying anything could lead to worse assumptions. I don't want to lie outright. Perhaps I can be vague enough to satisfy her curiosity?

"We met once before, but I don't know him very well," I say, choosing my words carefully, emphasizing them with a casual shrug. "I was surprised to see him on my first day. I'm sure that's what you were picking up on."

She studies me. "Probably. Where did you run into him?"

I think about telling her about the ice cream place and whole "roommate situation," but instead I say, "He's my neighbor."

That's not a lie. Not entirely. His room is next to mine. Once Hattie moves out, Carter will be my actual neighbor and that could easily explain any weirdness anyone might sense between us going forward. Also, it will eliminate any further questions as to why we have the same address. Someone at HR will notice eventually. In my sister's firm, we'd all filled out a sheet with everybody's name, address, and birth date. It was supposed to help bonding as well as possible car sharing.

"*Really?*" Gretchen's eyes widen. "Oh, man, that's gotta be weird being neighbors with your boss."

"You don't know the half of it." I briefly explain to her how I'd ended up in a posh apartment, carefully omitting all the details of the crazy date mix-up, of course, as well as the fact that Kate and Lewis's apartment wasn't quite ready for me yet, resulting in my unfortunate temporary stay at Carter's place.

"Wait, that would also mean you're possibly going to be running into him in your spare time too."

"Yup. That's very likely."

Gretchen makes an "I'm sorry" face, shaking her blonde head. "Rough deal. Imagine wanting to unwind after work and still bumping into your demanding boss. Well, as long as he doesn't try to rope you into working for him outside of office hours... Although, I will warn you that that is a possibility. He puts in more hours than anyone else and several of his other assistants had to stay late numerous times. That's why they quit eventually."

"I don't mind that. I plan on saving as much as possible during the next six months. That being said, I'm definitely not going to let him dictate my work schedule outside of the office."

In my mind, I know that's going to be difficult since I'll be staying in his apartment for two whole weeks, but I'm rather good at sticking to my guns when I need to. On the plus side, Gretchen makes me think of another ground rule I should set when we get back to his place: no discussing work outside of work hours.

"On the other hand," Gretchen smiles, "in New York, nobody knows their neighbors. You probably won't even see him when you're off duty."

You have no idea, I think, taking a bite of my crispy toast. "Don't worry about me. I can hold my own against Carter Bancroft. I just don't want any rumors spreading," I add truthfully.

Gretchen grins. "Oh, no worries, hon, your secret is safe with me. But be careful around Lexi. She's our gossip queen, as you might have noticed. If she knows, everybody knows. Ever since the news slipped through that Mr. Bancroft went to battle for a pay raise for his team and all of us assistants after winning that huge Granger account, Lexi has been enamored with him and dying for news. Best keep some things to yourself when she's around." Gretchen adjusts her red-framed glasses. "However, I did have another question. You seem pretty firm on that six-month time frame you mentioned. I never asked you why you came to the city for a few months."

"Oh, I don't think we have a long enough lunchtime to fill you in on all the details."

Gretchen laughs at my joke. "Get through as much of the story as you can."

I tell her about Rob and being left at the altar. How painful it had been for me, how I didn't even see it coming. She confides in me that she sometimes isn't exactly the best judge of character either and we bond over the fact we've both made bad decisions in the past, especially when it comes to matters of the heart. It's a nice, chill lunch hour. After my break, I go back to my desk, refreshed and ready to take on the rest of the day.

CARTER BARELY PAYS me any attention when he gets back. His afternoon is filled with back-to-back meetings, and the only instructions he gives me are sent via internal messages between appointments. Occasionally I go to the archive room to pull the brochures and reports he asks me for. Five o'clock rolls around, and when he doesn't return to the office or message me again, I pack up for the day.

I took an Uber in this morning, but since it's the end of the day, I decide to walk back to the apartment. I want a chance to stretch my legs and take a look at the city. I make my way from mid-Manhattan toward the Upper East Side, passing iconic landmarks like Bryant Park and Times Square.

Coming from a small town, I instantly feel lost in the sea of people—but not in a bad way. The crowd offers a kind of anonymity I'm not used to, and for some reason, I find it inspiring. I love walking among everyone, observing them, feeling the vibrant energy of the city pulsate around me, and I can't help but wonder about the people around me. Who are they? Where are they going? What are their lives like?

A forty-five-minute walk turns into an hour and a half. The air isn't as fresh as back home, but it has its own characteristics. Yes, there are noises, exhaust fumes, and oil from the many cars, but I focus on the food smells wafting from various directions. I pass the tall and majestic Rockefeller Center, charming shops nestled in the vibrant streets near Central Park, and upscale boutiques lining Madison Avenue. Along the way, street vendors peddle delicious-looking meals, and I also spot a few pizza restaurants and bistros I vow to try once I get my first paycheck. Finally, I reach the prestigious Upper East Side with its tree-lined streets, elegant townhouses, and refined ambience.

BACK INSIDE THE APARTMENT BUILDING, I pull some of the glossy brochures out of my handbag and tuck them under my arm to get to my phone and keys. While I ride the elevator up, I check my messages. There are a couple from Carter outlining tasks for the next day, but the final message tells me he's ordered dinner, and it will be arriving shortly. That's the only text I respond to, which is on purpose. When he gets home, I will tell him my new ground rule about contacting me after hours. Not just for my sanity. It's important that he gets relaxation in too, and by refusing to be at his beck and call twenty-four-seven, he'll have no other choice but to switch off the boss-mode.

I'm so busy on my phone that I don't hear Hattie's door open until I start fumbling with my keys.

"Evening, Eden, love!"

I jump in surprise. "Hattie! You startled me."

She chuckles from her open doorway. "Oh dear, did you perhaps mistake me for a ghost? Ha-ha, I'm not quite dead yet, you know. I do apologize, my dear. I assumed you'd heard me open the door. You're back pretty late, aren't you?"

"Yeah, I took a walk after work. I want to explore as much of the city as I can while I'm here."

"Oh! That's lovely, dear! As it happens, I've compiled a list of all the places I find delightful. And it's not just the mundane museums, you know! I'd be most pleased to share it with you."

"That would be great, thank you, Hattie. How was your day?"

"I've just finished grooming Myrtle and Mitsy. Ruth is up next. On top of that, I've sorted through some of my photo albums and diaries, preparing everything meticulously for the impending move. This old girl, has journeyed quite a distance, you know," she says, affectionately patting her round hips. "You'd probably be amazed by the tales I could tell you. I'm as British as they come, born and raised across the pond. But then along came an American doctor named Theodore, who whisked me away. Before I knew it, I had my bags packed and was crossing the ocean to embark on a new chapter. Theodore wasn't my first spouse, mind you. And he certainly wasn't my last, because after him, there was Conrad—"

Buzzz.

My phone goes off. A text tells me that the food is on the way. "I'm so sorry, I have to go prep for dinner, but I swear, Hattie, I'm going to need to hear the entire story of your life."

"And I shall be delighted to recount it all, my dear. And then you can enlighten me about what it's like to reside with your employer."

Whoa.

I almost drop my phone.

How does she know that? Yesterday, I only told her that we knew each other, but not from where or how. "How do you know he's my boss?"

"Oh, I just joined the dots, my dear. This old bat possesses a keen intuition, you see. Plus, you mentioned you've just returned from work and you're clutching his company's annual report and brochures under your arm." She laughs.

I look down and laugh too. *Duh.* "Good night, Hattie."

"Good night, love."

Now it seems both Gretchen and Hattie know more than they should about my living situation with my boss. Hopefully none of this will backfire.

10

EDEN
TWO DAYS LATER, THURSDAY

We board his private jet to Phoenix at about a quarter past six. During the early flight hours, Carter perfects his notes and talks me through his plan of action.

There are two major accounts he's been fixated on. The first is Granger Estates, a commercial construction firm he had previously brought onboard for Legacy. According to Gretchen, it's one of the biggest clients Legacy has managed to land, all thanks to Carter's efforts. The other even bigger one is Harbor View Developments, a massive real estate company Carter wants to get his hands on.

They're the ones we'll be meeting at eleven o'clock.

All day yesterday, Carter had involved me in preparing a presentation that's supposed to knock them off their feet and bring us that much closer to landing the account. I'd helped perfect the slides all day, aside from my normal tasks like scheduling, project coordination, and customer service. In the three days I've been there, it almost feels as if I've learned more than I did in the last three years at my sister's firm combined, and it's super fun doing so, especially when it comes to client relations. Interpersonal skills are a strength of mine, and I enjoy refining them.

· · ·

When Carter and I enter the imposing Harbor View building, I can't help but feel nervous, even though, or maybe because, it's more of an unofficial, intimate pre-meeting between the two CEOs and Carter. Apparently, we represent one of the three construction firms still in the running, and the personal visit is meant to give us a glimpse of their company and get a better feel for their vision before the main presentation at Legacy next week.

"The board thinks we have no chance," Carter tells me, his voice low.

"Our board? Legacy's board?"

He nods. "When I first reached out to Harbor View, I didn't expect anything to come from it, given that they operate on the other side of the country. Turns out, they are looking to expand on the East Coast, and that's what made the difference and helped us get a foot in. Lesson is, it never hurts to ask. They invited Huxley to today's meeting too, but he declined." Carter looks at me darkly, straightening his tie. "Now, let's prove our board wrong."

"Challenge accepted. We'll turn those naysayers into yay-sayers, let's do it!"

The potential clients, Joe Walsh and Adam Baker, greet us and lead us to a conference room where we settle in around a large black table. Both men are somewhere in their mid-fifties, dressed casually, and I assume it's to underscore the informal meeting. After the initial note exchange, Adam receives an urgent call and excuses himself, leaving his partner Joe to handle the rest. The conversation shifts to our team's approach to project management, and Joe asks some detailed questions. Carter answers all of them with ease, and I interject with additional information. We're a great team, highlighting Legacy's focus on communication, organization, and efficient problem-solving.

Joe seems increasingly impressed. "I can see why your company has such a strong reputation in the industry."

"We've worked hard to earn that reputation," Carter says. "It's the result of our team's dedication to consistently delivering top-notch solutions and building meaningful, lasting partnerships."

From there, Carter dives into the plans he has for Harbor View, showing some of the glossy brochures we brought along. Watching him, I'm in awe at his "No BS" approach. His communication is clear and to the point. His vision is *huge*. Carter has a talent for presenting groundbreaking, sophisticated ideas in an exciting manner, and in the relatively short amount of time he's had, he's managed to not just whet Joe's appetite for more but also leave him with his jaw hanging wide open.

As we say our goodbyes and walk out of the conference room, Carter turns to me. "Good job, Eden. You really held your own in there."

"I think we're in good shape for the main presentation." I smile, proud of him, but also of myself for contributing to such a significant meeting.

"We just need to keep up the momentum and really *wow* them with our pitch next week."

From there we fly to Las Vegas.

I've never been to Vegas before, and unfortunately, I don't really get a chance to enjoy the flight, or to relax. Believe me, I wouldn't be more nervous if it was a real wedding, not just us playing dress-up for a photoshoot in bride and groom attire. The distraction of work helps my jittery nerves. Carter is on the phone working pretty much the entire time. So am I. Either I'm taking calls on my work cell and forwarding the important ones to him, or busy with other admin tasks.

He's left me to organize everything for the wedding, and as his assistant, I'm there to make sure everything runs smoothly.

When the flight attendant serves drinks and food, Carter has me fill out and sign the "wedding paperwork" that includes the notation about the incredible bonus I'll be entitled to (and my account will be shocked to see deposited). His attorney overnighted the contract from the Easter Islands (Carter made him work during his vacation!), and he'll stop by in person with the NDA later this week.

The successful meeting and the positive atmosphere between us makes it easier for me to actually go through with the scheme.

However, despite my attempts otherwise, the whole experience makes me think about Rob. He had done everything he could to avoid marrying me, and yet with Carter, it's like he can't tie the knot soon enough. A sham marriage, of course, but still. When I said I was ready to be married, this wasn't exactly the unexpected turn I had in mind.

As soon as the jet lands, Carter whisks me away to a high-end jewelry store, foiling my plans of visiting a more affordable place. Seriously, I see a necklace that costs ten times more than my Kiki. We buy two wedding bands, which I can't stop staring at because they symbolize the eternal bond we do *not* share. At first, I'd opted for a simple gold band, but he insisted on me getting a diamond ring. He picked out a dazzling sparkly diamond set band that could probably fund a small country. It wasn't like I could refuse my boss's demands—so I politely and *humbly* accepted. (As if! I jumped on that opportunity like a frog on a lily pad.)

I'm deeply touched by his generosity, even though it doesn't change the fact that this marriage is a strict business arrangement. Just when I think I'll end up blinded by all the diamond-sparkles reflecting back at me from my new ring, Carter decides that I need an engagement ring too, with a diamond bigger than the moon. I mean, at this point, let's just say I don't protest too much. But I tell him we needed to get me sunglasses to protect me from all the brightness.

Of course, I'll return the rings to him once our fake marriage is over, but until his aunt flies back to France, I'll wear them, feeling like a princess. For a whole weekend, I'll relish the bliss of being the woman NYC's most eligible bachelor had walked down the aisle and taken as his "forever" wife.

It takes several hours for the wedding clothes to be custom altered to fit perfectly. Carter wants to make sure that everything is authentic. (Sidenote: If this *was* an authentic wedding, we would have used the waiting period to visit the Clark County Marriage License Bureau, where an authentic couple would have filled out the necessary paperwork and obtained a marriage license, but since we don't have to do that, we spend the time working.) Waiting for the custom alteration to arrive seems like an eternity. Boy, is it worth it though. Carter looks *dashing* in his tailor-made suit, and my wedding dress is a dream come true, fitting me so perfectly that I feel like a delicate flower snugly nestled in its petals. (It doesn't even come close to the simple dress I'd worn not too long ago, which now in comparison, likely made me look like a wannabe bride in a glamorous white potato sack.)

The photoshoot itself takes place in a small chapel on the strip. Even though I know it's all for the camera and Carter's aunt, I'm a little disappointed that there's not an Elvis impersonator to "fake" marry us. I'd done my best to get one, but Carter had said no when I'd told him my idea. I should have seen it coming that he wouldn't go for "such nonsense"—which I find hilarious given how funny our entire situation is.

The funniest part, though, is our photo session. It's a bit awkward at first, posing for romantic photos with my boss. Once or twice, the thought of Rob crosses my mind and I imagine how our photos would have turned out, but to my surprise, amid all his grumpy, bossy behavior, I find myself preferring to be Carter's fake bride than Rob's real one.

At one point, Carter accidentally steps on my dress and rips it. I burst out laughing, and the photographer captures the moment perfectly. Carter says he doesn't see the humor in it—however, I *do* see his lips quirk a bit. And so will the camera.

That's as close as I get to witnessing Carter smile.

I guess it's the closest thing we have to a romantic moment too.

Normally, the kiss is *the* romantic moment. Not in our case.

When the man pretends to pronounce us husband and wife for the camera, Carter doesn't kiss me on the lips. He doesn't even give me a quick peck. He doesn't kiss me at all. Not even on my cheek.

Jerk. He could have at least planted one on me.

I know this isn't a real marriage, but still.

Kissing wouldn't have been against my rule, but who knows, maybe Carter wants to be respectful and not breach our boss-assistant line.

Maybe he's worried that an intimate moment—like a kiss—would be too much. And he's right. It would be. I don't need the temptation after the heartbreak I went through.

Still, I can't help but wonder how it would feel to be kissed by a man like Carter Bancroft.

At least once.

Come to think of it, seriously, does this man not know how to kiss? When we were together last Sunday, his mouth had been busy exploring all parts of my body, and I wasn't about to complain. But in his rush to have me (because that's what it was: an *animalistic, unstoppable* surge), he'd forgone kissing my mouth. To make things even more infuriating, he has the most gorgeous lips on the planet. I can't stop staring at them when he's not looking: they're soft, inviting, kissable.

Somehow, it bugs me that I don't know if he's a good kisser or not. I'm in the dark about his hand-holding skills too. I mean, he doesn't even hold my hand as we exit the chapel!

Double jerk.

I force myself to think of something else other than kissing or holding hands with my boss. My fake husband. My fake boss husband. Fake husband roommate. My bossy roommate.

Damn, no matter how many combinations I try, it feels weird.

I stare out the window at the dark night, my fingers idly playing with the two sparkling rings on my finger.

Well, I guess I still get to be a sort of wife after all.

Silver lining.

We'd both changed back into regular clothes before we'd boarded the plane.

Carter sits a few seats away, still on the phone with work. It gives me a glimpse into how demanding his job really is—being here right next to him instead of just sitting outside his office has opened my eyes to his efficiency and to why he wants certain things done the way he does. He's under a tremendous amount of pressure. How does he even sleep at night? No wonder he hasn't gotten married or doesn't have a long-term girlfriend. He doesn't seem like he has the time for either.

We're about a half an hour shy of landing when he finally puts the phone away. He leans back in his seat and closes his eyes.

"Tired?" I ask.

"It's been a long day."

"I'll say." I keep twirling the rings around my finger. "You spent a lot of money on wedding bands that I'm only going to be wearing for two days. I would have been just as satisfied with costume jewelry or something."

"For the last time. No wife of mine, fake or not, is wearing costume jewelry. Don't worry about the price of the rings. Besides, you wanted me to be the doting husband who fawns over his wife, didn't you?"

"I meant flowers and hand-holding," *and kissing*, I think, but I don't say that out loud. Mentioning hand-holding feels audacious enough, but he doesn't react, so I add, "or showing me more of New York City, not blowing obscene amounts of dollars on rings that are just for show. But hey, it's your money. You do you."

Carter leans back in his chair, studying me for a moment. "Tell me about yourself."

"What do you want to know?" I ask. A spur of excitement rushes through my veins, until I realize he's just trying to use the time to collect data about me, so we don't have too much to go through tomorrow night.

"The basics. Where you come from, your parents, you know, things like that. Things I would know if I was your husband."

"My parents died when I was young. No grandma or grandpa. My sister, she's many years older, made sure I was fine. She took over Dad's company, a small home-based eco-friendly landscaping business. Also, it's comforting to know that I'll have a family and a job to return to in six months, when I leave New York again, just as I promised her. I owe her a lot, even though sometimes we don't see eye to eye."

"Why not?"

"It's a long story."

Carter glances at the watch on his wrist. "We still have time. What happened?"

I sigh heavily. "I'll give you the short version of events. I fell in love. I asked the man to marry me. He said yes. He left me during the ceremony. My sister never liked him, and when I told her I needed a change, she accused me of running away from my problems."

Carter studies me with his carefully controlled expression. It's hard to know what's going through his mind. When I finish talking, he makes a face. "What fucking lowlife asshole ditches their fiancée at the altar?"

"Rob. That's his name. Robert Winthrope."

"He has no right calling himself a man."

"On that, we can both agree. Apparently, he never loved me. I'm sure he's off sowing his wild oats and leaving a stream of brokenhearted women in his wake."

Carter narrows his eyes. "That has to be the most downbeat thing I've heard from you in the few days we've known each other. You've got a knack for keeping things positive."

"On the contrary, it's actually a very positive thought."

"How so?"

"He's gone." I try to laugh.

Carter nods, and there's warmth in his sincere eyes. It almost makes me keel over. It's a nice, genuine expression, and it makes his stunning face deadly captivating.

Then I remember that the topic we're talking about is quite sad. But still. It feels good to get it off my chest and be joyful, if even for a moment. I don't even want to think about the poor women who might fall for Rob in the future.

Our short conversation is over the moment my work phone rings again, and I answer it. Harbor View. Sure, it's late, and I could have just let it go to voice mail, Carter wouldn't have minded, but at this point—now that I've personally met them and know what's at stake—I'm fully invested. After pleasant small talk with Joe and a nod from Carter indicating that he'll take the call, I forward it to his phone.

. . .

A Bossy Roommate

NOT LONG AFTER, the plane finally lands in New York, and before I know it, we're back at the apartment building. Today has been such an emotional roller coaster. I'm exhausted. All I want to do is crawl into bed and sleep for as long as I can. I need to get some rest if I'm going to be useful at work tomorrow. The second we get off the elevator, Hattie's door creaks open, and she nosily peeks out.

"Nothing to see here," Carter says, unlocking our door and immediately stepping inside.

I ignore his rudeness and smile at Hattie. "It's just us. Sorry if we disturbed you."

"Oh, please don't mind me, I'm just a bit nosy. So...what might you have in that box?"

I look down at the box I'm holding. Inside is the wedding topper of our cake. Well, it isn't a cake-cake. With the short notice, I got a collection of cupcakes. (Okay, I would have gotten a cake, but I figured wedding cupcakes were way more fun and relatable after the "almost" fire incident, plus they won't go to waste like a huge wedding cake would have.) The cupcakes are decorated with a luscious vanilla cream topping and a bright red, succulent, juicy strawberry on top. Carter said they were only needed for photos, but I insisted on bringing them home because who wastes cupcakes? Nuh-uh. Not this one.

"Cupcakes. They're vegan and delicious. Here, have one."

Trying to keep my distance and avoid the cat hair that is no doubt clinging to her clothes, I open the box toward her, and she gasps. Heavenly fruity smells surrounded us. At first, I think she is really into those strawberry cupcakes, that's how big her eyes grow, but then her hand takes my left one, and she notices the rings.

"Goodness me, you certainly do work swiftly!"

Ah, shit. She doesn't miss anything. What should I tell her? I can't exactly tell her that we suddenly fell in love and got married. She'll never believe it.

"It's...complicated," I say.

"Indeed, my dear, all relationships are." She waves her hand. "This couldn't possibly be connected to a certain relative of his who's scheduled to visit, could it?"

How the heck does she know that?

Was she listening at the door? Or have I moved in next to a psychic?

At my alarmed expression, she laughs. "Don't panic, love. Eleanor and I are friends. She kindly gave me a ring to let me know about her impending visit. I had a hunch it would set her nephew into a bit of a flurry."

"So, you know about the marriage story?" I ask in a soft voice.

"As I understand it, she's quite delighted he's taken the plunge at last. But you know, I've also noticed that it's been *quite a while* since I last saw him with a lady. It's a sham marriage, am I right? Just for appearances? Please don't worry, I shan't unravel whatever plan he's cooked up in that head of his. It just concerns me that he's got you tangled up in it."

"It's all right," I say with a shrug. "I can handle whatever Carter throws at me. It's just for the weekend anyway."

"Might you be in need of any friendly advice, my dear?" she asks, biting back a cheeky smile, mischief dancing in her eyes.

"About what?"

"The wedding night."

I burst into laughter. "I think I'm all right on that front."

"Are you quite certain? It's just that I possess a multitude of tales on the topic. I myself entered the bonds of matrimony a total of six times, you know."

Holy shit. My elderly cat lady neighbor has six successful stories on the subject! She's not only the sweetest and funniest, but now officially the most unassuming old lady I've ever met.

"First, that's unexpected." I grin. "Second, I don't think there's going to be any real wedding night. This isn't a real wedding."

"My dear, if I were graced with a gentleman of such striking appearance, I wouldn't squander a single evening, if you catch my drift—genuine or not. Particularly if he happened to be my superior." She gives a playful wink. "Despite that ice-cool exterior, I reckon there's a fervent volcano smoldering inside..."

"*Ah!*" I playfully gasp. "Hattie, you minx!"

The old woman chuckles, grabs four cupcakes out of the box, and closes the lid. "En-jo-oyyyy," she sings playfully, pushing the box back toward me with her elbow. "The hour grows late. Myrtle, Ruth, and Mitsy require their midnight treats, and so do I. You'd best return to that fiery husband of yours."

I go back to Carter's apartment, amused by our interaction. My fiery husband is in the kitchen, pouring a glass of whiskey.

"Hattie knows."

"Well, of course she does," he says, unsurprised. "Fortunately, you haven't signed the NDA yet."

"Uh-huh." I know that he's teasing of course (at least, that's what I hope). He knows how observant Hattie is—but nonetheless, I feel guilty for not mentioning that Gretchen, too, has more info on us than she probably should have. At least Gretchen doesn't know anything about the fake marriage, and I'll make sure that she, like everyone else, never learns.

I set the remaining wedding cupcakes down on the counter, ready to get something else off my chest that Hattie just put into my head.

Something about the "wedding night."

Something I noticed about Carter's bedroom situation.

"Where does your aunt usually sleep when she visits you?" I ask him.

"Guest suite. You need to clear it until she leaves on Sunday afternoon."

"Where am I going to sleep?" The reason I'm bringing up this question—again—is because when I'd walked by his bedroom to get to the gym this morning, the door had been standing open and there *definitely* weren't two beds. What's even worse, even though his bedroom is quite spacious, the modern architecture and setting of the balcony, fixed shelves, and furniture doesn't even allow for a second bed.

"We've been over this. In my room, of course." He turns to me, giving me a "duh" face. "It's going to be our room for the weekend. We need to sell our marriage. I can't sleep on the couch if that's what you're suggesting, and neither can you. We're both sleeping in my room."

"But there's only one bed. You said there would be two. Right?"

"Right," he says.

"So?"

"So what?"

"A second bed wouldn't even fit into your bedroom...or would it?"

11
CARTER

"It wouldn't," I confirm.

"What do you mean?"

"There's only one bed, correct. Mine. We'll share it. There's no way around it. You have to sleep in my bed."

"What? No. You said there would be two beds."

"I lied."

"Carter!"

"Eden, we've already slept in one bed. I'm sure we'll manage again."

For once, she doesn't find the situation funny. "You're ruthless, absolutely ruthless. Ugh. And I already signed the contract."

"No, Eden, I'm not ruthless. I'm desperate."

Eden's eyes find mine.

Her expression softens, her shoulders drop, and she gives one nod. "Yeah, okay, have it your way. But no sleeping in the nude...you know..." The last two words come in a lower voice, and she motions in the direction of her balcony, referring to my naked state after unexpectedly having to prevent the building from burning down.

She's blushing. It's almost cute how embarrassed she is.

The moment lasts only a few seconds before her voice returns to its previous volume and determined intensity. "There will be no action. Zero. Zilch. Nada."

"Action?"

"Exactly. As in no husband-wife lovemaking, no chaining me to your bed, and no fiery eruptions."

Chaining her to my bed? Hm.

Drink in hand, I lean against the counter. "You can't stop thinking about sex with me. Can you?"

"I was just making sure. Good night."

With that, she turns and storms to her guest suite.

11.43 P.M.

I wake up to the sound of a shriek. It's similar to the one that interrupted my peaceful evening a few days prior.

My first thought is, *she's burning down the apartment again.*

I'm out of my bed and on my feet in two seconds flat.

Let me preface the next part by saying that I should have jerked off this morning. Or later in the day, or before going to sleep—at least before storming out of my room. With the interruption of her moving in with me, my routine is all over the place, and I feel pressure building up.

To disguise my "state," I hurriedly throw on my gray boxers, tripping and almost falling on my face before running to her guest suite. The door stands open. I rush inside, already seeing and smelling smoke. But her room is empty. So is the balcony. There's no fire. Not even the slightest smell of smoke. Her room carries a delightful scent, reminiscent of sweet vanilla.

"Eden?" I ask into the darkness.

No answer.

I didn't imagine the scream, did I?

I walk back out, listening intently. Some rustling noise leads me right next door to the small laundry room beside her guest suite. She hasn't turned the light on. It's dark, but by now, my eyes have fully adjusted to the darkness.

There she is in a white robe, facing away from me, not in the least looking like she needs rescuing. She's just closed the lid and turned on the washing machine. Water starts running into the cylinder while she reaches into a box on the counter to grab something with one hand and then reaches back in with her other hand. Our wedding cupcakes? Why would anybody need a sugar high at close to midnight? Holding one cupcake in one hand and biting into a cupcake in her other, she turns to leave the room.

When she sees me, she freezes in her tracks and shrieks again (luckily, this time muffled by the cupcake in her mouth). She stumbles back, to an almost sitting position on the washing machine, her legs parted to catch her balance.

"It's me, relax," I offer into the darkness.

"Carter! *Youfcarefeshifouofme*," she mumbles with huge eyes, chews, and swallows.

"Are you okay?" I ask, entering the small room, not bothering to turn on the light switch that's hidden somewhere behind one of the white shelves. Enough moonlight is streaming through the window to brighten her features.

"Jesus Christ, you scared me. I thought you were a ghost!" She visibly relaxes, still staring at me, cupcakes still firmly in her hands.

"What are you doing here?" I ask, stepping closer until my hip grazes the inner parts of her spread thighs.

She licks the frosting off the corner of her lips. "Eh...washing clothes." Her voice sounds breathy.

I lean farther in. "In the darkness?"

"I couldn't find the light switch." Her breathing is becoming erratic.

I find it satisfying that I have such an impression on her with my presence.

She's only in a white robe, probably after taking a shower. The fruity vanilla scent of her skin envelops me as my eyes drop to her neck, to the delicate curves of her decolletage. They're just revealing enough to raise an instinct in me to untie her bathrobe and explore what she's hiding beneath.

Visions of me pushing her robe open to soak in her dazzling beauty invade my mind.

My cock hardens at the thought of me exposing her tits and sucking in her left nipple and then her right.

To prevent myself from doing exactly that, I reach up to the shelves above her and hold on to it, positioning my arms on either side of her.

Eden gasps. "What are you doing…Carter?" Her eyes land on the ink on my arms, then follow my chest to my throat and up to my jaw. "I mean," she corrects herself, her gaze meeting mine, her voice raspier, "what are you doing *here*?"

Her chest heaves, rising and falling rapidly. Despite the relative darkness of the room, I see redness spreading down her chest.

"You woke me," I rumble, dipping my head down, grazing my cheek against her forehead. I lower my head further, grazing my beard stubble against the softness of her face. "I heard a shriek," I growl.

She doesn't pull away.

Her scent is invading my senses.

The thought of disrobing her slowly on that washing machine is replaced by the thought of *taking* her slowly on that washing machine.

I know it can't happen.

12

EDEN

I had shrieked. He's right.

But then I'd laughed immediately after, realizing it had only been my own reflection in the small mirror on the wall that had scared me.

I hadn't been able to find the switch in the small walk-in laundry room.

Instead, I've found myself in a sticky situation.

Him, between my legs.

Me, unable to move.

To think.

To process.

When his cheek brushes my cheek and his lips are only inches from mine, my senses start to go into havoc. There's a wild carnival in my head, and all of it is attacking me: sounds, smells, touch, his closeness, all mixed together in a jumbled frenzy.

His long lashes reflect the moonlight.

I can nearly feel them brushing my skin.

When I feel the side of his lip graze mine for just a millisecond, I almost drop the cupcakes I brought along for a mini midnight celebration.

He pulls back a little, slowly opening his eyes.

Locking eyes with him is like looking into a mesmerizing, starry sky. I find myself lost in their intense darkness, unable to look away.

"Did you scream to wake your husband so he could reward you for being a good girl doing laundry?" he rumbles in his deep, sexy baritone. "Or did you scream because you wanted him to punish the naughty little thing for waking him?"

"Eh…I wasn't trying to do either."

I'm at the point where everything is overwhelming.

Everything around me is intense.

His muscular arms, his presence, his hips pressed against my spread thighs. His *bulge*. I can feel it getting harder.

He moves his head to my ear.

Even the slightest touch of his stubble against my skin feels electrifying.

His head moves further, his lips grazing my ear. The moonlight casts shadows on his chiseled cheeks, making him look even more alluring.

"Are you trying to tell me that you're not eager to get yourself fucked?"

I mean…

I feel my cheeks flush as I stumble over my words, caught off guard. I have to take a moment to process what he said before I can respond.

"Of course not…" I whisper, my head light.

At this point, I can't even think straight. My vision is blurry, my hearing is muffled, and my sense of touch feels distorted. It's like my brain is putting all its power into me getting wet. I don't even hear the sound of the washing machine filling with water. All I hear is the sexy growl of his voice in my ears, and other parts of my body—parts of me that definitely shouldn't continue to listen.

"Because of your promise?" he growls softly, his touch against the shell of my ear sending more sensations down my spine.

"Uh-huh."

"Are you wearing anything underneath?"

I'm taken aback by his question, but can't deny the thrill it sends through me. His soft rumble is both exhilarating and disorienting. "I'm...not," I say truthfully.

Truth is, my nipples hurt. They hurt from being naked and rubbing hard against the cloth of the robe. They had peaked into an impossible state the moment he had reached up to grab the shelf, his broad tattooed chest hovering in front of me and his manly scent dizzying my senses.

"You're completely naked under that robe?" His head drops, and his jaw and his stubble graze softly at my shoulder, causing the robe to slightly open, enough for the cloth to rub against my tingly nipples, but not enough for them to peek out.

More wetness is pooling between my legs—which is so inexplicable.

Watching him with my nipples that are pulling toward him makes me wonder how someone's eyelashes can be so dark and captivating.

He tilts his head back up, causing his shoulders and back to move, and his hips to push slightly forward. It's an unconscious little move, but it has the biggest impact. He has no idea what has just happened—the robe I'm wearing is thick and the room is dark after all—but because of my sitting position and my parted legs, by this small adjustment, his cock has come almost in direct contact with my naked clit. He is maddingly hard under his gray boxers. The accidental stimulation takes me by complete surprise. Not only do I gasp, but I shift out of reflex, and so does he, but all that does is cause my legs to open a bit farther. Now, my pussy lips are basically clutching his shaft, and his tip is in an even *better* position, right at the very center of my clit ("jackpot" position).

His perfect eyes connect with mine, full of brilliance and beautiful stars. "You like this, do you?"

That's when the water *whooshing* stops.

That's when the machine starts its rhythmic washing cycle.

That's when my hips start to pulse against his cock, and my sensitive clit against his thick tip.

Another moan leaves my lips just as a groan escapes his.

"*Fuck*," he lets out as the cycle continues.

His eyes drop down, and his facial expression tenses, but his hips remain almost perfectly still, his arms still up and on either side of me, but now clutching the shelf firmer. My hands squeeze the cupcakes almost as intensely as my pussy lips are squeezing the head of his shaft.

I definitely have no idea what to do now. Firstly, I'm locked in. Secondly, still locked in. Thirdly, and believe it or not, still very much locked in.

And…my brain doesn't see any problem with that.

With the rumble of the machine, my clit is continuing to pulse against his tip, and with that, I'm losing all brain power.

All I can manage is to sit there, utterly powerless, absorbing the unfolding events, acutely aware of my complete loss of control and oh, dear, no, not now, *please* not this—an orgasm starting to form. A substantial one. A desperate one. One that promises to outlast any I have ever experienced.

In fact, somehow, I instinctively know that if I or an outside occurrence doesn't put an immediate end to this—maybe a power outage—I will come in exactly ten more cycling-rumbles.

Nine.

Oh, no.

Eight.

"Cart…" is all that escapes my lips, stopping mid-word when his lips graze my neck, kissing my skin, opening my robe farther.

Seven.

More grumbles escape his throat and continue to drive me insane.

Six.

He is just as turned on as I am. Another growl, this one with more tension, while the irremissible tip stimulation against my clit continues.

The washing machine and my hips are doing all the work, cycling against me, and all I can think of is how badly I want to come.

Five.

I can't come.

It would be so wrong to come.

Four.

However, my body does not see what could possibly be wrong with it. It's welcoming the continued friction between us. It wants to conclude what the washing machine started. Badly. Desperately.

Three.

There's no stopping this. My orgasm builds and builds and builds.

Two.

Another involuntary moan escapes my lips.

Another deep groan leaves his.

One.

"*Eden*," he rumbles.

With the growling of my name, there is no escape, and I tumble over the edge—coming, coming, coming—and dropping my cupcakes in the process.

He lowers his arms and pulls me against him. My trembling legs circle his waist, his thick cock still clutched between my drenched pussy lips.

"Ahh-ahhh." As he breathes heavily, his hips jerk up between my lips.

And jerk some more.

I feel warm fluid leaking through his shorts.

He presses me closer, his heartbeat loud against mine, his breathing heavy.

We remain like that for what seems like minutes, coming down from our highs, holding onto each other tightly.

Do not fall in love.

He moves his arms up, rests them on my shoulders, and presses his forehead against mine, one of his hands circling around my neck. Framed by moonlight, there's wonderful softness in his facial expression. The sparkle has changed, but it isn't any less intense. If anything, it's more vivid.

I want to kiss him, touch him, feel him inside me.

"We better say good night," he whispers in a hoarse voice.

"Yes, good idea," I quickly whisper back, nodding (as if I'm fully agreeing), still in a daze.

My body screams, *Why*. My hips chime in, *Please*. My pussy joins the chorus, *No*. Nobody here wants to let him (and his assets) leave. It's like a dysfunctional choir practice in the middle of an "O" symphony.

He nods, grabs my hips and lifts me from the running machine to put me on the ground. I'm careful not to touch him with my frosting-covered hands (squeezing too hard). He waits patiently until I—finally—regain my footing.

"Good night, Carter," I say when my wobbly legs offer me support.

"Need help with anything?" he asks, but I shake my head.

"No, thanks. I'm good. I'll clean this up." I gesture to the poor cupcake mess on the floor. They were a sacrifice I had been willing to make.

"We'll deal with it in the morning. Get some sleep. Good night." He lets go of me, tenderly closes my robe that threatened to come undone, and leaves the room.

Standing frozen with still stupidly tingly nipples, I hear the door to his room close.

I lick my hands.

13

CARTER

FRIDAY

The end of the workweek is here, and I'm busier than ever. Everyone is trying to wrap things up, me included, for once. Aunt Eleanor is due tomorrow morning, and I want as few interruptions as possible. Especially since Eden and I have blocked out time later this evening to get our stories straight.

At 4:47 p.m., I finally have a chance to breathe.

I enjoy what I do. The fast-paced, intense environment is where I thrive. A lot of my day is spent either coming up with new ideas, implementing procedures, or connecting with my clients for one reason or another.

Bradley's "whispers" about client poaching have more weight to them than I originally thought. Two more of my longtime clients have mentioned being contacted by Ecclestone Construction, which has left me wondering if they're attempting a takeover of my client base, possibly thinking they can outshine my long-standing relationships. It has certainly put me on high alert.

When I step out of my office for a break, Eden is typing away at her computer, focused on what she's doing. She wears a form-fitting navy skirt and light-blue blouse that draws my attention. The top two buttons have been left undone. From her seated position, I catch the barest hint of her cleavage. We haven't spoken about our midnight "encounter" in the laundry room. It had been a mistake. An incident arising from an accidental convergence of circumstances, one might say. It won't happen again. She knows it. I know it. Despite the unfortunate situation, both of us are maintaining our professionalism and are choosing not to bring it up—particularly within the work environment. We both recognize the importance of keeping a level head and not allowing personal matters to interfere with our work duties.

When I approach her desk, she looks up and smiles.

"Do you need something, boss?" she asks.

"I'm pretty much finished here. Let's get dinner."

"Sounds good to me, I'm starving." The way her eyes light up and her face brightens has me pausing for a moment. She lowers her voice, even though there's nobody around to overhear us. "Are you sure it's wise to be seen out in public with me?"

"You were the one saying you wanted to see more of the city and that I had to feed you. If you're fine with take-out again, then…"

"*Nope*," she says quickly, afraid I'm changing my mind. "Dinner out sounds great. It'll give us a nicer ambience to work up our battle plan for the weekend."

Appreciating but not reading anything into the fact that she said "our battle plan" instead of "a battle plan," I pull my phone out and bring up the Uber app. "I'm ordering a car to take you to the restaurant. I'm going to need a few more minutes to wrap up here."

"Are you sure? I can wait."

"No need."

She nods, and I know she understands my reasoning. There are still plenty of people around, and the last thing I want is for them to see me and Eden get in the same car or leave at exactly the same time. It's no problem for people to see us leave together now and then for a business lunch, a meeting, or a presentation, but people will get suspicious if we leave together every day at the same time. Rumors are the last thing I need. We've been doing well at keeping things at a distance, and I don't want to jeopardize that.

Eden shuts down her computer and grabs her purse. "I guess I'll see you in a bit."

I nod without a word and go back to my office. Eden's high heels click against the hardwood floor on her way out. It's been an interesting couple of days. The whole wedding situation aside, Eden's presence has been a pleasant change of pace in the office. She knows her stuff and is a hard worker. I'm impressed with how easily she picks up new things and how many clients have been starting to mention her in a positive way.

It feels good to have one thing off my plate. As long as everything goes well this weekend, the next six months will be a breeze.

For exactly twenty more minutes I finish up minor tasks and then shut my stuff down for the weekend.

Time to focus on my aunt.

I've told Aunt Eleanor a lot of stories over an extended stretch of time—she's curious like that. The good thing is, during the last few days, Eden has gotten a good insight on all things work related and other basics she would be familiar with as my wife. We still need to discuss how we met. If she gets even the slightest detail wrong, it could blow the whole charade. And I'm not going to let that happen.

We're planning to move her belongings into my room early tomorrow morning so the maid can prep the guest suite and rest of the apartment for my aunt before we return with her from the airport. Eden has surrendered to her fate and agreed to do so without any further objections. As long as we keep our stories straight for forty-eight hours, we'll be good.

THE RESTAURANT I sent Eden to is a small Italian place I've visited only once or twice, typically frequented by locals who enjoy authentic homemade pasta. I don't want to risk taking her to any of my usual places in case we're noticed or recognized. When I get there, she sits at a table tucked away in the corner, a complimentary drink and bite-sized appetizer in front of her, poring over the menu. When I join, she gives me another one of her bright smiles.

"Everything on the menu looks so good," she comments. "I'm having a hard time deciding." She lowers her voice. "There's no price. The price is missing."

"Pick whatever you'd like," I say, glancing at my own menu.

The waitress appears at our side, asking, "Good evening, may I take your orders?"

I look at Eden. She gestures for me to order first.

"I'll have the ravioli special with a glass of Chianti."

"One Ravioli del Maestro," the waitress repeats back to me.

After some friendly clarifications with the waitress, Eden says, "And I'll have the Gnocchi Sorrento with a glass of your house red."

"Are you sure?" I ask her.

"Of course," she says brightly.

"Two side salads."

"Oh, good idea, can I have a tomato salad?"

"One tomato salad, one green salad."

The waitress thanks us, takes the menus, and informs us about the estimated waiting time before leaving. It was refreshing to see that Eden didn't just fall in line with my food order. Instead of playing it safe, she'd ordered something completely different. I can see why she'd prefer her meal over mine. Eden has a sweet tooth, and her pick of potato-based dumplings with a sauce made from ripe tomatoes will be on the sweeter side.

She grabs a slice from the basket of warm artisan bread and dips it in one of the small individual dishes of seasoned olive oil. "This is a nice place," she says, scanning the restaurant. "Do you come here a lot?"

"I don't." I pull out my small black book. "All right, let's go over how we met."

She raises her eyebrow. "You have it in your notebook?"

"I took down a few pointers, yes."

"Why don't you use your phone?"

"The book is quicker to capture my thoughts on the go or while I'm on my phone when I can't access apps. I also don't have to worry about dealing with hacking or technical glitches." I flip through the pages, getting right to business. "I never said anything about your job, so it should be fine to tell her you just started as my assistant. Less room for error. We met four months ago when I was on a business trip on the coast. You were having lunch at the hotel where I was staying, and we ran into each other several times. I asked you to dinner the night before I was going to leave. We had a pleasant time. After that, we talked every day, and less than a month later you moved to the city, and we got married."

"Hmm. That doesn't sound too difficult to remember," Eden begins, something like worry crossing her features. "*But*...seems a little vague though."

"I approached you first," I go on, fully cluing her in. "You were sitting alone at the bar, and I sat next to you, asking if the seat was taken. I'd just closed the deal on an important account and was ready for a late coffee. Obviously, you were immediately attracted to me. We flirted a bit before I told you to have dinner with me."

"Wow, Carter, I didn't know you were such a ladies' man." She smirks while she enjoys her bread. "But I have to say, this is all very cliché. What's worse, it's one-sided. Also, it's hard to believe that we ran into each other all the time. And *less than a month* later, I'm moving to a whole other state to be with you—are you sure about that?"

"You cared for me so deeply you couldn't stand to be apart."

"Oh, yeah, that's totally believable and not at *all* like a bad movie. Hello? Your story sounds like it was written by a man."

"I am a man."

"*Exactly*." She takes a sip of her sparkling water. "How about this—something a *bit* closer to what actually happened, and thus, making it feel much more believable: We met at a cute, cozy ice cream place. I was at a nearby motel because my new apartment wasn't ready yet. I approached you first, because there was no other seat available. After a hilarious meet-cute that involved an unexpected rendezvous between my ice cream and your coffee, we engaged in conversation. Even though, when I asked about you, you transformed into a walking construction encyclopedia, I, for some uncharted reason, decided to throw caution to the wind and embrace this whole shebang. Obviously, your knowledge was impressive, and after we connected more, it became clear that not all bosses are the grandest peacocks strutting their feathers. Not all are like those commanding tower lights; some are more like those austere desk lamps, emitting an unwavering glow of dominant brilliance, while keeping us on our toes and never letting the workplace atmosphere get too dull as we scramble to find the 'friendliness-on' switch. Isn't that right, boss? I mean..."

I put my hand up to stop her. "That's too specific. It also makes absolutely no sense. We can't stray from what I've already told her, or she'll smell the lie. The reason why the story was vague and predictable was that it's easier to sell. Perfect to nod along to. The more weird details you give to a lie the more there's a chance it will be questioned."

"Well, okay, to each their own, but wouldn't it seem weird that a woman would drop her entire life just because some random guy made bedroom eyes at her one night? *Why*?"

"What do you mean?"

"I mean, I left my life for you, in under a month. For what reason? What did you have to offer?"

I raise my eyebrow and sit back in my seat. "What did I have to offer?" I repeat. "Eden, look at me. Look at where I live. Look at my life. I have *everything* to offer."

"Then why are you still single?"

"That's by choice. I'm choosing professional pursuits over the commitments that come with romantic relationships."

"Why?"

"It's just where my focus lies."

"Oh, I'm just dying to know more about your grand scheme for world domination." Eden sighs. "Carter, if we're going to sell this, I'm going to need to know a little bit about *you* and whatever else you've got up your sleeve, and not just details of your global takeover, a list of your clients, what motorcycles you're into, or how you prefer to drink your coffee."

The waitress brings over our drinks and places the glasses in front of us.

Eden smiles warmly at the waitress, thanking her for the wine. I pick up my glass of Chianti by the long stem and lift it toward Eden for a toast. We lightly tap the rims together, and I say, "Cheers to a nice evening."

"And a successful weekend!"

I swirl the deep red liquid around before taking a sip from the slightly flared bowl. The taste is rich and complex, and I savor the flavors, rolling them over my tongue before swallowing. I have to admit it's one of the best I've ever tasted.

I watch Eden try her house wine, a lighter red, the wineglass in a simpler design, shorter stem and made of crystal. Her eyes close in pleasure as she savors the taste. "Oh, my God...this is good!"

"I'm glad you like it." I set my glass down, having made a decision. "What do you want to know?"

"Everyday, mundane things I haven't been able to pick up on this week," Eden says after putting her glass back down.

"Fine. Ask, and I'll tell you the answer."

"How about instead of asking questions, I get to know you in a more human way. You know, through normal conversation and comradery."

"All we have is tonight before my aunt arrives tomorrow morning. We don't have time to do it the normal way."

"All right. Why don't you do relationships?" she asks. "And before you dodge the question again, I think it's pretty important to our cover story. How was I able to catch your attention when you weren't interested in anything serious?"

"I'm not particularly good at them," I tell her, observing her eat more of the bread. "I don't have time, and I don't have the patience for it. The few relationships I've had ended the same way. They always wanted more time than I was willing to give. And I also don't want children. Never have. Never been interested."

"Well, that's one question I can navigate if your aunt asks," she says, playing with the stem of her glass.

"Good luck with that. I already told her no kids, but that doesn't stop her from asking."

"Let's circle back to the relationship thing." She sips her wine. I watch the red liquid stain her lips, and her small tongue dart out to wipe it away. "What about sex?"

"What about it? Everyone has sex."

"You're okay with having sex with a woman for one night but not a relationship?"

"And? Sex and relationships are two different things. We had sex without a relationship, and you were okay with that too."

"I didn't say there was anything wrong with it," she says, on the defensive. "I was just curious about your thought process. Although now that I'm thinking about it, in big cities it's probably not really that weird, so maybe forget I asked."

"For somebody who doesn't want to have sex with me, you bring it up way too often."

"Carter, stop it."

"This is at least the third time you've brought up sex since we started our arrangement," I point out. I lower my voice to *that* register. "You just can't keep your dirty thoughts to yourself, can you? You're *that* eager to have sex with me?"

"*No.* Of course not! It was just a question, dear God." She sounds breathless, and her cheeks are pink.

She takes another sip from her wine—a long one this time—before she says, "So before you met my charming personality, you didn't do relationships. And because I was willing to compromise and not compete with your job, being quite the busybody myself, that's why you decided to marry me? Can't we make it a bit more romantic?"

Her abrupt change of topic speaks volumes. Clearly, she had been thinking about our encounters with each other. Just like I had.

She puts her glass back down, saying, "Romance goes a long way as far as a woman is concerned. Your aunt will more likely buy a romantic story, not some vague 08-15..."

"Eden." I interrupt her. "You're overthinking the situation. You don't need to think about all that stuff. All you have to do is act like you love me and sell that we're married. That's it."

"Fine, I was just trying to give our story more depth..."

"You love me, you moved to New York to be with me. Full stop. End of story."

Eden puts her hands up in surrender. "Fine, fine. If she asks, I can tell her why I'm attracted to you."

"Exactly."

Just when I want to move on from the subject, she starts listing, "I admire your determination, your bravery, and your resilience. It's inspiring."

I pause. My eyes find hers. I'm curious where she's going with this.

"Yes, you never give up on anything, no matter how difficult it gets. I will talk about how I realized that you have many qualities that people don't see from the get-go. If you want something, you go in full force. You're driven and focused, and you're not afraid to take risks, even when others doubt you. You're not just a boss, you're a leader. A true fighter. It shows in everything you do. I will talk about how much you care about your employees, even though it doesn't seem like it from the outside. And you're so giving, so generous, and always willing to help out those in need. You care deeply for people. It's in your actions. It's really impressive. And while you hide it all rather well because you're in boss-mode almost twenty-four-seven, you do have an excited, playful side..."

I'm taken aback by her words and feel a strange mix of surprise wash over me. Her words don't seem fake.

Is that how she really sees me?

Before I can lose myself in my thoughts, she props her elbows on the table and rests her chin on her hands, batting her eyelashes. "Now, what reasons did you give her as to why you were drawn to me?"

"I told her you were pretty, capable, and funny."

She shrugs. "Well, all right... if you think she will buy plain vanilla compliments, so be it, sweetheart."

"Sweetheart?"

"We're married. We need to have terms of endearment. When I'm in a relationship, I don't usually refer to my partner by his first name. Unless I'm angry."

She has a point there. "I don't like sweetheart," I say.

"That's fine. What about 'hot lips?'"

"Don't call me hot lips."

"How about 'sugar?'"

"No."

"Okay...wait. What about 'good-looking' or, I got it: 'babe?'"

I nod. "That works."

"All right. What do you call me? How about 'darling,' or wait, wait, no. You call me 'love.'"

I study her for a moment. Her expression says, *Am I pushing this?* She probably is. But my aunt will appreciate it. "Darling or love could work."

She beams, picking up her wine again. "I like both of those. By the way, I'm not letting you off the hook."

"Off the hook for what?"

"Off the hook for sharing *something* about yourself. Even if we can't do it the normal human way. The last few days all you did was talk about your work and your motorcycles. I'd like more info on you. I should at least know your birthday, where you were born, and all of that."

I'm not in the habit of being chummy with those I work around, with the exception of Bradley. Still, Aunt Eleanor is smart, and Eden's right. She would find it strange if my wife didn't know my birthday or much else about me.

"I'm thirty-eight years old, my birthday is August twelfth, I was born and raised right here in New York, and just like in your case, my parents passed away many years ago," I list. Her expression is one of surprise as she realizes that I remember what she previously shared with me. "What else do you want to know?"

The waitress approaches our table with her tray, and we pause our conversation to accept our food. Eden hands her empty glasses to her, asking for a refill.

"Who's the person you hold closest to your heart, besides your aunt?" she asks while we start eating.

"Bradley. Bradley Everhart. You've met him. He and I go way back."

"Tell me about the moment you guys bonded."

I think for a moment and enjoy her happy expressions about her food choice. "When Bradley and I were young—two broke kids in tattered jeans from Staten Island—we were dead set on getting our hands on motorcycles. I still remember that classified ad in the local paper and how we met that old, bearded biker in his rundown, dimly lit garage on the outskirts of town. After some negotiation, we sealed the deal, handing over the cash—our hard-earned savings from odd jobs and hustles. We rode our new rides out of that dusty garage, Bradley on his black Honda CB750, me on my blue Suzuki GS500, feeling like kings of the road. We loved riding through the countryside, exploring woods and hidden trails. The air in our faces. The open roads. The unknown. The motorcycle became an extension of ourselves. One day, we stumbled upon an old barn. From what we could tell, it was abandoned."

"Oh, like a scary place?"

"Yes, it was creepy looking. I wanted to explore it, but Bradley warned me, told me it was sketchy, that it wasn't safe. He said something about the *Texas Chainsaw Massacre*. I told him we weren't in Texas and that he could wait here for me, I was only going to take a quick look. But good buddy that he was, he said that Hell would freeze over before he let me go in alone. When we were climbing up the squeaky stairs, the wood gave way and Bradley fell, hitting his head on the way down."

She has stopped eating. "Oh, no! Please tell me you're joking."

"He was seriously hurt. There was blood everywhere. I grabbed his Honda—it was faster than my bike—and hauled ass to the nearest town to call for help. The ambulance rushed Bradley to the hospital. I didn't leave his side for a second. He wasn't even mad at me. Said it was an accident and that he would do it again."

She places her hand on her heart. "Aww. That's so heartwarming."

"That's not the best part. While he was recovering, we began dreaming of new adventures together. We decided to turn the old abandoned barn into a biker shop, where we could work on bikes."

"And you've been best friends ever since?

"Well, he still gives me shit from time to time, but yeah, that's pretty much it. He's like a brother to me."

"That's such a touching story. What happened to the barn?"

"The old owner eventually tore it down. It was a shitty idea to start a biker shop in the middle of nowhere. While it didn't lead directly to a successful venture, it did plant the seed of entrepreneurship in our minds. Shows you that sometimes a shitty situation can lead to something good."

There's a pause.

"I got goose bumps." She puts her cutlery down and shows me her arm. "It reminds me of my sister."

"Your sister? How so?"

"As you know, after my parents' death, Diane took over Dad's company. A fire hit the area. It caused significant damage and loss. Unfortunately, in recent years, the risk of wildfires has increased in the area where we live, due to factors such as land use and drought conditions. Anyway, after witnessing firsthand the devastation caused by a fire, my sister decided to shift our focus toward a more sustainable, fire-resistant landscape design approach, using plant materials and irrigation systems that could better withstand drought and heat."

"Has she managed to balance sustainability with profitability? Is there room for further growth and scale?"

"The company was heavily in debt when she took over, and while it's not making any real profits yet, the new approach seems to slowly be helping the firm grow and build a loyal customer base."

"I'm glad to hear that. If your sister is seeking to expand, I'd suggest collaborations with other companies or organizations to reach new audiences. Why don't you tell her to give me a call? Maybe I can open some doors for her."

"Oh, my goodness." With big eyes, she gives me a nod. "I will tell her. I appreciate that."

From there, we continue to enjoy our meals while engaging in conversation: fond childhood memories, books and movies we like, our favorite and least favorite foods, and we even scratch the surface of our hidden talents. Me: a talented survivalist who can rescue victims of unfortunate barn accidents, she: a skilled fire starter who can ignite a fire even in the unlikeliest conditions.

"What haven't you learned about me so far?" She smiles a bright smile when the waitress brings her dessert, a gelato with a cherry on top, and an espresso for me, with a small cup and saucer, accompanied by a glass of sparkling water to cleanse the palate.

When she offers me a taste of her dessert, I decline.

"You sure?"

"Oh, I'm sure."

"Carter, okay, since you dare to deny the opportunity to taste my sweet dessert—once again—I present you with a challenge! Tit for tat. Remember when I said something nice about you earlier? This is the moment you pay me, your brilliant roommate and fake wife, a genuine compliment back—not just the run-of-the-mill *pretty, capable, and funny*. Booo. It can't be predictable and shallow. You have to really mean it." She pauses. "I mean...you know, your aunt really might ask, and you want to be prepared."

"She probably will. Let's see. I learned that you're passionate," I start, watching her roll her lips over her teeth to take a bite of her ice cream. I shake my head, holding back an almost-chuckle. "I learned that you enjoy life, and you don't worry too much about the consequences, or about being goofy."

"Mmmm, fififfooooodelifiouf..." she mumbles as if on cue, and motions for me to continue.

"You never worry what other people think," I point out, "and you make your own decisions. You enjoy life to the fullest, and it's an incredible way to live. It sets you apart from others." She swallows her ice cream, looking at me, her face blushing. "I've also come to understand that you don't have a mean bone in your body. It's rare to find someone whose soul is untainted by the harshness of the world that can often be dark and unforgiving. But in you, I see someone who has managed to hold on to their goodness, and I think it's inspiring. If anything, it reminds me that there's still hope for humanity," I say as she listens to me intently, her eyes growing bigger and bigger. She has completely forgotten her ice cream. "That's what I've learned about you. Whether it's a career goal, a personal ambition, you're focused when you're in the moment, you're not afraid to say what you think, and you're not afraid to ask for what you want. I know you'll continue to achieve great things." I reach for my sparkling water. "And you're *flexible*."

She blinks, and I can see her swallowing—not ice cream this time. The blush on her cheeks almost matches that cherry. "How very sweet... I mean, that'll work when your aunt asks...except for the last part there, I don't think that last one is an appropriate thing for your aunt to know."

"What do you mean?" I ask her and take a drink of water. "I was referring to your commendable effectiveness and your 'no matter when or where or what' performance at work. So, good job."

"Carter! You were not." She laughs, and I can't help but lean back, thoroughly enjoying her amusement.

Am I playing with fire teasing her like this? Yes, I am. Is it a big mistake? Most likely. Do I regret it? At this point, no.

Because sitting across from her in the dim light, having this gorgeous woman looking at me like she is, feels good. Really good.

Despite all my protests, Bradley has one thing right.

I'm only a man. And when there's a woman like her giving me bedroom eyes, the excuses I've told myself start to sound just like that: excuses.

14

EDEN

The bill is paid, and Carter drives us home. It's nice to see him relax a bit. As the night has gone on, he's started acting more like the guy in the motel room and less like my boss. When he opens the platinum BMW's door for me, I tease, "I'm surprised you didn't call an Uber for me. Aren't you worried about us being seen together?"

"When we're going in and out of the office, yes. But it's a big city. The probability of one of our coworkers being in this exact same restaurant right now is slim to none. I'm not *that* paranoid, Eden."

"Yes, you are."

"Guess I shouldn't take you out to dinner anymore then." He smiles. Actually smiles. I didn't even think Carter knew how to smile.

And what a smile it is. There are cute wrinkles around his eyes.

The smile makes his face not only so much more handsome but adds an extraordinary charm that makes my heart skip a beat. There's so much warmth in it. Looking at him I have no doubt: his smile could illuminate the darkest corners and cast away all the blackness of the world.

"*No*," I say quickly. "I'm kidding. Keep taking me out to dinner." To strike a lighter tone, I add, "You promised to feed me before you married me. I take this promise very, very seriously."

Guess what? His smile doesn't only widen, he chuckles—actually chuckles—causing a warm flutter of joy to bubble up inside me.

"Noted, Mrs. Serious," he rumbles in his deep baritone. "Consider it done."

The back and forth is light and playful, the complete opposite of most of the conversations we've had this week. Also, I make a conscious effort to disregard any implications from him addressing me as "Mrs. Serious" and not "Miss Serious" (as if we're genuinely married).

Up until now, I had been a little nervous about how this whole fake marriage thing would play out, but after hearing more about the situation from Carter and being given some background on him, I'm confident we can pull it off.

ALL OF THAT is far from my mind when we get back to the apartment. I'm delightfully buzzed, and a teensy bit worked up from our flirting earlier. The idea of "no men or sex for six months" had sounded great at the time, especially when I'd found out another one had ditched me (at the motel this time) and was my boss on top of that, but after two glasses of wine and being alone with the same hot—surprisingly charming—man, my resolve has started to slip.

Hattie's door is closed tighter than a pickle jar. She's either dodging Carter, or she's simply in the midst of packing up for her move.

"I have an important question we haven't talked about yet," I say, kicking out of my heels the second we walk through the door. I pick them up by the straps, playfully swinging them on my way to the couch.

"What is it?"

"Where did we have our first kiss?"

I flop on the couch, carelessly dropping my shoes to the floor and propping my feet up on the armrest. I sneak a peek inside the box of wedding cupcakes I rescued from the laundry room this morning and gesture to Carter to see if he wants to indulge. There's just one left. When he shakes his head (of course, Carter never indulges), I close the box again. The generous swirl of vanilla cream frosting with that shiny, shiny strawberry on top is calling my name. I'll definitely indulge later.

"Our first kiss? Is that relevant?" Carter is aware that we haven't done any proper kissing yet (hot lip-brush moments do not count), and I feel that my question is legit. "It's a pretty big step in a relationship. If your aunt asks about it, I'd like to have something to tell her."

"We aren't teenagers anymore, Eden. I doubt my aunt is going to ask when we kissed."

"But what if she does? We should be prepared, just in case. Women never forget their first kiss, and they love to ask about it. Trust me, if she's as curious as you suggested she is, she will ask."

Stepping out of his shoes, Carter takes off his jacket and tosses it aside, regarding me curiously. I do my best to not stare at his lips.

"You tell me," he says, "where you think our first kiss should be."

This is new. Up until this point, Carter had made it clear he didn't want any of my input. What's changed? I almost ask but don't want to look a gift horse in the mouth. I mull it over for a minute before I sit up excitedly. "Okay, it needs to be romantic. So, how about after our dinner, we decided to go for a long walk and kept talking. It was dark, a little cold out. I was wearing a super-cute blue dress—but no coat. You gave me your jacket, and then you leaned in, and *muah*!" I make an exaggerated kissing sound.

"How romantic."

There's a slight tease in his tone I ignore. "Isn't it? Of course, not that I would know anything about what it's like to kiss you."

Carter raises his eyebrow at me. "Was that a hint of regret I heard?"

"Don't flatter yourself. I was only stating the fact that we haven't kissed, even though we had full-on sex together."

He snorts at my phrasing. "Full-on. As opposed to what?"

My brain is too enlivened to come up with the answer. "Um...not full-on. You know. Subtle. Reserved."

"I've never heard of subtle or reserved sex." He lowers his voice to a sexy growl. "You mean teasing washing machine run-ins?"

Quickly, I shake my head, hoping to get rid of any blushing. "No. No.

That wasn't subtle sex. That was a chance meeting beyond anyone's control." I ignore the almost unbearable clench between my thighs caused by the memory of me sitting uncontrollably in my white robe on that running washing machine, legs spread. "It doesn't matter anyway. It's your loss, you know. I'm an excellent kisser."

He smirks, clearly amused. "Is that so?"

"Yup. Best kisser in the world."

"That's a bold statement."

"One that you can't disprove since we haven't kissed."

"Fine. I believe you."

I look up at him. What's happened to Mr. Control Freak, and where has this agreeable man suddenly come from? "You do?" I ask him.

He loosens his tie a bit, then pushes the sleeves of his shirt up to reveal his strong, inked arms. Each muscle is defined like chiseled marble, veins subtly snaking beneath his sun-kissed skin. "You sound disappointed."

"I'm not."

"Good."

"Good." I shrug. I get up, ready to head to my guest suite. "I guess we'll never know."

"I guess not," he grumbles, observing me walk past him. "But to me, this whole interaction feels like a desperate attempt to get me to kiss you."

"It's not."

"Stop lying. I know you want to kiss me. You can't stop thinking about it. You wonder how it would feel. You're curious to learn if I'm a good kisser. I've seen you staring at my lips."

"I have not," I tell him. Just when I reach the door, I decide that lying doesn't suit me. "And even if I have, it was by accident."

"Hush, Eden." He's by my side in a second. "Get over here now." He pulls me back, and suddenly, I find myself face to face with him.

My brain shorts out for a second, and I stare at Carter, trying to process what I just heard. Did he just tell me to kiss him?

"Come again?" I ask.

"You heard me," Carter says, casually leaning against the doorframe, larger than life.

His closeness has me frazzled. The scent of his cologne overwhelms my senses and leaves me feeling lightheaded. It's a perfect blend of fresh orange, leather, and musk, screaming sophistication, confidence, control, and power.

"You said you're the best kisser in the world." He dips his head, but then he stills. "Prove it."

I can't tell if this is a bad idea or not.

I also can't tell if Carter is messing with me. I mean, we had been teasing each other during our dinner, so he very well could be joking.

But he doesn't look like he's joking.

He stares at me expectantly, as if it's a challenge. As if he expects me to back down.

Obviously, he doesn't know me very well.

Without thinking twice, I raise my head and take his face in my hands. He's way taller than me, and since I'm not wearing my heels, I have to stand on my tiptoes.

Suddenly, my mouth meets his.

The blow of feeling his soft lips on mine almost makes my heart stop.

I almost collapse. Worse. I almost black out.

Butterflies take off in my stomach.

A volcano erupts inside me.

Instant heat shoots through my body, and my knees buckle involuntarily, making me sway away. Carter catches me with his strong, muscular arm around my waist, dragging me closer against him while making sure our lips stayed connected. And not just our lips. His other hand slides into my hair, gripping my neck and head firmly, and keeping my whole body in place, flush against his.

Every thought I've ever had vanishes into thin air.

That magic of his touch and his mouth against mine controls my being. His lips are everything and more: soft, teasing, demanding. He tastes and nips at my lips until I open my mouth, feeling his tongue softly against mine before I have even a second to realize what's happening.

Desire clouds my senses, and my body aches for his touch. When his tongue teases mine again, more demanding this time, I can't help but let out a soft moan. Carter's tongue pushes deeper, past mine. His hand falls to my ass, gripping, pulling me closer, and squeezing. As if on their own accord, my hands move up his chest and broad shoulders, fingertips tracing the contours of his muscles, until my arms circle his strong neck.

We kiss like two people who have been deprived of kissing for far too long. We make out like our lives depend on it.

The sensation of his fingers in my hair, both his hands holding me close, and his tongue inside my mouth bewilders all my senses, sends them into a whirlwind of blissful confusion.

My heart does the twirly-whirley.

My knees do the wobbly jellybean jive.

My pussy does the giggly carnival carousel spin.

My soul does the swoony moonlit serenade.

Sweet Jesus, this man knows how to *kiss*. This man isn't just an excellent kisser, he's a heart-melting-jaw-dropping-panty-wrecking kisser. He needs to come with a warning label.

Everything is suddenly way too hot and way too overwhelming, and the urge to tear my and his clothes off forces me to break the kiss, gasping for air.

Part of me feels cheated that I didn't get his mouth on mine when we hooked up the first night, or when we got "fake" married, or when we happened to interlock in the laundry room. And all other moments in between.

Carter leans back against the doorframe, our gazes locked, both his hands suddenly cupping my ass. He just looks at me, saying nothing, his gorgeous eyes searching mine.

"See," I say, breathless. "Best kisser in the world."

Carter's lips quirk, and he slides his hands up and down and around my ass, the strength of his palms leaving tingling feelings along my body. "I might agree with you on that fact," he grumbles, his voice low and gravelly. "But best in the world?" One hand reaches up, pushes a loose strand of hair from my face and his thumb grazes my cheek. "Sorry, not convinced yet."

Cheeky bastard.

I'm acutely aware of the proximity of our bodies and that I'm frozen in place, physically incapable of moving away. I'm also acutely aware that his hand has moved back down to my ass. He pulls me closer, pushing my breasts against his torso and his length against my belly, deliriously hard. Sweet Jesus.

Yes, I was the one to swear off men.

And *yes*, he did say our night together was one time.

However—that was before I had those glasses of wine and that was before I accepted his challenge to kiss him. Or was it my challenge? At this point I have no idea. Because that was also before my panties were soaked. My libido is in full swing, and judging by the hardness in Carter's jeans, I'm not the only one.

"Eh...sooo..." I look up at him innocently, "how serious were you about that whole 'not sleeping with employees' thing?"

Carter arches an eyebrow. "I'm sorry, but didn't you swear off men and sex for the next six months?"

"I'm allowed to change my mind."

"Hey now," he rumbles teasingly. "One kiss and you're throwing your promise to yourself out the window? Don't you think it's me who deserves the title of the best kisser in the world?"

"Oh, please! No. Look, I'm a bit buzzed and horny, and you're hard and available. Tell me you aren't interested in a repeat of our first night."

Did I really just say that? Me and my big mouth.

I wish I had kept it shut and just let things progress on their own, because the second I challenge him, he removes his hands from my ass and gently pats my hips.

"I don't know, you were pretty adamant about your rule," he says, regarding me with an infuriatingly stern expression. "You shouldn't break it. It wouldn't be wise. You don't want regrets."

"Ha-ha, very funny."

"I'm serious. Far be it from me to make you fail to keep your vow of celibacy." He shakes his head and straightens. He really *does* mean it. Carter must see my disappointment because he grazes my cheeks with his knuckles. "Sorry. We can't have that."

"Okay," I say without thinking, "just the tip."

He stops mid-graze, his knuckles lingering on my cheek. The intensity of his eyes is stronger than before. His gaze is both intrigued and curious. "Just the tip?"

"You know, not full-on sex. Subtle sex."

I have his attention.

The right side of his lips twitch. He trails his thumb along my jawline, then he lowers his hand.

"As in just-the-tip sex," I add, as if I need to explain and he hasn't fully understood. "Also, it's not breaking any rules."

He chuckles, grabs my wrist, and pulls me back to him, bringing me and my breasts and my very pointy and tingly nipples against his chest.

His tongue dives tantalizingly into my mouth.

After another excruciatingly shameless kiss, he steps back and grabs my hand. "To my bedroom."

"Okay," I say, almost forgetting one important thing. "Wait, let me grab the last cupcake for later."

15

EDEN

Cupcake in hand, I let him pull me toward the hallway and lead me to his bedroom. My mind is in overdrive, eager and pleasantly surprised with how the events of the evening have turned. Part of my brain starts to scold me for changing my mind, but I tell my responsibilities *"To please frickin' hit the hay so I can play the night away."*

Not to mention, seeing the same Carter I'd met at the ice cream place has me beyond excited. I've missed that Carter, that excited, playful "Mr. Fun Time" side of him that's nowhere to be found once we step foot in the office.

Inside his bedroom, one large California king-sized bed greets us.

Carter undoes the knot of his tie, letting the fabric hang loose around his neck. His eyes never leave my face.

I barely have a chance to admire the beauty of his eyes before he picks me up and turns us. He sets me down on one of the narrow cabinets that only hold a few thick magazines.

"You won't be needing this now," he says, taking the cupcake out of my hand and placing it somewhere on the shelf above me.

He pushes himself between me, wraps my legs around his waist, trapping me between his strong body and the cool wall.

My arms anchor themselves around his neck.

"Never had just-the-tip sex," I mutter between kisses, more to myself than to him.

"Me neither. We'll change that tonight."

"It's definitely something I've wanted to try, so please, continue," I say, as if we aren't all over each other already, and still have the physical and emotional ability to suddenly stop. We don't.

Carter kisses his way to my throat, teasingly, torturously, and my head falls to the side, giving him better access. I suck in a deep breath when I feel his teeth drag teasingly. My skin rises with goose bumps when he breathes into my ear.

I've been craving this, I think. Or maybe I even say it out loud. I can't tell. Going from hot and heavy to hotter and heavier makes my head spin. Granted, it's already spinning from the rush of endorphins, but the additional dose doesn't help.

"I know, I'll make it worth your while," he rumbles into my ear.

I squirm, laughing, needing more, wanting everything. "Honestly, as long as it ends with orgasms, I'm up for a lot of things."

"Orgasms. Plural?"

I nod, breathless. "Yeah…"

His whiskers graze across my skin from my ear to my mouth, and I think he's going to kiss me again. But he doesn't, letting his lips hover just over mine. "Perfect."

I enjoy his touch breathlessly, my lips softly touching his.

He teases my lips with featherlight brushes with each word, growling, "Just. Like. You."

I gasp, and Carter pulls me into another knee-buckling kiss. Lips on mine, he places me into position, both hands clutching my waist, pulling me closer, and pushing my legs wider with his hips. He devours my mouth like he can't get enough. I meet him enthusiastically, making up for all the kisses we didn't have before.

His hips roll forward on their own, grinding against me.

My skirt rides up, and I go along, grinding myself against his hard bulge.

After minutes of him devouring my mouth, and simulating rhythmic thrusts, my panties are soaked all the way through, and I'm sure he can feel it through the layers of clothing between us.

Dear heavens, I'm so turned on that it almost hurts. I need more. I need to feel him inside me—his tip, that is. Only his tip. Not his thick, long, *full* shaft.

"Let's take these off," he growls and pushes my skirt all the way up, leaving it bunched around my waist and sliding my wet panties down. I lift myself and maneuver my panties off, tossing them over the side onto the bed.

The sound of his belt and zipper fills the room, and there's rustling as he takes the time to lower his jeans. Once our offending garments are out of our way, he positions himself back to where he'd been and grabs my legs to straddle him. Hot desire shoots straight to my core.

"Better. Much better," he growls.

The smooth shaft of his dick slides between my legs, and I gasp in delighted pleasure. Grinding against him now, I bite my lip in excitement. I'd hoped we were beyond teasing, but that's not the case. His rhythm meets mine, dragging his dick through my folds tantalizingly but making no effort to enter me. He begins simulating deeper thrusts.

"Carter, you're torturing me."

His hands leave my waist when he leans forward, latching his mouth onto the back of my neck, the head of his cock teasing my entrance. "Don't worry, we'll get there."

He grabs my wrists, bunches them in one hand and pins them against the wall, forcing my arms above my head. With one hand, he reaches for his tie and folds it around my wrists, locking me in, still holding my arms up. Then he draws nearer. His hips push my legs farther apart, letting air hit my pussy and clit. The new angle forces me to stay still, trapped between his chest and body, unable to move. It would drive me crazy if his free hand hadn't started to unbutton my blouse, his strong hand eager to cup my breast through the material of my bra. Once my blouse is unbuttoned, he pulls my bra down, fingers closing around one of my nipples and pinching just enough to draw another moan out of me.

After making sure my nipples are the hardest they've ever been, his hand leaves my breasts to lightly brush down my belly over my waxed pussy and deeper down between my folds. I gasp when he brushes right over my wet clit, just once. A firestorm of sensations rushes through my body at that one touch.

"Carter," I moan as he denies me more of the pleasure I desperately need.

"You're so fucking wet. Perfectly ready for me."

"Please do that again," I beg.

He doesn't listen. Instead, he grabs his cock, now harder than steel, strokes himself a few times, distributing the wetness his tip has collected. He gives himself time to connect his eyes with mine, watching me squirm, enjoying how badly I want him inside of me. Then he positions himself back at my entrance, pushing more eagerly this time.

I gasp, my nerves getting the best of me, moaning at the feeling of his soft skin against mine. Never in my life have I been happier to be on birth control.

Slowly—excruciatingly slowly—he pushes his tip inside of me, stretching me open.

"Ohh..." The suddenness of feeling about one inch of his crown in my body is so intense I can't help but release a moan.

I want to push myself against him, pull his hips against me, taking all of him at once to bring our bodies flush together.

But I'm not physically able to do so. I'm trapped and my movements are limited. In a protesting response, I try to lower my arms, but remember they're still tied. I need them to push myself against him, but a shake of his head forces my arms back into their original position.

"Stay still," he whisper-orders.

He can be such a boss sometimes.

In defiance, my muscles clench around his head, too overwhelmed by the intensity of the situation. He moves his hips slightly, hardly even a quarter of an inch, causing his tip to slide out and back in. Every thought leaves my brain except for Carter, me, and the torturous way we're connected. The position is hotter than I thought it would be. Feeling his tip inside me is hot enough, but the way he's trying to control himself and not push into me makes me want to force him against me with every fiber of my being.

"Do not move your hips," Carter rumbles. "Stay like this. Keep your arms up."

"Okay," I rasp, feeling almost dizzy from arousal.

Even though I want to immediately sling my arms around his head to his shoulders for support and pull my hips against his, I remain in position. Yep. Frustratingly obedient, I keep them up and my hips still as he ordered. His strong hands are digging into the flesh of my hips. Everything in me hopes he will pull me closer, but instead, he prevents us from moving. It's hard enough to leave a mark on my skin. But I want him to mark me, to claim me, and leave a reminder of what we're doing. No one would know if he thrust into me completely. I wouldn't tell. It would be our little secret, and the thought thrills me more than it has any right to.

"Carter," I moan, squeezing down on him. "You feel so good. Please. Please go deeper."

He groans and pushes himself in a tiny bit more, barely, maybe half an inch, if that much, but pulls back out to where he was, absolutely preventing his hips from gyrating and keeping him only the one damn inch deep and not all the many, *many* inches he could possibly be inside of me. Anytime I try to somehow pull myself forward, he holds me tight, keeps me flush, not even giving me one fraction more of his cock.

"Just one more inch," I beg. At this point, I'm happy to get anything.

"I can't. I won't be able to stop," he rasps. "I want to fuck you so badly I can barely think."

This is hard enough, his eyes tell me.

With his forehead leaning against mine, his hands run from my hips up my naked belly to my breasts. My blouse had fallen closed when I'd lifted my arms, and he folds it back open. He cups my breasts, and his thumbs graze my nipples, teasing and pinching them over and over, while his lips find mine.

Doing all this, he doesn't move his hips. He remains perfectly still.

Except for his hands. One hand circles my throat while his other drops to my sensitive clit. When he brushes it with his fingers, I moan into his mouth. Relentlessly, he starts playing with it, circling it, and I'm lost in the sea of sensations that overtakes me, clenching onto his tip, relentlessly.

He was right, and I was wrong.

This position isn't subtle. This is in no form or shape subtle sex.

This is agony.

Pure torture.

But I'm perfectly happy staying right where I am, arms up, feeling his fingers where I need them most, gearing up for the impending Big O explosion that's rapidly sneaking up on me. By rapidly I mean I'm drawing nearer too quickly, remarkably close...almost...there—when Carter suddenly moves.

His hands leave my body. He pulls out of me. *Wait, what, no. Noooo.* The sudden loss of him drags a whimper out of me, but when I glance back to see what he's doing, I'm greeted by the sight of him tearing his shirt off.

Oh, good thinking.

His inked torso is fully naked now. On either side of his chest are designs that wrap around his arms and shoulder, made up of bold, black lines. The sight is mighty impressive, to say the least. Cool, manly strength. Uncontained energy. That's what I see. But when my eyes focus on his chest, my jaw drops open. Carter's torso boasts a tattoo of a fierce hawk in a moment of unbridled ferocity, exuding a primal, untamable spirit with muscles rippling beneath its dark feathers. I blink. A predator. The hawk's piercing eyes lock onto me, its wings spread wide, a warning in its gaze and a threat in its poised talons, ready to unleash powerful strikes at any moment, daring any challenger to cross its path.

"Arms down for a second," he growls.

Oh, finally. I let my tired arms fall, and Carter undoes the tie that binds them, then slides his hands down my shoulders to lower my blouse. With quick work, he unclasps my bra, which I happily toss away with the rest of my clothing.

His cock is swollen and pointing straight at me from above his jeans.

Being completely naked now, I make a move to get him closer again, but he stops me with a firm hand and pushes me back to where I was.

"No, you stay like this." He grabs a pillow from his bed and shoves it under my ass, then pushes my legs apart with his strong hands.

His stubble nuzzles my hair as he kisses the shell of my ear.

"I like it this way. You completely naked, wet, eager to be fucked. That's what you are, ready to be fucked. Am I right?" he rumbles, his fingers teasing the sides left and right of my clit, denying me another direct hit of pleasure. "Tell me."

At this point, I can't even think straight. I want his touch so badly. "Yeah."

"Good. Let me fuck your tight hole with my tongue. Arms back up."

I gasp, obeying.

Since my wrists aren't bound this time, my hands hit the shelf above me.

The cupcake he'd placed there earlier tumbles down between us. With a *thump*, it lands on my belly and rolls down, leaving cream in its wake. I tremble. The cupcake stops on my pussy, creamy side down.

I start to snort-laugh.

There's a cheeky grin in Carter's gaze, and when his eyes take me in like that, my pelvic muscles squeeze.

"Stay still, don't move," he orders. He leans down, grabs the end of the cupcake, pushes my legs farther apart and smears the vanilla cream between my pussy lips, right on my clit and entrance. He takes the plump, ripe strawberry that had been jumbled into the cream through the fall, between his teeth by its stem and places it among the cream at my entrance.

"Carter, wha...ohhh."

With the cupcake that has now lost all of its vanilla swirl (and its strawberry too), he stands, and removes the luxurious cupcake liner that helped to keep it fresh (and typically also prevented them from getting crushed or damaged). Putting the deliciousness between his teeth, he leans in.

Take a bite, he gestures with his eyes.

And I do. I bite into our wedding cupcake. While I savor the goodness, vanilla and strawberry smell invading my senses, he leans in to allow me another bite.

The taste isn't too sweet. There's a nice vanilla and orange citrus flavor that I love and could bathe in, as I savor the small pieces of strawberry and real vanilla in my mouth.

Our lips graze, and not only does my heart jump, but my pussy releases electric shockwaves.

Feeling the softness of his lips on my mouth and the softness of the cream on my sensitive clit, my pussy clenches. He finally indulges in a bite. Sharing a cupcake with Carter in the sweetest—and hottest—way possible, only heightens the significance of the rare moment. I can't help but feel a flutter in my chest.

Pleasant surprise is written all over Carter's face, even though I'm not entirely sure if it's caused by the taste of the cupcake and its subtle sweetness or by the whole situation in general. All I know is that he isn't into sweet things—except for me, *ha!*—but the delicious flavoring seems like a treat, even for him.

With a sexy gesture, he offers me the last bite, his lashes lowering in a moment of quiet intimacy.

The warmth of his touch lingers on my skin as he leans in closer and whispers in my ear, "Ready to be fucked by my tongue?"

I nod, eagerly, desperately, as I realize that I'm about to fall for him harder than I ever expected.

"I'm going to devour that pussy."

He begins kissing down my neck, to the top of my breasts, over my nipple that is basically poking into his mouth. He sucks it in eagerly, first my left one, then my right. Doing all this, teasing both my nipples, licking from one stiff bud to the other, he takes his time—knowing full well that his announcement is already creating havoc in my mind. He proceeds to trail his tongue down my belly, licking up the vanilla cream spread on my naked skin.

This experience sure gives "getting your pussy eaten" a whole new meaning.

He licks through my folds, eating the cupcake cream, eating my pussy, no, *feasting* on my pussy, feasting on everything, but evading my swollen clit (so frustrating, no, irritating!) and glides to my entrance. There, he sucks the strawberry in and holds it by its end with his lips, then he begins to fuck me with it.

Don't ask me why, but it's so hot—life's sweet surprises!

Finally, I can take "getting fucked by a strawberry" off my bucket list.

He stands, strawberry (slightly mangled) in his mouth, a small smile playing on his lips. The strawberry is covered in cream and my wetness. Slowly, he places the fruit against my lips. We remain like that, looking into each other's eyes.

"Lick it," he grumbles, without dropping it.

I lick over the skin. The cream is delicious. It tastes like vanilla, and me. He watches me lick it and eat it, as the warmth of his touch lingers on my skin.

"Atta girl."

I swallow.

He leans in, growling, "I bet you want my attention on your clit, don't you?"

With a happy nod, I whisper, "Yeah..."

"I got you, baby." He smirks, his long and stunning eyelashes framing his eyes. "You know exactly who this sweet pussy belongs to."

"You. Only you."

Nodding, he traces his tongue back down to my pussy, licking off the remains of the cream on the way, evading direct contact with my clit again, torturing me, running to my entrance, and licking across it.

"Damn right," he growls and fills me with his tongue.

I gasp. With thrusting motions in and out, he tongue-fucks me, making me clench, making me moan, until I'm a breathing mess. He licks his way back up, hovering his wet tongue just over my clit that's still covered in cream. I try to push my hips up, but to no avail.

I can feel him grinning at my despair.

When I whimper his name in agony, he gives in and—oh, so lightly—brushes over my clit, licking parts of the cream off, causing me to jerk. He brushes over it again. And again. He proceeds to circle it in soft lazy circles, cleaning me, eating me, as I continue to gasp and moan and jerk and feel the orgasm building with each caress.

"You taste delicious," he growls in between another set of delicious licks.

"Carter..." I somehow manage to respond.

"I'm not talking about the frosting. It's your taste that I love." Just when I'm about to stumble over the edge, Carter gets up. "Don't come just yet."

"Whoa...."

"I want you to come on my tip."

His idea stops any lingering protests. In fact, my *entire* being likes his idea. He hovers in front of me, placing his inked arms on either side of me against the wall, caging me in. His shaft is teasing my clit as he moves his hips against me in rhythmical motions, getting us both off, causing my orgasm to start knocking at the door.

"I'm so close..."

His eyes connect with mine. "Not yet. Hold on a bit longer for me."

He's such a controlling jerk. A *hot* controlling jerk.

"Okay." Obviously, I've lost my mind, simply agreeing to that, especially now that I'm teetering on the edge, poised to erupt with the slightest touch. "Please, Carter, I can't..."

I moan even louder at being suddenly filled with his tip again.

It's just as intense—and just as frustrating—as it was before. If not more. He simply refuses to push himself all the way in. I spread my legs farther apart, hoping to cause him to slide in deeper. Carter's mouth is all over my throat and shoulders, nipping and sucking on the sensitive flesh. I grip the sides of the pillow I'm sitting on, twisting it each time he pushes and pulls in and out of me by just a fraction of an inch.

I've never been this frustrated and never this turned on. Yes, we've had sex before, but his control brings a new level of intimacy, closeness, and horniness I haven't experienced before. My pussy is drenching his hard tip and squeezing it uncontrollably. Wetness is pooling on the pillow under my ass. With shaky movements, I try to rotate my hips, and try to steer his tip deeper.

"Stay still," he orders.

"*Carter....*"

"The last fucking time. Stay fucking still," he grumbles sternly. "Don't move, or I will have to fuck you. I only have so much willpower."

Carter's hands and mouth are all over me, his tongue inside me, his cock *not* inside of me (enough), one hand clasping my throat, the other brushing over my drenched clit, but all I can do is be there and take it. Or *not* take it. I have to accept all he's doing to me. And what he's not doing to me.

Sensing by my uncontrollable moans that I'm at the brink, ready to tumble over the edge, he continues his teasing, his thumb circling my clit. I'm beginning to lose it. "Yeah, come for me, baby. Come on my tip."

I explode hard and loud, squeezing his tip over and over, chanting his name as I ride out my orgasm, coming and moaning and squeezing.

I have barely come down from that high when his fingers release my swollen clit, while he sucks on the junction between my throat and shoulder.

There's definitely going to be a mark.

"Carter," I moan when his hands are on my breasts, caressing my nipples, stiffened from my orgasm. "Give me more. Push in. Please. I'm serious, please."

His head draws away, and he raises his eyebrow, watching me beg while his hands are still playing with my hard nipples, now plucking and twisting them, his hips moving in those agonizing tiny thrusting movements.

I can't take it anymore. I want Carter to take me, hard and fast.

I want to get stretched by him, feel painfully full of him. Full of his cock.

I want the air filling with the sounds of our moans and skin slapping skin. I want to feel him thrusting, pumping his long, steel-hard cock into my willing body.

"Take me...please, Carter," I plead, my voice cracking from the intensity of the desire coursing through my veins. I want to be his, and allow him to do all the dirty, unimaginable things to me, to be fucked and used by him as he pleases.

Carter must be just as eager as I am because he doesn't say anything.

His stormy eyes bore into mine, more intense than ever. Piercing. Dangerously fierce.

He lowers his hands from my breasts and firmly grips my hips and ass.

He's ready to thrust in.

I want him to.

Badly.

Desperately.

Ding-dong. Ding-dong.

We freeze.

"Fuck," Carter grumbles through clenched teeth.

"Who's that?"

"My lawyer. Vance. With the NDA."

"*Now?*"

He glares at me. Carter doesn't have to explain. He already mentioned on the plane that his lawyer would stop by this week. Like with anything else, Carter doesn't want any loose ends, and his attorney had interrupted his vacation to fly out to see us.

Apparently, that's not all he has interrupted.

The timing couldn't be worse. Did his attorney have to come at this exact moment? Despite a flood of frustration crashing down on me, I can't help but find the situation a tiny bit amusing. Okay, I find it hilarious, especially now that my body has released all those happy "O" hormones, and they're having a dance party within me.

"Let's ignore him," Carter rumbles darkly when he sees my grinning face, and leans back in.

"We can't, we have to answer."

"No, we don't," he urges, one hand now on my throat and jaw. "We don't."

Ding-dong. Ding-dong. Ding-dong.

"I doubt he'll leave. The best lawyers are the most relentless ones," I argue.

"*Fuck.*"

Carter brushes his thumb across my jaw, retracts his hands, slides his tip out of me, slowly, attentively, then straightens and pulls up his boxer shorts and jeans. Next, he puts on his shirt, and after making sure that his arousal isn't visible, he rushes out to answer the front door, while I try my best to get back into my clothes and cover up my rumpled, disheveled appearance that's a dead giveaway of me just having had cupcake cream smeared all over my naked body, complete with a delicious strawberry, not on top, but inside of me.

You know, the usual night at the Bancroft residence.

"So, does this happen often? You know, people signing NDAs in the middle of the night?" I ask after saying hello to the lawyer, trying to inject a touch of humor into the circumstances and smooth out the awkwardness.

"Let's just say it's part of the job," Mr. Vance Lombardi says matter-of-factly in a thick Italian accent. I can't tell if he's being serious or joking.

Just like we had with Carter's family lawyer, we both put on our game faces and get down to business. Despite seeing the humorous side in all this, I can't help but feel acutely aware of the situation. The lawyer had interrupted a very, uh…intimate moment between me and Carter. Mr. Lombardi seems unfazed, though, as he starts explaining the terms of the agreement—in excruciating detail. I try my best to pay attention, but all I can think about is how I'd almost broken my promise, and gladly so.

Signing the papers, I feel a tightening in my heart. While our physical connection is strong, our emotional connection is almost nonexistent. It's just a business arrangement, and as much as I'm enjoying the oh-so-hot physical aspect of it, I know I can't allow my heart to get any closer to him.

"I should get some sleep," I say through a pretend yawn when Vance pulls out more papers, related to different projects he wants to urgently discuss with Carter.

Carter doesn't look too happy, at least I think that he doesn't, but what can he say? *Sorry, Vance, get out, I have to go fuck?*

"Good night, Eden," Carter says instead, his tone of voice back to boss-mode, and Vance gives me a polite nod, immediately taking back Carter's attention.

ONCE IN MY BED, I check my socials. More people have unfollowed me on Insta. "Good riddance." I reassure myself that they were never true friends to begin with, though I can't entirely dismiss the twinge of pain in my chest knowing they believe the false stories Rob is spreading about me. After he robbed me and distorted the truth about what had actually occurred, Rob simply vanished. He's nowhere to be found, as if he has been swallowed by the earth itself.

I try to reach my sister, missing her voice. Informing her about the uplifting news Carter had conveyed over dinner will not only brighten her evening but also improve my own mood, which has been negatively affected both by finding out how many people continue to believe Rob, and by the lack of a response from the legal aid I reached out to last week.

As always, my sister's phone rings, and rings, until it jumps to voice mail. I leave her a quick message, telling her to call me back, that I have good news. Two minutes later, she calls back, telling me that she's packing for a short trip to see her husband's granny who has broken her leg.

"Oh, I'm sorry to hear that!" I say.

"No worries, she's going to be fine. Just needs a helping hand for a couple of days. So how's New York?"

In light of the NDA I have just signed, and my sister being busy packing, I opt to provide her with just a brief response. I tell her that NYC is fine, and that I'm enjoying my job at Legacy.

"How's your boss?" she inquires with a mischievous tone, fully aware of her own tough nature.

"Carter Bancroft is determined, relentless, tough, but also so—"

"Wait, what? Did you say Carter Bancroft? *The* Carter Bancroft? The construction king of New York?"

"Yeah. How do you know him?"

"I might be a small-town girl from tiny Ellsworth, but they do have Internet here, you know? He was featured in several articles for having catapulted that Legacy Construction firm from the million-dollar mark into the billions in record time. They say he's a force of nature, that he faces challenges head-on, moves with precision, never backs down with his unbreakable spirit, and overcomes obstacles that would make others throw in the towel. Is all that true about him?"

Oh, you have no idea.

For some crazy reason, immense pride fills my heart. On top of that, hearing the excitement in my sister's usually much more serious demeanor gives my mood a little boost. "Yep."

"Oh, my gosh! Why didn't you tell me earlier? Getting to work for him, that's like winning the jackpot!"

Wait 'til you find out that I live in his apartment, I think. *And that he's my fake husband. And that I know what he looks like naked. And what it feels like to orgasm on his tip.* I'm itching to reveal that, but: NDA. However, once the contractual obligations are met, she'll be the first person to receive the information (excluding, perhaps, *all* the tantalizing details—certain *berrylicious* aspects are best kept between two sets of minds).

"And Carter Bancroft is expecting your call."

"Say whaaaat?"

"I told him about your fire-resistant landscape design approach. He wants to help the company expand."

"Are you telling me I need to hold on to my gardening gloves because we're about to see green and witness that company bloom brighter than a garden in full springtime splendor?"

"Uh-huh, yep."

"Sweet heavens! How do I best get in touch?"

"Great question. Via me." I give my sister the best contact info, and she promises to reach out promptly. "Okay, happy packing, talk to you soon!"

"Waitwaitwait. How are you holding up?" she asks. "How's the heart?"

Keeping things vague, I tell her, "I might have met someone."

"What?" There's silence. "Spill! When? How? Who?"

"Eh...it's complicated. And special. And impossible. And I want to break promises that I made to myself because of Rob...and I know I shouldn't..."

"Sweetie, listen. You can't let the fuckface get to you any longer. That's how you got into trouble after he left you. And you sound like you did then. I know you don't openly display your emotions for everyone to see, not even me. But promise me something. If it gets like it was before, you'll call me."

It had been a bad time when Rob broke it all off. A really bad time. "I promise I will. I'm all right. Don't worry about me."

"Just take your time. Don't rush into anything. But if you like this guy you've met, don't let the experience you had with the fuckface ruin it for you. Don't let the fuckface wreck the rest of your life. Or stand in the way of the possibility of a new relationship."

I love my sister. I'd hated when she'd called him fuckface back then. I love that she does now.

"You deserve to find love," she continues. "I've been saying this forever. Now, I may have been a tiny bit hesitant about you using New York as an escape plan, but if—by some crazy chance—you have happened to stumble upon that special man who'll show you the moon in the Big Apple, I'll be the first one to bust out the party hats and celebrate like there's no tomorrow. Got that, sis?"

"Got it."

"Good. Be ready for this epic chapter in your life. See you in six months!"

Oh, I'm ready for an epic chapter, but I'm not sure if I can turn the page. "Love you, Diane."

"Love you too."

An hour later, I hear the front door close, and half a minute later, there's a soft knock at my door.

"Are you awake, Eden?" I hear Carter ask.

I don't answer. It wouldn't be right to invite him in. We have to be up early to get to the airport.

16

EDEN
SATURDAY MORNING

I don't get much sleep.

Not because of the call with my sister.

All I can think about is that my boss had subtle fucked me into oblivion.

Lying here alone in my guest bed, I know that from this day on, I will never be able to enjoy cupcakes the same way again, especially vanilla ones with strawberries on top.

I've also lost count of how many times I've replayed our just-the-tip sex. Disclaimer: In my mind, the just-the-tip sex hadn't stayed just-the-tip sex. Oh, no. In my mind, after the lawyer had left, I'd opened my door to Carter and invited him into my bed. All damn night, we were all over that bed and all over each other, entangled, glued together, deeply inside of each other.

In my dream, after our hot tip-including-all-the-cock sex, we fell asleep together in my guest bed—my head on his chest, cuddled up against him, feeling him still inside me.

The just-the-tip sex has made me desperate to have real sex with him.

It was a horrible mistake that cannot happen again.

When the alarm goes off at half past six, I pop my head up and push my crazy hair out of my face to find that I had fallen asleep facing the end of the bed.

Carter is nowhere in sight. Not in my bed. Not in my room.

Once I get up, I noticed his is empty too.

Though my dream was excruciatingly vivid, it's hard not to have a sense of déjà vu, but I quell any lingering anxiety. First off, we didn't have real sex last night. He didn't even sleep in my bed. Second, it's his place, so there's really no sense in running off if he wants to ditch me. And third, I can smell coffee coming from the kitchen.

The fresh coffee brew is like a magnet.

Humming, I follow the alluring smell down the hallway. Carter is shirtless in only a pair of white workout shorts. By the way his hawk glistens, it isn't hard to tell that he's just finished his workout. He sits at the kitchen table, sipping black coffee as he studies his phone. There's a second steaming mug left out for me, next to a plate of food: French toast with bananas and orange juice.

"Morning," he greets me as soon as I come closer, without looking up. "Made you something quick. You might want to hurry; we have to head out in a few."

"What time do we leave to pick her up?" I start to shovel the toast into my mouth. "Mmm. *Foooyummy!*"

"In about forty minutes." Carter downs the rest of his coffee and gets up. "I'm going to jump in the shower."

"I should probably do the same. I imagine I look like hell."

Carter pats my wild hair, a smile dancing on his lips. "You look thoroughly *debauched*," he grumbles, his voice dropping low as he leans down. I thinks he's going to give me a kiss, but he nips at my throat instead. Not hard but enough to tease a moan out of me before he walks away like nothing happened. It's cute, and sexy.

I'd be lying if I said there wasn't an extra pep in my step.

. . .

ONE SHOWER LATER, in our separate bathrooms, of course (and me singing my all-time favorite, "Empire State of Mind" by Jay-Z and Alicia Keys, followed by "Fly Me to the Moon" by Frank Sinatra), we move my things into his bedroom, say hi to the over-punctual maid, tell her to start with the guest suite first, and head out the door.

"All right, I'm getting a little nervous," I admit as Carter pulls into traffic.

"Don't be. She's very frail right now," he explains. "It might take her a little while to get around so just be patient."

"Of course. Did she tell you what she has?"

"No, not specifically. I don't think it's one thing, I think it's a combination. Which is not surprising since she's sixty-six."

"Actually, it *is* a little surprising, isn't it? Sixty-six isn't that old."

"That's what I keep telling myself."

"I think it's very sweet that she wanted to come for a visit," I say. "The fact that she's still so active and willing to travel is a good sign. It also shows how much she loves you."

"She's my special lady."

I've never heard Carter sound so soft and sincere. It makes my heart melt that this tough-as-nails, no-nonsense man has a soft side for his elderly aunt. I can't wait to meet her. Between what he's told me about her and the fact that she's good friends with Hattie, she has to be an amazing lady.

We pull up outside the airport with a few minutes to spare. "Wait here." Carter puts the car in park. "I'm going to go in and meet her."

"Okay. But wouldn't it be better if I came with you?"

"No, let's not overwhelm her."

Just as he steps out of the car, the airport doors open, and a tiny old woman steps out. I instantly know she's his aunt because she's the epitome of class and glamour. I've never seen someone so glam and eye-catching in my life.

Eleanor Toussaint doesn't just catch my eye, she catches *everyone's* eye. She wears a tailored pantsuit that's a deep purple and accented by the elegant fluffy coat with fur draped around her shoulders. Carter had given me a heads up that she might don fur, but he'd quickly assured me that her love for pets was too strong for her to ever give in to wearing the real thing. He'd also enlightened me that she remarried in her late fifties, tying the knot for the second time with a gentleman named Henri Toussaint, a French industrialist, who had left her a substantial fortune. Her body is adorned with various jewels, from rings on almost every finger to a delicate string of pearls around her neck and pearls dangling from each ear. Her long gray hair is slicked up into an elegant twist, and her eyes are covered by big round sunglasses, which she whips off when she sees Carter. She reminds me of an older Audrey Hepburn, capturing that same timeless elegance.

"Cartie! *Mon cheri!*" she coos under her flawless makeup, not pancaked on but rather lightly used to highlight her facial features. Just enough that I can tell she's wearing some but not so much that it's comical—except for the eyelids and eyebrows which are "slightly" overdone. "Come here, Cartie, and give your auntie a big hug!"

Cartie? Oh, my God, I love her already. I dare not look over at him for fear I'll spoil everything by laughing, but I'd give almost anything to see the expression on his face.

Carter does as he's told. "Hello, Auntie." He gathers her into his broad arms. "You look younger each time I see you."

"Oh, Carter Donovan, did I not teach you not to lie to your aunt? But thank you, you are not wrong." Chuckling, she pats his arm before her face turns toward the car and she catches sight of me. "Is that Eden? What are you doing sitting in that fancy car? Come on out here and give your aunt a big hug!"

She doesn't need to tell me twice. Swept up in her warmth and pageantry, I jump out of the BMW and let her pull me into a hug. Her wiry frame is stronger than she looks, and she hugs me so tight it almost cuts off my breathing.

"It's nice to meet you, Mrs. Toussaint," I say, hugging her back.

She scoffs. "*Nonono.* What is with the formality? We are family, dear, are we not? You will call me 'Auntie.' Yes, I insist you do!"

"Okay, Auntie."

She draws back from the hug and takes my face between her boney hands. She leans back in and lightly kisses each of my cheeks, starting with my left one. Carter has already explained that it's a social custom in France that has been around for centuries and is deeply ingrained in French culture. In the same breath, he'd also cautioned me about his aunt's "French," the delightful outcome of her "Franglais" escapades, to the extent that even the Eiffel Tower might arch an eyebrow. According to Carter, she believes that adding a French word to everything she says makes it *très chic* (which, honestly, I find so endearing!).

"Oh, *mon Dieu*! So beautiful! Carter, you lucky man."

I grin over at him. "You hear that, *babe*, you lucky man?" It's both odd and awesome to call him babe. He plays along perfectly, doesn't even bat an eye, as if he's used to me calling him that.

"So lucky." He pulls his aunt into another hug. "Why don't you get into the car, and I'll go get your bags."

"Oh, I already had some help from a handsome young man. *Où est-il*? Ah! There he is! Jack!" A security guard steps out of the airport with a cart full of luggage. Aunt Eleanor steps up to him and pats his arm. "*Merci*. Such a helpful young man. Handsome, too. Here, this is for you."

I watch her take a roll of cash out of her fluffy coat and slip it into the small pocket on the front of his uniform shirt. His cheeks turn red. "Oh, no thank you, ma'am. I can't accept this."

"*Absurdité*! I *know* they do not pay you nearly enough for all you do. Hush now. Accept the tip and buy yourself something nice." She motions for Carter to take the cart before turning back to me. "Do an old lady a favor and help her into the back seat."

"Oh, you can have the front," I offer immediately, motioning to the open door. "I insist."

"Such a sweet girl."

I help Eleanor into the front seat while Carter loads her six bags into the trunk. We catch each other's eye, and I don't need words to know we're wondering the same thing. If she's only staying for the weekend, why does she have so much luggage? That has to be a typical French thing. Aren't French women famous for always looking immaculate? I know she's American by birth, but living in France has clearly rubbed off on her.

Once she's settled, I close the passenger-side door and climb into the back seat. Carter finishes loading her bags and gives the luggage cart back to Jack. He accepts it with a nod and waves goodbye to Eleanor, who gives him a warm smile and a wave back.

"You must be exhausted," Carter says as soon as he starts the car. "We'll get you home and you can take a long nap."

Eleanor waves a dismissive hand. "I slept enough on the plane. Besides, I am not going to miss a moment getting to know my nephew's beautiful new bride."

Carter doesn't get a chance to pull out of his parking space. His phone starts to ring. He gives us an apologetic look as he answers it. "Bradley, you know I'm not available today. This better be an emergency."

I can't hear what Bradley says, but by the look on Carter's face, I can tell it's not good. He glances over at his aunt, who's staring at him with her intense blue eyes. "Uh-huh. Yeah, all right. Thanks."

He hangs up, but before he can say anything, his aunt says, "Well, that did not last long."

"I'm so sorry, I really am." Carter puts the phone in the cup holder. "There's an emergency at the office. They need me."

"Can't someone *else* handle it, babe?" I ask, emphasizing the word so he knows exactly how I feel about him trying to bail.

"Save your breath, *ma chère*." Eleanor interjects with a wave of her jeweled hand. "Carter and his work are joined at the hip."

"I can't apologize enough." Carter pulls out of the parking lot. "I swear I'll only be gone for an hour, tops."

"Yes, yes, I have heard it before." Eleanor smiles and reaches into her handbag to pull out her hand mirror and check on her eyebrows. "Do not worry, Cartie. We will be fine. In fact, it will give me and Eden a little one-on-one time."

Now, I'm a pretty positive person and know I can handle myself. But the thought of being alone with Carter's elderly aunt when she's in poor health and believes we're married and that her nephew is deeply in love has me more than a little nervous.

Carter gives me "You got this, right?" eyes.

I offer a subtle nod.

You can handle this, I tell myself and smile back at her beaming face. It's just an hour alone with an elderly lady. What could go wrong?

WE MAKE it back to the apartment, and Carter takes the time to bring up all of Eleanor's bags. After he takes them to the guest suite, he gives his aunt a quick peck on the cheek. I look around. The maid is gone, and everything is perfect.

"One hour," he repeats. "At the most."

"We'll be fine." I offer him a smile, playing the loving wife to the T. "And you can make it up to us later."

To my surprise, he leans in and gives me a kiss on my lips. The impact is so strong, it leaves me breathless. Even though it's only a brief press of our lips, it still has my knees wobbling like the night before. In the heat of the moment, I forget I need to stay in character. When he pulls away, my head is spinning, and then I remember his aunt and that the kiss was all for show.

Right. It was all pretend. *Don't get too invested*, I warn myself.

"I'll be back as soon as I can, love," he says.

Sweet heavens. He called me "love." During our just-the-tip sex he'd called me "baby." Now, he'd called me "love."

Don't get emotionally attached, I warn myself.

Carter leaves, and I'm alone with his aunt. I can feel her intense eyes watching me as I turn away from the door.

"Young love! My heart!" she coos when I finally regain my senses and turn to face her.

Apparently, the happy face I'm wearing due to him calling me "love" is an Oscar-worthy performance.

"I *know*." I beam. "How about we get you settled in the guest suite?" I suggest, ready to help her unpack.

"Oh, *nonono*, we do not have to do that right now." She shakes her head, making her way to the couch. She takes off the animal-friendly coat, and it makes her look even smaller. Without it, I can see that Eleanor is more fragile than her charisma suggests.

She lets herself sink onto the couch.

I follow, taking her coat and hanging it on the rack by the door. "Can I get you something?" I ask when I return to her. "A snack or some tea, maybe?"

"Tea would be grandiose." She makes herself comfortable with a pillow. "How about Earl Grey? As long as you make a cup for yourself and join me."

"I'd be happy to."

"*Ma chère*, I have a *ton* of questions."

17

CARTER

The only reason I'm going into the office is because I know it's an emergency.

Bradley wouldn't have called me otherwise. He knows my aunt is in town and that it's important for me to spend time with her and sell the whole marriage thing. But when two board members call a secret meeting and one of them is Huxley, I can't sit back and not get involved.

Bradley is waiting for me in the parking lot when I pull in.

"You know, for someone who lives in Connecticut, you sure are here a lot," I comment, getting out of my car.

Bradley bumps my fist, giving me a once-over. "Something's different."

"Yeah, I'm not in my suit. You caught me right on the way back from the airport."

"Nah, that's not it. You seem way too relaxed." Bradley studies me closely. "Wait a minute, I know that stance. You had sex."

"Not quite." I shake my head, annoyed. "Get out of my ass."

Part of me is glad I'd taken Eden up on her offer, even if Vance's showing up couldn't have come at a worse time. The cupcake sex was hot as fuck. I can't stop thinking about what would have happened if

Vance hadn't appeared. Us rolling between the sheets all night, that was what would have happened—naked, sweaty, sticky. Luckily, I jerked off this morning. Hard. Twice. Still, there needs to be a repeat performance, and soon—this time preferably with an uninterrupted outcome.

Bradley claps his hand on my shoulder. "Not quite? Not quite means yes. I knew it. I knew you couldn't be fake married to your assistant and not get your dick wet again."

I give him a dark look. "Hey, watch it." It comes out harsher than I intended.

Bradley's eyebrows shoot up. "Sorry, bro." He lifts his hands in surrender. "Didn't realize you were that into her. My bad."

I grab my tablet from the driver's seat and tuck it under my arm, calming my nerves. Bradley's a loyal friend, and we go way back, so he knows how to push my buttons better than anybody. Usually, I appreciate him for his "No BS" attitude, but the unexpected meeting has thoroughly soured my mood.

I bump his knuckles. "Also, don't fucking say I'm married. It's only a fucking show." I close the car door. "And it's supposed to be between us, remember?"

"Then you might want to get rid of that." Bradley eyes my left hand, where I had slipped on the wedding band before picking up my aunt.

"Fuck. Good call." I take the ring off and put it in my pocket as we head into the building. "Any idea what this meeting is about?"

"Nope. Just that Huxley called it, and my boss told him to make sure you were there. I figured he hadn't said anything to you, which is why I called."

"Of course he didn't inform me. Huxley never misses a chance to cut me out of things."

I'm not worried about being kept in the dark—pissed off about it, that's what I am. Huxley knows damn well I'd planned to be tied up with my aunt's visit, and he's using the time to try to go behind my back. Joke's on him though because more people are loyal to me than they are to him.

In the conference room, I find Saul Huxley and CEO Nathan Bernie sitting and speaking in low voices. Without knocking or waiting to be acknowledged, Bradley and I walk right in. Huxley sits at the head of the table, and Bernie is in the seat to his right.

Immediately, I take the same seat I'd occupied during our last meeting, so that Huxley is forced to look directly across the table to meet my gaze. It puts both of us in positions of power, and I can see the vein in his temple twitch when he notices me. Bradley takes the seat next to his boss, not choosing sides. He doesn't need to sit next to me for me to know he has my back.

"Good morning, gentlemen," I start. "Seems like a strange time to hold a meeting."

Huxley looks me in the eye, but his expression is a cool mask of indifference. Good poker face, I have to give him that. He doesn't reveal whether he's surprised or not that I'm here. It's not a good sign, and I know not to trust him.

"Good morning, Bancroft," Bernie says, leaning back in his chair. "I'm sorry to call you in on a Saturday, but Huxley said this meeting couldn't wait."

"Oh, really? Then by all means, do tell." I'm relaxed and confident that whatever this is, I'm not going to let Huxley get the best of me. I never allow myself to be rattled by what he does, and I won't be this time.

"As you know, we've had numerous discussions about your future here at the company," Bernie addresses me. "You're an excellent worker, Bancroft, and your loyalty is greatly appreciated. The work you've done to expand our revenue is unparalleled, and I want you to know that your determination has not gone unnoticed."

"But?" I ask.

"No but. I know you've been looking for more and it's been discussed, and we've decided to give you more responsibility."

I keep my emotions in check and my expression passive. On one hand, I'm satisfied that things are finally moving forward the way I want. However, considering the odd circumstances and Huxley's chill demeanor, I'm on high alert.

"What do you have in mind?" I press.

"Obviously you're aware of the Granger account?" He raises his brows.

The Grangers are a highly influential family throughout New England and even a few of the southern states. Their firm is a major player in new commercial construction areas. Our firm scored them as a client several months ago. And by our firm, I mean me and my team. It took two years of work to win that account, and as soon as they signed on to work with us, Huxley swept in and took it over. Needless to say, I was pissed.

Yet now Bernie has the nerve to ask if I'm aware of the account?

"Considering I was the one who worked on getting them to sign with us, I am aware of them," I reply.

"Well, they have been adamant about wanting you on the account, to personally work with them. Up until now, major accounts like theirs are typically handled by the partners. We have decided to make an exception. Starting Monday, Granger Estates will be in your hands again."

Translation: Huxley has fucked up in some way, and it's now my job to fix it. It's not the first time in the last several months. Bradley keeps me informed of mistakes he manages to overhear on his end of things—they all wear Huxley's name. The partners have had to cover for him on at least three separate occasions.

I look at Huxley for any tell-tale signs that he's fuming. He has to be. There's no way he can't be pissed that Bernie is taking the account away from him. But all I see is a smile and a relaxed stance.

No. I don't trust it.

"Is there anything I need to know going in?" I continue questioning them.

"They have high demands for their renovation project," Huxley says. "They recently bought a small chain of restaurants, and all of them need major construction and updating. Their timeline is short, and their budget extremely specific."

There it is.

Short time frames with small budgets are nightmares to organize.

Especially for highly involved clients who have specific needs and are already wary due to fuckups. No wonder Huxley isn't mad that the account is being taken away from him. He doesn't have to deal with the mess he's caused. But that's the major difference between us. He sees those types of clients as annoying—I see them as a challenge.

I never back down from a challenge.

"Great, can't wait to get started," I say. "Unfortunately, I can't do so today, gentlemen. I have to leave right after this meeting. But I'll do what I can from home and lay the groundwork for the transfer first thing Monday morning."

"This is a big client," Huxley suddenly jumps in. "The reason we're having this meeting on a Saturday is that it can't wait. I'm surprised you would delay getting to work on such an important client."

Laughable. Huxley really thinks he can goad me into dropping everything to stay at work. He knows I have family obligations. Of course, he doesn't know exactly what I have happening over the weekend since it isn't any of his damn business. But if he wants to go that route, if he wants to try to make me look bad in front of Bernie, he's in for a surprise.

For one thing, I put in more than enough work to deserve a weekend. Second, work doesn't come before my aunt. The only reason I felt comfortable enough to leave her for an hour is that she always takes a nap after her flight, but mostly because Eden is with her.

"The reason why I have to leave is because my elderly aunt is visiting, possibly for the last time," I announce. "I have someone staying with her at the moment, but I need to get back soon. The rest has to wait."

I can feel the energy shift in the room. Bernie looks uncomfortable, and Huxley's smile falters. "You could have told us," Bernie says, shifting in his seat while absentmindedly running his hand through his thinning hair. "We could have rescheduled or done a remote meeting."

"Unfortunately, I didn't have enough time. I got the call about the meeting on my way back from the airport."

At that, Bernie looks at Huxley sharply. "What is he talking about? I told you about this meeting two days ago."

Two days ago? Bastard. Not telling me earlier about an important meeting is exactly the kind of shit I've come to expect from Huxley. It's a good thing Bradley had called me to let me know the meeting was going on. Huxley probably wouldn't have said anything at all.

"I swear I sent the message yesterday," Huxley says. "Must be that new assistant you have. Shame, I thought she would work out well. You might want to rethink her position here. How many assistants would that be now? You go through them so fast it's hard to keep track."

All right. He wants to play dirty. Bastard is already on thin ice trying to throw me under the bus. His going after Eden is where I draw the line. I know with absolute certainty that if she had gotten that email before she'd left work, she would have immediately put it in my calendar, or at least told me about it when we'd gone to dinner.

He had sent the email after hours, knowing full well I wouldn't see it in time.

"As you know, anything last minute like that should be CCed to me as well or sent directly to me. I have explained on multiple occasions that my assistants don't work after hours or on weekends and therefore she would not have seen it until it was too late," I inform him, keeping my voice calm and cool, yet glaring daggers at the asshole who sits across from me. "I will also say, she's been working with us for a week already and has proven to be competent at her job."

Huxley nods. "You are right, that was my mistake. I forgot about that." He smiles. I can count on one hand the number of times Huxley has smiled at me that wasn't a sneer or smirk.

"Anyway, it doesn't matter. What matters is that I'm here and we've discussed what we needed to. Is there more or can I return to my guest?"

"Yes, of course," Bernie says. "There was something else I wanted to go over, but the full details can wait." He turns to Bradley. "Everhart, can you make sure to fill Bancroft in on the other items we discussed?"

Bradley gives a curt nod. "I will."

"Enjoy your visit with your aunt," Huxley throws out. "I'm sorry to hear that she isn't feeling well. Please let us know if you need anything."

What the hell is going on with him? He's being way too nice and understanding, which is unlike him. I know he has to be pissed that his plan to keep me out of the meeting failed spectacularly. I'm sure he has something else up his sleeve.

Any other day I would have dived headfirst into work to stick it to Huxley. But my mind is preoccupied with Aunt Eleanor, and I'm anxious to text Eden to check in, announcing that I might need a bit longer than the promised hour, so she won't have to worry. Without a word, I get up from the table, and Bradley follows me out of the room.

When we're far enough away that we can't be overheard, he says, "Well, that could've been worse."

"I don't trust anything that just happened in that conference room," I tell him as we head toward my office to discuss our battle plan.

"Why? Huxley seemed pretty chill about the whole thing."

"I know. When have you ever known Huxley to be chill about anything, unless he believed he had all the strings in his hands?"

"Fair point."

18

EDEN

I go to the kitchen and put the kettle on for Aunt Eleanor and me. I've taken time over the last few days to get to know where things are in the apartment, that way it looks more believable that I spend all my time here. While the tea is going, I open the cabinet and pull out a box of rum balls Carter bought specially for his aunt, saying that they could come in handy as "her absolute favorite distraction."

I arrange everything on a silver tray I find in one of the cabinets. When the Earl Grey is ready, I carry it into the living room. Eleanor isn't on the couch where I left her. I'm about to get worried when I see her coming down the hall with a red box in her hands.

"You are an angel, dearie," she says. "Now, before I forget, I have a little something for you." She sits back on the couch, and after she gestures for me to sit next to her, she places the box on my lap. On top is an envelope graced with beautiful calligraphy that says, "Mr. & Mrs. Carter Bancroft."

"This is for you, *ma chère*," she says. "Technically, it's for you and Carter both, but I'm giving it to you as a wedding present."

Without waiting, I pull out the card, smiling at the gorgeous gold trim and wording.

The card reads:

Congratulations Carter & Eden,
Your marriage made my heart the happiest it has been in a très, très long time.
Although I wasn't able to be there in person to witness it, your wedding brought endless joy and light into my life. May your amour be like that beloved unbreakable teapot in my cupboard—comforting and eternally enduring.
Love, Auntie Eleanor

As I read the lines, I feel a wave of guilt and sadness wash over me. I can't bear to look up, afraid my eyes will give me away. The words on the card feel like a weight on my chest. In the box I find a beautifully hand-crafted sign that reads "The Bancroft Family." The dark wood has a perfect glossy finish, and I can't help running my fingers over the engraved letters. "Wow, I don't know what to say."

Aunt Eleanor beams at me. "Welcome to the family, my dearest Eden."

"Thank you. It's beautiful."

"I had it made special," Eleanor says proudly, picking up her teacup. "So, tell me how you and Cartie met."

Gently putting the sign back in the box, I swallow my feelings away and launch into the story Carter and I discussed, trying to sound as love-struck as I can. I tell her all about how we met four months ago when he was on a business trip on the coast. How I was having lunch at the same hotel where he was staying, and how we ran into each other several times.

Eleanor smiles and nods along with the story, calmly sipping her dark tea.

"He approached me first, alpha man that he is," I continue to tell her, and she nods in agreement. "I was sitting alone at the bar, and he sat right next to me, asking if the seat was taken. Next thing I know he told me to have dinner with him."

We both grin at that.

When I finish talking, I actually feel pretty proud of myself for keeping the whole thing straight. Not one detail did I forget or mess up. By the way she smiles at me, I've sold the loving part enough for her satisfaction.

"That sounds very romantic," Eleanor declares, and inwardly, I sigh in relief.

Perfect. Carter will be proud of me.

She puts a rum ball into her mouth. "Now, tell me how you *really* met."

My jaw drops.

I know I'm in trouble. If there was ever a competition for the worst poker face, I'd be the grand prize winner. Seriously, my face is more expressive than a toddler's on Christmas morning. I couldn't hide the shock if I tried.

"I don't know what you mean," I utter in the weakest of weak attempts, reaching for a rum ball.

"Come now, Eden." Eleanor gives me a look that says she clearly isn't buying it, and I need to stop BSing her. She swallows the chocolate. "I was not born yesterday, dearie. Let us not play coy. I love my nephew to death. But I have always had my suspicions about that story."

I stuff the rum ball into my mouth. Internally, I'm trying desperately not to high-five her with a huge grin (I've had my suspicions about the story too!)—*and* not to panic (I have *no* idea what to tell her). Carter had been confident in his deception, and to sit with his aunt and have her tell me to my face she doesn't believe him has me scrambling to respond.

She grabs another rum ball.

I grab another rum ball.

I place it into my mouth, feigning innocence and hoping to buy myself time to come up with a suitable response. Chewing, I busy myself by standing up and propping the new family sign on the mantel. These rum balls taste kind of...healthy, like they've forgotten the sweet stuff. Is there even any alcohol inside them? Feeling drunk might have calmed my nerves and stopped my cheeks from blushing.

"What's so suspicious about the story?" I ask her, sliding the family sign down a bit, a bit more to the left, no, a bit more to the right again, no, back to where it was—

"You are making me dizzy. Please sit back down. I will gladly tell you what is so suspicious about it. It is too vague. Neither you nor Carter mentioned why you visited the hotel in the first place. It is ridiculous that you kept running into each other and mostly," she narrows her eyes on me, "why would you—all of a sudden—give up your life and move to a different state for him? In *less* than a month?" Her eyes are fixed on me, big and expectant, imploring me to provide an answer that will unravel the *ultimate* mystery.

I can't help it. I laugh. I look back up to face her, and she smiles, watching me trying to pull myself together. "I told Carter the same thing."

Eleanor laughs this time as she shakes her finger at me. "See, I knew it. I knew there was something up with that boy's story."

"We met in an ice cream shop here in New York City, late on a Sunday evening, and from there we went into a bar," I explain, sitting back down. There's no reason to double down on the other story since she clearly doesn't believe it. "It was a chance encounter just not as… clean as Carter made it sound." Technically, I'm not lying. It may have only happened a week ago, but it's still the truth.

"Now, *that* sounds more believable," Eleanor says with a chuckle. "I am sure my nephew thought I might balk at the idea of him dragging his wife from a cute ice cream parlor into some dingy bar. But the truth is, I could not care less where he met you. I am glad he did."

She pats my knee with her bony hand, and I reach out to lay my hand over hers. "Carter thinks the world of you, Auntie," I tell her. "I can tell that he loves you very much. He's been talking about this visit all week. I'm happy that you're here with us."

"I'm happy Cartie found such a lovely woman to settle down with." Eleanor smiles and squeezes my hand. "I know he's consumed by work,

work, work. I'm well aware of his relentless pursuit of becoming a partner at that firm. I am sure you know that he started from nothing—a young boy from a rough neighborhood—and tirelessly worked his way up the ladder, and now it is driving him mad that the CFO stands in his way. You see, coming from a background of limited means, he had to overcome immense challenges and work relentlessly to carve out his path, and his journey has been full of sacrifices and relentless perseverance."

Carter had alluded to his humble upbringing, but hearing Auntie speak about it sheds a whole new light on his character and who he truly is.

"Oh, I am so proud of him," she goes on. "The thought of not achieving his goal would devastate him, not only that, but it would shatter his aspiration, especially considering how close he is to attaining it. It is within his reach, just at his fingertips." She gives my hand another squeeze. "I genuinely wish for him to succeed, but it's refreshing to see something else finally capturing his attention. Indeed, a woman who supports his goal is exactly what he needs. So. Where did you first kiss?"

I knew she would ask, though I had no idea she was going to pop the question so soon. But after the turn of events, I can't possibly tell her the made-up story Carter and I had agreed on—you know, the one where he heroically handed over his jacket due to the low temperatures and leaned in for a kiss. "Quite honestly, I managed to coax him into kissing me. I told him I was the world's best kisser."

"Well, well, well, looks like curiosity didn't just kill the cat, it caught the man too! That was the perfect way to lure him in." Eleanor laughs and so do I. She grabs another rum ball. "What do you think about children?"

Again, she's not afraid to cut to the chase and ask the tough questions. Carter had warned me that she wouldn't be shy.

I grab another rum ball. Quickly, I place it into my mouth, thinking.

Carter had been incredibly clear on the subject, and I'm not about to feed Eleanor some line about "playing things by ear" or "maybe someday." She has already proven to be of sharp mind, and while she does look frail, I doubt this would be something she couldn't handle. Eleanor strikes me as a woman who could handle anything. I swallow the sweet goodness.

"Well, in general, I like children…" I start confidently and truthfully, watching her sip down her chocolate with some tea. "In fact, I like them a lot…"

"Carter was never much interested in children, even when he was one." She interrupts, gently placing her teacup back on the coffee table. "He always says he doesn't want kids, but don't you worry, dearie, with the right woman, he will. No doubt. I remember one time when he was in his early twenties, a distant cousin had a baby, and when we went to visit them, he practically melted and showered it with endless affection."

My shoulders drop, and I release a happy snort. Not only is the visual of bossy, tough Carter melting downright hilarious, but the idea of him softening for a tiny baby is incredibly heartwarming. It dawns on me that Eleanor is the perfect resource for getting to know Carter. After all, she had raised him. She knows him better than anyone. "What was he like as a kid?"

"Oh, *très sérieux*. Always so serious, but smart as a whip. He was never officially tested, but dearie, I was always sure that he was nothing short of a genius. He was always curious about everything, which made him a real pain to take on a museum tour. But it made him a good listener too, and mostly, a natural born problem solver. No challenge was too big for him to tackle. School was a breeze for him. College was a breeze for him. He graduated early. With honors."

"Wow, really? That's *amazing*…I mean yes, I knew that."

"Right. That boy has a wonderful mind. He was determined to make something of himself, and lo and behold, he was able to do just that. He didn't have it easy growing up, having lost his parents early, I admit that. But he never needed much discipline from me—well, at least not when it came to working. His love life, on the other hand, is a whole other matter entirely."

"I bet he left a few broken hearts in his wake." I prop my chin on my hand, wondering how much of Carter's life she's willing to share.

"More than a few," Eleanor confirms laughingly. "He is handsome and smart—must have been my good genes. You know what they say? The apple doesn't fall far from the tree." She chuckles. "Looks like my sense of humor didn't make it through the gene pool though. He's got everything else, but no jokes. Poor kid. I guess I'll just have to settle for being the funny one in the family. Anyway, as soon as he entered high school, *all* of the girls had their eyes on him, but nothing came of it other than a couple of dates. Of course, he would know better about his love life than I would. Still, I always felt like he was looking for something specific. Soon I understood that the girl he would choose as a girlfriend was a girl he would choose as a wife."

That's the greenest flag if there ever was one.

I stop my jaw from dropping, reminding myself to stay in character and mostly, not read anything into her statement.

Also, I'm still stuck at her "all of the girls had their eyes on him" comment. "Sounds like he was a very popular kid, huh?"

"Only with the ladies. He didn't have much by way of friends, as far as I can tell, except for a handful of true friends he kept in touch with all those years, to this day. I suspect he prefers it that way. But let's not dwell on that. For now, let's celebrate that he has you. I'm grateful that he does. I can tell he loves you."

"Oh, you can?" I can't help it. My heart does a little flip-flop and butterflies sprout wings in my stomach.

"Oh, absolutely, dearie. You can tell that a mile off. Without a doubt."

My heart melts a little at her words. If only she knew the truth and that all of it is nothing more than acting. I need to do a much better job of not letting her words get to me.

The more she talks, the more I realize how tired she looks. Her hands shake when she lifts her teacup again, nearly spilling it before I reach out to help. Despite what she said earlier, I'm sure the long plane ride has taken a lot out of her.

"Auntie, why don't we get you settled into your room for a nap?" I suggest. "You've had a long day, and I think it would do you some good to get some rest."

This time she doesn't protest. "You're right, dearie. That jet lag gets me every time. It has been a long trip, and I am positively *fatiguée*." I make a move to help her, but she declines. "I can stand on my own. By the way, no need to fuss over me, *ma chère*. I'm not planning to meet our lord and savior quite yet. I still have plenty of good health in this body, so stop worrying. It's true, I may not be able to do everything I used to, but I'm not completely helpless."

"Of course you aren't. We haven't known each other long, but I get the feeling you're a tough one."

"Smart, beautiful, and an excellent judge of character." She laughs. "And impeccable taste in husbands. Keep doing you, dearie. I can see why my nephew was so drawn to you."

I FEEL relieved once I see her guest room door close. Things may not have gone exactly as planned, but thankfully I haven't ruined the whole cover.

Buzzz.

I pull my vibrating phone out of my pocket.

> CARTER:
> We're almost done here. Everything okay?

> ME:
> Auntie is asleep. FYI, she didn't believe the hotel bar story for a minute. Had to improvise.

The second I hit send I see the three dots appear, and I have the mental image of Carter somewhere between an angry heart attack and a furious rage. Before the three dots stop dancing, I quickly respond.

> ME:
> All good!

A Bossy Roommate

> Told her we met at the ice cream shop and went to the bar, but still stuck to most of the story. She liked it.

> Thumbs up emoji.

CARTER:
> Damn it. I'm on my way. Don't say anything else.

I roll my eyes as I tuck my phone back into my pocket. He's worrying about nothing. Aunt Eleanor adores me and doesn't seem to care about anything other than the fact that we're married.

Since she's resting and Carter is at work, I figure I'll take the time to get some rest myself and head up to Carter's room for a well-deserved nap.

19
CARTER

"All right, Bradley, let's get this shit over with." I slide my phone back into my pocket. "I have to get back home."

"I can just email it all to you. Expect it in your inbox before you hit the sack. You can get back home."

Normally, I would tell him just to tell me now since I'm already here. But I'm desperate to get back home and decide to take him up on his offer. Giving him a slap on the back, I nod. "Thanks, man. Sorry you came all this way for no reason."

"No problem. Don't sweat it, Carr." He waves me off. "You have more important things to focus on. Although I've got to say, Eden has done a number on you."

"What the hell are you talking about?"

Bradley shrugs. "I don't know, man. You seem different. I've never known you to be in such a rush to get out of the office."

"Yeah, well, when you find out your only family is struggling with their health, it really puts things into perspective. If it weren't for Eden, I wouldn't have come in at all," I huff.

"Relax, bro, I was just teasing. But you trust her that much already? Damn, you really *are* that into her."

I think about what's happened between Eden and me over the last few days.

It's been a roller coaster.

I'd be lying if I said there isn't *something*.

We head to the elevators.

"I'll check my email later tonight once my aunt is settled. If anything else comes up, just text me. I may not answer, but I'll at least handle it when I have a chance," I tell Bradley.

"Don't worry about it." He offers a bro-fist, and I bump it. "I'll take care of what I can. Hope everything goes okay with your ladies."

Huh. My ladies. I actually don't mind the sound of that.

I GET HOME AS FAST as I can. When I enter the apartment, I'm surprised to hear absolutely nothing. With a frown, I check the living room and, aside from a tea tray on the coffee table and an almost-empty pack of the "Not-So-Rummy Rum Balls" from a small local bakery, it's exactly as I left it this morning. The "Not-So-Rummy Rum Balls" are a non-alcoholic, low-sugar version of the classic treat. However, Auntie doesn't know that.

I glance toward the guest suite and see the door closed. Aunt Eleanor must have gone to lie down. Poor thing. She's probably exhausted after her long flight.

That doesn't explain where Eden is. Or does it?

I walk to my bedroom and am greeted with the sight of Eden curled up in my bed. Her pants and bra are discarded on the floor, and she's asleep in only a thin nightgown. Seeing the shape of her beautiful curves and other details shine through the thin cotton like that, I'm tempted to crawl in next to her.

I hear the sound of a door opening.

Aunt Eleanor must be awake.

I caress a strand of hair away from Eden's face, silently close the door behind me, and go back out to the living room to greet my aunt.

"Hi, Auntie. Did you have a nice rest?" I ask, pulling her into a hug. She feels so fragile in my arms, it tugs at my heart.

She's changed into a different pantsuit, this one made of softer material and clearly meant for comfort. She has removed her rings and necklaces and put on a pair of pink fuzzy slippers. It's been a long time since I've seen her in person, and without her huge fur coat and endless jewelry, she looks a lot smaller. However, she has freshened up her makeup.

"Oh, I tried, but could not turn my brain off. Too much on my mind." She hugs me back, kisses both my cheeks, before taking a step away and slapping my chest. "Shame on you, Carter Donovan Bancroft!"

"What did I do?"

Aunt Eleanor huffs. "You lied to me!"

I freeze, staring at her. "I did?"

"Why didn't you tell me that you dragged Eden into a bar on the first day you met? Did you think I would be so snobbish that I would not understand?"

"No, of course not. I'm sorry, Auntie," I say, relieved.

"Apology accepted." She smiles and makes a move to pick up the tea tray, but I take it from her. Aunt Eleanor has never been one to hold long grudges. That's something I've always appreciated about her. "Eden told me about that special first kiss you both shared..."

"Did she?" I stop in my tracks.

"Yes! How romantic!"

Surely, Eden had stuck to her own suggestion that we'd discussed earlier, namely of our long walk and me handing her my jacket because it had gotten cold. "Well, I am a gentleman," I say.

"What do you mean, son?"

I stare at her, blank. First, I consider telling her that I meant that anybody would have given her a jacket, but then I pause. What version did Eden tell her? Obviously, something doesn't match up. "Well, a gentleman doesn't kiss and tell."

"Oh, you! You charmer! For a second, I thought you did not

remember your first kiss. How she told you she was the world's best kisser."

Ah, so that was the version she'd told her.

"Are you hungry?" I ask, impressed that Eden had gone with the truth, but not ready to risk any more mismatched reactions or answers, and turn with the tray toward the kitchen. "Bruno will be glad you're visiting. Last time I saw him, he said he'll have your favorite dish ready whenever you want it. We can order in."

Every time Aunt Eleanor visits, she insists on going to a small fine dining restaurant around the corner. Since she's not doing well, I know the chef will be more than happy to pack up her favorite dish for delivery.

She follows me into the kitchen. "Oh, *quel trésor*. But why would we order take-out? We should go and get our favorite seat."

"Auntie, you're supposed to be resting and taking it easy. I don't think going out into a busy restaurant is a good idea."

She pauses. "Oh, you're probably right. Fine, I'd be more than happy to enjoy dinner here tonight with you and your lovely wife. As long as you open a bottle of that spectacular pinot noir I know you keep on the top shelf of your wine rack."

I put the tea tray next to the sink before turning to frown at her. "Aren't you on medication? I would think drinking wouldn't mix well with your meds."

Aunt Eleanor waves her hand and takes a seat at the table. "One glass of wine isn't going to make a major difference."

"Since when have you ever stopped at one glass?"

"Oh, Carter, the things you say! Forget about that tray and come sit with me. I have a few things I want to say to you...and ask you."

Well, that doesn't sound good. Never one to disobey my aunt, I take a seat next to her at the table.

"Why did it take me making this long trip to finally be introduced to Eden? Did it really have to take months and months for the two of us to meet?"

"I'm sorry it took this long," I tell her, and I mean it. "But you know how crazy work has been. Taking time off to go to France hasn't been in the cards. Not just for me but for Eden as well."

"Right. What does she do again? I don't think you've said. Unless you have and I just forgot. My mind is not what it used to be, Cartie."

My heart aches when I hear that. "You didn't forget anything," I assure her, taking her hand. "I didn't tell you what Eden does. She recently started as my assistant. It's not something we typically talk about, especially not at the office, because we don't want others to get the wrong idea."

"What?" Aunt Eleanor removes her hand from mine and studies me with those piercing eyes of hers. "Your wife is your new assistant? And nobody knows about it? That sounds like it could get complicated *très, très* quickly."

"We have ground rules. Work isn't discussed outside of the office and our home life isn't discussed inside the office."

"Translation: you're keeping your marriage a *secret*? Is that why you're suddenly not wearing a ring?"

I try a calming smile, noting I'd forgotten to put the ring back on after the meeting. Well, one less thing to worry about. "Nothing gets past you, does it?"

"Nope. I may not be the woman I used to be, but I'm still sharp when it most counts."

"You're every bit the woman you always were. Maybe you should consider moving back here to New York City."

She opens her mouth to say something but am cut off by a series of deep coughs. I stand and immediately get her a tall glass of water. When I try to hand it to her, her hands shake so bad I have to steady the glass for her. After several sips, the coughing subsides, and Aunt Eleanor lets out a tired sigh.

"Thank you, Cartie," she says, reaching over to take my hand.

"Do those coughing fits happen often?"

"No, no. I'm fine."

I take her small hand between mine and squeeze it. "Tell me, how long do you have? Did the doctors say something?"

First, she looks at me blankly. "Oh, I wish I knew," she finally says. "That would make things a lot easier."

"You need to see a specialist, get a second opinion. Let me make a few calls, I'm sure I'll get the best—"

"No." She squeezes my hand. "I've seen enough doctors. They all say the same thing. Cartie, I'm getting older. Sixty-six. At my age, any number of things can slow me down. I don't want you to dwell on this though. I've made my peace with it. Let's just enjoy what time we have together."

A door opens and closes, and I look up to see Eden coming down the hall. She's wearing her brown hair in a high ponytail and looks pretty in her orange summer dress, the same one she wore on the day we first met. No, not pretty. She looks spectacular.

I only realized I'm staring when Aunt Eleanor chuckles. "Ohoohoo. Look at that lovestruck face," she teases, pinching my cheek.

Eden approaches with a smile. I lean toward her, indicating that I'm expecting a kiss on my lips as she joins us at the table. She leans down and obliges, giving me what I asked for. Am I an asshole using the situation to my advantage? Yes, yes, I am.

"Did you have a good rest, Auntie?" Eden rubs my aunt's shoulder, her face a little flushed as she sits down.

"Please, I haven't had a restful sleep since I was forty-four. Only to be young again." My aunt looks back at me. "Cartie, you haven't shown me the marriage license! In my day, we used to have them proudly on display."

There it is.

Eden's eyes meet mine, shock written all over her features.

In the back of my mind, I hoped Auntie wouldn't ask and Eden had a better poker face, but I should have known better. "Let me get it."

"And bring the wedding photos too!" my aunt demands.

Giving a calming glance to Eden, I get up and go over to the neat pile of mail and papers on the kitchen counter. There, I grab my tablet. Auntie is forgetful. She won't remember if I distract her long enough.

My aunt's eyes light up when she sees our marriage photos, and I can see a tear or two slide down her cheek. "Oh, will you look at that?" She gives me a radiant smile. "My little Cartie is finally married. Gosh, you're even smiling in this one." She looks at me. "Why didn't you print them out and assemble a wedding album? This one, where you stepped on her dress, is hilarious!"

I was glad I hadn't sorted it out. It's the one photo that feels the most genuine, real. For our situation it's more than ideal—it makes the whole wedding believable. "Well, I figured if we put them in an album, especially that one, I'd have a constant reminder of my legendary move."

"Exactly. It is the perfect antidote to a bad day! Right, Eden?"

"I'm glad my wedding day included some comedy," Eden says happily. "I'll forever cherish it."

After my aunt looks through all of the photos, she hands my tablet back. "Carter, now the marriage certificate."

"I'm hungry!" Eden blurts, suddenly drawing our attention, hand on her belly. "Babe, when do you think we can put that food order in?"

"Oh, how silly of me," Aunt Eleanor says. "Carter, feed your wife. Of course! I am sure she is famished. After all, a woman in her condition needs sustenance."

I furrow my brow in confusion, putting the tablet down. "What condition?"

"You know..." Aunt Eleanor leans in for a loud whisper, saying, "In a *family* way."

She beams at us. Then she gives us a playful wink, as if sharing a secret joke.

I give Eden a look. She seems as baffled as I am. "What are you talking about?"

"That's why you two married after such a short time, isn't it?" she asks. "Because of the baby?"

Eden's cheeks turn bright red, and she bursts into laughter. I put my face in my hand. I thought I'd given her a convincing enough story and a decent timeline, but she has a wild imagination.

"Auntie, I think you have the wrong idea."

"What do you mean?"

"I'm not pregnant," Eden speaks up. "That's not why we got married."

Aunt Eleanor huffs. "Oh, don't you try to pull the wool over my eyes. I told you I am as sharp as a tack. It is the twenty-first century, and I am well aware life is different than it was in my day. I am not here to judge."

"Seriously, Auntie," I insist. "Eden isn't pregnant. We didn't get married because of a baby."

"Well, why not?" Eleanor asks. She looks over at Eden. "What are you two waiting for? When we talked earlier, I thought you said you wanted children?"

Goddammit, Eden. I give Eden a look that says: I was clear about what topics to stay away from when talking to my aunt. Children and babies were two of them.

Eden gives me a look that says: Sorry, not sorry.

She turns to my aunt. "You asked what I thought of children, and I said I liked them," Eden clarifies. "...A lot. But I never said we were going to have any."

"I know what you said, *ma chère*. I read between the lines."

"There were no lines, I can assure you."

I love my aunt, but God, can she be a pot-stirrer. She understood Eden perfectly. Her fake confusion is her way of trying to prod us into changing our minds about having kids. Which would not happen even if this was a real marriage.

"Auntie, don't," I say in a firm voice. "You know how I feel about kids, and I know Eden didn't tell you she wanted any."

My aunt huffs again and gets to her feet, surprisingly energetic. "I never understood why you're so adamant about having no children. Kids are wonderful."

"*You* didn't have kids," I point out.

"We're not talking about *me*. We're talking about *you*."

She beelines into the kitchen, and I watch her go on her tiptoes and grab the bottle of wine she'd mentioned earlier. I glance over at Eden who looks like she's trying not to smile. Her hand covers her mouth, highly amused by the whole situation.

At least one of us is.

I get up, storm into the kitchen after her, and take the bottle of wine away from my aunt as she scours the drawers for a bottle opener. "No wine," I say in a firm tone. "We already talked about this."

"Carter, I am a grown woman, and if I want a glass of wine, I damn well will have one. Open the bottle. *Now*."

"Why don't we order dinner?" Eden asks, trying to change the subject. "I hear you like to have something from Bruno's every time you come to New York. I've never had their food, is it good?"

"Is it good?" Aunt Eleanor repeats. "Oh, dearie, Bruno makes the most *amazing* dishes. The best in the state."

She goes back to the table, and I give Eden a thankful look, taking pleasure in the cooperative dynamic we have as a team. She offers a warm smile in return before giving my aunt her full attention as the woman raves about Bruno's cooking.

The rest of the day is, well, *manageable*.

Once Aunt Eleanor gets off her children train of thought, it's fairly smooth sailing. The food comes quick and is as delicious as ever. Aunt Eleanor is insistent about the wine, and I pour her half of what she requests. She isn't thrilled about it but doesn't complain. Instead, she asks about the wedding itself, and Eden takes the reins, giving an embellished account of our quick Vegas wedding.

Aunt Eleanor loves every minute of it. "Oh, that sounds beautiful," she gushes as I clear the plates from the table. "I'm sure it would have been more beautiful in person. Not that I'm bitter that you didn't invite me."

"No, of course you're not," I tease. "This is only the third time you've mentioned it in the last five minutes."

I carry the plates into the kitchen and put them in the sink. While I prepare to slice into my aunt's favorite authentic New York cheesecake from the same local bakery I got the Not-So-Rummy Rum Balls from, I notice Eden quietly swipe my aunt's empty wineglass, along with the dishes I wasn't able to carry. I'm glad because I saw my aunt eye the bottle, and I know she would have poured herself more when we weren't looking.

"Well, you know I always wanted to be at your wedding," Aunt Eleanor says from the other room while we get the dessert ready. "I am glad you are married, but I would have loved to have been there."

Eden carries fresh plates to the table while I bring the cheesecake.

"Don't be mad at Carter, Auntie," Eden tells her. "That one was on me. I wanted to do something small and intimate with just the two of us. For personal reasons."

I'm surprised Eden has taken the blame for that. But I can see my aunt's demeanor immediately change. Her expression softens and she reaches over to take Eden's hand.

"I'm sorry, dear," she says, with genuine concern in her voice. "My heart aches for you. It must have been such a difficult decision not to invite friends and family to your special day. Did something painful from your past influence this decision?"

Eden sits back down with a nod. "I won't delve into the specifics, but yes, something happened the last time I was preparing to walk down the aisle that caused me to lose not only my heart, but also my finances, and many of my close friends. It felt like a knife had been plunged into my chest. The pain was so intense, I couldn't even cry." She gives a brave smile. There's courage in her expression, but also hurt, deep hurt. Her heart, she guards it with care, and it isn't just her smile or braveness that holds one captive. She's a force to be reckoned with—smart, unpredictable, stimulating, and full of nuance.

But the cloud surrounding her worries me. While she had mentioned to me that she'd been left at the altar by some douche, she hadn't *explicitly* stated that the event had caused her financial hardship. I can only surmise he was the culprit behind her financial downfall and the loss of her social circle. Nonetheless, I don't want to make decisions based on mere assumptions. An insatiable curiosity to delve deep into her world rises within me, starting with the fucked-up act carried out by some worthless fucking scumbag.

Aunt Eleanor reaches over and pulls Eden into a tight hug. "Oh, dearie," she says, rubbing her back. "I do not understand how some men can be so awful. Let me tell you, some of them are about as useful as a chocolate teapot! But don't you worry, now that you've got Carter, you will never have to deal with that kind of rubbish again! Right, Carter?"

"Right."

"And the cherry on top? You've got me in the mix now. We are your family now. Now and forever. Right, Carter?"

"Right. Cheesecake, anyone?" I ask, gesturing to the plate I've placed in the center of the table.

"Cheesecake is my favorite," Eden points out as Auntie is clapping. "I can't wait to try New York-style cheesecake."

"Oh, it's the only way to have cheesecake," my aunt insists. "So many people change the flavor or put fruits and things on top. Utter nonsense if you ask me, and a waste of ingredients. Plain is the best."

I serve Eden her slice first, as per my aunt's gestured request. "You're in for a real treat." I turn to my aunt. "Auntie, how big a slice?"

"Lay it on me! There's always room for cheesecake."

The conversation becomes much lighter. I can tell that Aunt Eleanor adores Eden. The way she starts fussing over her and trying to make her laugh makes me smile. Deep down, I feel bad because of the deception. She has already accepted Eden into the family. The two are getting along like two peas in a pod—even more of a reason to make sure Eleanor doesn't find out the wedding was a sham.

It's late by the time we finish eating and talking. Aunt Eleanor looks exhausted, and her eyes start to droop as Eden clears away the dessert.

"Come on, Auntie," I say, getting to my feet. "You've had a long day, and you need to get some sleep. Tomorrow is going to be equally as long."

She doesn't argue. Instead, she nods and extends her hand toward me. "Sleep sounds lovely. Help me up."

I help her out of her seat, and she shuffles over to give Eden a tight hug. "I enjoyed getting to know you today. Cannot wait to spend more time with you tomorrow."

"Likewise, Auntie."

She gives Eden a kiss on each cheek, and in her fatigue, she skips her customary three-kiss routine and obligatory French linguistic flair, before reaching for me. I slide my arm around her waist and hold her hand as I lead her down the hall to the guest suite. She has unpacked a couple of her bags already, and the bed is neatly made, even though she had laid down in it earlier.

"You know, I don't notice my age until the end of the day," she says. "There's a certain point where these old bones and joints hurt."

"I'm sure you'll feel better in the morning. We'll take it easy tomorrow."

She smiles at me. "I am so happy for you." She reaches up to squeeze my cheeks. "Eden is a wonderful woman. You make sure you take good care of her, you hear me? You love her back with all your might and never make her sad."

"I promise, I will try my best."

"Good, you do that."

I place a kiss on her forehead. "Eden is a tough woman. She can handle herself. Just like someone else I know."

"A tough woman still needs a shoulder from time to time. Good night, Cartie."

I wish her goodnight, and she quietly closes her door.

20

CARTER

Eden is sitting at the kitchen table with a steaming mug when I find her, not noticing me at first. It's like she's focused on something far away. The usual bright smile she always wears is nowhere to be found.

When I step closer, she looks up at me and the smile returns. "She certainly is something."

"She's a pistol. Always has been." I take the seat next to Eden. Softly, I brush a strand of brown hair from her face. "You didn't have to get so personal, you know. I never expected you to share private stuff about your past." I can tell that it pains her to be reminded and I want to kick myself.

"I know, but I wanted to. Your aunt seems to value the truth, and I wanted to give her a legit reason why we didn't invite anyone to the wedding."

"If you really got married, would you not invite anybody? Not even your sister?"

She fiddles with the coffee mug for a minute before taking a sip. "Right now? I don't know. Maybe I would. Maybe I wouldn't. My sister didn't like him—and that's an understatement. She even warned me. I should've listened."

"I'm sorry about what happened. Care to discuss it further?" I offer, bringing her into a hug, and for a moment, she rests her head against my chest. Her hands cling to my shoulders before quickly pulling back.

"Don't worry about it." She adjusts herself, grabs her mug and takes another sip. And just like that, she hides her sadness under a thick layer of composure. "I have to say, I didn't know what to expect when you said your aunt was visiting."

I lean back. "What do you mean?"

"I mean, I've only seen you at work or in the throes of passion. I didn't know how you were going to act around your aunt. You surprised me. You're actually really sweet with her. I can tell you love her and really care about her."

"She's my family. How did you think I was going to treat her?"

Eden shrugs with a small laugh. "Bossing her around and telling her to shape up."

"Hey, who do you think I learned it from?" I wink at her.

Eden laughs. I chuckle at her response. I love my aunt. True, it probably is a side I hardly ever show to anyone. Getting onto the battlefield and among the lions as a young buck, I had to build a reputation over the years in order to be taken seriously. I have to maintain it at all costs, especially with guys like Huxley breathing down my neck.

Eden and my relationship, for lack of a better word, is already so god damn different. My rules have been thrown out the window or stretched. So have hers. We're treading unfamiliar territory and, for once, I don't mind playing things by ear.

"I'm exhausted," she yawns, "and I have a feeling your aunt is going to be up early because of the jet lag. We should probably get some rest."

"We should."

She finishes her coffee and gets to her feet.

We quickly clean up the kitchen and head to bed. Eden and I take turns brushing our teeth and preparing for bed. When I get out of the bathroom, she's combing her hair, already in her nightgown. I watch her walk over to her side of the bed. Wait. No, not *her* side. Just the side she's picked to sleep on. We're only going to share the bed for one night. Then my aunt will be gone, and Eden can take over the guest suite again.

I watch her climb into bed.

We have one night.

Without a moment's hesitation, I pull my T-shirt up over my head and let it fall to the floor. She watches me as I do, and I enjoy her eyes roaming my naked chest. I press the button on my phone to dim my bedroom lights. After removing my socks, I climb into bed, still wearing my jeans. Eden gasps as I crawl over her, cradling her, one arm supporting my weight. With my free hand, I push her hair away from her throat and lean down to kiss it.

Eden moans softly. "What are you doing?" she whispers.

"What's it look like I'm doing?" I grumble against the soft skin of her neck. "I'm going to fuck you so hard."

It was she who had told me last night—before Vance rang the bell—to do what I'm about to do.

I slide my hand inside her nightgown, seeking warm curves. My fingers are rewarded with beautiful soft nipples that immediately start to harden under my touch. Without a second thought, I pull her gown up over her breasts and lean down to brush my lips over them.

That's when her fingers wrap around my wrist, stopping me.

"Carter...why are you doing this?" She sounds breathless.

"Because I want to." I suck in her puckered nipple.

"Wait..." Eden shakes her head, whispering, "We're not having sex with your aunt right here, right next door."

"She won't hear anything." I straighten and look into her eyes. "The soundproofing in this place is great, and she sleeps like a log. Trust me, she won't be up until the morning."

"Are you sure?"

"I'm sure."

Seeing as she lets go of my wrist, I continue my exploration, running my hand over both her breasts and back down over the sweet curve of her belly. Her breathing quickens as I kiss her jawline, her cheek, and the corner of her mouth. My hand slides deeper, leaving delicious goose bumps along the way as I spread her legs wider with my knees. Just before my fingers reach tender flesh, she stiffens.

"Carter, stop." She breathes out and whispers, as if my aunt is right here with us, listening, and not in the next room, deeply asleep. "I'm firm on this one. We can't. There's no way we're doing *that* while she's staying with us. Sorry, but you're going to have to wait."

"You're messing with me, right?" I whisper back.

"I'm dead serious."

Well, shit. I was hoping to wrap up the day on a high note—she filthy wet, me filthy hard, on track to creating some seriously dirty memories. I'm not entirely convinced that she isn't messing with me in some way. But her expression is serious, and she doesn't look like she's joking. Fuck. Oh, well.

"Fine, whatever you say."

I'm never one to be pushy. If she doesn't want to continue what we started yesterday, that's fine by me. I'll just have to wait.

Eden turns her back on me. I get up to get myself ready for bed, and after I put comfy gray boxers on over my still-hefty erection, I press the button on my phone to turn my bedroom lights completely off. She shifts a few times and is still, her breathing eventually evening out.

Wish I could say I fall asleep fast.

My dick doesn't seem to want to go down, and no matter how many times I try to think of something to make the stiffness go away, it won't budge. When did I turn back into a horny teenager who can't think of anything but fucking all day long? I turn my back on Eden and purposefully shut my eyes, willing sleep to come and my cock to go down. It doesn't.

Fuck this.

Without a second thought, I reach down and palm myself through the fabric of my boxers. My breath comes out as a hiss. "Ssss." I'm so worked up that it's almost painful. I shove my hand underneath the band and take hold of myself. With nothing but my knowing that Eden just now had felt perfectly slick, creamy, and hot, I start to jerk off. My only thought is to get off quickly so I can get some sleep.

The sheets rustle, and the next thing I know, a warm mouth has latched itself onto the nape of my neck. Soft tits push into my shoulder blades. Eden's hot body is pressed against my back.

"Didn't realize you were so impatient," she whispers softly in my ear.

I stop, only to feel her grab me where I want her hand the most. She gasps when she feels my enormous size. Her smooth palm and slender fingers have my cock weeping for more. Feeling her touch around me, I can't remember the last time I literally ached for a woman. Except yesterday, that is. Or in the motel. I push my boxers down just enough to release my steel-hard cock, biting back a groan at the lack of restriction.

Wrapping my hand around her smaller one, I start to guide it along my shaft, up and down, up and down, showing her the exact pressure and speed I enjoy most. "Just like that, baby."

"Psssst. Got it, Carter," she whispers, indicating to let go of her hand.

After two more strokes, I release my hand from hers. Eden works me with a firm, knowing grip. I relax into it, enjoying her strokes and those curves that keep pressing and pushing into my back with the movement of her arm, perfect nipples piercing my shoulder blades.

It feels fucking good. Her hand is all over me. My tip, my shaft, my balls. All I can do is lie there, bucking into her hand and getting closer with every passing second.

"Keep doing that. Yeah," I rumble quietly.

Next thing I know, she pulls my hips toward her. When I begin turning onto my back, she follows my movement and her mouth latches onto my cock. Whoa. Is this fucking paradise? Eagerly, she starts sucking me in.

This has to be paradise.

"You look so pretty with that mouth on my cock," I growl, unable to stop myself, praising her quietly.

She does. Absolutely gorgeous. Breathtaking.

My cock is made for her mouth, because the moment her warm, soft lips capture my length, I lose it.

"*Ahh-ahhh...fuck.*" I come hard, with a strangled groan, shooting hot liquid into her sweet mouth.

Immediately my body relaxes, and an intense feeling of satisfaction washes over me.

"Better?" Eden murmurs, licking her lips.

I can tell she's smirking as I caress her chin and cheeks, but I have no response, no witty comeback, because I'm too wrapped up in my haze.

"Sleep well, babe," she whispers.

She rolls away and settles back into her spot on the bed, while I lie there trying to catch my breath.

What the fuck just happened?

I glance over. She lies there, motionless. In one fluid motion, I pull her back close against my body.

No protests.

Am I fucking dreaming?

21

CARTER

5:14 A.M.

I roll over to find she's not there. The sheets are cold, and when I sit up and listen, I can hear her humming to herself in the kitchen. I take a second to collect myself and get up. After my bathroom routine, I splash my face with cold water. Why the fuck am I allowing myself to get worked up about this?

No, I know what the problem is.

The power dynamic. She's my assistant, and I'm the boss. I set the ground rules and she follows them. I have always been that way at work and in the bedroom.

Friday night after our kiss, something had changed. Last night, things had gotten worse.

She's gotten under my skin.

I need to work out, to channel my energy into something else. After throwing on a pair of black workout shorts and black sneakers, I head to the gym like I do every morning. I avoid even looking in the direction of the kitchen, not wanting to get distracted by Eden.

The familiar burn of my muscles is a welcome feeling. I run on the treadmill, watching the news.

I haven't been going for more than five minutes when I hear the guest suite door open, and my aunt pokes her head in. "Oh, Carter, good morning, I figured that was you," she greets. "Stop that running nonsense. I think your beautiful wife is cooking us a big breakfast... Mmm. I can smell pancakes."

"I'll be there in seventeen minutes, Auntie."

"All right, *mon chéri*."

I work out until I can't run anymore. By the time I step off the treadmill, I feel a lot better. I jump in the shower and throw on a fresh pair of blue jeans and a white T-shirt before joining Eden and Aunt Eleanor in the kitchen.

She was right: Eden has made a large breakfast.

There are veggie omelets, toast, and vegan pancakes. It surprises me, considering she's never given any indication that she's interested in cooking. There's even a colorful fruit salad, and, lo and behold, chocolate cupcakes. It's a nice gesture from her to make my aunt feel welcome.

"Good morning," Eden sings, far too cheerful for the early hour, wearing her summer dress, and pouring orange juice into three glasses.

"Good morning," I rumble.

I walk over to her, put my fingers under her chin, turn her face to me, and place a soft kiss on her lips, followed by another one.

"Good morning," she repeats breathlessly, spilling half the juice. I like that my kiss affects her that much. Her eyes are laughing, so are mine, but she quickly catches herself and wipes away the mess, addressing my aunt. "What do you want to do today, Auntie?"

My aunt's plane is leaving in the early evening, and I'm glad there are many hours to fill with memories. "Yes, Auntie, anything special you'd like to do?"

"Oh, you don't have to go making such a fuss. As long as I spend the day with the both of you, I'll be happy."

"Auntie, I must say, you are positively glowing today," Eden says. "Did you sleep well last night? You seem to be full of vitality and vigor."

Just as Eden asks that, my aunt goes into a coughing fit, and Eden hurries to get her some water while I kneel by my aunt to check on her.

"Try to take a deep breath," I order.

"I'm all right, I'm fine." She drinks from the glass Eden pushes into her hands, and after a moment, the coughing stops. "There, see? All better."

I keep my eye on her as we eat breakfast. She seems fine, chatting away with Eden as the two of them lay out the plans for the day. Straying from her initial insistence of our activities not being important to her, my aunt is on a mission to take Eden and Hattie around to see not one or two but every single one of her favorite sights NYC has to offer.

"I am bringing Hattie with us, folks," she announces. "Hattie's always telling me about her wild youth, and I need to see some of that excitement in action. You know what they say: the more, the merrier!"

She's in the middle of a lengthy talk about touring the Museum of Natural History when I interrupt.

"That's a marathon," I tell her. "Auntie, I really think we should consider doing something less strenuous. I know you want to spend time with us and show Eden and Hattie the places you like, but I don't think this is the best way to do it."

"Carter, I am not spending the entire day cooped up inside this apartment. Eden is family, and so is Hattie, and I want to spoil the three of you while I can." Her tone is firm. "This is not up for discussion."

"We'll take frequent breaks," Eden interjects, trying to ease the tension. "We'll rest, and make sure there's plenty of down time. But my husband is right, you don't have to take me to see everything, Auntie."

When she drops the H-bomb just like that, an odd feeling shakes through my chest. My aunt catches on to it and smiles at her. "We won't see everything, dearie. Just the places I know you'll love."

I can tell Eden is trying to find a compromise, but when Eleanor has her mind set on something, compromise isn't an option.

I'm outnumbered two to one.

WE SPEND the better part of the morning touring the city, Hattie Hutton in tow. We take a ferry ride to Red Hook, Brooklyn, first, then Aunt Eleanor drags us into a department store, trying to buy things for us: a cat-shaped shower head that sprays water out of the ears and nose for Hattie, and two books for Eden: *How to Train Your Husband* and *How to Survive Your Husband's Midlife Crisis: A Guide to Coping with a Balding, Harley-Riding, Leather-Wearing Man*. Last but not least, she finds—according to her—the perfect gift for me: a T-shirt that reads "I'm not bossy, I'm the boss" (which I actually like).

Hattie and Eden staunchly refuse to accept the gifts at first, but my aunt keeps insisting between three coughs, telling them she will feel much better if they would let her spoil them. Eden and Hattie give me pleading looks—Hattie because she's trying to declutter since she's moving and isn't ready for "that level of wackiness in her life," Eden because she doesn't want to jinx things by accepting gifts that offer the best advice on "how to navigate tricky marriage dynamics."

I know better than to interject. A shrug and a cheerful smile are the only things I offer.

"I'm sure this one will be a real page-turner," Eden says to Auntie when we stand by the register. They're still joking away about my midlife crisis that's apparently a breath away.

"You know what would really help me cope?" I ask. "A brand-new sports car."

The three women turn to me, slack jawed.

Eden beams at me. "Did Carter Bancroft just make a joke?"

"Yep, told you I'm a fun time."

T HE DAY WOULD HAVE ACTUALLY TURNED out nice if not for the phone call I receive around noon.

We've just sat down for lunch at The Good Fork, a cozy and charming neighborhood spot, when my phone goes off. It had happened a few times throughout the morning, and I'd ignored it. However, this time, I look at the screen and see Saul Huxley is the one calling.

Fuck.

Eden must see the expression on my face. "Why don't you answer it, babe? We'll tell the waitress we need a few minutes to decide."

I nod and get up from the table, answering the phone. "What is it, Huxley?"

"Bancroft, I'm sorry to disturb you on a Sunday," Huxley says, not sounding the least bit sorry. "But I just received an...interesting phone call you need to be made aware of."

"What happened?"

"The Grangers have decided not to renew their contract with us."

No.

My stomach drops, and my hand curls tighter around the phone. "Why the hell not?"

"A myriad of reasons. It looks like they're talking to Ecclestone. I'll forward the email to you. But suffice it to say, this doesn't look good for Legacy. As you know, the Grangers are a very influential family. First thing tomorrow morning I'll need you to gather your team and prepare for damage control. I'll likely be out all day, but I'll check back with you. No doubt others are going to hear about this, and it's not going to be pretty. But I'll leave you to the rest of your day. How's your aunt?"

What a dick move.

Huxley is such a fucking bastard. I can't even begin to list the reasons why I want to curse at him. He did all this on purpose, called me right in the middle of my day to tell me horrible news. He wants to ruin my time with my aunt, knowing I'll be distracted, wracking my brain, and powerless to do anything until Monday.

"We'll talk tomorrow." My voice is tinged with the barely contained rage I feel. Without waiting for a response, I hang up on him.

I go back to the table, where Aunt Eleanor, Hattie, and Eden regard me with triple looks of concern.

"Everything all right, Carter?" my aunt asks.

"Everything's fine. Nothing that can be done right at this moment." I force a smile, and my aunt relaxes. Eden knows something is up, but she also knows not to press and turns her full attention back to my aunt.

Lunch proceeds uneventfully. I wish I could say that I push Huxley's phone call to the back of my mind, but that would be a lie. I'm itching to get back to work so I can try to solve the Granger situation. I know if I'm able to talk to them, I can convince them to reconsider. When the ladies are refreshing in the bathroom, I fire off an email to Bradley.

Between that mess and the fact that my aunt is insistent on continuing our outing, despite her clearly being exhausted, I'm getting impatient. Still, I agree to a leisurely walk through Central Park and a stop at a coffee shop or bakery along the way for a coffee and some pastries.

"All right, what else is there to do?" Aunt Eleanor asks as we climb back into my car in the afternoon. Eden takes her seat next to my aunt in the back, which I'm happy about. "Oh! We could pop over to the Museum of Natural Hist—"

"We're going home, Auntie," I say, trying to sound breezy. Hattie, sitting next to me in the passenger seat, gives me a thankful glance. She, too, appears exhausted, and her expression says it all: *Museum, you say? Dreadfully dull! Let's beat a hasty retreat!*

"Carter, we still have time," my aunt argues.

"I don't care that we have time. We've been out all day, it's been exhausting, the weather is getting hotter, and you have a plane to catch this evening," I say, trying to keep the frustration out of my voice. "I think it's best if we just take the next couple of hours to relax."

"I'm sure stopping by the museum wouldn't be so bad," Eden counters. "It's not far from here. There's A/C. We wouldn't have to stay long."

"I said we're going home," I snap. "End of discussion."

My aunt huffs. "There's no need to get testy, dear. We heard you the first time."

Hattie smiles at me, grateful. It's the first time I've ever seen her smile warmly at me.

In contrast to that, in the rearview mirror, Eden is glaring daggers at me. Because I'd insisted we take the less-exhausting ferry ride first and now have no time for my auntie's beloved museum. If we had started with Auntie's beloved museum first, we'd all have been exhausted for the rest. Strategically, it had been the better choice. Not just strategically, mentally too. I can feel Eden's disappointment, and I know she's biting her tongue to stop herself from arguing with me in front of the ladies. She has to move on from it, simple as that. I've been on edge for hours and am tired of arguing. It's time for a break.

When we pull into the parking garage, I notice that my aunt's hands are shakier than usual. "Are you all right?" I ask and see Eden immediately grab her hand, concern written all over her face.

"Just fine. I think perhaps you were right, and I need some rest. Help me upstairs."

I help my aunt out of the car, and Eden goes ahead of us with Hattie, calling the elevator and holding the doors open as I usher Aunt Eleanor in. Once we all say goodbye to Hattie—rather shortly, in which the two elderly women only quietly wave at each other—and enter the apartment, my aunt goes to lie on the couch.

An hour later, Eden re-fluffs one of the throw pillows my aunt is lying on. "No worries," she tells Auntie. "You just stay here on the couch, and Carter and I will prep your things for your flight."

"I'm sorry, dearies, but I don't really think I'm in any state to travel," Aunt Eleanor says, slowly lowering herself back onto the couch.

"I'm taking you to the emergency room." I immediately reach for her. "Eden, grab one of her bags."

"No, no! No doctors!" Aunt Eleanor exclaims, outraged. "I don't need them to tell me what I already know. I'll be fine in a couple of days."

Out of the corner of my eye I see Eden looking at me, but I don't meet her gaze. "Auntie, I don't think it's a good idea for you not to get checked out," I insist. "We shouldn't take any chances. If you're too weak to fly—"

"Carter," Aunt Eleanor says in a firm voice, "I am *not* going to the hospital and that is final. All they are going to tell me is that I need to rest. I do not need to waste time hearing what I already know."

"I'm sure she'll be okay," Eden says, trying to be positive.

I'm not having any of it. "I don't like this, Auntie," I insist. "You're playing with your health."

"It is my life, Carter. I will do with it as I please. Eden, help me to the guest suite, *s'il te plaît*, I wish to take a nap."

Eden pushes past me to do as my aunt asked. As they walk away, I make for the kitchen. I need a drink. A strong one.

I pour myself a large glass of whiskey and drink half of it in one swig. It burns my throat all the way down. I shut my eyes and revel in the feeling, trying to figure out what the hell I'm going to do. It's not my aunt's fault that she's grappling with a medical issue. However, her behavior today didn't help the situation and has most likely made it worse. That, coupled with the loss of the Granger account, has me at the end of my rope. The beginnings of a headache have started to take route.

After another quick drink, I go to my room.

"She's resting." Eden joins me a few minutes later. "Care to tell me why you're acting like this?"

"Not now, Eden. I'm not in the mood."

"Well, it's not about *you*, Carter. She's tired. If she says she's not up to traveling, then so be it. We'll deal."

I spin around to face her, but speak quietly. "That's not the point, dammit. Look me in the eye and tell me you aren't frustrated with this whole thing. She spent the entire day dragging us around the city, refusing to rest and take it easy. And now, unsurprisingly, she's not feeling well. I'm fucking scared. Of *course* she's not going anywhere. I wouldn't let her on that damn plane even if the flight attendants were all damn doctors. And on top of all that, I get a call from Huxley that Granger Estates, the client I spent two years working for, suddenly doesn't want to renew our contract. How am I supposed to focus on work when I'm too busy trying to get my aunt to take her health seriously?"

"You'll figure it out. It's not the end of the world, Carter."

"For fuck's sake." I shake my head. "How can you always be so damn optimistic, woman?"

"What, you want me to be grumpy and pissy like you?" she asks, gesturing at me with a glare. "I wish you could hear yourself right now. You have an aunt who loves you and wants nothing but the best. You have a successful career and clearly tons of money. From where I'm standing, you have a hell of a lot to be thankful for, yet all you've done today after that phone call, is brood and think negatively. Get over yourself, Carter. Ugh!"

"Your volume, please, keep it down." I gesture to the room next door where my aunt is resting. "Save your vocal exercises for the shower, or is that asking too much?"

She shoots me an irritated glance. "You really have a knack for ruining the mood, you know that?"

"You have no idea what I'm going through."

"And whose fault is that? Do you want to know why I try to be so optimistic? Because if I really examined where my life is right now, I'd spiral hardcore. I was left at the damn altar and robbed blind by the man I loved and thought I was going to spend the rest of my life with. I was under the impression that he loved and cared for me deeply, but he shattered my heart by confessing that his feelings were never genuine. All of my friends turned their backs on me, believing his deceitful claim that it was me who robbed him, instead of the other way around. Now I'm left with just my sister, who had been warning me about him from the start. Talk about getting a bitter taste of her 'I told you so'!"

There it is. My instincts had been spot on. What a poor excuse for a man. Eden had mentioned it before and had always more or less played it off like it wasn't a big deal. I can sense the magnitude of her suffering. Clearly it had been bad enough for her to run away.

"The woman down there is old," she says, pointing next door. "She's frail and *still* made the journey across a flipping *ocean* to see you. All she wanted to do today was have fun, to spend the day active like everyone else. And you want me to feel sorry for you because she wouldn't listen to you? Yeah, that's not going to happen. She's an adult, she's allowed to make her own choices." Eden is visibly agitated in a manner that I've never witnessed before or deemed possible of her. "If you actually started paying attention and stopped trying to think you know best about everything, you would see what she's *really* trying to do."

Yes, I'm frustrated that my aunt is playing loose and hard with her health. But more importantly, I'm frustrated that she won't take my concerns seriously. After all, I only want what's best for her.

"Eden, please," I say, calmly. "You've known her for two days—I've known her my whole life."

"Sometimes it takes someone from the outside to see what you're blinded by. I know you love her. It's obvious she means a lot to you, but in your haste to take care of her, you're ignoring what she wants, which is not to be treated any differently than you treated her before. There's a reason why she's here. And by the way, I think your aunt has plenty of energy and health left in her, and she'll be around for many more years to come. That's what she told me yesterday, and I'm confident that's exactly what's going to happen."

Although I have my doubts, her words have a calming effect on me. Despite the circumstances, I, too, can sense that my aunt still has unfinished business and is far from ready to take her final bow. Still, I won't take any risks.

"Speaking of being blinded," I say, not letting Eden off the hook. This is about her as much as it's about my aunt. "Did you ever stop to think that in *your* haste to stay positive, you're ignoring what you're really feeling?"

"Who says I'm ignoring anything?"

"I do."

Her eyes flare. "I think I know my own thoughts and intentions better than you."

"Do you? Because in the little time I've known you, you've been back and forth on your feelings so much it gives me whiplash."

"What the hell is that supposed to mean?"

"Your 'no sex for six months' rule. How is that going by the way?"

"Ugh! Look in the mirror! How is your rule going about not having close relationships with employees?"

"Quiet. We're not alone, remember?"

Eden glares at me. "Oh, now you care about that? I'm done here."

"Wait. Don't run away. Please don't."

She turns abruptly, storms toward the door, and, in her haste, knocks a thick investor's magazine from a nearby shelf. As she tries to avoid it, she bumps her foot into something. The next thing I hear is her cry of pain.

"Ah. Oh, my God! Ah...*ahhh*," she moans in pain.

"*Fuck*." I'm by her side in less than a second, holding her. "Does it hurt, baby?"

"*Ahh-ha*. Yes."

"Oh, fuck."

I crouch down to take a look.

"*Ahh*, Carter, oh, my God," she whines and moans. "*Ahh*."

I haven't even touched her. "Eden, wait..."

"Carter! *Aaaahhh*."

What the fuck?

I've yet to make physical contact with her foot.

Close by, a door slams.

We freeze.

Her wide eyes meet mine.

I stand back up, and we're glaring in the direction of the door. We listen to my aunt's footsteps draw closer, and all I can think is, *I fucking hope she doesn't think what I think she's thinking.*

"Carter Donovan Bancroft?" she asks through the closed door.

I have to take a second to answer, trying to come up with what to say, how to approach this, form the right words. "Yeah?"

"I'm feeling well again. I'm going over to Hattie's. For a glass of...a cup of Earl Grey."

I can't bring myself to say no. After all, she's supposed to be resting, and a cup of Earl Grey sounds restful to me. "Okay."

"Oh, and...next time just ask me if you want some alone time. I know what it means to be newlyweds."

We hear her shuffling footsteps quickly fading away.

The front door closes.

"Wait, what?" Eden stares at me. "Please. Does she imagine we were doing *that*?"

"Yep."

"No, seriously. Does she think we had sex just now, and that I... *orgasmed*?"

"*Yep*."

"Stop her! We need to explain."

I laugh out. "I can't."

"You *have* to."

"I can't."

"Carter!"

"*Impossible*. How would I explain this? 'Auntie, we did not have sex. Eden dodged a falling magazine and, in the process, she bumped her toe, meaning, her cries were cries of pain, not of passion?' She'd never believe me. She'd think it was a poor excuse. It'd make things worse."

Eden palms her face, peeking through her fingers. "This is *so* embarrassing."

"I know."

"She thinks we're having angry sex."

"I *know*."

She drops her hands, and her outraged eyes meet mine. I half-expect them to pop out of her head.

That's when I erupt into laughter. I let myself fall against the wall, pulling her with me, unable to stop laughing.

She bursts out too, snort-wheeze-laughing, curling into my chest, holding her stomach. With my arms around her, we watch each other laugh, only to stop and start again. Her laughter does something to me. It's been a long time since I've laughed with somebody the way I'm laughing now. Seeing her laughing eyes, her laughing face, truly loving the moment snaps my resolve and has me reacting without thinking.

I grab the back of her head and pull her against my chest, my lips descending hungrily onto hers. The second my mouth touches hers, our laughter stumbles briefly—but doesn't come to a complete stop.

We kiss-laugh.

I mean, I kiss-laugh, she kiss-snort-laughs.

But eventually the kissing gradually replaces our laughing until all that's left is us kissing. Hungrily.

We kiss like two people possessed.

I'm losing sense of time.

My hands are all over her body. Over her tits. Over her ass.

Next thing I know, her hands seize the front of my shirt, twisting the fabric as she pulls away from me.

She straightens, thanks me for the "nice kiss," (What the fuck?) and slips out of the room.

It takes everything in me not to pull her back. I want to fuck her so bad I can't think straight. I'm glad she's out of my grasp. At this point, I can't guarantee my actions. I'm impatient, greedy. Hungry. A wild beast. Something in Eden brings out this side of me, and Jesus Christ, I would have fucked her into oblivion.

I let myself fall onto the bed, landing on my back, arms outstretched.

SOMEWHERE BETWEEN THE kiss and two hours after that, I doze off. In my half-asleep state, the dreamy events that follow our kiss are different—to a *slight* degree.

Marginal, really.

We kiss like two people possessed.

My hands are all over her ass and tits.

Next thing I know is her hands seizing the front of my shirt, twisting the fabric as she pulls me closer, urging me to take it off.

My shirt is gone in no time, and I press her against the wall.

Seeing her all fired up has me hard as a rock.

"You're mine," I growl. "Nothing will stop me from hearing you scream my name."

I tug at the waistband of her pants and slide my hand underneath the tight fabric. Her skin is hot. If she thinks I've forgotten her favor the night before, she's sorely mistaken. Ultimately, I'm all set to reciprocate the gesture. I slip my fingers into her panties, causing her to spasm against me. She's wet. Drenched.

Her hands are harsh and impatient when she tugs at my belt. She's going straight for the jackpot, that's how wild she is for me. Once the buckle is undone quicker than I can blink ("good job there, *wifey*"), she goes straight to rubbing my cock over my jeans.

Without warning, I brush my fingers against her clit while simultaneously biting down on her bottom lip. Her gasp is breathless and beautiful.

My lips trail down her chin to that silky smooth neck of hers. I nibble, bite, and suck on the sensitive flesh while my fingers coax an orgasm out of her. Already her thighs tremble, and her kisses are feverish. She won't last long.

"Carter…" she breathes out in a harsh whisper.

I know what that means.

With one hand still between her legs, I use the other to push her panties down the swell of those tantalizing hips. I've never seen anybody step out of their clothes and kick them away as eagerly as Eden does. Urgency unlike anything I've ever felt with anyone else takes hold of me.

We move in tandem, my erection rubbing against her belly. I grab the back of her thighs, and she hops up, wrapping her legs around my waist as I walk us to my bed where I lay us down.

"Baby, spread those legs even wider. Tell me, 'Fuck me, babe.'"

She does. When she whispers the words, my heart almost stutters.

With one quick, hard thrust, I push my cock into her heat.

Thank fuck.

This time, both of us have to struggle to keep our voices down. For the record: in my dream the whole building is completely soundproof, effectively contravening Eden's suggestion of Mrs. Hutton and my aunt listening with turned teacups held against the wall.

Heaven. Fucking heaven.

Eden's mouth claims mine in a breathless kiss.

I fuck her against the mattress.

In my mind, fucking her is a desperate need. An insatiable hunger.

But it's more. It's an irresistible force that renders me powerless. Every fiber of my being longs for her and craves the sensation of touching her.

She rocks up and against my dick like she's made for it, made for me—and me alone. She molds against me perfectly. We fall into a steady rhythm as I cradle her against me, my tongue in her mouth, my cock inside her, and I fuck her slowly, savoring every precious second, relishing the sweet ecstasy of that moment.

I hold her tighter, breathing hard. "Oh fuck. *Oh fuck.*"

Neither one of us is going to last long. It becomes a competition to see who'll give in first. Clearly, I'll win. It's not as though she has any doubts about it. But she sure as hell is trying to fight for the place. Every time she squeezes or clenches around me, shockwaves of pleasure ripple through my system—they make me move faster, fuck her harder. Fuck her more thoroughly. Fuck her like she deserves. Making it impossible for her to greet the next day without still feeling me, feeling our connection.

My hands grip her ass, giving me the leverage to ground myself deeper into her addictive heat. She twitches and rocks along with me, her kisses growing desperate, her breaths becoming ragged, her hands digging in tighter.

She comes first.

She comes hard.

Harder than she's ever come in her life.

It's the most beautiful sight of my life. Also, the hottest.

Throwing her head back against the mattress, a beautiful moan escapes through her clenched teeth, with my name on her lips. Her sweet pussy squeezes and pumps me, making me groan.

I can't stop coming.

I come, and come, and come, holding her firmly in my embrace.

I keep going until there's nothing left, until all I can do is press my weight against her, my forehead against hers, only my arms supporting me.

When I open my eyes to hers, our breathing still heavy, she looks at me like I'm all she's ever needed.

As I attempt to pull out, her pussy squeezes me like a vise, preventing me from sliding out, so I remain inside her. Her eyes smile at me. Mine smile back.

Next thing I know, I fucking wake up—lying in bed, alone, begging, pleading for this not to be just a dream.

22

EDEN

It goes without saying, the rest of Sunday is more than *a little* awkward.

I'm mortified that Carter's aunt heard "my orgasm," and even though I try pretty damn hard to think of a way to bring up the topic and clarify things, Carter is right: There's no way I can look the older lady in the eyes and start talking about sex with her nephew. Heck, I can *barely* look her in the eyes when she returns from Hattie's a few hours later, a "knowing" smirk on her face.

We don't know when she'll feel well enough to travel back to France. It means we'll have to keep up the marriage charade a bit longer, however, I have confidence we'll be able to handle it.

Of course, I tell Carter no sexy times (and definitely no kissing, either), until she's gone. The last thing I want is for her to hear me in the throes of passion again. It was the reason I had made it a rule in the first place.

The kiss had been mind-boggling, yes, but our fight is still ringing in my head, especially when he called me out for going against my own rules. What the hell is going on with me?

Kissing doesn't count as sex.

Getting somebody off doesn't count as sex.

Neither does just-the-tip...sex. Okay, maybe it does count, a tiny bit.

I try not to dwell on it too much. Everything is so upside down that it's best to go with the flow. It's not a crime to have a little fun, and every time he even looks at me with his stunning eyes, my knees buckle.

MERCIFULLY, Monday morning comes fast enough, and Aunt Eleanor is going to spend the day with Hattie, who promises to take good care of her and inform us immediately if Auntie gets worse. Carter and I head to work, separately of course. For the first time in months, I'm excited to go to work on a Monday, and not just to flee the mayhem of my personal life. I enjoy working at Legacy Builders, and having my own workspace is a godsend. It's one of the few times I can be by myself to concentrate on work I'm passionate about.

Carter comes in and out throughout the day. Though, for the most part, he stays in his office or in meetings. I'm happy to quietly listen to music while working on all the tasks he's assigned me. When lunch rolls around, I meet up with the girls, and we have a wonderful time. This time, even honey-blonde Gwen from the front desk, with her ever-present friendly charm, joins us. It isn't until late afternoon that Carter walks by my desk after returning from his lunch meeting.

I can instantly tell he isn't in a good mood. "How are you holding up?"

"Good." His voice holds his usual sharp bossy tone he uses when waving his authority over his employees. I don't take it personally and shrug it off, having become used to it by now. I hand him high-priority papers he asked me to get ready ASAP. "If it's all right with you, I'm going to start wrapping things up soon. Unless you need anything else from me?"

"No, that's okay." He shuffles through the papers and then pauses. With a heavy sigh, he meets my gaze. "Sorry, Eden, I didn't mean to snap at you."

My eyebrows shoot up so fast I think they're going to fly off my face. Did he really just apologize? "I'm sorry, what was that, Mr. Bancroft? Do you want to say that again?"

"Ha-ha, very funny." A smile tugs at his lips.

I can count on one hand the number of times he's smiled in the office. Actually, I'm fairly certain this is the first time.

"It's been a long day," he says. "Have we received any response or call back from the Grangers yet?"

"No, I'm afraid not. Do you want me to try again?"

"No, I will try to get in touch with them myself at a later point." He rearranges the papers and looks at me. "I just had a call from Aunt Eleanor."

"Is she okay? Do you need me to rush home?"

"No, no, she's fine. She says she wants to talk to us when we get back."

Uh-oh. No wonder he's tense. "Did she say what it was about?"

"No. She only assured me that she felt fine, and then scolded me for sending a doctor over to check on her."

"You did *what*?"

"Eden, I'm concerned. She needs to be examined."

"I'm surprised she didn't come here to tear your head off in person." I laugh with a shake of my head. "She's a pretty headstrong woman *and* has been clear she doesn't want to talk to a doctor."

"That doesn't mean she still shouldn't. Besides, Dr. Mayweather is a family friend. He's retired. Technically, he stopped by 'accidentally' to 'surprise-visit me' since he was 'just in the area.' I figured it would be low-key enough that she wouldn't get upset."

"And how did that work out for you?"

"She kicked him out." A long, drawn-out sigh escapes Carter's lips. "Anyway, I wanted to give you a heads-up that she's probably going to be in a mood when you get home."

"Thanks." I break into a smile. "Should I get my bulletproof vest ready?"

"No, but ensure mine's within reach."

A Bossy Roommate

Suddenly, the glass door to our office lobby opens, and Mr. Huxley stands there. His appearance is so abrupt and sudden that it takes both of us by surprise. For one thing, Mr. Huxley is supposed to be off site all day, holding meetings with some bigwig clients in an attempt to replace the hole left by Granger Estates. My stomach drops, anxiety taking root. That door is not soundproof. It's possible he caught some of our conversation on his way in—how Carter and I both referred to my place as our "home." The chance is slim, but not impossible. Carter, too, observes him with a raised brow.

However, as I think it over, it seems increasingly unlikely. We would surely have noticed a motion out front—it's a *glass* door for crying out loud. As far as his presence goes, maybe there had been an unexpected change of plans in his schedule. It happens all the time.

I straighten my shoulders.

"Hello, Mr. Huxley," I say cheerfully, not letting any of my concern show. "Is there something I can help you with? I don't have you on the appointment list…"

"No need, Eden." His attention is fully on Carter. "We need to talk."

"In my office." Carter motions to his open door.

Huxley struts past him. Behind his back, Carter and I exchange looks.

"You're good to go home, Eden." Carter's voice is back to his formal work tone. "I'll see you tomorrow."

"Okay, Mr. Bancroft. Have a good evening."

I have a feeling whatever conversation is going to happen is one I want no part of. As quickly as I can, I finish the task I'm working on and gather my things. I'm sure I'll hear about the impromptu meeting when Carter gets home. I startle Gwen with a greeting as I walk by—as always, she's completely absorbed in her work—but she quickly recovers and waves back warmly.

I DON'T BOTHER to use the train or an Uber, needing the long walk to help clear my mind. I'm not as worried about Auntie as Carter is, only because to me she doesn't feel or look sick, and she's expressed to us plenty of times that she doesn't want us to treat her like a helpless invalid. And her coughing fits? It's almost as if they make their appearances precisely when it's most convenient for her.

Still, I take Carter's concerns very seriously. What if he's right and her health has deteriorated to the point it's clouding her judgment? And what if she decides to stay longer? What will the next few days look like? I hate the thought of her being alone in the apartment should something happen. Then I remember Hattie, and that helps ease some of the worries. Hattie will keep a watchful eye on her. After all, she watches that hallway like an eagle guarding its nest.

On a complete self-centered train of thought, it's obvious that the sizzling spark between Carter and me isn't going to stop any time soon. The tension between us is...hot. It's undeniable. Strong. Powerful. And it's getting hotter. That's what makes the whole situation so very difficult and...so very, *very* enticing. The push and pull between us makes me want to forget my vow and rules. It makes me want to ignore the fact that Carter has the potential to shatter my heart even more profoundly than Rob ever did. Worst of all, I know that the idea of our marriage charade and how two days are quickly turning into a whole week should make me concerned, but it doesn't. Deep down, it makes me excited.

I sigh heavily and try to push the swirl of thoughts to the back of my mind. It's going to be okay. It'll be fine.

My stomach grumbles as I pass a few food vendors on the street. I can't wait until my paycheck. One of the first things I'm going to do is try one of these delicious-smelling delicacies such as the hot, freshly baked pretzels. Next on my list are the decadent, mouth-watering cinnamon rolls, with a side of roasted nuts. The artisanal ice cream with seasonal fruit looks yummy and refreshing too. And what in the name of all that is holy are *gourmet* plant-based hotdogs? *Heaven have mercy.* As I venture farther, the peaceful serenity of Central Park envelops me. I love this city. Walking the NYC streets brings me a comfort I hadn't expected. The city has already started to feel like home to me, and if I think about it hard enough, I can see myself possibly staying longer than six months—

and as far as Carter is concerned, that would undoubtedly be the worst idea ever.

When I get back to the apartment, Hattie's apartment door opens. "Oh, Eden, good evening!" she calls with the brightest smile. "Did you have a good day at work?"

"Hi, Hattie. Yeah, it was nice, thank you for asking."

"Eleanor and I had the most lovely day, and now she has returned to your reside—" As if she has a sixth sense, Hattie suddenly frowns and steps out of her apartment toward me. "Something troubling you, my dear?"

"Nothing."

"Come now, Eden. I've lived long enough to discern when a lady is holding a concern within her heart."

"Can't get anything past you, can I?" I try to smile. "It's nothing major, I assure you. I've had a lot going on, and it's been a little difficult juggling all of it."

Hattie gives me a sympathetic look. "You do have a lot on your plate, my dear. The recent move, the new job, the shared dwelling with your boss who's now your," she makes quote fingers, "*husband*, no less…" She motions to Carter's apartment, "…and to top it off, a guest who has chosen to extend her visit."

Her voice is low, thankfully, so I'm not worried about Auntie somehow hearing through the wall. Unlike the apartment itself, the hallway is a bit more soundproof.

"How is she doing, by the way?" I ask. "What did you do together?"

"Oh, we had a marvelous time with the cats. The energy that woman possesses is really remarkable! Rest assured, she is in excellent spirits. But enough about us—let's discuss you, dear. You know, if ever you feel the need to unburden your heart, I'm always here to lend a friendly ear."

"Thanks, Hattie. I really appreciate—" I suddenly sneeze and, sure enough, when I look past Hattie, three furry cats have wandered out of her apartment to see what's going on.

Hattie shoos them back in, but one of them, Myrtle, won't listen. As she fights to get the cat back into the apartment, the elevator pings, and Carter steps out.

"Hey, you're home earlier than I thought you'd be," I tell him, hastily trying to wipe my watery eyes on the back of my hand.

"Are you just getting in?" He glances at his watch. "You should have been home like thirty minutes ago." In one smooth motion, he extends a handkerchief to me.

"I walked. Needed the fresh air to clear my head," I explain. I motion to Hattie, but when I look, she has disappeared back into her apartment, shooing the cats in. "Everything go okay with Huxley?"

Carter makes a noncommittal noise, and I watch him reach to unlock our door. But before he slides in the key, he turns, and in a low voice he says, "Wait. Before we go in, we need to talk about what to do about my aunt."

"What do you mean?"

"If she's going to stay with us, I'm going to have to insist that she at least talk to Dr. Mayweather and then have him give us detailed instructions on how to navigate, let's say, *extremely difficult* patients, and mostly, how we can help her should something serious happen."

"Do you think she'd go for that?"

"Oh, she most definitely won't," Hattie chimes in from behind us. She had returned when we weren't looking. "Good evening, Carter."

"Hi, Hattie. Excuse us. We'll take our conversation inside."

She waves a hand at him. "Oh, no need. I already know all about this whole situation, remember?"

"Right," Carter says.

"Why don't you both just have a chat with Eleanor? She's very understanding, you know. I'm sure you can come up with some sort of compromise. You could tell her, 'If you follow my advice, I'll get you a rum cake. If not, I'll enjoy it all myself!' Unless you have a better suggestion?"

"Good night, Hattie." Carter unlocks the apartment and ushers me inside.

Hattie puts her wrinkly hands up in surrender. "Very well, my dear, I understand. I shall refrain from meddling."

I don't even get a chance to thank her for her concern before Carter closes the door behind us. "Well, that was rude," I tell him.

"You don't know Hattie like I do. There would have been another thirty minutes in the hall with her, at least."

Auntie isn't in the living room, but there's movement down the hall as she slowly emerges from her room. Like the other two days she stayed with us, she's wearing her signature pantsuit and is well groomed. But she moves significantly slower, which makes my heart hurt to see. I should have taken things more seriously. Carter's right. But wait...didn't Hattie just now talk about how well Auntie's doing, and how much energy she has? Was she talking about the same person?

Carter meets his aunt halfway and offers his arm. "How are you feeling, Auntie?"

"Tired, but that is par for the course. I am glad you two are home. There is something I want to talk to you about."

"Are you going to scold Carter some more for the stunt he pulled with the doctor?" I ask, trying to lighten the seemingly thick, dark mood that's hanging around us. "Because I'd love to witness that."

Carter shakes his head while Aunt Eleanor starts laughing, a wispy, raspy sound that makes me smile back. "She is a keeper, Cartie," she says, easing herself onto the couch with her nephew's help. "Quick as a whip that one. You better watch out! No, it is not about that. It's about the two of you."

My stomach does a flip-flop from nerves, but I try to keep my expression neutral, not wanting to betray my worry. I glance at Carter. He glances back at me, taking a seat next to his aunt. I sit on her other side.

"First," she begins, "I want to apologize."

"You have nothing to apologize for, Aunt Eleanor," Carter says, and I put my arm around her bony shoulders in agreement.

"That is sweet, but yes, I do. I know extending my stay was a last-minute decision that threw you both off. I should have double-checked before deciding to postpone my return. Which is why, I have decided, for the rest of my extended stay, I will be moving into Hattie's spare room. She'll have it ready for me tomorrow."

"But, Auntie," Carter protests, "Hattie is moving out in one week, on the twenty-fourth. You need rest and relaxation. You won't be able to get that while she's packing and cleaning up the place."

Carter's right. I'm not sure how her staying with Hattie will work in the long term. Sure, not having her around the apartment all the time will take some of the weight off our shoulders since Hattie will be in her presence around the clock. Also, we won't have to be in full "pretend we're married" mode for hours at a stretch. But I can't disagree with Carter: Her moving in with Hattie isn't an ideal solution.

"It would give me something to do," Eleanor insists. "She has been in that apartment for decades, and she will need all the help she can get while she prepares to move."

Carter shakes his head. "Auntie, you're supposed to rest and not overexert yourself even more."

Eleanor ignores Carter's objection. "At the end of the week, we'll see how I am feeling, and then I will decide if I am going to go home or stay longer. If I do decide to stay, I can make other arrangements."

"You don't have to do all that. We have a perfectly good guest suite. I even promise to stop calling Dr. Mayweather on you."

"Carter's right," I pipe up. I want her to understand that we both want her here with us. Sure, our whole fakery would be easier if she wasn't, but neither one of us care about that, so long as she's safe and getting the rest she needs.

Eleanor shakes her head. "Nope! No debate. I have made up my mind, and you cannot talk me out of it. Hattie and I had a long talk today, and staying with her and her lovely cats will be so much more pleasant than staying here all day alone while you two are at work. And again, nothing will make me happier than to help her wrap a spoon or two or offer her good advice in preparation for her move. At least being at Hattie's will keep me close so I can still spend time with you both. Hattie told me she thinks it's a great idea and can't wait to welcome me."

Good old Hattie. That sweetheart of a woman keeps racking up the cupcake points in my book. Once I get paid, I'm going to send her a huge bouquet of flowers. I move my eyes to Carter, whose expression is annoyingly vague.

"Are you sure?" he asks.

Eleanor huffs and gently pats him on the arm as she makes a move to try to stand up. "Of course I am. I already packed the bags I won't be needing tonight. We just need to move them over."

"I'll take care of that," Carter says, forcing her to sit back down. "You stay put. I ordered us some dinner, and it should be here in a few minutes." He kisses her on her wrinkly forehead before he stands.

As he goes off to handle her luggage, I take Eleanor's hand. "If things don't work out at Hattie's, you're always welcome to come back here," I tell her.

She smiles sweetly and pats my cheek. Then she lowers her voice and gives me a mischievous smile. "I'm old enough to know when I am overstepping. You two need to be together now, as a couple. Not with an old bat like me hanging around."

I stare at her, knowing exactly what she's implying. "Oh, stop that! It's nothing like that! You're good. You're fabulous."

"Does not make me any less old," she says with a chuckle. She lowers her voice even more. "There is one thing you can do for me though, before Carter gets back."

"Anything."

"Glass of merlot, a vintage year if there is not one open already."

I raise my eyebrow at her. "Aren't you not supposed to drink?"

She giggles. "It will be our little secret."

23

CARTER

I'm skeptical about my aunt moving into Hattie's spare room. Not necessarily about my aunt's safety or anything like that. I'm sure the two of them will have a good time, and she'll be well taken care of. With each visit over the years, the two women have grown closer. The last time Auntie visited, she told me she and Hattie were as inseparable as Waldorf and Statler (the two puppets on *The Muppet Show* who sit in the balcony and talk shit about the others), and while I could see her point, I always thought the comparison was flawed. The two elderly women are rather good at observing, that's true, and they love nothing more than to make fun of themselves as well as others, which is true as well. But they both have an admirable positivity about them that is in stark contrast to Waldorf and Statler's cantankerous personas.

What I'm concerned about is Hattie spilling the beans. Eden assured me that she wouldn't, and while part of me wants to believe that's true, another part isn't as confident. We've never really been that warm toward each other, even though I believe our family trip might have helped in that regard. While I don't think Hattie will say anything to be malicious, she isn't exactly known for keeping a secret. Half of our conversations over the years have been her trying to fill me in on the gossip happening in the building. No, thank you.

However, with the way things are moving at work, I have no choice. I have to take Eden's word that Hattie has things handled. At the very least, it sets my mind at ease that Aunt Eleanor won't be alone all day. I certainly prefer her being here with us instead of in France. The good thing is, Hattie has clearly developed a soft spot for Eden, and I hope that closeness will be enough to convince her to keep our secret to herself.

∼

Wednesday is a big day.

Legacy is on the brink of landing a huge contract, one that will replace the loss created by Granger Estates and then some. Months of late nights and intense legwork have culminated in representatives from Harbor View Developments coming to the office to meet face to face so we can pitch our ideas and sign the papers. If it all goes through without a hitch, it'll be the biggest contract I've ever organized. Even bigger than Granger Estates. Unfortunately, the Grangers have decided in favor of Ecclestone. To my dismay, I was unable to convince them to change their minds: My attempts to establish communication with them had consistently been impeded.

Harbor View Developments work mainly on the coast. They specialize in flipping houses and properties for a profit. They'd started small about twenty years or so ago but quickly grew, expanding into the Pacific Northwest region. Their growth was the reason I reached out to them in the first place, only to find out that they were looking to expand on the East Coast and New England States, which led me to believe we were an ideal partner for their endeavors. With so many branches and properties, they need a company like ours to take over the construction side of things, so they can focus their efforts on sales.

It's a huge deal.

Following our visit to Phoenix, they flatly rejected every single offer put forth by Ecclestone Construction, as well as declining an offer from one of our main competitors, Humphries Properties. Apparently, my work with the Grangers was what convinced them to proceed with us in the first place, and this time, I'm not going to let such an influential client get away.

It's unnecessary to explain to Eden how important Harbor View Developments is to us. In the weeks she's been working as my assistant, she's already become fully in the picture.

With Aunt Eleanor safely at Hattie's, Eden and I start the day bright and early. So early in fact that I ignore my "we can't drive in together" rule, because we both need to be in the office as soon as possible to prepare. These are tumultuous times, and nobody will think twice about me and my assistant working closely together day and night. We're early enough that even Gwen, our front desk manager, isn't there. It's still the night guard who stifles a yawn the moment we step off the elevator. The entire drive in and way up to the office, I fill Eden in on any last-minute changes she needs to know.

She takes the whole thing in stride, pounding down the Starbucks coffee and their breakfast sandwich I ordered in the drive-thru for her before she heads off to the conference room to get it ready.

While she handles the small details, I go through my notes one last time. My numbers are sound. I've run them several times with the board and gone through line by line myself. I've given hundreds of presentations throughout my life, and while I'm not the least bit nervous, there's still a nagging feeling in the back of my mind—like I'm waiting for the unexpected twist, the other shoe to drop.

I hear Eden open the glass door and walk in, and a few seconds later, I stand to meet her at her desk. "I need you to double-check the file I just sent you and print out four more sets," I say, my eyes focused on the tablet in my hand.

When Eden doesn't respond, I look up at her. Immediately I can tell something's wrong by the look on her face. "What's going on?"

She holds up her finger to tell me to wait. My eyebrows jolt upward, and right before I press for an answer, I see Huxley walk by the glass door and disappear into his office. I glance at my watch. It's still early, and he's never been in before eight o'clock.

Eden lowers her finger and gives me a look that doesn't sit well with me. She closes the glass door and keeps her voice low. "I overheard Mr. Huxley while I was setting up."

"Judging by your expression he wasn't making a social call."

"Hardly. I don't think he knew I was there because he was taking the call just outside the room." She nudges me toward my office where we're out of earshot. "I could tell he was talking about the meeting."

"Today's meeting with Harbor View?"

"Yes."

"How? What did he say?"

"He was saying that the contract provides a loophole. Something about locking them into the quote they were given."

I exhale. I know exactly what she's talking about and what Huxley meant. "That's it? That's standard. We tend to aim on the higher side for our quotes to cover any unexpected changes or deals with the suppliers. It's normal procedure."

"Yeah, I get that. That's not what I'm concerned about. I don't know who he was talking to, but he mentioned something about not having an itemized breakdown of the cost or something and that he can use that to his advantage to get twice as much from them without them suspecting a thing."

My eyebrows shoot up. "Really?"

"Yes. He used the term 'milking the cow.'"

"Does he know you overheard his call?"

"I don't know."

"Anyway, it won't happen, not on my watch," I assure her. "He's not the project manager. I am. And I don't charge my clients for shit they don't ask for."

"Maybe you can offer the breakdown without the client having to ask for it," she suggests. "It would provide full transparency about the project and would probably reassure them."

"Of course, it's procedure. Providing an itemized breakdown of costs is a common industry practice and is part of the bidding and contract negotiation process. A breakdown like that allows clients to see exactly where their money is being spent and helps them—and us—make informed decisions."

"I see, but once a project is underway, the client's point of contact would be the contractor. Is it possible that the contractor can somehow bypass this step?"

"Technically speaking, a contractor could choose not to provide an itemized breakdown, but that's not going to happen here. The contractor is responsible for coordinating with subcontractors and suppliers, and ensuring that the project is completed on time, within budget, and to the client's satisfaction, but he still has to relay everything back to me."

"Unless he's reassured, he can skip that step. Looks like somebody is trying to make a huge profit by trying to not openly provide the info at one point or the other. You should call Huxley out on it."

I know Eden's heart is in the right place, and I appreciate her input, but first, I need to hear what we're dealing with before making decisions on how to smooth over any client's lingering doubts.

"I'd rather tread carefully. We need the client to feel that we're a united front."

Eden doesn't seem put out. She shrugs and returns to her seat. "Whatever you say. You're the boss. Oh, oh! I have a thought! How about we meet them when they arrive in the lobby and bring them up?"

"That's what we'll do. Even better, we greet them in the parking lot."

"Oh, brilliant idea, *yes*."

TEN MINUTES BEFORE THE PRESENTATION, a call from Gwen informs us that our driver who picked them up from the airport is two blocks away. "All right, we better get going then."

I look at my watch. They're on the dot. "Let's go."

"Let's go. Let's do this. Let's knock 'em dead." She gives me a bright smile that entrances me, and I have to admit, her cheerfulness rubs off on me. I find myself in a positive mood as we leave the office. It's reassuring to have a reliable ally in my corner.

On our way to the elevators, we cross paths with Huxley, who's heading to the conference room. He ignores me completely, talking away on his cell. Judging by his conversation, I assume he's on the phone with someone from the board.

"Yeah, yeah, we should wrap this meeting up within the hour," he's saying. "I'm confident we'll nail this. And if we don't, you can take it up with the project manager."

When he ends the call, I give him a look. "Subtle, Huxley."

"I wasn't trying to be." He slips his phone into the front pocket of his jacket and looks at me. "We both know how important this meeting is. Do you think you're up to the challenge?"

"When have I not been?"

"I've been doing this longer than you've been alive. This isn't the only big-ticket client you're juggling. And given what happened with the Grangers, I wouldn't be surprised if you were a little off your game."

"If you're trying to psyche me out, you're doing a poor job of it."

We part ways.

When we reach the parking lot, the limousine arrives, and we greet Joe Walsh and Adam Baker.

"Good morning, Joe, Adam," I say, and we shake hands. "Glad you could join us today."

Meeting them outside and bringing them up has provided a nice, personal touch.

While they're both businessmen, they wear dark jeans and button-up flannel shirts, unlike the finely pressed suits Huxley and I wear. I enjoy their decision to maintain a casual dress code during our meeting, despite the high stakes of the billion-dollar deal we're discussing today. Passing them on the street, you'd see two men who were used to getting their hands dirty rather than signing multi-million-dollar deals. I'm not judging—I've found the experience of working with them to be highly favorable compared to, let's say, other business types.

"Thanks again for the driver and for meeting us downstairs," Joe says as we all sit down in the conference room and the introductions and small talk are done. "This place is so huge, I'm certain we would have wandered around aimlessly if you hadn't met us at the car."

"Well, we're always here to rescue lost souls in this labyrinth of a place." Eden smiles.

"We understand that our facility can be expansive," Huxley says, his tone subtly correcting her charming response, apparently oblivious to the fact that they've already met, and that her playful reply had been spot on, "but we're pleased that you have found your way, and we extend a warm welcome to you."

Everything goes smoothly after that. I give the presentation with zero issues or interruptions. I've made several refinements to the existing plan that further clarifies our objectives and strategies, and the new ideas provide additional direction to our plans, making it clear that our proposal is the best possible option.

In my mind, the meeting really is a formality to sign the contracts and seal the deal. At least, that's what it's supposed to be.

Once I finish the main talking points, I ask, "Any questions?"

"Yes, I have one." Adam twirls the pen he's holding in his fingers.

He'd been the one who'd left our meeting in Phoenix early. I haven't spoken much with him over the phone or through email. Most of my dealings have been with Joe, which means I haven't been able to get a read on Adam's personality. Of the two partners, Joe seems to be the more personable one while Adam keeps to himself.

"I'd be glad to answer it for you," I say. "What would you like to know?"

"I know what you quoted us, and your presentation was noticeably clear on what you could do for us within our budget. But I also know construction isn't always so cut and dry. What if there is something unexpected that comes up?"

"We've prepared for any and all possible changes or adjustments in the original quote," I assure him. "And, if for some reason something happens that we didn't prepare for, you, of course, will be consulted before we go ahead with those changes."

Joe smiles and nods along as I talk, while Adam remains still and stone-faced. He doesn't look convinced or overly impressed.

"Let *me* answer your question. I am the Chief Financial Officer and branch manager here, after all." Huxley speaks up, sitting straighter in his seat. "See, I was in real estate once upon a time as you both are, and I know what concerns you face moving forward with such a massive project. Rest assured, Carter has done all the legwork, and the quotation we are providing you with represents the optimal price for the services you require. Of course, if there are still concerns, allow me to set your mind at ease."

I know exactly what he's doing. Because I've seen him do it before. He's trying to endear himself to the client, to get on their good side and butter them up so they'll feel more comfortable with him, the individual who's perceived as reliable and supportive of their interests—as opposed to me. I don't know what bothers me more, the fact he would be so full of himself to make such a shitty move or the fact I know it could work.

"I understand cost and budget are major concerns," I interject, barreling over whatever Huxley is going to say next. "Unless you have further specifications regarding the proposals presented today, we will—of course—put together an itemized breakdown of the cost for you. This breakdown will include a detailed list of all the services and materials required for the project, as well as their corresponding costs. Also, you will have my direct number. This way, even when our contractor takes over, you can always reach me with any concerns."

Out of the corner of my eye, I see Huxley freeze.

I'm not about to lose this client, especially not to Huxley. My words are exactly what Adam needs to hear.

His shoulders relax, and he finally nods. "That would be appreciated, thanks," he says. "I don't mean to be difficult, but the reason I ask is that we've been screwed over before."

"Our reputation speaks for itself," I tell him. "Transparency is important to us. Our goal is to provide you with clear and concise information, so you have a full understanding of the scope of the project and the associated costs. The contractors and our accounting department will be happy to provide any invoice with a detailed price breakdown before it's sent. Sound good?"

Huxley agrees hastily. "See, gentlemen? Legacy is the best for a reason. We deliver personal service and have your interests at heart."

For the first time since he arrived, Adam's face cracks into a smile. It's a small one, but it's there. "Yeah, sounds good." He looks over at Joe. "You ready to sign this thing?"

It takes another twenty-five minutes to go through the contract and sign and initial every line, however, once it's done, I shake their hands.

I don't trust Huxley's good mood and the sway of his sail for a second. One minute, he's trying to screw the client over, and the next, he's applauding my decisions. Eden's accidental eavesdropping on his phone call leaves no doubt that it's an act, but I can't address it at the moment.

Once everything is signed and the meeting concluded, Eden bids our guests farewell, subtly hinting that she has tasks to complete before her boss grows displeased. Adam and Joe chuckle, clearly charmed by her. They regretfully decline my lunch invitation due to pressing work obligations that require them to return to Phoenix, and I personally walk them down to the lobby myself. I don't want to risk Huxley or anyone else throwing a curveball on the way out.

"You know, one of the things that really sealed the deal was your assistant," Joe says as we ride the elevator down.

"How so?" I ask, my curiosity piqued.

"During our interactions in the last few days, she couldn't stop praising you or the company," Adam explains. "The way she went out of her way to answer all the questions with a genuine interest in offering us the best possible solution, I would have sworn she had worked here for years. We were surprised when she said she'd been around for a fraction of that."

"Our father always said, if your assistant thinks the world of you," Joe adds, "you must be doing something right as a boss."

"Exactly," Adam agrees. "So, congrats on hiring her!"

A pleasant sensation spreads through my chest. It's the second time

I've felt genuine pride at having Eden as part of my staff. By the sound of things, she weaseled around telling them that she started here less than two weeks ago. It's comforting to know I have such a savvy assistant on my team.

When I part ways with Joe and Adam, I enjoy feeling confident at the outcome of the meeting.

As I walk back into the building, Gwen gets my attention. "Mr. Bancroft?"

"Yes?"

"Your aunt just went up about ten minutes ago."

My heart stops. "What do you mean my aunt just went up?"

Her smile falters at my tone, and she quickly adjusts her glasses. "Mrs. Toussaint stopped by to see you. I'm sorry, was I not supposed to send her up? In the past, you've given your permission."

Shit. I have to get back to my office fast.

"No, it's fine, thanks, Gwen." I make a beeline for the elevator.

Why? Why is my aunt in the office? Is she okay? And why in the world is the damn elevator taking forever today? When I finally arrive, there's Aunt Eleanor, chatting with Eden at her desk like she hasn't a care in the world. When she sees me, she smiles brightly.

"Cartie! Sweetheart! How was your meeting?"

I relax.

"Auntie, what are you doing here?"

"I came to take you two to lunch," she says as though it's completely obvious, and I should have expected it. "*Surprise!* I know it is a little early, but you both work so hard, and I was feeling much better, so I thought it would be the perfect time to stretch my legs."

"You shouldn't be making the trip all the way here. You know you need to rest."

"Oh, please, it is not like I walked. Hattie dropped me off after our pedicure. Honestly, Carter, stop worrying so much. You worry way too much, am I right, Eden?"

"Eleanor, why don't you and I head out to lunch and Carter can join us in a few minutes," Eden gently suggests, putting her arm around my aunt. "He has a few things he needs to wrap up before he's ready for his break."

Just like earlier, Eden has my back. She's trying her hardest to get my aunt out of the office without everyone seeing the three of us leave together as the "happy family" that we've apparently become.

"Oh, excellent idea," my aunt says to my relief. "But Eden, dearie, didn't we agree that you call me 'Auntie'? Did you already forget? Cartie, *mon chéri*, we'll meet you at the restaurant. What's that place you like to go to with your clients?"

"Actually, I saw a wonderful new little bistro on one of my walks," Eden recommends. "The Sweet Spot. I've wanted to try it for days now. How about we go there instead?"

"Love it!"

"I'll walk you two to the elevator," I say, holding the door open for them. I'm not about to let my aunt wander out of my sight without at least some form of support—and without making sure that she doesn't run into anybody and "accidentally" spill the beans about our secret marriage. The last thing I want is to give Huxley any kind of ammunition.

After making a call to Gwen to arrange for a driver, Eden grabs her purse and the two walk arm in arm out of the office lobby. I don't think anything of it since my aunt is slow-moving, and I know people will assume Eden is being polite. We're almost home free until we turn the corner, and I notice a small group hanging by the elevators. I recognize Huxley's assistant Gretchen, and the two other administrative assistants, Lexi and Jaylin.

"Oh, Gretchen!" My aunt beams, dragging Eden to Huxley's assistant. "*Bon jour*! How nice to see you again!"

My aunt has met her a couple of times over the years when she's had to fill in occasionally. Dammit. The longer she stays in the office chatting with everyone, the higher the chance of something going wrong. I understand that she wants to catch up, but if we don't get her onto the elevator soon, there's no telling what will come out of her mouth.

"Hello, Mrs. Toussaint. It's wonderful to see you again," Gretchen greets her politely. "To what do we owe the pleasure?"

"Oh, just visiting. Thought I would take my nephew and his new wife out to lunch."

And there it is.

Gretchen appears confused, and the others stare at me and Eden with wide eyes.

"Assistant." Eden laughs. "She means new assistant."

Damn, she's fast.

"This one, always trying to marry me off," I say, motioning to my aunt, easily downplaying the slip-up. I know I should be unsettled that my aunt had just called Eden my wife in front of our staff—but I'm not. Eden is calm, cool, and collected, and so am I.

The doors to the elevator open, and Eden urges my aunt onto it. "Come on, Eleanor. Let's go down to the lobby. Your nephew will join shortly."

The last thing I hear before the doors close is my aunt saying, "Did I misspeak?"

Eden and I share a look before the door shuts, and I'm faced with the small group in the hallway, each of the three women giving me curious looks.

"It was nice to see your aunt again." Gretchen is the first to speak up. "She looks so vibrant, as if she hasn't aged a bit."

Jaylin nods in agreement. "That's what I noticed too. How long is she staying in New York?"

"Hold on, wait...did your aunt just call your assistant your *wife*?" Lexi interrupts with a giggle. "That's such a funny mishap, Mr. Bancroft! After all, she *is* kinda your work-wife, isn't she?"

Keeping things professional, I clear my throat. "Please, excuse my aunt. She's struggling a little with her health lately and not doing well. She's staying in the city until she gets better. Have a nice day, everyone."

Of course, my aunt's health issue is physical rather than mental, but

I don't need to tell them that. Gretchen, Jaylin, and Lexi nod in understanding, accepting my answer at face value like I knew they would. Eden's response had been quick and genuine, really selling the whole thing as a mix-up. No one even bothers to ask why my aunt would be taking me and my assistant out to lunch—it's plausible that I'd simply asked Eden to accompany us. My curt statement seems to drive home the point that it actually is none of their business.

"Have a nice day too, Mr. Bancroft." Lexi beams at me.

"Hope your aunt gets better soon, Mr. Bancroft," Jaylin says.

I turn to go back to my office, carefully scanning my surroundings for Huxley. He's nowhere in sight. Good. I'm glad he wasn't present to witness anything that might have raised his suspicions. With everything else going on, I need to stay on high alert. The bullshit he had pulled in the meeting—or at least tried to pull—is troubling. Did he know Eden had overheard him? Maybe Huxley had even banked on her telling me. Over the last few months, he's made it perfectly clear—at least to me—that he doesn't have the company's best interests at heart.

I wish I had a way to prove it.

Determined not to let Huxley spoil the rest of my day, I make a few last calls, change from my three-piece suit into a dress shirt and jeans, before joining my ladies out to lunch.

24

EDEN

When we get down to the lobby, Gwen smiles at us from the receptionist's desk, peering over the rim of her glasses. "Ah, Mrs. Toussaint, I see you've found Eden," she says in a friendly but louder voice.

"Oh, I have. Gwen, *merci*." Eleanor pats me on the arm. "Come on, Eden, show me that little bistro."

"Your driver is already waiting," Gwen confirms when I look at her.

"Thank you, Gwen."

It isn't until we get into the car that she finally speaks about her slip-up a few minutes prior. "I'm sorry about that, Eden," she says, squeezing my hand. "I was not even thinking. I know you and Carter wanted to keep things quiet. I completely forgot. I hope I did not just ruin everything."

I'm confident that Carter will quell any rumors or talk about what happened. "Don't worry about it, Auntie," I say, squeezing her hand back. "Carter will handle it. Forget about all of that. How are you feeling?"

"Oh, you two make such a fuss over me! I'm perfectly fine! I mean... as good as to be expected."

"We fuss because we care. I'm sure you would be fussing too, if you were in our shoes."

Eleanor sighs dramatically. "Oh, I am sure you are right. I am sorry, ma chère. It is just that I am a very independent woman, I always have been. I have never had to answer to anyone, and I do not intend to start now. That is how I raised Carter."

"You know, there is a difference between independence...and stubbornness."

She turns to look at me, and even though her huge sunglasses take up half her delicate face, I can still feel the intense gaze through the dark lenses. She blinks twice. I smile brightly in return, daring her to deny my statement. A second later, it's like a switch has been flipped and suddenly her face lights up, and we both start laughing.

"You are going to keep that boy on his toes for the rest of his life." She gives a cute little giggle.

The driver pulls up outside of The Sweet Spot, and I thank him. Eleanor and I enter the small but cozy bistro. Even though it's the lunch rush and most of the tables are full, the atmosphere is calm and quiet. Exactly what the three of us need. At least, it's exactly what I need.

We settle ourselves in a booth toward the back, and just when we're being handed our menus a few minutes later, Carter enters, dressed casually, helmet in hand, looking around. He'd hopped on his motorcycle and zipped through the sea of cars, dodging traffic to make it here in record time.

"I've never seen this place before," he admits, taking the spot next to me. Aunt Eleanor sits across from us, her face hidden behind the large menu.

"Everything good?" I ask him in a low voice.

He nods and throws me an "I've restored order" wink, dropping his arm casually across the back of the booth, not quite around my shoulders, but as close as he can get, given the situation. It's so casual and intimate that it takes me a moment to process. He seems relaxed, which is strange, considering his aunt has just blown our cover to several employees.

He leans in close, looking at the menu I'd totally forgotten I was holding. "What's good here?" he asked.

Smelling his aftershave and feeling the heat of his body has my libido immediately taking notice. I have to swallow past the lump in my throat before I can say anything. "I don't know. This is my first time." The last time he and I had been this close was when we were fooling around, and my body knows that.

Carter studies his aunt while I try to get my head on straight.

"Auntie, I'm not mad. You're fine. We're good."

She immediately lowers the menu. "Oh, Cartie, *mon chéri*, I'm so glad! I was sure you'd be as mad as a wet cat stuck in a bathtub, but I'm relieved to see that's not the case!"

He smiles at her warmly. "Did you make a choice?"

"I feel like a kid in a candy store! I hope my dentures are up for the challenge."

"Hi, I'm Bess. What can I get you folks?" Our waitress, a peppy young girl with blue hair tied in a floppy bun and a pencil tucked behind her ear, places a basket of steaming rolls on the table.

We order our food, and Carter and his aunt talk the whole time. I'm not sure when it happens, but eventually, Carter's arm slips down to rest around my shoulders. The booth is small, and between that and our legs pressing against each other's under the table, my brain can only focus on him and him alone.

Cold water. Ice-cold water. Now. Quick. Where's Bess?

Don't ask me why his closeness does what it does to me. We've been in *much* closer moments. But this, somehow it feels real.

Pressing his leg against mine isn't for show. It's for...me.

I can barely remember what I ordered. All I know is the food is superb, and by the time we leave, my head is spinning. After helping Eleanor into the car, Carter instructs the driver to ensure she arrives home safely since she insists on traveling alone. "I better go home right now and nap off this food coma. It's a good thing I wore my stretchy pants. Cheerioooo, you two! Let's make it a weekly thing!"

. . .

We return to the office, on his bike. Picture this: first, Carter wanted me to squeeze into a car with Auntie, go all the way to work, and then let the driver take her back home, which is like, the complete opposite direction. But then I gave Carter the cutest puppy-dog eyes and begged him to take me on his bike instead.

And guess what? He actually said yes.

As I plop myself down onto the bike's seat behind him, the warm metal beneath sends a shiver of excitement down my spine. It's like I'm straddling a wild beast—*and I'm not talking about the motorcycle.* There I sit, unable to stop a sense of déjà vu from washing over me. It wasn't that long ago that I had been in this exact same position, zooming toward a motel with the same handsome man sitting in front of me. But this time, everything has changed. He's not a total stranger anymore—in fact, we've gotten to know each other pretty darn well over the past few days. He's let me peek behind the curtain of his life and see the real him, and I've let my guard down and shown him the real me. And you know what? He hadn't run for the hills or made a beeline for the nearest exit. Neither had I. As unexpected and scary as that is, I've grown to appreciate Carter Bancroft on a deeper level. All of it feels like a little miracle and has turned my world upside down. I have to pinch myself to make sure it's real.

I wrap my arms around his waist, feeling his strong muscles flex beneath my fingertips. His body is warm against mine, and I snuggle closer to him, reveling in his scent and the feel of my body against his. I lean into him, feeling safe and secure.

In the parking lot in front of the big Legacy building, I step off Carter's motorcycle, hand over his jacket and helmet, smiling at him.

In another world, I would have leaned in to kiss him. Can he sense the shift in the air between us as well?

Just then, my phone goes off.

I look down at the screen and am surprised to see it's the attorney I had contacted prior to coming to New York.

"Everything okay?" Carter asks.

"My attorney is calling." I think for a moment, looking at Carter. This is a private call, and my lunch break is technically over.

"Answer it," Carter tells me. "It could be important." His eyes say: It's not like I'm going to dock your pay for taking a phone call in the parking garage.

I give him an "Okay, thanks" nod and a small wave, then swipe right while Carter heads inside the building without me. "Hello?"

"May I speak to Eden Ryan please?" a female voice on the other end asks.

"This is Eden speaking."

"Good afternoon, Eden. This is Sarah Robertson from Robertson & Associates. I understand you're in need of legal advice."

"Hi, Sarah," I say. "Thanks for getting back to me." *At last.* I dismiss the ungrateful thought from my mind.

"Of course. I received your email regarding a joint bank account, and I'm sorry to hear about your situation. Can you please confirm some of the details for me?"

Uh-oh. Somehow, I have a bad feeling. Her voice doesn't sound as if she has great news. Carter's pessimism is rubbing off on me. "Sure."

We talk for about twenty minutes.

The information I get from her boils down to this: If my former fiancé took all the money from a joint bank account without my consent (which I didn't give him), it's considered illegal, and I might have legal recourse. However, if I can't prove that my fiancé took the money from the joint account without my consent (which I can't) I might not have a good chance of winning the case. Legal fees can range from a few hundred dollars for a simple case to tens of thousands of dollars for a more complex case that goes to trial. If my fiancé has left the state (which I hear he has), it might be more difficult to track him down and enforce a judgment if I win the case. This could increase the cost and time involved in pursuing the matter.

There's much more she said than that, but ultimately, I can sum up the call in eight words: I have no chance of making him pay.

Regrettably, I have no evidence to present, while he's enjoying the backing of numerous individuals. It already stings that I can never get back the money I spent on the wedding itself, the fact I can't hold him accountable for his wrongdoing is even more aggravating. The expenses I would incur could surpass any potential winnings, even in the event of a victory.

I can't breathe.

It takes every ounce of willpower not to scream.

I close my eyes, trying to force myself to take a deep breath. It takes a while to manage, and when I do, it's more of a huff than an actual breath. I take another, and another, until most of the fury has subsided. I'm still pissed. Rightfully so. However, at least I'm not seething and can walk into the building without looking like I'm on a murder spree.

Gwen greets me as I hurry by, and even though I smile, my emotions must still be clear because she hesitates for a moment before addressing me. "Good to see you, Eden. One of our visitors dropped this off." She holds up Carter's small black notebook. "Mr. Bancroft must have lost it by the elevator. Would you be so kind as to take it?" I thank her and am relieved when the elevator doors closes behind me.

I ride the elevator up on my own, focusing on my breathing. All I want is to get back to my desk and throw myself into my work. For a second, I see another option: throw myself into Carter's arms. It's the only thing I know will make the anger really go away, and that scares me to death. It would be the worst thing I could do right now, because our relationship, if you want to call it that, is temporary.

It's not about proving a point to Rob. Not anymore.

It's about proving a point to *me*.

It's a chance to overcome the disappointment and get my life back together. It's about standing up for myself. It's about finding closure, that sense of peace after enduring the wreckage of a horrible breakup—after having been left emotionally broken and scarred, struggling to pick up the million shattered pieces of my heart, while fighting to reclaim a sense of self-worth that had been trampled upon by a remorseless individual. It's about not letting an asshole get away.

Gretchen is talking to Jaylin and Lexi when I arrive on my floor, but instead of joining them, I walk right past. I swiftly enter Carter's office to hand him his small black book. He's on the phone and gives me a curt nod, before I make my way back to my desk. By the time I sit down in my comfy chair behind my huge desk with my incredible view of NYC and a world of possibilities just waiting for me, the anger has mostly subsided, and I can breathe easier.

About a minute later, Gretchen messages me.

> **GRETCHEN:**
> Everything okay? You looked upset.

> **ME:**
> Oh, you know, meddling phone call regarding my past.

> **GRETCHEN:**
> Oh, damn! Do you need to talk about it?

> **ME:**
> I'm good, girl. Thanks. Just want to get some work done.

> **GRETCHEN:**
> I'm here if you need me. Smiley emoji

I smile and type a "thank you" back before I take a final deep breath and get back to work.

I HAVEN'T BEEN at it long before Carter's mahogany office double door opens. He holds his tablet and is looking at something on it as he approaches my desk, not bothering to look up.

"Hey," he says, "so I was just looking over those reports I asked you to pull, and we're missing a couple of our smaller accounts."

"Sorry, I'll rerun it."

There must have been something off about my response because Carter looks up and frowns. "What's wrong?"

"Nothing, I'm fine."

He raises his eyebrow, not believing me for a second. "Eden, I'd like to think I've gotten to know you pretty well by now. What's going on? Was the phone call bad news?"

"Nope, no bad news. Just unfortunate news." I keep my explanation brief, not wanting it to derail our work conversation or distract me. "I'm sorry about the report. I'll fix it right now."

I turn back to my computer to do just that when Carter puts his tablet down. He leans on my desk, forcing my attention back to him. "Would you like to discuss it?" he asks, with a quiet and gentle tone. "I'm here to listen, Eden. Please come into my office."

My heart suddenly begins to race. His expression is soft and one I so rarely see, especially in the office, that it takes my breath away. I'm tempted to talk to him, to tell him everything the attorney said, and vent my frustrations. But now isn't the time or the place.

"I appreciate it, but I'm okay," I say. "It's not something I want to talk about here."

He nods in understanding, picking up his tablet again. "We'll open some wine this evening and you can tell me about it. So, anyway, back to this report."

And just like that, he's in work mode.

He goes right back to "Boss Carter."

The switch gives me whiplash, and I find myself having a tough time keeping track of what he's saying. Expectedly, Carter has drawn a clear line between what is appropriate to talk about at work and what needs to be kept out of the office, and I agree with that, one hundred percent. But for him to be the one to get personal, to offer to listen, has thrown me off. Not because he hasn't done it before. It was the way he did it. He'd said "please." He'd said, *"Please* come into my office."

I feels like something has shifted between us, though I'm not exactly sure when it happened. Or what that means about our relationship.

Trying not to read too much into it, I rerun the report for him and handle several other tasks.

. . .

A Bossy Roommate

THE REST of the day passes without incident. My mood improves even more when the afternoon comes and someone from HR hand-delivers my paystub.

"I had *completely* forgotten it was my first payday," I tell her.

I hadn't forgotten, but it feels cool to say it. Then I immediately apologize for saying it because: karma. We laugh, and once she's gone, I do a quick check of my bank account on my phone and breathe a sigh of relief. *Thank God* for direct deposit.

It feels good to have more than fifteen dollars to my name. A lot more. The amount that smiles back at me displays not just my salary, but also the weekend marriage bonus I'd deposited from Carter's check, though it had taken a while to appear in the bank. A huge weight is lifted off my shoulders, and I can breathe. Finally, I can afford to gas up Kiki, fix her windshield wipers, and start driving to work. *In case of emergency*, I correct myself, immediately thinking of my sister and her efforts to run an ecological and sustainable company. Every contribution counts, and I'll walk the distance or use the train as often as I can without penalizing myself for occasionally using Kiki.

As usual, when the end of the day rolls around, I leave before Carter does, welcoming my walk home. It's become a reliable source of exercise and a way to clear my head after a long, busy day. The route is now ingrained in my memory, and I could walk the same path blindfolded if I needed to. While I walk, I consider taking the sweet offer by HR—that had been sent through by Carter—to leave my car in the parking garage both in the mornings and afternoons to save money and to avoid it heating up.

With money in my bank account, it's time for a celebratory treat. Without a second thought about the scales and healthy choices (screw that!), I stop at one of the many delicious food places on my route. Since Carter had mentioned wine and dinner, I opt to visit a bakery and pick up something sweet for dessert. Since their mouth-watering cinnamon rolls are sold out (a moment of silence, please!) along with any cupcakes (oh, the memories! *Sigh!*), I settle on their iconic NYC black-and-white cookies. They're *way* more expensive than any cookies would have been in my hometown. But by now—bougie as I am—I'm used to New York's hefty price tag.

When I get home, I make my way to the apartment, humming to myself. At some point this afternoon, I'd let go of the frustrating news Sarah had given me, not wanting it to mar the rest of my day. I'm glad I did, because when I manage to reach the apartment, I remember that Aunt Eleanor is going to be staying with Hattie—meaning Carter and I will be...alone.

Only the two of us.

Completely isolated.

We'll have the place to ourselves without having to worry about someone interrupting, listening next door, or walking in on us—during or after the fact.

Hattie's door opens right when I get to mine.

25

EDEN

Seriously. How does Hattie do that? Does she have a hidden camera somewhere? Does she stand by the door, looking out the peephole to see when I'm coming? I need to know how that woman always seems to be ready and waiting to greet me when I come home from work.

Except this time, it isn't just Hattie. Eleanor stands with her, both of them ogling me. I have a brief moment where my brain goes, *Oh, no, there's two of them.*

They both say my name enthusiastically.

"Eden! There you are, dear!"

"Eden! Welcome home, *ma chère*!" Eleanor pulls me into a tight hug, and I do my best to balance the cookies in one hand as I return the embrace.

Likewise, she has a glass of wine in her hand that she's careful not to spill. "We were just going to sit down to a game of Scrabble. You should join us!"

The idea of sitting with two elderly ladies playing Scrabble and drinking wine actually sounds ridiculously fun, especially with these two ladies specifically. But there's still the issue of being allergic to Hattie's apartment—and there's Carter. Completely isolated Carter.

I offer a sad expression. "I'd love to but—"

Hattie speaks up for me. "I'm quite certain she would prefer to spend her evening with her husband, love." She smiles, and I swear I can see her nudging Eleanor's arm before looking back up at me. "We certainly wouldn't want to intrude upon what might be a romantic date night."

"Oh, yes, yes, of course, I get it," Auntie says. "You don't want us four-wheeling on your date night. We'll just be over here, on our best behavior."

I nod with a bright smile, seizing my opportunity. "Which reminds me, I should go get ready before he gets home. Oh, care for cookies?"

"Funnily enough, we were just on the verge of whipping up our own batch," Hattie says, "but we'd be delighted to sample yours instead, my dear."

I extend the box of cookies, and Auntie's gaze immediately lands on it.

"Cookies? Oh, I thought you said 'cocktails,'" Eleanor says. "Good, we'll take the cookies, anyway."

They reach into the box and grab some.

"We'll pretend we made them ourselves," Eleanor says. "Don't tell anyone!"

I laugh. "Your secret is safe with me. Have fun, ladies."

I let myself into the apartment. As embarrassing as it is that they know exactly what Carter and I will be getting up to, at least there'll be no interruptions this time. It's practically guaranteed after that conversation.

I put the cookies on the counter and then head to the bedroom and then to the bathroom to take a quick shower (belting out the lyrics to "Can't Help Falling in Love" by Elvis). It's not until I start going through my minuscule wardrobe that I pause and realize what I'm doing. Hattie had been the one to call it a date, not me or Carter. Why am I acting like it is one? Carter and I have dinner all the time—what the hell makes me think tonight will be a date? He never said it was and hasn't given me any indication it will be.

Crap.

I sit on the bed, taking a moment to collect myself. Without noticing, without even realizing it, Carter has wormed his way into my heart. How has that happened? *When* did that happen? That can't happen.

I can't have feelings for him. I *shouldn't* have feelings for him.

There's a laundry list of reasons why, but it really all comes down to the big three: he's my boss, our marriage is fake, and I'm leaving in six months.

I hear the door open and the familiar sound of Carter's boots across the hardwood floor. Pulling myself together, I put away the clothes I had been ransacking and go to greet him.

He's in the kitchen already, shuffling through a stack of mail. Standing there all casual, with a hint of scruff on his jawline, he looks effortlessly irresistible. His leather jacket is folded over one of the kitchen chairs, and he's untied his tie but left it hanging around his neck. The top buttons of his dark-gray shirt are undone, and he's rolled the sleeves up past his elbows.

How dare he?

Inked sleeves. *Heavens.*

There's something about a well-groomed man being half-dressed, showing off his tattoos that makes me clench my thighs together. Especially *this* well-groomed man.

"I ordered dinner before I left, so it should be here soon," he rumbles, not looking up from his pile of mail.

"Awesome," I chirp, trying to act like my libido hadn't shot through the roof the second I came in. "I got cookies. They're in the kitchen. Did you see your aunt?"

"Yeah, I stopped by there a minute ago. Had to scold Hattie for making sangria, but lord knows they won't listen to a damn thing I say." He puts the mail down and removes his gray tie all the way, wrapping it around his hand in the process.

My mouth drops open a little. If only my hair could have such fun...

When he finally looks up at me, he stills. Next, he playfully raises his eyebrow. "You see something you like?"

Busted.

Shit. Am I drooling?

"Not really," I lie, moving across the room toward him. "Not sure what you mean." I'm a lying liar who lies, and he knows it. My whole body screams, "*Take me!*"

Carter's gaze still on me, he picks up his jacket and makes his way around the table. "That's not what I heard."

"What do you mean?" Damn. Did I say something out loud? Surely not.

"I mean, two ladies just told me that my wife had plans for a date night tonight. I wasn't aware we had a date night."

At that, I laugh and shake my head. *Thanks, ladies!* "Oh, my God, those two are going to be the death of me. *Hattie* was the one who said the words 'date night.' All I did was try to politely bow out of a conversation."

"I warned you."

"Yes, yes, you did."

"So, no date night then?"

My heart skips a beat. "You were the one who talked about wine and dinner. I should be asking you the same thing."

"After that phone call, it looked like you needed it."

Instant mood killer. I've been doing my best to *not* think about the call, and it had worked very well up until he mentioned it. I make a face and sit on the nearest chair. "Ugh, don't remind me."

For two seconds, Carter puts his hand on my shoulder—my heart stutters for those two seconds—as he walks by on his way to our room. His room. Not our room.

"We'll open some wine," I hear him rumble, "and you can tell me all about it. Let me take a quick shower first."

"I don't think you have enough wine to cover the whole story."

"We'll make do."

While he goes to shower, all naked and tattooed and hot, I busy myself in the kitchen. I need to find something to focus on, something other than the pounding of my heart and the casual comfort Carter is willing to provide. Add to the fact my brain decides to think about all our special encounters, including how close he sat next to me at lunch, how his arm was around my shoulders, and I know if he comes into the kitchen and touches me in any way, I'm going to jump his bones.

Ding-dong. Ding-dong.

Luckily, dinner arrives, distracting me.

"I've got it." Carter comes to answer the door, dressed in black jeans and a black long-sleeved shirt. The shirt is tight enough that I can see his muscles just barely straining through the fabric. I force myself to look away, because if he catches me staring—again—I'll never live it down.

Instead, I unpack the food and finish setting the table, while he goes to pick out wine. He's ordered pasta with marinara sauce this time. The delicious smell of tomato sauce elevated by sautéed mushrooms and assorted vegetables fills the room. I didn't realize how hungry I was until I fill our plates, and when he returns with a bottle of white wine a minute later, I'm already picking up my fork.

"All right, spill," he says. "What happened?"

I spend the next ten minutes telling him about the phone call with my attorney, revealing the harsh truth that winning a case against Rob is outright impossible. That it feels like I'm getting farther and farther away from any sense of justice because I have no proof. I admit to Carter that it was a consequence of my own actions, my own foolishness. I had placed my trust in a man who had turned out to be a master manipulator of words. His extensive network of friends and connections are a result of his expertly crafted façade, and I can't compete with that.

By the time I'm done, Carter is shaking his head. "Ridiculous. I don't want to accept that."

I sigh, pushing my food around with my fork, not very hungry anymore. "And you want to know what the most screwed-up part is?"

"All of it?"

"Besides that. I was the bold one. I was the one who took the leap and asked him to marry me. I even told all my friends about it, feeling so proud that I'd made the first step, defying conventional rituals."

I pause. Oddly enough, I don't find it as difficult as usual to admit to why I'm hurting—especially to a man who hardly ever messes up. Gathering up the last shred of bravery I have, I finally voice what is causing such turmoil that I hadn't even shared it with my own sister. "Finding that one true love has always been my biggest dream. To be with one man for the rest of my life, knowing that we can overcome anything together, from reconciling after the worst arguments, to wholeheartedly backing us in all our crazy pursuits and heartfelt endeavors, and ultimately, growing old together, hand in hand...you know, being able to share everything without the fear of being abandoned..."

I pause and look at Carter. His gaze is tender, soft even, and he nods once, slowly, as if this thought is new to him, but not necessarily a bad thing.

"In short," I continue, "I wanted to be loved for who I was. I thought Rob was the man who loved me unconditionally." I take another deep breath. "So, I popped the question and asked him to become my husband. Consequently, it came back to bite me. He claimed that I 'forced myself upon him' and he justified his actions of safeguarding our joint financial resources as a means to protect himself from potential misuse. According to him, I was driven by my bruised ego after he backed out. It struck a chord with those who were unaware of the truth, despite my numerous attempts to set things straight. But I guess it was a good life lesson...luckily, I found out before I said I do. Imagine being stuck with him, ugh!"

"Don't do that."

I frown, glancing up at Carter. He stares at me with a serious expression. "Don't do what?"

"Don't backtrack."

"I'm not backtracking. I'm trying to stay positive."

"You don't have to put other people's feelings before yours to be positive."

"That's not what I was doing. I was only saying that I could take it as a good thing that I wasn't stuck in a shitty marriage with a man who doesn't love me and doesn't deserve me."

"Why is that a good thing when the outcome of everything was a complete disaster? You know, Eden, let me share with you one of the most profound realizations I've had in my lifetime: Shit happens."

I snort, grateful that he made me laugh.

"There's no point in blaming yourself when it's blatantly evident that you're not at fault," he continues. "You move forward, focusing on your goals. And you never backtrack, and you never apologize for standing your ground. Simple as that."

For once, I have no response. I sit there for a moment, thinking about what Carter said. "I see your point," I tell him.

"But also give yourself more time to process the fact there are plenty of shitheads around, and while you do that, don't let a shithead get inside your head. Just like with Huxley. You met the CFO, and pretty much immediately, you realized he's one of those shitheads."

I nod. Carter's right. I had disliked Huxley from the very beginning, not just because of his outdated, condescending 1950s attitude toward working women.

"Can you imagine that he managed to deceive even me once?" he asks.

"You? *You* fell for Huxley?"

There's something in his gaze, something vulnerable that oddly makes him appear even stronger. He nods, a grin turning up his lips. "I was young and inexperienced. Under his direction, I devised a strategic plan aimed at yielding favorable results for the company. During my presentation, Huxley diverted the conversation by introducing doubts and questions about my plan." Little by little, the smile fades. "I'm serious, Eden. You know how much Legacy means to me and how hard I work every day to become partner. It's not just about being the best, although that's pretty important to me. I want to strengthen Legacy in every way I can. I want to be part of something bigger and meaningful— of a company where we create opportunities, where we drive innovation and shape the direction of the industry. Where people enjoy working.

Where they get job stability and the salary they deserve. Where we're cultivating the best out of people and giving them ownership and opportunities for growth and leadership as we continue to expand. Where we *empower* them. It's always been like that. The nine-to-five routine and a picket fence existence," he gives me a mischievous look, "that has never been what I wanted."

My heart melts. I know Carter is a strict but fair boss, but hearing him reveal a part of his soul—a very hardworking and ambitious soul—stirs and awakens something inside me.

"Back to Huxley," he continues. "It didn't take long for me to see through him, but unlike you, I took that mistake as a lesson and moved on. You should do the same. With Rob."

That's actually good advice, and his words make me smile. For some reason, they calm my stormy heart. Hopefully, giving myself time and space to understand and accept this new phase in my life will help me come to terms with my shaken sense of self-worth.

"Thank you, Carter."

"You're welcome. Anytime." Carter holds his wineglass out in a toast, and I tap my glass to his. "Also, I'll talk to Vance, if you're okay with it. There must be something that can be done, and the fact that your lawyer took so long to call you back is unacceptable—and pretty shitty. Your ex-fiancé is not going to get away with this. This will also help you get some closure."

"Really? I wouldn't want to waste your lawyer's time. I might not be able to pay for—"

"Hush," he interjects, his tone filled with the assurance that he will handle it. "Vance is the best in his field."

"Carter, I don't know what to say. I wasn't expecting you to ask about it, much less while at work today. You're always so adamant about not getting personal in the office."

"I'm not a robot, Eden. I do feel sympathy and empathy. When my usually happy and level-headed assistant has a twenty-minute phone call and comes back clearly upset and distracted, I'm not going to ignore it."

"Well, whatever the reason, I appreciated it."

"Also, thanks for that quick thinking with my aunt. I still cannot *believe* she showed up and spilled the beans like that." He laughs. Actually laughs.

"Don't mention it." Just the sound of his laugh is enough to make me break out into a fit of giggles.

"Ready for the good news?"

"Absolutely." I beam.

"We sealed the deal with Harbor View, and I have you to thank for that."

My eyebrows go up in surprise. "Why? You were the one who did all the work. All I did was assist you."

"No, that wasn't all you did. First, you warned me about Huxley, which I greatly appreciated, and your advice was spot on. Joe and Adam were on the fence, but our conversation provided me with a clear understanding of how and where to tackle the problem to drive the account home. On top of all that, they couldn't stop singing your praises."

Thrilled is an understatement. I'd never imagined my overhearing Huxley's phone call would lead to such a favorable outcome, especially after Carter had initially more or less dismissed it. I'm also struck by the fact the clients had mentioned me.

Carter finishes the last bit of wine in his glass. When he puts his glass down, he reaches over to grab my hand. "How about dessert?"

The smolder in his eyes and the smirk on his face lets me know he's not talking about the cookies that sit waiting on the counter. Smiling back at him, I down the rest of my wine as well and allow him to pull me to my feet.

We're done playing around.

We're done waiting.

I've barely pushed my chair back when his mouth is on mine, his hand reaching up to cup my cheek. I melt into his embrace, pressing my body against the solid warmth of his chest. He kisses me like he's starved, like we haven't kissed in weeks when it has only been a day.

Melting under his kiss, I prepare myself for the wreckage.

"I want to break our rules," he rumbles in his baritone.

"Okay," I breathe.

Just like that.

In a heartbeat.

The next thing I know, he lifts me off the ground.

With a squeak of delighted surprise, I wrap my legs around his waist. His hands cradle my ass as he carries me down the hall and kicks the door of the bedroom open.

Everything feels tight, like I'm on edge, waiting for him to touch me, to light my body aflame again. With one hand holding my back, he lowers me onto the bed, the weight of his body sending a thrill of excitement through me. I love feeling him on top of me, feeling the powerful lines of his muscles and the way his hands explore every bit of me he can reach.

Carter only breaks the kiss to pull my shirt up over my head, and slide my skirt down, dropping the items off to the side. The moment they're out of the way, his mouth returns to mine and his hand slides up my torso to my breasts.

When he draws back, it's not my body he stares at.

He gazes into my eyes as if he wants to delve into the depths of my soul.

"Baby," he whispers, his lips brushing over mine.

"Yes?"

"Now," he pauses for a moment, murmuring against my mouth, "I will take care of you. I will fuck you happy, baby. That's a promise."

And just like that, I know I'm a goner.

He pulls me close. His hot breath grazes my neck as his lips trail down my body, his mouth devouring mine, and his hand touching, groping, exploring my body. His hands roam hungrily over my skin, intensifying my desire for him thousandfold. His grip tightens, almost mercilessly, as if he can't bear to lose physical contact for a second. Despite the need in his eyes, he holds back, and I feel my pleasure growing and growing until it's unbearable.

I probably fell in love the moment I saw him in that ice cream shop. Carter makes me come alive in ways I didn't think were possible.

With a growl, he sits back on his heels, taking the hem of his shirt and pulling it up and off. I can hear the rustling of clothes and the sound of his breathing as he inhales and exhales like some sort of beast.

I can almost feel the muscles moving beneath my fingertips and the hair on his chest. I long to touch his tattoos. Each are a part of him. Each tells a story. On Carter's muscled body, the ink dances across his skin. Maybe it's just my imagination, but the hawk on his skin appears hungry. It looks as if the predator is poised to swoop down and consume its prey. From what I can see, it seems likely it will achieve its goal. In fact, it's the most compliant quarry he's ever come across. I can't help but run my hands up the hard planes of his chest, touching the beast, sucking in a breath as the muscles twitch under my palms.

The world turns. Every breath is a rumble of thunder, every heartbeat a dull drum beating to the rhythm of our passion. My skin feels hot and feverish under his fingers.

Carter hovers over me, only in his jeans now, but this time, the kisses aren't for my mouth. They're for my cheek, my throat, my collarbone, the valley between my breasts…lower and lower he moves until he slides between my legs.

I run my fingers through his hair as his tongue slips inside me.

With each kiss, nibble, and lick, I find myself losing every ounce of control. Not that I have much to begin with when it comes to him. I hadn't had that first night together, and I sure as hell don't have any in this moment. Every nerve screams for him, every muscle clenches and waits for the pleasure this man brings.

His expert touch sends ripples of pleasure through my body, and I bite my lip to keep from crying out. Carter's mouth and fingers are magical, bringing me closer to the brink repeatedly before backing off, leaving me sweaty, shaking, and wanting. I beg for that sweet release, shamelessly writhing, and moaning his name until he's merciful enough to give me what I want.

An electric pleasure rushes through me, crackling like powerful sparks. I can feel Carter in every nerve in my body as I come beneath him.

When I return to myself, he's on his knees in front of me, his fingers nimbly undoing the button of his jeans. He pushes them and his boxers down, letting me finally get another look at him. Knowing that he not only wants to fuck, but love me, rid me of the pain in my heart, is almost too much.

I reach for him as he lowers himself on the bed. My arms circle his neck, and I kiss him, trying to pour everything I'm feeling into one simple action. I want him to know what he does to me, to my soul. I want him to know how much I want him in case it isn't obvious that he can turn me to ash with one fiery look. He lies on top of me, fits us together, this time skin to skin, my breasts pressing into his pecs. His cock is pressed against my thigh, hard and ready to be inside me.

With his arms left and right of my shoulders, caging me in, he nudges my legs farther apart with his knees.

"Tell me, 'Fuck me, babe,'" he growls.

I do, without hesitation. "Fuck me, babe," I whisper.

Slowly, he pushes into me, only to still when his tip fills me.

His eyes connect with mine.

He peers at me through his long, dark eyelashes, winks, and patiently waits.

Just when I'm about to protest, he pushes deeper with one smooth thrust.

"Ohhh..." I gasp and slide my arms around him, pulling him into another kiss.

Carter doesn't move at first. He stays there, buried inside me while he kisses the life out of me, leaving me breathless and wanting more. "See how perfectly you were made for me."

He begins to move, the pace of his thrusts slow, leisurely even, like everything else has been tonight. He fucks me with a delicious force I can't get enough of. He won't stop kissing me, will leave my lips only to growl into my ear, tell me how perfect I feel, how flawless I am, how deliciously I squeeze his cock, how much he loves fucking me. That my soul, my body, and my pussy are his. And that he will fuck me as long as it will take, until I start to believe again.

I cling to him, my legs circle him.

I can't say what I want to say.

I try to let my body do the talking. I let myself go and give every part of me to Carter. I'm his, heart, body, and soul. And I will never ever say it aloud.

He starts to go faster. I know when he's close. His pace becomes relentless, and his mouth travels away from my lips to release a groan, to latch onto my throat, kissing and sucking the sensitive flesh.

"Fuck, baby, *fuck*," he groans.

My breathing and moaning take control of me. I'm surrounded by him, enveloped by the scent of his skin, the feeling of his hands, mouth, voice, his cock, and when I can't hold back anymore, I give in and let him consume me.

I fall over the edge, moaning his name.

His forehead presses against mine, mouth slotted over mine, stealing what little breath I have left. I feel his hips jerk, dominantly, hard, once, twice, and then he's still, locked into place as his cock pulses and his own release takes over, followed by a final groan.

We collapse.

For a few endless moments, we remain locked, not letting go of each other.

When he slides out of me, he lies down by my side, pulling me with him so we're face to face, giving me a chance to finally move. If I could. My body hasn't started working again, so I'm perfectly content to just lie there, struggling to catch my breath.

"That was perfect, baby," he rumbles, his voice hoarse and his eyes hooded with post-orgasmic bliss as he pulls me closer against his body.

I tuck my head under his chin, pressing myself against his broad chest. "Yes, more than anything. Not sure if I'm going to be able to walk tomorrow."

Carter reaches out to slap my ass. "If you're not sure, then I haven't done my job properly."

"Trust me, you did it well and then some." I roll over onto my back, half-snuggling into Carter and half spread out. "By the way, that position is maybe my new favorite."

"It's maybe my new favorite too." He chuckles and glances at the alarm clock on his nightstand. "We should get some sleep," he says through a yawn. "We have to be up early to get to work."

"And here I thought we were going to keep going until we passed out from exhaustion. That's too bad."

Carter raises his eyebrow. "Was that a challenge?"

"It could be."

In the blink of an eye, I find Carter on top of me again, his mouth colliding with mine in a kiss that leaves me even more breathless than I already am.

He growls my name, his hand cupping my breast while he lowers his mouth to my nipple. "Don't say I didn't warn you."

26
CARTER

The end of the week is coming, and Aunt Eleanor's preparing to fly home. I was actually surprised when she told me she'd bought her ticket, only because I'd sworn she was going to extend her stay further. And trust me, I want her to.

My aunt staying means Eden and I need to keep up the charade and stay in character, spending our nights in my bedroom. This arrangement will grant us those precious extra hours together, and, perhaps most importantly, ample time for those much-needed date nights.

Eden is one of the best assistants I've ever had, probably *the* best if I really draw up comparisons. But I know it's not why I want her here. It has nothing to do with work and everything to do with her as a person.

Somewhere along the way, what had started as a business transaction has begun to morph into something else.

"Are you sure you're okay to travel?" I ask my aunt, not letting her answer. Her health is my main concern. "I don't think you should. You need to stay. You shouldn't rush things. I wish you would at least let me call Dr. Mayweather just in case to check you out."

I'm with my aunt in her room at Hattie's place, helping Hattie pack Auntie's things—and by helping her pack, I mean *not* helping her pack, but instead trying to prevent her from leaving. Eden is in my apartment, avoiding the plethora of cat hair like the plague, and assisting with tea and sandwiches. The owners, Lewis and Kate, have a cleaning crew scheduled to come and disinfect the entire apartment on Monday before Eden moves in—which will give her and me an extra day or two together at my place.

After that, I'm determined to find a way to keep her by my side.

Tied to my bed, if necessary. Naked, to be precise.

"For the last time, Carter Donovan Bancroft. Will you stop fussing over me already?" My aunt shakes her head, lightly batting at my arm with her boney hand and then tiptoeing to give me a kiss on my cheek. "I'm perfectly fine. If it makes you feel better, once I get back home, I will go right to my doctor and have a full exam."

"You'll be all the way across an ocean. I can't hold you to that. But just know if you don't, Eden and I will book a ticket and fly out ourselves to make you go."

"You really found a good one, Cartie. That wife of yours is a gem."

"Yeah, she is," I agree without hesitation.

Smiling warmly, Aunt Eleanor sits down on one of the suitcases and pats the chair next to her. "Come, sit with me for a minute." When I do, she reaches out and takes one of my hands in both of hers. "Cartie, do you know why I've been hounding you so much to get married?"

"Because you like to see me sweat," I tell her.

She laughs immediately. "True."

"And," I continue, "because that's the way things were done when you were my age."

"Where did you get that nonsense from?"

"From *you*. You've outright said it to me. More than once."

She chuckles and slips her arm around mine. "Smart advice. You should listen. But no, jokes aside, the honest to God reason why I wanted you to get married is that, when I am gone, I do not want you to be in this world alone."

Her words hit me like a bus. The raw truth is almost too much to handle, and I have to breathe for a moment and process what she just said. With everything she's had going on, all her health issues and scares, my aunt has never once mentioned her death. She's implied it with the usual offhanded, "I'm not going to be around forever you know!"

This is different.

"Well, that's not happening any time soon, so you don't have to worry about it," I tell her firmly, wrapping her in a large hug.

She chuckles and pats my back. "I know, I know, it's not. But let's not kid ourselves, Cartie. I'm in my late sixties. Who knows how much longer I have on this earth? But at least now I can rest easy knowing my little one is going to be taken care of."

"I'm hardly little anymore, Auntie."

She pinches my cheek. "You'll always be my little one. I also know you don't need Eden to take care of you, not in the physical or traditional sense. Emotionally, however, you have always been a lonely boy. Even when surrounded by friends."

"I like the solitude."

"I know you do. But I have seen how you are with Eden. I have seen how you light up when she enters a room, and how she lights up when you enter a room...how you two are naturally drawn together. I'm happy, Cartie. So happy that you have found someone who makes *you* happy. It is important to have people by your side who will be there for you when you make the tough decisions, and who will help even when you don't think you need it. I don't think you realize how much that girl loves you, and how special it is to find someone who is so perfect for you."

I open my mouth to respond, yet for once, I find myself at a loss for words.

Eden had seamlessly fitted into my life overnight. Our connection is so strong that it's easy to forget that we were practically strangers just a short while ago.

"Carter." My aunt squeezes my hand. "You treasure that woman and do not let her go, even if it gets tough."

I smile and give her another hug. "Love you, Auntie."

"Love you too. Now, let us finish packing up my things."

For my aunt's last night in New York, she has dinner with me and Eden at my place. We invited Hattie, but Hattie excused herself, stating she had commitments elsewhere. "I must apologize, but it appears that young Myrtle is feeling rather lonely today. Whenever I'm not around to keep an eye on her, she tends to get into a bit of mischief, I'm afraid." But I can tell in her eyes that she wants to give us the time with my aunt.

From across the table, I watch Eden and Auntie, pleased at how close the two have become during my aunt's visit. I'm not sure what they're talking about—I'm too lost in my own head.

I keep looking over into the living room, seeing the Bancroft family sign on the mantel. We're a family, albeit an unexpected one.

Somehow, Eden has become part of my family.

~

Sunday

The next morning, I wake up early. Aunt Eleanor's flight leaves at an ungodly hour, which means we have to get up at 4:00 a.m. in order to get ready and make it there on time. Eden starts to dress. I didn't ask her to come with us, didn't even expect it from her. Once my aunt is on the plane, our whole arrangement will be over. She does it anyway, without a moment's delay.

In the quiet of the early morning, the three of us load up my car with all of Aunt Eleanor's things. We drive to the airport in silence.

After we've unloaded her ridiculous amount of luggage onto a nearby cart, checked her in, and accompanied her as far as we're allowed, she pulls both of us into a tight hug. It's emotional.

While I'm happy she'll be going back home where she's surrounded by her friends, loved ones, and doctors, my stomach is in knots. Eden's hand comes to rest on my back, and I wrap my arms around her and my aunt's shoulders to pull them close.

Both Eden and my aunt cry, and I almost crack.

I want to take Aunt Eleanor and those damn bags back to my apartment, insisting that she stay forever. I can't. The lie will come out. I would break her heart, and that's something I can't do, no matter how much mine hurts.

With tears prickling at the corners of my eyes, I bring them closer, feeling the sobs that emanate from them as they cling to me, and I tighten the embrace.

"Love you, Auntie," I whisper.

"I know...Cartie," she sniffles, her voice soft and trembling. "I love you too."

My arms strengthen, pulling them closer in the embrace. "I know." I lower my head and place a kiss to my aunt's wrinkled forehead.

We stay that way for what seems like an endless time—it's not long enough, and it never will be—holding onto each other firmly, not wanting to let go.

Eventually, I allow them to reluctantly pull away, knowing it's time to say goodbye. It's a bittersweet moment, but I know that the memories of our time together will stay with me forever.

"You've been quiet," Eden says when we get back into the car, and I pull into traffic. "I know you're worried about her. When you handled her bags, I made her promise to video chat with you as soon as she was checked out by her doctors."

"Thank you, Eden."

"She also made mention of us coming to visit her for our honeymoon."

"She did?" I smile.

"Yes, but I think I was able to direct her away from that idea when I told her how crazy work is." Her pause is filled with a warm smile. "Of course, if you *did* want to visit her and she was insistent I came along, I wouldn't mind."

"You wouldn't? Have you ever been to Paris?"

"No, never. And that wasn't me fishing for a trip out of the country," she adds hastily. "I was just telling you what *she* said."

"I know. I didn't think you were fishing for anything. Paris is a gorgeous place. I'll take you sometime."

Eden grows silent. When I look over at her, her cheeks are pink. Her eyes sparkle. "You'd take me to Paris? To the city of love?"

"Sure. Everyone should go there at least once in their lives."

I try to keep my voice casual—however, I know she likes to tease me, talking about *love*—but the second she asked me, and the words came out of my mouth, there was no other answer. I didn't have to think twice.

Eden has weaved her way into my life and into my heart without me realizing it.

What had started out as a fake marriage to appease my aunt has turned into something more, something real. There are feelings here that I've been trying to suppress, trying to put aside, because I know what's happening between us is temporary.

And yet, despite all that, I'm beginning to fall for a woman who's set to leave for her family's company in just a few months—which, ironically, I'm helping to make a success. Eden's sister Diane is pleasant to work with. With her practical no-nonsense approach, we immediately saw eye to eye when she first called. Hopefully, she won't insist on bringing Eden back earlier than the six months she'd announced. In order to meet the growing demands, Diane will soon need to expand her staff.

Eden seems flustered by my unexpected response. "Are you sure?" she asks, bringing my thoughts back to the topic of visiting Paris with her.

"I'm always sure."

When we get home, Eden puts her finger to her lips and all but tiptoes off the elevator so that Hattie won't hear us and come to the door. For once, I wouldn't have minded a chat with the woman who kept my aunt so happy. But we don't want to wake her. With the moving company due to arrive at her doorstep at 10:00 a.m. the following day, it's evident she has a long day ahead of her. She needs all the rest she can get. Nonetheless, I intend to pay her a visit later on to inquire if she requires any help.

Once our door is closed, however, I can't take it anymore. I do what I have to do—I pull Eden into a kiss. Kissing her has quickly become my favorite thing, my obsession, my need. A delicious moan escapes her, one that makes me fit her closer against me. The way her body molds to mine, how her hand buries itself in my hair, how her mouth automatically opens for me to explore—it drives me absolutely feral, and I want to claim every part of her.

I'm in trouble. I know that and yet, I don't give a damn.

With her face cradled in my hands, I kiss her like I'm dying, like she's all I need, like there's nothing else on this earth that I want more than her.

Because, at this moment, it's the truth.

When I draw back, she slowly opens her eyes. They're cloudy, staring back at me as if in a daze. Before she can speak, I kiss her again, maneuvering us toward the couch, too eager and too lost in the moment. Her back hits the couch cushions, while I cover her body with mine, diving in for more.

I need to feel her lips on mine, feel her trembling with need, my body inside hers, like I need air to breathe.

We probably should talk, should discuss the unspoken things between us that I've been avoiding. But when I draw back to look down at her, and she looks back at me, her eyes shining with excitement, all other thoughts fly out of my head as I begin unbuckling my belt with one hand and leaning down to capture her lips once more.

"Carter?" she moans, spreading her legs under my weight.

"Yes, Eden baby, I've got you."

I press my forehead against hers, caging her with my arms. She clings to me, beautifully, radiating with excitement, warmth, and love.

I thrust into her.

TWO HOURS later

Just when I raise my hand to knock on Hattie's door, it swings open.

"Greetings, there you are!"

"Is there anything I can help you with, Hattie? Lift something heavy?"

She looks at me as though I've just suggested something absurd, like petting her cats.

"Oh, dearie me! No, no. I've just had a call from my new landlord, and it appears that my moving plans for tomorrow have been scuppered, after all that."

I stand there, utterly flabbergasted, bewildered by the revelation.

She continues apologizing profusely, telling me that she doesn't have an exact date, but it's only a matter of time as my mood lifts with every word she says. "I just wanted to find out whether you'd be willing and able to put Eden up for another few days?"

"Absolutely," I assure her immediately, without batting an eye.

"I've already got in touch with the moving company," she continues to update me on the situation, a hint of uncertainty in her voice as if not entirely sure if she's misinterpreted my words, "and I've made the necessary calls to both Lewis and Kate. Oh, and I've contacted the cleaning crew as well."

"Good. Let me know if you need anything else, Hattie. Have a good day."

"Ooh, dearie me!" She beams at me. "You too, love, you too!"

With a victorious stride, I enter my apartment, ready to pop some bubbly.

27

CARTER

Two weeks pass in the blink of an eye.

Eden still lives with me. It looks like the moving gods still aren't on Hattie's side—clearly, they're on mine. Apparently, there have been "even more unexpected delays" at Hattie's new place. I don't ask what exactly has happened to cause the delay—I don't want to tempt fate—and Hattie doesn't bother getting into detail. I'm satisfied by reasoning with myself that it's a common issue in the cutthroat world of the New York City real estate market.

Eden's presence in my place has become a comfortable part of my life without me realizing it. I, for my part, can't wait to see how our shared experiences will unfold. Now that Aunt Eleanor has left, Eden and I are continuing to share a bed and a room. She said it doesn't make sense for her to move everything back to the guest suite only to have to pack it up and move it again when Hattie finally does leave, whenever that is. I'm *one hundred percent* on board with that. Sleeping alone? Not when I could have this beauty curled up beside me. I enjoy having her lying next to me every night. Especially when she drapes herself with that soft hair and skin over my chest and clings on to me like there's no tomorrow.

We haven't discussed where things will go or what we'll be. I'm in uncharted territory. Point is, I don't want to overwhelm her. I know how much her heart has suffered, and that I need to tread carefully. I can't risk hurting her by making a mistake, or driving her away by a bone-headed or worse, overhasty move.

Instead, I need to give us both time to figure out what we want.

While I'm at work, I receive a call from Vance, who provides me with the latest intel on "Eden's case." After concluding the conversation, I begin scrolling through my emails when suddenly my aunt calls me. As soon as I pick up, she says she has some news. I brace myself for the worst, but she quickly reassures me that everything is okay.

"I went to the doctor today, as promised," she announces cheerfully, "and I'm happy to report I'm in excellent spirits...for now, at least, until the lab work reveals its verdict in a few days' time..."

It has been worrying me, and I'm glad to hear her voice. "Let's keep our fingers crossed."

"...the only downside is that the doc told me to put a cork on the bottle."

"Looks like you'll have to find other ways to have fun."

With a sigh and a promise to stay in touch, she declares that she'll do her best to keep her inner wild child in check.

As we hang up the phone, I can't help but feel grateful that she's under medical supervision, appears to be doing well, and taking care of herself—even if it means no more wild nights out on the town—and immediately get up to tell Eden about it. She always loves hearing about my aunt's antics, and this time is no different.

Work goes from busy to insanely busy. We're swamped, I'd even call it hectic. Between planning the details on the first Harbor View project and handling the other clients I've been assigned, it means late nights at the office.

Eden is right there with me the whole time.

Between work and home, we're with each other almost all day every day. She starts to stay later to help keep me organized and, since we're almost always the first ones to arrive and last ones to leave, she drives with me. Sometimes we drive in my car, sometimes we ride on my Ducati, sometimes we take the extra-long tour. I still remember her huge eyes when I surprised her with a pit stop at Ashford Motors to get her her own helmet and jacket.

Because: life isn't all work.

But today has been a particularly rough day. I'm annoyed by a delay in materials that were supposed to be delivered two days prior. Eden has been on the phone for hours with the suppliers, trying to figure out where the hell the shipment is. I'm in my office, putting our backup plan into motion in case she can't straighten things out.

I hear her swear—which she rarely does—and she marches into my office positively fuming. Before I can even get a word out, she hugs me. I'm not expecting it and sort of stand there shell-shocked. I'm not surprised that she touched me, no, I'm used to it by now. I'm surprised by her throwing her arms around me *during work*—she's never done that before. At that specific moment, her in my arms, it doesn't even occur to me that I should say something about touching in the office. All I do is hug her back and kiss the top of her head.

"Sorry," she says, quickly pulling back. "I just... I needed a hug."

Without a second thought, I pull her back in, and rumble, "You don't have to be sorry about that."

I hold her for a few moments before she takes a deep breath.

With the cutest smile, she says, "Thanks, all better," and goes right back to her desk.

It's the only line we ever cross at work and it's so endearing and wholesome that I don't care. My office doesn't have security cameras. One hug won't start rumors.

The sex we save for home. It becomes an unspoken ritual. We'll get to the apartment after a long day, and one of us will shove the other against the wall, or we'll fall into bed, hands eagerly tearing at each other's clothes. The sex we have is dirty, filthy, always thorough, but on occasion, slow, loving, and mesmerizing.

And yes, sometimes we indulge in cupcake sex.

It never ends subtly.

Either way, it's a good way to unwind and makes the days a *hell* of a lot better.

~

LEGACY CONTINUES TO EXPAND, and we're busier than we've been for the last few years since I've been COO. I like my work, and I like what I do. I run a tight ship and have a good relationship with my staff, our clients, and our distributors. Delegating tasks is essential to getting things done. Over the years, things have fallen into place and are running like a well-oiled machine.

And yet, all of a sudden, it's like nothing can go right.

My staff tell me on several occasions that there's a delay of sorts, or our contractors are calling us to ask where shipments and payments are.

Not only that, but rumors also start circulating in the office. Not normal office gossip and nothing about Eden or me. These are old rumors, rumors that have surfaced before, yet always die down. They're the ones Bradley warned me about a few weeks ago, referring to them as "whispers."

The major difference this time is, they're not the good kind, and they're not going away: It's believed that someone at Legacy is talking to Ecclestone Construction, revealing company secrets and making it easy for them to swoop in and take clients right from under our noses. Granger Estates isn't the only account we've lost recently. Two smaller clients have also started to opt out of renewing contracts, and another one is insisting on making changes to current projects.

One Friday morning, Eden knocks on my office door.

Normally, if my double doors are closed and she has something to tell me, she'll either call, send a quick message, or wait until I come out.

I can tell by the look on her face that I'm not about to like our conversation. "What's wrong?"

"Sorry to interrupt. There's something I think you should know. Rumors have been going around..."

I'm immediately annoyed.

"...about Huxley."

I look up. "Do you think there's any basis to it?"

"Well, normally I don't, but I think this time it's different." She closes the door behind her and takes the seat across from my desk. "I've been talking to Gretchen, and Huxley is up to something."

Yeah. No surprises there. Huxley is always up to something. He's been on my radar since I'd first heard about the irregularities. "Any specifics?"

Eden bites her lip as she shakes her head. "Well, she mentioned that he's been very secretive lately. Like, going out to have meetings that aren't scheduled on his calendar or having a lot more phone calls go directly to his line instead of having Gretchen answer them like she normally does."

A few months back, I would've instantly brushed it off. Eden's words give me pause. Huxley is always one to rely on his assistant a little too much. Every little thing he can push onto her, he does. It's a wonder Gretchen has stayed around as long as she has.

"What else do you know?" I ask.

Eden shrugs. "That's it. I haven't seen him in the last few days. But with your meeting coming up later, just...be careful."

"Don't worry. Thanks, Eden."

Eden winks as she stands up. "I've got your back, boss."

"And I've got yours." I pause and throw her a wink back. "Especially when you wear that skirt."

She snort-laughs. "Keep it in your pants, *boss*."

Eden goes back to her desk, and I mull over what she told me. Ever since our meeting with Harbor View, Huxley has been suspiciously absent from my day. Normally, I can't get rid of him. He's always there breathing down my neck, second-guessing every decision I make.

Therefore, him keeping his distance can only spell disaster. He's not one to give up so easily.

Neither am I.

The main problem I have, however, is that everything I've heard sounds sloppy. Huxley is a lot of things. Sloppy isn't one of them. If he's the one talking to our competitors, he wouldn't be so bold as to do it during office hours. Then again, maybe he's that sure of himself and his position in the firm.

Not less than an hour later, I get a phone call to my direct line. When I check the caller ID, I notice the call is coming from the conference room.

"Hello?"

"Hey, Bancroft, it's Bernie. Can you come to the conference room?"

"Sure, I'll be there in a minute."

"Good. And if you could bring your assistant with you, that'd be great."

He hangs up before I can say anything else. What the hell is Bernie doing here? And what the hell does he want me in the conference room for?

With a sinking feeling in my stomach and my defenses up, I leave my office. The second I step into the lobby, Eden looks up from her work. Her eyebrows are knitted together. "Everything okay?"

"Bernie just called. He wants to see us in the conference room."

Her face pales. "Is this a normal thing? Does the CEO often show up and call unannounced meetings?"

I shake my head. "No, he doesn't. I either hear it from him or Bradley that they're coming to New York. Let's go."

Eden nods and stands up. "Maybe it's a good surprise. Of course! They are going to promote you to partner for having landed Harbor View."

I doubt they would give me a promotion, but I don't want to negate her hope.

As we walk out of the office, I can tell she's nervous, despite the smile she gives me. I want to reach out to take her hand, to squeeze it and try to provide some kind of comfort, but all I can do is give her a reassuring look.

BERNIE ISN'T the only one in the conference room. Huxley sits at the table, as well as all the members of the board. Shit. This is bad. Very bad. I can count on one hand the number of times I've seen them all in one room during my career at Legacy.

They never gather like this unless it's pressing.

"Gentlemen," I say.

I sit next to Eden. Her hands are on her lap, fidgeting with nerves. I place my foot against hers to let her know I'm there with her—she doesn't need to worry. I don't know what's going on. However, there's one thing I know for sure: if they try to drag Eden into whatever this is, I won't sit idly by. I'll fight tooth and nail to defend her.

"Thank you for meeting with us on such short notice, Bancroft," Bernie says, avoiding direct eye contact for too long. "And you as well, Ms. Ryan."

"What's this about?" I ask, not wanting to fake pleasantries. I don't like any of this, and I especially don't like the way Huxley is smiling.

Bernie clears his throat and sits up in his seat. "I'm sorry we couldn't be meeting under better circumstances, but there's a serious discussion we need to have."

"Let's hear it," I press, trying my best to not let my impatience show.

"Slow and steady wins the race," Huxley pipes up. "Slow down a bit, Bancroft. No need to be pushy."

I regard him with a mask of indifference, fighting with my patience to deal with whatever bullshit he's about to throw my way. "Maybe I don't enjoy being kept in the dark or being summoned to a 'serious meeting' without any preparation or knowledge of it beforehand."

"Then I guess we'll cut right to the chase." Bernie folds his hands. "We're giving Harbor View to Huxley."

My first instinct is to say nothing. Weeks ago, I would've exploded on them and demanded an explanation. After all, I'd worked my ass off to land that client, by putting most of my time into it and asserting myself against all naysayers. Judging by Bernie's face, this isn't the end of the unwelcome news. This is just preparing for the kill.

"All right, if that's what you feel is best." I lean back in my seat. "I don't see why we had to have a whole meeting about it."

"That's not all we wanted to talk to you about."

I remain silent.

"It has just come to our attention that a handful more of Legacy's top clients have decided to end their contracts with us." He mentions the two smaller clients that I'm already aware of, but then he goes on to name three of our larger and closest clients—Miller, Banks, Parker—who I hadn't anticipated would terminate their association with us in the near future.

"Why?" I ask, this time unable to keep my voice cool.

It doesn't make any sense. As far as I'm aware, those clients are happy with us. I've personally spoken to most of them myself, and they've never given an inkling that they were unsatisfied with the work we're doing. The work *I'm* doing. The ones who have officially left (aside from Granger) are small fish in a big pond, hardly the kind to make a dent in our earnings.

"In a nutshell," Bernie says, "it seems one of our main competitors, Ecclestone Construction, has offered them more for less."

Huxley shakes his head in frustrated agreement, but he doesn't say a word.

"That's it? That doesn't seem like a good enough reason to terminate year-long contracts with a company as trusted as we are."

"It isn't just about the money," Bernie explains, fixing his eyes on mine. "During the last month, several of our clients have had issues at building sites and complained about mismanagement. We've had contractors poached, shipments lost, projects delayed, and that's just to name a few—"

"All of those clients are yours," Huxley jumps in, pointing his finger at me, "and were given to you to oversee. It has become apparent to us that you can no longer handle your position here with the company."

I hear Eden inhale sharply, no doubt ready to say something. The quick glance I give her silences her.

"Gentlemen," I say, keeping my cool. "You know me. You know that if I make a mistake, I'm upfront about it. Projects have snags all the time. None of these outside issues you mentioned were caused by mismanagement, and I don't see how they fall onto my shoulders. Especially since I've spent those same weeks successfully fixing each of those matters. Which, you know, is my job. My team and I have been working around the clock putting out fires left and right."

"Ah, yes, your team," Huxley says, turning his attention to Eden. "Let's talk about your lovely assistant. Or should we call her...your *wife*?"

Eden stiffens, the tension radiating off her in waves. I press my leg against hers, so she remains focused. "Excuse me?"

"Yes." Bernie nods, having the decency to appear uncomfortable. "Saul has brought it to our attention that the two of you are married."

And there it is. The reason why Huxley has been avoiding me.

I'm not going to let them get a rise out of me. "I don't see how that's relevant to this meeting."

"It's a marriage that was arranged to fool a poor old lady battling a severe ailment," Huxley adds. "Which, if I'm honest, is one of the most *despicable* things I've ever heard. And I'm sorry, dear board members, but do we really want to have such a ruthless, corrupt, lying individual on our staff? Let alone on *our board*?"

Huxley looks like the cat that got the canary. The rest of the board members murmur to each other. Huxley's expression is smug, giving me all the reasons to want to punch him in the face. So that's what he's been up to the last couple of weeks.

Someone must have told him that Aunt Eleanor had referred to Eden as my wife, and he had decided to investigate. How he learned of the other stuff—the reasoning behind it being to fool my aunt—I'm not sure. But the one slip-up had been enough for him to decide to dig deeper.

"That's *not* true," Eden speaks up, glaring daggers at Huxley.

I anticipate her response—however, I can't allow her to go through with it. If faced with further questioning, I don't want her to become entangled in a web of deceit. Despite having her sign a non-disclosure agreement, which, I admit, was a dick move on my part, considering that Eden is the epitome of trustworthiness and loyalty, it's time for me to put an end to it.

Under the table, I take her hand, squeeze it. I feel hers stiffen, but only for a short moment before she squeezes back, holding my hand tightly. I'm not hiding how close we've become, not in the least. If circumstances were different, I would have raised our joined hands, shown them that we're a team, but this isn't the time. Huxley would use it against us, against her, and that's not a risk I'm willing to take.

"You're only half-right, Huxley," I say, turning back to the board. "Eden isn't my wife. Yes, she is living with me until her own apartment becomes available, but we're not married. The only reason we never said anything about the living arrangements is because I'm a private person and Eden didn't wish for any special treatment. It hasn't been easy for either of us, but we have maintained the utmost professionalism while in the office."

"Please. You want us to believe you?" Huxley asks, leaning forward. "It's obvious that you're hiding something. If you're not married, did all the rumors just come out of nowhere? Where there's smoke, there's usually fire—and I'm seeing flames on all sides. Wait..." Huxley rises from his seat, "...unless you're *pretending* to be married? To fool a poor old lady? Is that it? That's even worse. It's horrendous! Outright evil!"

"Is that what's going on?" Bernie raises his eyebrows at me. "You're pretending to be married to your assistant?"

"I have," I say without pause, watching everybody's jaw drop.

I sense Eden tensing up beside me.

"Do you have a reason?" Bernie asks.

"As far as the reason goes, since it's not against company rules, I did not *and* do not feel I have to explain myself on why I made the decision to take certain actions."

Huxley raises his arm, still standing, pointing directly at me. "Yet the fact is, you're a two-faced schemer, are you not?"

"Yet again, I will state that I don't see how my private matters have any relevance to this meeting. Yes, I asked Eden to fake being my wife in front of my aunt for the length of her visit. The cause pertains to a private family issue." I take a momentary pause, steadying my tone. "I will only say this much: It was a decision of the heart—one I don't regret and would do again."

It's so silent you can hear a pin drop.

I know I've taken some of the wind out of Huxley's sails. Sitting down, he doesn't seem as smug as he did a moment ago. From the look he gives me, he'd been prepared for me to argue and lie and to tell the board he was wrong so he could present some bullshit evidence and wave it in my face. Even if I had been able to convince everyone else Huxley was mistaken, the damage would've been done anyway.

I glance at Eden. Her eyes are wide, mouth slightly agape. I can see a tear starting to form. When it slides down her cheek, she quickly brushes it away before anybody can notice. I exchange a warm glance with her and gently brush my thumb against hers, eliciting a hidden smile from her in return. I turn back to the rest of the table, still holding her hand.

Looking at the board members, I say, "I'm confident you will make the decision you think is best. If the body of my work up until this point doesn't speak for itself, then I have nothing else to say."

I've given my life to this company. No one is more determined and loyal than I am. I don't have regrets. I don't yell or call Huxley names—funnily enough, the thought never occurs to me. I know my decisions are the right ones. In a way, I'm glad the secret about me and Eden is out, and we can stop hiding our relationship. Her hand is solid in mine, and it's a bond I don't intend to give up.

The board members talk among each other. After a moment, Bernie looks at the others while he shifts uncomfortably in his seat and runs his hand down his face. "While I appreciate your truthfulness, and can understand why you decided to keep all this a secret—"

I know where this is going. No matter what I say, they've made their decision. I can't save my job, but I can save Eden's. I can't make her pay for my involving her in private matters.

"Eden wasn't my assistant when we first met," I argue. "In case there are any questions about the validity of her hiring, you can speak with HR, and they will tell you that I wasn't part of the process. Eden earned this position on her own. The successes we achieved were due to her involvement and dedication," I say, refusing to let her suffer any consequences. "I took her lack of housing to my advantage. It's important to note that she bears no responsibility for any of this."

Out of the corner of my eye, I see her head swivel toward me.

"Regardless," Bernie says, continuing as if I hadn't said anything, "you can see how all of this puts us in a delicate position. Therefore, I'm sorry, Carter, but we are going to have to ask you to step down from your position."

It's not typical of him to address me by my first name. I can sense his inner turmoil, the weight of his regret. "No," I say.

Huxley's eyebrows shoot up and even Bernie looks surprised. "Excuse me?"

"I said, no." Letting go of Eden's hand, I stand and adjust my suit jacket. "If you no longer wish for me to work here, then you can fire me. I'm not going to step down when there's no wrongdoing on my side."

Silence once more.

Even if the mentioned incidents had happened on my watch, landing Harbor View more than makes up for any losses—it triples Legacy's market value and will guarantee upwind for years to come.

I don't break eye contact with Bernie, even though I know Huxley is staring at me, smirking at me.

Bernie sighs deeply, running a hand through his thinning hair. "I'm sorry, Carter. But my hands are tied."

While Bernie is the CEO and thus the top executive with significant authority, the board holds the ultimate decision-making power. That's what has just happened. The board has exercised its authority and overruled the CEO's position.

I nod. Years of work, of giving myself to Legacy has amounted to nothing.

"I understand," I say calmly. "Gentlemen. It was a pleasure working with you." Next, I turn to Eden. "Let me express my gratitude for the assistance you have provided the company and me, Eden."

She wants to get up and come with me, but I signal her to stay. Bernie, too, immediately motions for her to sit back down.

I walk out of the conference room without any regrets.

28

EDEN

The boardroom erupts after Carter leaves. I'm stuck there in shock, trying to process what the hell has just happened. I had been more than prepared to deny everything, to tell them that Carter and I were simply employee and employer. After all, that was what we had said we would do in case we were busted. And yet, Carter had blown me away. He'd not only admitted that we had been fake married, but he'd also said he didn't regret it.

He had stood up for me, and even praised me for everybody to hear.

My heart is racing and my mind is being torn in different directions.

I want to run after Carter, to talk to him about what just happened. He was fired, that much is clear. But what about me? Am I going to be let go? None of the board members have said anything specifically, except for Mr. Bernie who urged me to stay and wait. Do they plan on discussing my fate now? Should I quit? Do I even want to stay?

I look around the room, trying to figure out what the hell I'm supposed to be doing. The board members are now hunched together, discussing with Mr. Bernie and Huxley, not loud enough for me to hear.

When he catches my eye, Mr. Bernie quiets everyone down. "You two are not married?" he asks, probably double-checking on Mr. Huxley's request.

"We're not."

"And your apartment, when will it be available?"

"In a few days." As fate and Hattie will have it, but that's none of Mr. Bernie's business.

He exchanges glances with the board, then turns back to me. "Eden, you may return to your desk. I will meet with you in a few to go over the next steps."

"I'm...not fired?" I have to ask because I can't quite believe what he's saying.

"No, you're not. If you were married to Mr. Bancroft, we would have to reconsider your employment. It seems to me that circumstances led to your involvement in a situation that was beyond your control. You only followed Mr. Bancroft's orders...and since we don't question your ability to carry out your duties effectively without him, and there have been no performance or misconduct issues on your part, you are permitted to remain employed with us."

I desperately want to get out of there. The moment Mr. Bernie dismisses me, I slowly get up from my chair and walk out of the room. Then I book it. I have to catch Carter and talk to him before he leaves. I need to know what he wants to do next.

Also, did he really mean what he had said? That he didn't regret anything? I've never known him to say something he didn't believe in, but I need to know.

Unfortunately, when I get to the office, Carter is nowhere to be found. His office is just like he'd left it.

I grab my phone and fire off a text.

ME:
Where are you?

HIM:
Going home. We'll talk later.

> **ME:**
> Wait for me. I'm coming with you.

> **HIM:**
> No, stay. Don't throw the job away because of me. I'm fine.

The three dots appear, indicating to me that he's writing another message.

I wait. Those are the longest twenty seconds of my life.

> **HIM:**
> You remember our conversation? Always look forward. Maybe this is the kick in the ass I needed.

I briefly close my eyes. As much as I want to believe that Carter will get over the fact that he's just lost the job he'd lived for, it's unlikely. Yes, he's incredible, and I don't put it past him that not even fifteen minutes later, he's able to roll up his sleeves and move on. But even he has to feel that the rug has just been pulled out from under him under absolutely unfair conditions that force him to start from zero again. The way those idiots in the executive suite had treated him makes me unbelievably angry.

I'd bet my last cupcake that by tomorrow he'll have at least five serious job offers, that everything he's done for Legacy up until this moment—and that's a damn lot—will pay off.

That doesn't make things any better.

I sink onto my chair, staring off into space. Now, I've been in several meetings with Carter since I started working here and admire the way he easily navigates speaking with clients and staff. The way he handles himself is another level entirely.

Then, after he'd walked out of the meeting room, he didn't even stop at his office.

He'd just left the building.

What a man.

Of course, now I'm left with a spinning mind and no one to talk to.

That doesn't last long. About two minutes later, Gretchen swings the glass doors open and rushes into the lobby, her blonde hair almost unraveling from its knot, looking concerned, her eyes huge behind her red-framed glasses.

"Hey, what happened?" she asks. "I saw Mr. Bancroft leave a few minutes ago and then you ran out and back. Everything okay?"

"Nope, it's really not." I figure she'll find out sooner rather than later, and wanting her to hear it from me, I say, "Mr. Bancroft's gone."

Gretchen's eyes go even wider. "*What*? They fired him? You've got to be kidding me. Why?"

"It's a long story, and I don't know how much time there is before Mr. Bernie comes, but you remember when Aunt Eleanor called me Carter's wife?"

She nods right away. "Yeah…"

"She wasn't entirely wrong. We were pretending to be married to make her happy."

Concern morphs into shock as Gretchen slams her hands on her face, causing her glasses to nearly slide off her nose. She swiftly pushes them back into place. "Oh. My. God. I have so many questions."

"And I'll answer them as soon as I can. Not right now though. I still have my job, but I'm hanging on by a thread here. I don't want to be caught gossiping when Mr. Bernie comes back."

"Man, if it were me, I'd grab my stuff and go."

"Don't think I didn't want to. I nearly did, but Carter was insistent I stay."

So is Mr. Bernie.

The more I calm down and think about the whole situation, the odder it feels. I'm not entirely certain why Mr. Bernie hadn't let me go, and why he'd made himself strong for me during the meeting, but I know this: I have to use my chance. I want to know who has made it seem as if Carter is at fault for the lost accounts.

I won't tell anybody—including Gretchen—about my plan to investigate the setup. Because that's what this is—a setup. I need to clear Carter's name.

I'd bet my next month's salary that the miserable bastard Huxley is behind it, but...under no circumstances can I be biased. I need solid evidence that will withstand Mr. Bernie's critical gaze, because if he hasn't put Huxley in his place so far, the accusations from Carter's fake wife certainly won't either. No, I have to follow Carter's lead and, with a cool head but iron determination, uncover the essential proof.

Point is, I have to stay at Legacy until I accomplish this task. For whatever reason, I can't shake off the suspicion that Mr. Bernie has allowed me to stay on for this exact reason, despite his inability to make it overtly apparent. Not that I can be certain of that. It's possible that the reason behind his decision is straightforward, such as having sympathy toward me or recognizing that retaining me will benefit the firm. It's no secret that I have a good relationship with our clients, and getting rid of both Carter and me at the same time might have raised too many concerns.

Either way, I'm ready to hold the person who's responsible for this whole mess accountable.

Huxley. Based on everything I know about him so far, he's a despicable individual, but he doesn't have the energy to dig up the things about Carter that he put on the table today. Besides, nobody, and I mean nobody, likes him enough to casually exchange gossip with him.

There's unmistakable evidence of someone within the company aiding him.

The three people who witnessed Auntie's slip about us being married were Gretchen, Lexi, and Jaylin. One of them must have informed Huxley. I doubt that Gretchen has any involvement, but I could be wrong. Heck, I've been wrong and too trusting on many occasions...*cough*—Rob—*cough*.

The million-dollar question is: out of these three women, who is most likely to be a spy for Huxley?

It could be any of them.

I really hope it's not Gretchen, even though some of the evidence

A Bossy Roommate

points to her. She's Huxley's assistant. And I'd told her about my living situation with Carter. My shoulders fall. Oh, no.

Gretchen shakes her head, still in shock. "Okay, but I want to know *all* the details as soon as possible. How about lunch later?"

"Sorry, Gretchen, can't," I inform her, masking the dawning suspicion with a casual shrug. "I really need to get all this work done. I can text you when I have a second."

"Don't use the office messenger though, it's been on the fritz."

"Good to know. Weird. It was working fine yesterday."

"Yeah, not sure what's up. I've already called IT."

"All right, thanks."

"Now get back to work!" Affectionately, she shoots me a grin over her shoulder as she heads for the door.

Despite the intense situation, I attempt a smile. "I'm on it!"

I TRY to take the advice and get back to work. However, it's next to impossible to think of anything other than that meeting. About ten minutes after Gretchen leaves, Mr. Bernie enters the office lobby. I try to keep my cool and act professional. It's difficult to be faced with one of the men who had fired Carter, but again, he'd stood up for me against the board, and without him, I would now be jobless.

"I am sorry you were dragged into this mess, Ms. Ryan."

I immediately get up. "Sir, I need you to know that everything that was said about Mr. Bancroft was done to paint him in a bad light," I say firmly. "I know I've only been here a short time, but he loves this company and has always put work before his own personal feelings or matters. Nothing that's been happening lately is his fault."

"I appreciate what you're saying, but as I said previously, my hands are tied," Mr. Bernie says firmly. "Other information has come to light that wasn't mentioned in the meeting. We had no other choice. We had to let him go."

"What information?" Probably some BS Huxley conjured up out of the blue.

"You don't need to worry about that."

"Yes, I do," I insist. "I'm his assistant, I know his day-to-day better than anyone else. Whatever you think you know, I guarantee is wrong."

I know I'm treading on thin ice, but what else am I supposed to do? I can't sit here and be quiet while Carter's good name is smeared.

"I appreciate your dedication to your former boss," Bernie says, his tone taking on a sharpness that lets me know I've pushed my luck, and he doesn't intend to explain himself any further. "Now, in the interim, Mr. Bradley Everhart is on his way from Connecticut and will be filling in Mr. Bancroft's vacant position until further notice."

That amazes me. Everyone knows Carter and Bradley are close associates. It confirms my suspicion that Mr. Bernie is taking advantage of the opportunity to discredit the allegations against Carter and bring him back.

"In the meantime," he continues, "cancel all of Mr. Bancroft's appointments and tell them you'll be rescheduling at a later date. They don't need to know just yet that Mr. Bancroft was let go. Am I understood?"

I bite my tongue. There are so many words I want to say to him, and if I had any evidence, I absolutely would. Instead, thinking about my self-imposed quest to redeem Carter, I swallow them down and nod. "Understood."

He leaves after that, and all I can do is sit and stare at the computer screen.

Unsurprisingly, I have a challenging time getting much of anything done. I keep checking my phone on the off chance Carter has texted. He does, only to ask what I want for dinner. It's such an innocent question yet speaks volumes. If I were in his shoes, dinner choices would be the last thing on my mind.

MR. EVERHART COMES a few hours later. He walks through the glass double doors, talking to Mr. Bernie. They continue speaking as if I'm not there. "If you find anything out of the ordinary, compile it all, and we will go through it," Mr. Bernie is telling him in a hushed voice.

"Understood."

Mr. Bernie leaves, and Mr. Everhart sighs deeply as he turns to acknowledge me. "We're a team here, and I want us to be on equal footing. No 'sir' or 'Mr. Everhart.' Just Bradley will do," he offers. "Carter and I are friends, and I know about the fake marriage agreement."

"You have to know that Carter is innocent," I blurt without acknowledging anything else he said. "He would never do anything to jeopardize this company."

"Trust me, I know that better than anyone. This is all bullshit—it has to be. The problem is, we need proof."

I sigh with relief. "Thank God you see that. I don't know why the board can't."

"Because you and I know him personally." Bradley shrugs. "We both know how much this place means to him and what he's sacrificed."

"Mr. Huxley has to have something to do with it."

"Of course he does. The thing is, we need evidence."

"What should we do first?"

Bradley looks at his watch. "Start fresh in the morning," he says when he realizes the time. I'm startled to see it as well. My mind had been spinning so fast I'd lost track. "I'm sure you're dying to get home. Tomorrow, you and I will go through all these files one at a time and see what we can find." He points at a bunch of folders of Carter's clients that have decided to not renew their contracts with Legacy Builders.

Feeling relieved that there's some semblance of a plan, I nod with understanding. "Sounds good to me. I'm glad you're taking over the position for now. At least I know I can trust you."

"Likewise," Bradley states firmly. "We're going to figure this out."

THE ELEVATOR DOORS open on our floor and Hattie's door is already ajar. She comes out to meet me. "I have to ask—is everything quite all right? It seems like Carter has returned home early, but he doesn't seem to be in a terribly chatty mood, I'm afraid. And you, love, you've never got home quite so late!"

"Everything's fine." I try to rush her along while still being polite. "How's the move going?"

At that, Hattie winces. "Ah. Actually, I've been meaning to speak to you about that. Bit awkward, I'm afraid... but after careful consideration, I've come to the decision that I won't be moving, after all."

Oh.

Well, *of course* she isn't. Because why would anything go according to plan? I can't even begin to wrap my head around anything. My mind is already consumed with other more important things.

"What happened?" I ask. "You were so excited."

"Oh, my dear, I just thought 'why on earth am I uprooting myself?' The thing is, my feline companions have a distinct aversion to change—and, truth be told, so do I. Relocating to a bigger place just so I can accommodate more cats may have been rather an ill-advised idea, I must admit."

I can understand that. Honestly, I don't fault her for it. "As long as you're happy, Hattie. That's all that matters."

"I do apologize, my dear. I'm completely aware that my decision means you won't be able to have the apartment."

"I'll figure something out. Have a nice evening, Hattie," I say, turning to unlock my door.

"Oh wait, there is another little thing I should probably tell you..."

"Can it wait until later, please? I really need to talk to Carter."

She nods. "Of course, it's probably of little consequence... or so I hope, anyway. It may well be quite trivial, in fact. Well, I must get on with unpacking now. But should you see Eleanor, please do convey my heartfelt thanks. It was her persuasive words that convinced me to stay, you see."

My jaw falls open, but Hattie doesn't give me time to respond. She steps into the apartment and closes the door behind her.

. . .

A Bossy Roommate

I'M MORE than a little distracted going into Carter's place. First Carter was fired—possibly because of me, because I'd entrusted Gretchen with info I shouldn't have—and now the apartment I was supposed to stay in isn't going to be available anymore.

My conversation with Hattie is forgotten when I walk inside.

Carter stands waiting, two glasses of wine in his hands.

"There you are! Welcome home," he says.

The kitchen table is decorated with a large bouquet of vibrant roses and white calla lilies.

My heart skips a beat. Maybe even two. "What's this?"

Carter looks at the table and then back at me. "Well, we have a lot to talk about, and I figured we were overdue for a proper date. The kind with flowers, good food, and not just moonlight as an added perk."

"You didn't have to go to all the trouble. Especially not after what happened today…"

"Yeah, I did. Come, sit down."

My feet carry me to him even while my brain races to process what's going on. The loving way he smiles takes my breath away, and my hand shakes when I reach for the wineglass. "I take it you meant everything you said in the meeting?" I ask, my throat suddenly dry. "That you had no regrets and would do it all over again?"

"You know me by now, Eden. When have I ever said something I didn't mean?"

He's right. I know he wouldn't have said the things he'd said if he didn't absolutely mean them. My question probably came from deep insecurities left over from what Rob did to me, a lingering scar that had started to heal the moment I met the man standing in front of me. Carter is nothing like Rob. I know I can trust him, that what he says is one hundred percent true (except for that one time he told me there were two beds in his room).

"I…don't know what to say."

Carter puts his glass down and holds the chair out for me. "Sit."

I do. Carter takes the chair next to me and lifts his glass, clinks it with mine in a small toast before we take a sip. "There's a lot we need to talk about." He reaches over to take my hand. "Let me get straight to the point."

"You could have denied it!" I blurt out.

Briefly, he finds himself uncertain of my implication. "What do you mean?" he asks.

I know I've interrupted him, but I need to get it out, to come clean. "I would have gone along with you. Because now I think it's my fau—"

"Eden, I don't have any intention of talking about work right now. I just got off the phone with Bradley, and he's keeping me in the loop. There's something else I need to tell you. Something important."

"Uh-oh…what?"

29

CARTER

"I found Rob."

Her shoulders drop. "You what?"

"Well, Vance's PI did. Alexei. He wasn't hard to find. I got the call from Vance earlier."

Thinking about the embarrassment she'd lived through still makes my gut churn. Rob had made the breakup out to be her fault, made her believe that she had tricked him into a marriage that he never wanted, and had dug the knife even deeper by telling her that he never loved her. Truth is, the piece of shit had found out that "he didn't love her" after one of his deals went downhill and bankrupted him. The people within their social circle have rallied behind him, swayed by his influence, and captivated by his crazy little story. Little do they know he was broke and that she had financed his life after he took a severe dive on several investment deals.

He'd lied to save face, the fuckhead. Then robbed her and turned it on her, knowing full well that she lacked evidence and has no social backing for her accusation against him.

She'd not only been left at the altar, brokenhearted, without money, friends and support—but on top of all that, he'd made her out to be the culprit.

Getting cold feet before a marriage was one thing, but he was a piece of shit for leaving her at the altar. As far as the rest goes? Unforgivable.

And *I'm here to make things right*. Eden had entrusted me to do so when she had agreed to place the matter in Vance's capable hands.

If there's one thing I can do to salvage this, I can make sure she knows there's a man who will stand up for her, have her back, no matter what. Who won't use her and drop her like a hot potato after he's fucked her, physically and mentally.

"He will face legal consequences," I declare as she stares at me, wide-eyed. Initially, there's disbelief, but she can clearly read in my expression that I wouldn't joke about any of it. "Vance filed a police report, a defamation lawsuit and a civil lawsuit to recover the stolen funds."

"Carter, I know Rob. He will deny any wrongdoing—"

"Let's just say, he agreed he made a mistake."

"Just like that?"

"Just like that."

"Wait a moment," she interjects. "This PI didn't…"

"—resort to physical violence?" I finish the sentence for her. "No, that wasn't necessary. Someone else had already taken care of that. Alexei found Rob in some third-rate hotel, nursing his wounds, quite literally."

I wouldn't mind giving Rob a black eye (at the very least) myself, but in the end, that scumbag isn't worth us getting our hands dirty.

Eden looks at me, eyes brightening, still processing.

"He also agreed that he will never bother you again," I add, pulling her into a hug.

She tenses up in my embrace. "Why? Carter…tell me, is he severely injured, or *dead*?"

I look at her and kiss her forehead. A smile tugs at my lips. "No, but if he ever tries to come near you or tries to assert any kind of pressure on you or your loved ones, or any other person for that matter, I'll make sure he'll wish he was."

"What about the fees?"

"Vance is going to make a compelling case for an award of attorney's fees. He anticipates the court's recognition of your position and expects a resounding verdict that will decree your ex-fiancé responsible for the entirety of the legal fees and expenses."

Her shoulders ease, and her eyes remain locked with mine. Those sad eyes that she usually hides under a thick wall of optimism. She trusts people, always tries to see the best in them, and despite her disappointment, it hasn't brought her to her knees. It hasn't made her bitter. Just incredibly hurt.

If there's anything I can offer to expedite justice, I can't envision a more worthwhile investment of my time.

She blinks slowly.

And with that one blink, a tiny sparkle appears.

A subtle shift occurs in her eyes.

They almost gleam, reflecting an inner fire.

"If this doesn't earn me the Husband of the Year award," I tease, "nothing else will." I say husband, not "fake husband," and it's not by accident. I'm making a point.

She zips right past it. "Husband of the Year? Carter, this might just earn you a *lifetime* supply of backrubs and an extra slice of *dessert* every night."

She holds onto me tighter.

"We can arrange that. Now to the second, equally important point on the agenda."

"Uh-oh...what?"

"I want you to stay right here, with me."

She blinks again, letting go of me, leaning back. "What do you mean?"

30

EDEN

"Come here. I heard a certain older lady isn't moving after all," he answers, pulling me back. "Which is why I've been on the phone with Vance, twice today. He's speaking to the landlord and will draw up a new lease agreement with your name on it. That way, no matter what happens, you always have a home."

My mouth falls open in shock. I can't even properly process what he said. Mostly, I can't wrap my head around the fact that he was fired a few hours earlier, and instead of looking for a new job or fighting back, he busied himself with the whole "Rob business," and on top of all that, he's prepared a romantic date and told his lawyer to add me to his lease.

"You'd do that for me?" I ask.

"It's already done. We'll sign the papers tomorrow."

I can't contain myself anymore. Throwing my arms around his neck, I kiss him with as much passion and vigor as I can manage. Yes, the satisfaction of finally being able to put Rob to rest makes me want to scream in joy, and yes, the fact that I will always have a roof over my head is a tremendous help, but it's Carter's affection that has me smiling like a crazy person, even while I try to kiss those gorgeous lips off his face.

Carter stands, bringing me with him. I wrap my legs around his waist, trailing my lips down to his neck, which I playfully nip and suck. If he thinks I'm not going to leave hickeys now that we don't have to hide anything, he has another thing coming.

"Here's what's going to happen," he grumbles into my ear as he carries me. "I'm going to show you—despite today's outside interferences—who's still boss, and always will be, all over the apartment, in every room, all weekend long, starting in the bedroom. Any objections?"

"No." I laugh. "None."

"That's a good fucking girl."

In his bedroom—*our* bedroom—he lays me on the bed.

I need him, need to feel his solid chest against mine, need to remind myself that this is really happening.

I'm actually getting my happy ending.

Carter sits back, clearly enjoying my eyes on him, his black T-shirt straining against his muscular chest. I swear he wears those shirts on purpose because he knows what they do to me.

Slowly and with one hand, he pulls the shirt off from behind his neck, and before he even has a chance to toss it to the side, I run my hands up that chiseled torso, feeling his primal energy, sensing the hawk's intensity, and grabbing his broad shoulders so I can pull him back down into another kiss.

His deft fingers undo the buttons of my blouse, not even bothering to take it off before folding it open and reaching in for my bra-covered breasts. I moan into his touch, arching my back to bring myself as close to him as I can.

Everything this man does sets my body on fire. His touch does things to me I never dreamed possible. I had known love before, at least I thought I had. But everything with Carter is different. He's different. Not only in comparison to the other men I've been with, but to the version of him I'd met not too long ago.

Even tonight, something has changed. There's a shift between us, and I know exactly what it is.

We're all in.

Both of us are committing to this relationship, to each other. Tonight, we're not two people seeking a comforting touch and a few hours of pleasure.

We're Carter and Eden, officially living together—and becoming more than just a fake couple that accidentally share an apartment.

Regardless of our status, honesty and communication are the foundation of any relationship, particularly in its early stages. I know I need to inform Carter about Gretchen and my inappropriate disclosure of certain information to her.

"Take off your clothes, baby," he growls into my ear, and I shudder at the rub down he gives me, grazing the shell of my ear with his jaw.

With that and the deep, leathery musk that invades my nose, I forget all of my good intentions.

Somewhere very, very deep inside of me, a voice assures me that I can tell him everything later, after all, there's really no point—absolutely zero—in raining on the parade of a perfect moment with a half-baked hypothesis.

So, without a care in the world, I shrug out of my blouse, desperate to feel Carter's bare skin against mine. Kissing me, and giving me more of that sexy stubble, he reaches around to undo my bra. Once the fabric is impatiently discarded by me and tossed somewhere across the room, two strong hands cup my naked breasts.

"So fucking beautiful. You have gorgeous breasts, I noticed the first time I saw you," he snarls against my lips, giving them a squeeze. "Perfect size and shape."

My nipples pucker and ache under his touch.

"Perfect for my hands," he growls, his voice dripping with satisfaction.

I release a little whimper, and my hips buck involuntarily against his growing bulge.

I kiss my way to his neck, and I feel him shudder as my lips brush the sensitive spot just below his ear. I wrap my lips around it and suck greedily, and I'm so caught up that when he plucks my nipples and pinches them lightly between his fingers, I break off to moan in sudden pleasure.

"And perfect for my mouth."

He leans his head down, and my hands are in his hair as his tongue licks around my nipple. Every nerve starts tingling with happiness. A prickle awakens between my legs when his tongue circles once more and then softly, almost accidentally, brushes over my nipple. Slowly, he begins to suck it in, sending tingles of pleasure through my body. After he releases the swollen bud, he blows air across it, watching it harden.

My hands fall to his shoulders, gripping hard when he flicks my other nipple with his tongue and then sucks on it rougher, almost biting me.

I moan in pain and pleasure, as my breathing grows even heavier.

"You getting wet for me, baby?"

He continues sucking and teasing, causing more shots of intense pleasure to race through my body and straight to my already-soaked clit.

"I want to see that sweet pussy slick and pulsing," he growls, "and your little clit throbbing for me. I've been thinking about your gorgeous tits all day long. And about your pussy. How exactly I'm going to fuck you so good."

My breath hitches. "So that's...what a COO does all day?"

"If you ask me, that's time well spent," he remarks with conviction. With a final kiss on each peaked nipple, he moves back up, pulls me back close against him, my nipples pressing into his chest, and the outline of his cock pulsing against my center.

My hands fumble with the button of his pants, finally able to open it and pull his zipper down. I need to touch his dick, to make him feel as good as he's making me feel.

With a nod, he pulls away, this time to push his jeans and boxer briefs down over his hips, freeing his cock. He's hard. Thick. Angry. I wrap my hand around his length, still thrilled by the size in my palm.

I stroke and squeeze, swallowing the swears he spouts.

With a groan, he tugs my skirt down. "This needs to go. Now."

I lift my hips to assist, and when it—and my wet panties—are gone, there's nothing left between us.

No barriers.

Except for one maybe: my conscience.

"I can't wait to lick you clean, baby," he growls, interrupting my thoughts.

He doesn't lick, or eat my pussy, he *devours* it. There's no other way to describe it. By the time he's done destroying my clit, I'm a breathing, panting mess, begging him to do everything and anything he wants with me.

I'm crazy for him, ready and willing.

We kiss when he pushes in. He steals my breath as I gasp, his hand cupping my cheek while his hips start moving back and forth, taking me slowly at first. "God, you're gorgeous. You're perfection, baby."

My body is more alive than it has ever been.

"Carter...I have something to tell you," I blurt.

I need to tell him.

He looks up without stopping his thrusting motions, continuing to fuck me. When I don't say anything, he raises his eyebrows, softly rumbling, "What, baby?" He keeps thrusting without breaking his rhythm, or waiting for my answer.

I know at once that no matter how many times we do this, it will never be enough.

I'm always going to want him.

"Nothing," I whisper.

And as we make love that night, as we lose ourselves in each other's arms, I know I'm where I'm supposed to be. In his arms. Under his body. Owned by him. Loved by him. Every experience, every triumph and setback, every twist and turn filling chapters and chapters has ultimately led me to this page, where destiny has united me and him. Carter.

He pulls me up into a tight embrace. His hand cradles my head, gathering my hair into a circle around his wrist, and then he tugs my hair backward, causing my mouth to open and my head to tilt backward.

"You're mine, all mine."

He thrusts in.

～

Even with the unknown hanging over Carter's professional life, I try to relax. By Monday morning I've convinced myself that it's not Gretchen. I tell myself that I'm not *that* bad a judge of character, and I honestly believe it.

Despite wishing for more time to spend with Carter, I'm excited to hit the ground running when my alarm goes off.

I know whatever comes next, we can handle it, together.

But the sooner Bradley and I clear Carter's name, the better I'll feel.

"Any plans for today?" I ask Carter as I'm getting ready for work.

"Yes, I have a meeting with a friend who wants some investment advice."

"I've gotta say, babe, you're handling this firing way better than I would," I tell him, picking up my coffee mug. "Aren't you mad?" I've heard him on the phone with Vance once or twice, seeking advice and discussing potential courses of action. Ultimately, it all comes down to one crucial requirement: tangible evidence.

"I'm mad as fuck. My blood is boiling. In fact, I want to strangle the damn bastard who's responsible for this. Huxley, that miserable conspirator. But there are more important tasks demanding my attention right now. I see the potential for a new beginning."

I swallow the lump in my throat.

"That's a great way to see things," I say, making an effort to convey a supportive tone, but feeling terrible. His words align perfectly with his beliefs, about the significance of progressing and concentrating on goals rather than holding on to harmful influences.

"Maybe it's because of you," he adds, putting the tablet down and reaching under the table to lay his hand on my knee. "Maybe I'm feeling good because you're staying with me."

I had informed him of my plan to clear his name. He'd told me not to. He'd told me a number of times that I shouldn't do that for him because it was risky and could cost me my job—a job I'd been more than just excited about. But it matters to me. *He* matters to me. They're wrong, and I'm determined to prove it.

"It's not fair." I take a drink of my coffee. "I'm a positive person, at least I try to be, but this is some bullshit, and I won't stand for it."

He leans down and kisses the top of my head, then my lips. "All right, I have to head out. Don't work too hard."

By the look in his eyes, I can tell that he's proud of me for sticking up for him (if only he knew)—but I can sense that he holds doubt regarding my chances of uncovering evidence of his sabotage.

"Okay, babe," I say, "have a good day."

"I'll call you on your lunch break."

I watch him leave, thinking what a change a little over a month could make. When we first met, we both were so adamant about pretending our first night hadn't happened. Now, we're living together like we've known each other our whole lives. I waited years to find a loving man like this, and he had fallen into my lap when I least expected it.

I take a couple of bites of my breakfast, but it doesn't settle right. Ever since Carter was fired, food hasn't been even remotely appealing.

I finish getting ready for work early and head out not too long after Carter leaves.

BRADLEY and I are full steam ahead in our investigation. However, by the time Wednesday rolls around, I'm thoroughly exhausted. Bradley and I weren't able to find any glaring issues with the client files at our first go around, and even though what we're doing has priority, actual work obligations demand our attention. There's no set date for when they'll find a permanent replacement for Carter, and between his work in NYC and the duties he as COO still has in Connecticut, Bradley is all over the place.

Gretchen has been subtly trying to help me and Bradley—which I'm taking as a good sign that she isn't part of Huxley's deceitful machinations. Yet I can't dismiss the possibility that she simply wants to remain in the loop to provide updates to her boss.

Taking a deep breath, I square my shoulders and set about going through my daily routine. I check emails and phone messages, update Bradley's calendar, and make sure new client files are ready for him to review. Once all that is said and done, I pull up the "CDB" folder I created to store the information we've gathered so far.

It's not much. A lot of it is reimbursement receipts for town cars and dinner meetings that Huxley had charged to the company account. Gretchen is going to dig into Huxley's calendar for the last month, and together we're going to cross-reference them with the days his calendar was empty. If he had taken meetings yet didn't have them on the books, it definitely will be suspicious.

A little while later, Bradley comes in. He looks as tired and unhappy as I feel. "Morning, Eden."

"Morning, Bradley. I have those files you wanted to go over."

"Thanks. Have you heard anything from IT about the messaging system?"

"Not today."

Our internal office messaging system hasn't been working for days. IT is trying to solve the issue, yet it seems that every time they think they have figured it out, it goes down again. Which makes things more than a little annoying.

Bradley sighs. "Ridiculous. We've never had a problem with it before, I don't know what the hell is going on."

Something clicks, and I look up from the computer. "Wait a minute. It's been down since that day—the day Carter was sacked. That cannot be a coincidence, could it?"

"What do you mean?"

"I mean, what are the chances that the *day* Carter is set to be handed the pink slip our trusty messaging system suddenly stops working. And now every time our highly capable and intelligent IT department fixes it, it goes down again? You just said it yourself: We haven't had this problem before."

Bradley's eyes go wide. "Call the head of IT and tell him I need to pay him a visit ASAP. Today. I don't know why I didn't think of that before."

"Neither of us did. We've been too damn busy."

He steps into his office while I reach for the phone. I've called IT so many times already that I know the number by heart. Once I arrange the meeting, I jump back into my investigation. I can't let Carter down.

When the end of the workday arrives, I decide to take my leave, too exhausted to wait for Bradley's return and the outcome of the potentially lengthy IT meeting. Since I haven't received any updates, I guess the outcome was insignificant, and Bradley had gone home afterward.

ONCE I GET HOME, I'm ready to immediately kick off my shoes and collapse onto the couch. Carter won't be home yet. I recall him mentioning a late interview.

"Good evening, love," Hattie says with that cheerful smile of hers when I step off the elevator. There must be a strange look on my face because her smile falters. "Are you feeling all right, dear? You're rather pale, if you don't mind me saying."

"I'm fine, thank you," I assure her. "Just feeling a little under the weather."

"You mentioned that the other day, as well, didn't you?"

"It's just exhaustion, it'll pass." There's no point in trying to explain to Hattie how my possible guilt over Carter's firing is draining me.

Hattie doesn't look convinced—however, she's learned by now that it's hard to argue with me when I've already made up my mind. I turn to unlock my door.

"Hang on just a moment, dear. Do you remember that I had something to tell you other day? Perhaps it does turn out to be significant after all. It's about a woman who was here not too long ago."

My heart in my throat, I turn back to her. "What woman?"

"Well, my dear, a couple of weeks ago, a woman turned up here. She arrived around noon, appearing somewhat perturbed when I answered the door. She claimed to have lost her way, and we had a bit of a friendly chat. She inquired about my neighbors, to which I replied that you and your husband reside here—to which she seemed a bit puzzled. Tell me, did I act correctly in divulging your marital status? I presume that is the image you wished to project to Eleanor and all others, is it not?"

Oh, no.

"What did the woman look like? Was she blonde with glasses? A couple of years older than me?"

"Ah, yes, that's the one, my dear! That describes her exactly. A very elegant and amiable lady, I thought. Do you know who she might be, love?"

Gretchen.

Oh, no.

Even though Lexi has glasses too, both she and Jaylin have dark hair.

"Somebody from work," I say, feeling sick to my stomach. "I've got to go. I'll see you later, Hattie."

"Goodbye, love."

Once inside the apartment, I collapse onto the couch—face down.

After ten minutes of hell, I drag myself to our bedroom. Along the way, I shed all my clothes, not caring about leaving them on the floor. My body feels like lead. I climb into bed in my nightgown, rolling myself into the comforter like a burrito.

However, as tired as I am, my brain has a tough time quieting down.

It's my fault that Carter got fired.

I trusted Gretchen and told her we're living in the same apartment, just next door to each other—basically a thin wall and an eyebrow raise away from "living together." My story must have sounded so fishy she figured we were practically sharing a bed. She'd come to check. She'd informed Huxley. Huxley had had Carter fired. Once again, I'd made an error in judging someone's character. And this time, it's Carter who paid the price.

I feel dizzy.

What am I going to do?

I drag myself to the balcony to get some fresh air.

What will he do once he finds out? How angry will he be? Will he somehow think I did it on purpose? Kick me out?

I want to strangle the damn bastard who's responsible for this. Those were his words.

And that damn bastard is...me. I'm responsible. I'm the one who lit the fuse. I'm the one who plunged the knife. I'm the one who pulled the trigger. Yeah, it was Huxley who seized the opportunity, but ultimately, I had placed my trust in the wrong person. Again.

Wild thoughts spin over and over in my mind as I sit there on the balcony floor, wondering what I'm going to do.

I'm the one who destroyed the future he had tirelessly worked toward for numerous years, dedicating endless nights, winning strenuous battles, and proving himself to those who doubted him.

The irony is, he had fought for me there in the boardroom. He had abandoned his dream job, ensuring I would keep mine, so that *my* dream of working in New York City would continue.

Nobody has ever fought for me like he had. He even fought for me when it came to Rob.

And what did I do?

I'm the reason why he can't live his dream.

He even warned me about the gossip.

I didn't listen.

Certainly, Carter will no longer want me to stay with him after he finds out I've turned his life into a shattered mess.

There's no point in me staying.

I start to pack.

31

CARTER

If someone had told me six months ago that I would be let go from Legacy, I would've thought they were insane.

One meeting has turned my life completely upside down. I'm jobless for the first time since I was a kid and, honestly? I don't hate it. Not one bit. While it sucks that I wasn't made partner and that all that work I'd put into Legacy hasn't amounted to what I'd hoped it would, I feel genuinely excited for what's to come. I'm embarking on a new adventure, a new phase of my life—and I can't wait to see where it leads.

And I know why.

It's Eden. She's made all the difference. She'd strutted into my life with those green eyes and those laughing lips, kicking the door of my heart down with her cheerful personality and breathtaking beauty. She brought with her that infinite ray of sunshine and kindness she carries around and has made me see things in a new light. I have something, *someone,* in my life who loves and cares about me.

What my aunt said now makes sense. To have someone like that, someone to be there for you through thick and thin is life changing.

But as happy as I am that she's staying, I'm also concerned.

I've noticed that on top of being exhausted, she hasn't been saying much unless I strike up a conversation first. Even then it's quick, usually one-word answers. Clearly, something is bothering her. She's always upbeat and positive—to see her quiet and withdrawn makes my concern jump to outright worry.

Worst of all, I've seen some of the sadness return to her eyes. Even the morning's humming through the apartment and singing in the shower has stopped. Funny enough, it's something I find myself missing. And I'd given her so much shit about it. Is she having second thoughts? About me? About us?

Or is work getting to her?

While I appreciate her work ethic, I know how thoughtless the company can be in that regard, and I don't want her to hurt herself trying to please them. She's been working too hard. Everyone needs a break from time to time, and she's no exception. I gave years to that place, and they wrote me off without a care. I don't want the same thing to happen to Eden.

Ever since word has spread that I've left Legacy, my phone hasn't stopped ringing. I'm receiving job offers left and right.

Several construction giants have reached out to me and shown interest in having me on their staff. I've agreed to meet with two. Thorne Architects. Humphries Properties. The work seems interesting on paper, but I need to learn more. After all the time and work I put into Legacy, I'm not about to take the first job that falls into my lap. I know my skills and my worth, and I'm determined to only accept opportunities that align with my capabilities.

I haven't talked with Eden about it yet, but there's another reason why I've been declining most of the other interviews. I've given my career a lot of thought, and I've realized that in any new place I join, any job I take will require starting over in some capacity. After everything I've been through, I honestly don't *want* to start over. I want more.

But I take the interviews to keep my options open. I don't want to decide without exploring what's out there.

By the end of the first meeting, my brain is elsewhere. While the company has their ducks in a row and I see a lot of potential, the prospect doesn't sound even remotely challenging. The company wants me to manage their sales team, and also implement the same strategies and changes I had put into practice at Legacy. True, they pay a lot and there are many perks. But for what? To redo what I've already accomplished? No, thanks.

The main thing I loved about my job at Legacy was providing my expertise in the construction field, and making solid decisions based on my knowledge. Being fired hasn't taken any of that away. Former clients and friends are texting and emailing me asking for that advice. What if I start my own company? Clearly there's a market for it. Then I could focus on what I want to focus on instead of what some board dictates.

The idea is in its infancy, and I can't wait to present it to Eden. It's funny. Not too long ago, I wouldn't have thought twice about deciding what to do. I have the space, the time, and the money. I could start my own company. But I don't have just myself to worry about anymore. I have Eden. She's my partner. My decisions affect her just as much as they affect me. I find myself wanting to share it with her, wanting to get her opinion and thoughts because I value what she has to say.

I love her. I love her more than I have ever loved anyone.

And I want the best for her. If she decides to give us a chance, I'm going to make sure she never wants for anything for the rest of her life.

She's a girl I know I could steal horses with.

Through thick and thin.

I need to show her how serious I am about her, about us.

I want to avoid any possibility of doubts or hesitation on her part that could jeopardize our relationship, particularly considering the numerous uncertainties she's faced in her past.

She had been dumped at the altar, her dream shattered, and shortly thereafter, I'd asked her to fake marry me.

It's up to me to make things right.

After the second interview, I hop on my motorcycle and pull out my phone to call Eden. I want to say hi. Hear her voice. Tell her that the interview took longer than expected—even though I left as quickly as possible without appearing impolite—and that I'm on my way. She doesn't pick up. She's probably chatting with Hattie.

Before I can text her, I get a message from Bradley.

All it says is:

> Call me.

Shit. That doesn't sound good. I hit dial, and it only rings once before it goes to voice mail. I leave him a message saying that I can't reach him.

I kick down.

Everything is still up in the air. Eden is the one thing I have to "nail down," and *not* in the bedroom. I want—no, need her with me, always. While the future is unclear, one thing is evident: She has to be an integral part of it. The rest will unfold in due time. First, I have to stop by the jewelry store. Next, I need to visit our local bakery.

Time to celebrate.

WHEN I GET HOME, cupcake box in hand, Hattie pokes her head out and tries to greet me. I hurry past her, glad that I don't have the time to stop. I'm not a monster—I'm busy, knee-deep in things to tackle. I need to talk with Eden. I need to ask her something important. Putting everything else out of my mind, I unlock the door and head inside.

In the apartment, everything is quiet.

"Eden?"

Something seems off. Without taking off my boots or anything else, I march straight to our bedroom, hoping she's maybe gone to bed.

She's not in bed.

She's not in the bathroom either, or on the balcony. She's not in the laundry room.

I rush to the gym. It's empty. When she first moved in, I'd given her an earful on how it was off-limits during my sessions, how it would throw off my entire routine. Just this morning, I thought how I yearn for nothing more than to have her by my side, and not just in our gym or singing loudly in the shower, but everywhere we go, accompanying me throughout all my endeavors, extending to every aspect of our lives.

She's not in the guest suite either. "Eden, baby girl, where are you?"

I rush back to our bedroom.

That's when I finally notice. All her stuff is gone. Her clothes, her shoes, all her bags.

She's left.

What. The. Fuck.

She ran away?

She ran away *from me*?

Here I was, thinking we were fucking happy, and she's run off? What the hell has happened?

Rushing around like a madman, cupcake box in one hand, fishing for my phone with the other, I check every single room of the apartment. I dial her number, but she doesn't pick up.

Blood rushes in my ears as I try to comprehend, make sense of the situation.

What had happened in my absence to make her flee without saying a word?

Has she seriously made up her mind about us?

I shouldn't have waited to tell her how I feel—instead, I should have made sure there was no fucking doubt in her mind that she was my woman. My heart lodges in my throat, and I instinctively straighten up.

I rush out and knock at Hattie's door.

"Where's Eden?" I ask, noticing her lingering just beyond the cracked door, but it swings wide immediately.

"She left about twenty minutes ago. With all her belongings in tow, by the looks of things."

"Did she tell you where she was going?"

"I'm afraid she didn't, love. She seemed pretty upset. It's quite possible she has returned home to her sister's, I presume? Gosh, what's happ—"

I'm already running down the stairs, realizing that the damn parcel from the bakery is still in my hands. What the *fuck*, Eden?

Her car is gone.

I storm to my bike. Before hopping on, I stuff the cupcake box in the saddlebag. I kick down. Damn cupcakes. If I hadn't made a detour to get them, I wouldn't have missed her.

I haul ass.

Has she really fucking gone back to Maine?

It's cloudy, and as if to mock me, it starts raining. Heavily. Thick drops of rain are soaking through my jacket and jeans as I race at full throttle.

I'm facing a long and arduous drive, made even more challenging by the fucking rain.

After covering numerous miles, I drive past the motel we'd stayed at when we'd first met. My gut churns at the memory.

I waste no time thinking back, my focus returning to spotting a small blue car on the road ahead of me.

Maine: 451 miles.

A part of me knows how foolish it is to search for a blue car in a metropolis like New York, but the thought of never seeing Eden again makes me lose all sense of reason. I have to make her understand that she and I belong together.

With the onset of night, the task grows steadily harder.

32

EDEN

I have to stop because it starts raining too heavily.

Kiki's yet-to-be-fixed windshield wipers are like, "Nope, not today!" When it gets worse, I stop at the first motel I come to. It's *our* motel. The one Carter and I had made love in the day we met. It's late, and I know I can't drive through the night to Maine, let alone a rainy one.

Sure, there are a few other motels around, but I'm familiar with this one, so it makes it a no-brainer for me to pull into their parking space. But if I'm perfectly honest with myself, not only is it the familiarity, it's also the need to catch my breath, the *necessity* to stop.

Truth is, driving back to Maine is the last thing I want to do.

Tears stain my cheeks, and more fill my eyes.

Here I am, looking at the motel bed.

Our motel bed.

The memory of his eyes, how he'd looked at me, makes my heart ache. Bittersweet, the scene plays vividly in my mind. His gaze had been fixed upon me with such intensity. The emotions overwhelmed me as I remembered the warmth of his embrace on that bed, how tightly he'd held me, pressed closely against his body, providing warmth and relieving my pain.

I can almost feel his embrace. I can almost feel his presence. A man of unwavering determination, who doesn't give up until the last card has been played.

"It was a decision of the heart, one I don't regret and would do again," he'd said at that last meeting. Those were his exact words.

More tears roll down my cheeks.

I should have waited until he'd returned before I left, but in my haste, in my panic, I'd packed my things. Now I wonder how I could have been so stupid. I didn't even leave him a message explaining my reasons. If he finds I'm gone and all my belongings with me, he'll assume the worst.

I ran.

I'll never run again.

I remind myself that it's never too late to do the right thing.

Wiping my face and mascara spiders, I grab my phone and dial his number. He doesn't pick up. I try again, with no luck. In my "Recents," I find that he tried to reach me earlier once.

It will be hard to face him, the hardest thing I'll ever do, but I need to tell him how sorry I am for my actions that have drastically altered his future.

How do you even confess to someone that you obliterated their dreams? Is there a roadmap for that?

There are no words to rebuild what I've broken.

While I know it won't alter the outcome, my confession will provide us with the closure we both need.

I'll miss his unwavering determination, his emotional intelligence, the meaningful glances we exchanged, and his unique humor he reserved solely for me.

Quickly, I grab my bags.

I have to return to him at once, try to explain.

I should never have just left—not without talking to him first.

I reach for the door to open it, already firing up the Uber app. I'm startled by the huge, tall shadow standing in front of me.

Stumbling back, I drop all of my bags.

A face with dripping wet hair stares down at me.

Carter.

Through the heavy rain, I hadn't heard his footsteps. I hadn't heard anything.

"Eden, baby, what the fuck?"

Worry is written all over his face. I don't know how he found me, and even when he asks me, I can't get the words out. Not at first.

"Baby?"

"How did you...?"

"Find you? I made a fucking U-turn. I had an inkling, and then I saw your car." The concern in his eyes, the way he reaches for my hand, doesn't help. I inch back. "Were you running away?"

"No. I promise it's not what it looks like," I say as I step farther back. "I wasn't running away. I mean, at first, I was, but just now, I decided I was coming back. I panicked. I didn't know what to do."

"Panicked, why?" He steps into the room and closes the door, his jacket dripping. "Why did you panic, what's going on?" He runs a hand through his wet hair.

"You're wet...let me grab you a towel."

"No. First, tell me what's going on."

The hem of my shirt is in my hands, and I keep twisting and untwisting it. My teeth dig into my bottom lip. "You're going to want to strangle me," I say in a soft voice.

He reaches out to take my hand, but I pull it away. "Eden, why would I do that?"

I avert my gaze, unable to look him in the eye anymore. "It's..." My voice breaks, and I trail off.

"Eden, baby, whatever it is, we'll handle it together."

"You say that now..."

"Hey," he says in a sharp voice. "Come on, sit down. Over here on the bed. You know you can tell me anything."

He takes off his wet jacket, and sits next to me on the corner of the motel bed. The frame lets out a subtle squeak under the added weight. I take a deep, shaking breath and finally lift my gaze to meet his.

I open my mouth, and no noise comes out.

Carter's expression softens. "I never want you to be afraid to tell me anything. Baby, if it isn't clear by now, let me spell it out for you: I'm serious about you, about us. I don't see us just as boyfriend and girlfriend, I see you as my wife. Not a fake one. A real one. In the course of all this craziness, you've captured my heart. I don't want to lose that."

My breath catches in my throat.

What?

I blink. Twice.

"That's why you left, isn't it? Because you thought I was stepping away from what we had? That I didn't want to hold onto you, just like your ex-fiancé didn't? That I wouldn't sense how awful it might feel for both of us to lose what we've become—even if it had been planned? No. Let's give this marriage a proper shot. Stay with me, Eden, forever."

My eyes sting with tears, and I try to hold them at bay. This is all so overwhelming. It's all too good to be true. I can't speak at first. I sit there, staring into his expectant eyes, at a loss for words.

Isn't this what I've always wanted? To be a wife? To have a man love me so much he wants to spend the rest of his life with me?

I shake my head. "I can't..."

"I'm headstrong. I don't know if you noticed, but once I make up my mind about something, I stick to it. I won't accept a no. I want to be the man who gives you a world of dreams, who fixes what was done to you, who deserves your trust, who makes all of this right. Having said that"—he gets down on his knee in front of me, and I gasp—"I figured you'd respond more to action than words."

"Wait..."

Not listening, he reaches into his pocket and my heart stops when he pulls out a small, gray satin box. The way he smiles at me makes my heart melt.

When he opens it, I about fall off the bed.

The most beautiful diamond ring sits on a small pillow. It glistens with a unique, asymmetrical cut, casting fractured rainbows in the dim motel room light.

"*Carter...*" is all I can say.

"Do you want to be my wife, baby?"

I shake my head, tears falling. "I'm sorry, so sorry, Carter, but I can't. You're not going to want to marry me. You're going to hate me..."

"I would never hate you."

"Uh-huh..." More tears stain my face.

"It's all right, it's going to be okay. Take a deep breath. Please, baby, don't cry." He gets back up and sits next to me. "Now relax and tell me what happened."

When I manage to speak, my voice is barely above a whisper. "It's me who got you fired." Tears start to fall again, and my breathing picks up. God, why is it suddenly so hard to breathe? It's like something was squeezing the air out of my lungs.

He narrows his eyes at me. "How?"

Ring-ring.

Carter grabs his phone and quickly pushes the incoming call away. "Sorry, baby. Go on."

"I told Gretchen about us living together and she showed up in the apartment and then she talked to Hattie, and then she told Huxley, and Hattie just told me...and it's all my fau—"

"Hey, hey, whoa," Carter says, sliding his arm around me. "Stop. It doesn't matter, baby."

"Yes, it does, Carter, it—"

"Not to me."

Ring-ring.

"Goddammit." Carter grabs his phone. "It's Bradley again."

"You should take it," I say just when he's about to turn off his phone. "It seems important. I'll go grab a towel for you, and freshen up a little."

33

CARTER

"What's up, Bradley?"

"Who's your best friend in the entire world?" Bradley greets me as I'm drying off my face with the towel Eden handed me before disappearing behind the bathroom door. The sound of running water fills the space behind it.

Bradley sounds cheerful, which instantly puts me at ease. "Probably Eden," I answer to get a rise out of him.

"Ouch, dude. That hurts."

"It's nothing personal."

"I get it, I get it. You've seen her in ways the rest of us can only dream about, you lucky devil. Fair enough. But seriously, you're going to be kissing the ground I walk on."

"Cut to the chase, I don't have much time." Only Bradley has the perfect timing to call right in the middle of my proposal, and he's the only person who could get away with it. But this doesn't mean we have to drag things along.

"I caught him. I caught Huxley."

My heart jumps into my throat and I straighten, letting the towel drop. "You did? How?"

"The new internal messaging system. Actually, your *wifey* was the one who pointed out how weird it was that the system went down right when you got fired. So I met with IT late this afternoon, and we did some quiet digging. Guess what? Huxley bribed one of the IT interns to manipulate the system, causing all the disruptions, likely as a means to obscure his tracks. There's still tons I have to read through, but so far, we've uncovered a slew of deleted messages between Huxley and Gwen, telling her to hold back calls or sabotage orders."

"Gwen, the front desk manager?"

"Yeah. Gretchen and I went through his calendar and cross-referenced with some expense reports, and let's just say, Huxley has a lot of explaining to do."

I can't believe it.

Eden, Bradley, and Gretchen risked their jobs and reputations to prove my innocence—and they succeeded. They didn't have to do that, I definitely didn't expect them to. I'd even told Eden not to. And yet, they did.

That new messaging system had never quite clicked with me. My gut had been screaming at me back then, but I'd foolishly brushed it off. Hindsight is twenty-twenty, and now I realize I should've trusted my instincts from the get-go. Lesson learned, the hard way.

"Did you talk to Gwen?" I ask him.

"Sure did. Gretchen and I intercepted her just after work. She started shaking like a leaf and admitted to everything. Told me that Huxley had ordered her to keep an eye on you. Offered her big bonuses for any dirt she could dig up. So she did some digging, all right, and even stole your little black book, which proved to be worthless for Huxley. However, there were a few cues about 'your wife' that likely aided him in thinking along the right lines."

My black book. I recall the day Eden had returned it to me, just a few moments after I'd been searching for it, certain I'd left it on my desk the previous day. I'd assumed Eden had taken it to synchronize my appointments, as she'd done on numerous occasions.

"Next," he continues, "Gwen saw you and Eden ride in on your motorcycle in a tight embrace on the day your aunt showed up for lunch, and that sparked her curiosity. She investigated your addresses—as front desk manager, she has the means—and when they were a match, she even went so far as to pay a visit and talk to your old neighbor, Hattie Hutton. Hattie confirmed that you two are married. Told her all about your lavish Vegas wedding with huge diamond rings, custom tailored dresses, and shiny limousines."

Hattie, for Christ's sake. She meant well as far as I know, but she definitely needs to be careful who she gossips with in the future.

"So what happens now?" I ask him.

"Now I have to take all of this to the board," Bradley says. "I already called an emergency meeting which, I have to say, was a baller move on my account. You should have seen the look on Bernie's face when I told him." He chuckles. "*Damn.* Huxley has no idea we're onto him yet."

Other than relief, I'm not sure what else I feel about everything Bradley has uncovered. I have no idea what any of the information will change. I highly doubt the board will hire me back, and if they do, will I accept? Not likely. At the very least, I'm willing to wait and hear them out. If they have any shred of decency, they'll let Bradley present his case.

"Seriously, Bradley," I say, "this means a lot. Thanks for having my back."

"Anytime, bro. I'll let you know how the meeting goes. I wouldn't have uncovered half this stuff if it weren't for Eden."

"I'll let her know. Talk to you later, bro."

"Later, Carr."

We end the call.

A storm of emotions rolls through me, and I'm having a difficult time keeping track of them. Part of me hadn't expected them to uncover the truth. I thought it was too much to hope for. And yet, they have. They're actually going to be able to clear my name.

"Eden," I call toward the bathroom. "Good news."

34

EDEN

"It wasn't Gretchen. It was Gwen," Carter says as soon as I open the bathroom door, drying my hands.

I stare at him blankly. "*What*? No."

He gestures for me to sit back down, and I do. "Yeah. Bradley and IT found proof on Huxley. Gwen was his helping hand. Huxley paid her big bonuses for her side gig. Bradley explained the whole thing, how she stole my black book, saw us on my motorcycle on the day we took Auntie out to lunch and started to become suspicious. Gretchen helped him to gather all the evidence this evening. Bradley told me you were the one who got him on the right track, so if it hadn't been for you, we might have never known."

I can't believe it. Gwen?

The kind, inconspicuous Gwen was in cahoots with Huxley?

"But..." The words die in my throat. He's looking at me with such amusement and even admiration, it startles me enough to start laugh-crying. My brain is working overtime, thinking of everything that happened. More and more things start to fall into place. Gwen's hair has a honey-blonde hue, and she, too, wears glasses, just like Gretchen! As front desk manager, she would have the necessary access, the contacts, and the possibilities to perform certain duties without raising any suspicions. On top of that, she's good friends with all the assistants of the top dogs. Why had I never thought of her?

Poor Gretchen. I feel bad for even accusing her. But then I let out a sigh of relief—never in my life have I been happier in knowing that I hadn't mistakenly accused her directly to her face, sparing us both any unnecessary discomfort or awkwardness.

Carter rubs my arms comfortingly, and then wipes the new tears softly away with his knuckles. Luckily, I hadn't gone for a fresh round of mascara just before this. Dealing with those stubborn black stains is already enough of a battle.

"Carter, I didn't have Gwen on my radar, at all. She, too, has bright hair and wears glasses. When I talked to Hattie, and she confirmed that the woman who asked about us fit Gretchen's description, I didn't even consider anybody else. I just put the obvious one and one together without even questioning it properly."

"That's the gossip game for you. It twists and turns, and takes on a life of its own. That's why I prefer to operate on facts and facts only. But I'm glad we figured it out."

"What's going to happen with Huxley?"

"There will be a board meeting soon. Tomorrow evening, most likely. Or the day after."

"So you're going to get your job back?"

"You know, at this point, I don't want to rush things. Let's wait and see what happens. I might have other plans I want to talk to you about." His face lights up, his eyes falling to the small ring box he's still holding in his hand. "But now is not the time or place to delve into such matters and risk derailing the current discussion."

"But wait. It's still my fault that Gwen saw us on your motorcycle. I asked you to give me a ride instead of driving with your aunt."

"Hush. Eden, look at me. It's nobody's fault. Shit happens. Sometimes it's not just regular 'shit happens,' but more like 'mega shit happens.'"

I snort out loud.

He places the ring box next to him, tilts my chin up with his fingers and forces my eyes to meet his, which I have subconsciously been avoiding for the last few seconds. "If anything, it's my fault for leaving my black book lying around—no, for involving you in the fake-marriage scenario in the first place."

He pulls me into a kiss.

It shocks me so much I can't reciprocate at first.

Once I realize what's going on, once I register that he's not going anywhere, the fear and anxiety melt away, and I lean into him, sliding my hand into his hair.

My body comes alive, and the tears dry.

He's not angry or upset with me. Nor has he withdrawn and kicked me to the curb. The rational part of my brain, which has been shut off for the last couple of days, scolds me for thinking those things about him. I've been so consumed by fear and paranoia that I allowed my imagination to get the best of me.

When we break apart, he still holds me close, a smile spreading across his face. "Sweet Jesus, I'm so relieved. Give me a second. I was expecting the worst."

I blink, unsure if I've heard him right. "I can't believe you're not mad."

Carter shakes his head, pushing loose strands of hair away from my face. "No, Eden, I'm not mad. Not mad at all. I'm actually happy. Really happy."

"But, you said—"

"I know." He gently cuts me off. "I know what I said about romantic relationships. But that was before when I never thought I'd meet someone like you, someone who has changed how I look at life. Having those things changes a person, makes them see things in a new light. You're the girl I want to have a family with, babies, things I never thought I would want. Eden, don't you see what you do to me?"

My heart melts. "I was so sure you were going to be furious. I was scared to tell you."

"How could I be? It's good that it happened. That *all* of this happened the way it did." He takes my face in his hands and looks at me deeply. "If anything, it showed me that you're the perfect girl for me. It showed me that I want to do everything in my power to be the perfect man for you—if you'll let me. I want to spend the rest of my life proving this very point to you until there's no doubt in your mind. Again, I'm headstrong, and I have no doubt in my mind that I'll succeed." He winks at me, and it's the cutest wink I've ever seen. "All I ask of you is to trust me, with all your heart, and to know that I'm going to bring you a piece of heaven. A large piece, at that. So colossal, it'll make angels jealous. I love you, Eden. I've loved you from the first moment I laid eyes on you."

This is the first time he has said those words. He's implied, and I've hoped but to actually hear him say them brings more tears to my eyes, and I'm rendered speechless.

"Deep down," he says, "I knew right then, you're the one for me. You're my love, my life." His eyes lock with mine. "Baby, I was never pretending."

My mind is blank.

No words, only feelings.

Well, one feeling. Intense, overwhelming love.

"I've been without a family for so long," he continues, bringing me closer, "I forgot what it was like. Then you came along, and you brought my aunt and me closer than we've ever been, and from the moment you moved in with me, you became my family."

I hug him, finally finding my words. "I love you too, Carter. God, I love you so much."

"Oh, I know you do," he teases, grinning at me, and I start laughing.

Chuckling, he grabs the ring and slides it onto my left ring finger. "Figured I should get you a diamond that symbolizes the right intention," he says, as I admire the way it looks on me. He brings us to a sitting position, holding me tightly, and I crawl onto his lap so I can touch as much of him as possible.

"It's all a little backward, don't you think?" I tease, tears sliding down my cheeks. "Also, pretty sure I'm not supposed to get several diamond rings."

Carter laughs. "So what? We do things our own way. You'll definitely get a second wedding band too."

I stare at the newest ring, my vision swimming. "This is too much." Instead of having to pawn my wedding ring and having none, I now have all these.

"Nothing is too much for my soon-to-be wife." He wipes the tears away, gently cupping my face.

"We need to get me those sunglasses. Ultra-protective."

"You got it. Sunglasses coming right up!" We laugh. "Anything for my beautiful fiancée."

I kiss him this time, needing to feel his lips on mine, to taste and hug him. To remind myself that this is real, all real. When I draw back, he smiles the warmest smile, his hand coming to rest on my chin.

"I can't believe it," he says. "We're going to get married."

The awe in his voice makes me smile back. "Yeah, we are."

He kisses me again. The emotions I'm dealing with are endless. Excitement, anxiety, and some fear is there, but they're quickly overpowered by more positive ones, like hope, happiness, and love. God do I love this man. I love him more than I can even quantify.

And he loves me.

What started off as a beneficial arrangement has somehow morphed along the way. It's become something else, something deeper and immensely powerful.

Carter's firm hands clutch me close and surround me with warmth. The warmth of his kisses, his touch, his body. It's all overwhelming in a wonderful way.

I gasp into his kisses, chanting his name once his mouth trails down to my throat. Every time we touch it feels like the first. I have the same rush of adrenaline, the same flood of emotions. They've only gotten stronger. I lose myself in the sensations, in Carter's show of love. I'm going to spend the rest of my life with this man, this wonderful, generous man who knows me better than I know myself.

I want it to always be like this. I want us to always love each other and want one another so much that when our skin touches, it's like coming home. Even now, I could swear we sizzle. Shocks of heat flow through my veins, fueling the flames of desire. Carter's mouth steals my breath while he pushes into me.

Finally, we're connected, mind, body, and soul.

We move in tandem, hands grasping, mouths tasting, hearts beating as one. He takes his time, touching and kissing every bit of me he can reach. With every kiss, I feel our love surge through my veins, igniting a flame that will never die.

When we come, when I feel the heat of him inside me, tears run down my cheeks because it reminds me that our love is strong and will be able to conquer anything.

Carter holds me after, my back pressed into his chest so his hand can reach around to trace absentminded patterns on my stomach.

"I love you," he says again with as much firmness and conviction as the first time.

"I love you too, Carter. This has to be a dream."

"Why?"

"It's too good to be true."

He strokes my hair. "You're allowed to have what you want, Eden. Look at where you are, what you did. You're so damn strong. You left everything you knew because you wanted a better life for yourself. I'd have to be brain dead not to notice what an amazing woman you are." He pauses. "And that's why I have one more thing for you. It's clear that you possess an inherent passion for celebrating in style. In fact, if anybody knows how to make celebrations memorable, it's you."

"Me? What do you mean?"

"I have one more surprise. The ring wasn't your only present." With a kiss on my head, he gets up. In one swift move, he pulls on his jeans, delectable abs in full motion. The hawk emits an exhilarated cry, its talons outstretched, poised for takeoff. "Be right back."

He runs out, and a minute later, when he comes back in, he hands me the sweetest and funniest surprise. A box of...cupcakes.

With strawberries on top.

35

CARTER

After indulging in the cupcakes in various delicious ways, places, and manners—the inevitable happens. With a loud crack, the bed frame collapses beneath us. A crash echoes, cupcakes fly. We look at the mess, then at each other, and erupt in laughter. After paying for the damages, we maneuver all of Eden's stuff and us back into our apartment, where we drift off to sleep wrapped in each other's arms.

The next morning, I wake at my usual time: 5:00 a.m.

However, instead of getting out of bed to exercise, I stay for half an hour longer, enjoying her sleeping presence. I decide to let her sleep in as long as she can afford and wake her after my workout.

Eden stirs and rolls over onto her back, her green eyes sliding open to meet mine. The beautiful soft smile that spreads across her face tugs at my heart.

"Good morning," she mumbles, voice hoarse from sleep.

"Good morning, baby. You sleep okay?"

She nods, stretching her arms above her head and letting out a quiet groan, which goes straight to my dick. "Better than I have in days," she says. "Probably because of the unforgettable night. Even the bed couldn't handle us."

"It's seen better days, that's for sure."

"It was fun, though," she says with a mischievous glint.

"Absolutely." My hands still itch with the memory. I can barely keep them to myself. No matter when or where, I can't help wanting to touch her. Even now, I push her hair away from her face and place a kiss on her forehead. "What do you want for breakfast?"

"You know what actually does sound good? A smoothie. I bought the stuff the other day…"

"Say no more. I'm on it."

I give her another kiss on the forehead before climbing out of bed. I slip on a pair of black shorts and a white T-shirt, then head to the kitchen to make my woman her drink. How quickly things change. When Eden had moved in, my main concern had been the disruption of my routine, and yet here I am, happy to break it so I can make sure my woman gets something in her stomach before she leaves.

I've been so wrapped up in the news and what Bradley told me, that I haven't had a chance to tell her my start-up idea. There's a lot we have to talk about and not enough hours in the day to do it.

By the time Eden is finished getting ready, I have her smoothie and lightly buttered toast waiting for her. She gives me a kiss as she joins me at the table.

She's barely taken a few sips from her glass when she points to my phone. "Ready to call your aunt?"

"Yeah."

One thing we'd discussed before we'd fallen asleep, was inviting Aunt Eleanor to our wedding. It won't be an easy call, but we know we have to come clean about our fake act. In our hearts, we hope she'll let it slide once she gets the invite to our "official" grand wedding. Ensuring she'll get first-row seats and be the very first to know, may also sway her heart to be lenient about the disclosure. Okay, who am I kidding? The shitstorm that's about to hit us will be fucking massive.

However, we agree that delaying will only make matters worse.

Glancing at the screen, I dial her number and try my best smile when I see Aunt Eleanor's picture pop up. She's accepting a video call, something Eden had shown her how to do before she left.

"Good morning, Auntie."

"Cartie! Finally!" she exclaims, the phone too close to her face so all I see are her eyes and forehead. "Am I doing this right? Can you see me okay?"

"Just pull the phone back a little." When she does as I say, I can see her full face. "There, perfect."

Eden leans in close, allowing my aunt to see us both. "Hi, Auntie!"

"Oh, Eden, you look beautiful this morning. How have you two been?"

"We're fine, Auntie," I tell her. "Listen, we would like to invite you to our wedding. To our real wedding. Eden and I haven't been married. We were faking being in love."

Yep, that's exactly how I say it. Direct. Honest. To the point. I prepare for the tsunami to unleash its fury upon me.

"Cartie, I know. I'm old, but I'm not stupid."

Eden's jaw drops.

My jaw drops.

Aunt Eleanor counts down her bony fingers while I stare at her, processing. "First, the story was ridiculous. Second, you didn't have a marriage certificate. Third, you didn't even go on a honeymoon. Fourth, keeping it a secret at work, *please*. Last but not least, Hattie confirmed my suspicions."

Eden snort-laughs. Me, I don't. I breathe in and out, still trying to wrap my mind around the news. "Why didn't you tell us anything?"

"Isn't it obvious? Because I could see deep and profound affection, *vrai amour*, true love, devotion in its purest form, so I played along. Also, because Hattie said I shouldn't so she wouldn't get into trouble for telling me."

"Sweet Jesus." Those two will be the death of me.

"I will gladly come to your wedding, Cartie! Of course! Congratulations to the both of you. About time! I've been waiting for this call. Make sure to invite Hattie too."

Eden leans closer to the phone. "Thank you! We will, for sure. Auntie, how are you doing? Have your coughs improved?"

"Yeah," I jump in, not wanting to drag the whole thing out. There are more important matters to focus on. "Any updates regarding the lab results?"

"Right, see about that..." My aunt's face twists, and she suddenly looks guilty.

I already know I'm not going to like where this conversation is headed. "About what?"

"The whole going to see my doctor thing..."

"Auntie, what happened?" I feel like I'm missing something, like she's holding back information. "Tell us everything."

"I'm not really dealing with a medical issue."

I sit there for a moment, stunned. Her words register, yet I can't react until I process them. Eden looks as shocked as I feel, but then her lips quirk.

"What do you mean you aren't dealing with a medical issue?" I demand.

"Okay, now, before you get angry, just know I had a perfectly good reason for faking poor health."

Faking? She had been faking poor health this whole time? What in the world? "I should hope you have a good reason," I try to keep the tension out of my voice. "Explain."

"Cartie, you were consumed by work, never taking time for yourself. I knew you weren't going to bring 'your new wife' to see me and I wanted to see you both so bad. I needed a serious enough reason for you to drop work. So, I told a little white lie."

"That wasn't a white lie, Auntie. A white lie is telling someone you like their shirt when you don't. Pretending you have an illness is not a white lie, it's a nightmare!"

She raises an eyebrow. "Look who's talking."

I huff. "Auntie, faking an illness can't be compared to faking a wedding."

"I beg to differ. I at least never, not once, said I was ill. I just implied it."

"Stop being stubborn."

"All right, maybe I shouldn't have done it. But it worked, didn't it?"

I'm speechless. Eden looks way too amused, as if she had suspected it all along. She grabs the phone. "Auntie, I'm glad you're healthy, you're wonderful, but don't you do that ever again."

"I only did it because I thought my nephew needed to be reminded that there were more important things than work. Now that you're taking the plunge into the wonderful world of marriage, this old lady can finally retire from the 'tying the knot' business, right, *mes chéris*? It's time for me to kick back, put my old feet up, and enjoy watching you two embark on your journey of eternal love!"

Unbelievable. Un-fucking-believable. She'd faked everything and had me worried sick for absolutely no reason. I want to be mad at her—hell, I feel like I *should* be mad at her. But honestly? I'm relieved she's okay. A huge weight lifts off my shoulders, and I'm able to take a breath. I take the phone back from Eden.

"Despite the fact that you're a crazy, wicked woman, I'm not angry," I tell my aunt. "I'm just glad you're okay."

"Me too! My goodness. Now, I know you two have work to do so I'll leave you to it. Let's do this video thingy again soon. Don't forget to send me the date, time, and location as soon as you can. I love seeing your smiling faces. Say hi to Hattie for me."

"Wait. That's right. About Hattie—is that why you told her to stay put?"

"But of course! Nothing gets past you. And aren't you glad I did? That and pretending to be unwell was the best idea I've ever had. You know I'm right. All right, gotta run. Bye, you two. *Au revoir! À bientôt!*"

"Bye, Auntie."

We hang up, and Eden and I sit there in stunned silence. Eventually, my eyes meet hers. "I...have no words."

"She's a trip."

All of this, the fake marriage to Eden to give my aunt closure, everything we'd gone through when she was here, it had all happened because of Aunt Eleanor's "illness," and it turns out that that "illness" didn't exist. Part of me is utterly relieved, part of me is still in disbelief.

"I can't believe we went through all that hard work," Eden says, "and she turned around and conned us. We can't even be mad at her."

"We honestly can't."

"Dear God, now I know where you got it from."

That makes me chuckle, it's so damn ridiculous. Eden's right. My aunt and I had played the same game on each other. She'd faked being sick to draw me away from work and try to show me happiness, and I'd faked being married to make sure she was happy. Eden joins in laughing, and before I know it, we're both cracking up—more from the ease of nerves and the sheer liberation that Aunt Eleanor is fine.

Eden wipes the tears from her eyes, still chuckling. "My God, does the universe have a twisted sense of humor."

"That's one way to look at it."

Eden shakes her head and goes back to her morning smoothie and toast. "What are your plans for today?" she asks, mixing her smoothie with her straw.

"I had an idea that I wanted to run by you. Remember when I told you about working on other plans?"

Eden looks up. "Yes, of course! You want my input?"

"I'd like to hear what you think."

She gives me a wide smile and props her chin on her hand as she leans on the table. "Shoot. What were you thinking?"

"Instead of getting a job at another construction firm, I'm debating on starting my own consulting business," I explain. "People have been asking for my advice for years, and it would be the perfect time now that I'm not working at Legacy anymore. If I went off on my own, I could handle things the way I want without a board to answer to."

Eden's eyes light up. "Yes! Do it. I think that's a fantastic idea!" She reaches over to lay her hand on my arm.

I take her hand in mine and squeeze it.

"It'll be a lot of work, but it wouldn't be as difficult with my connections to find clients and eventually investors."

"You would do *amazing* consulting people. Hell, you did it all the time when working with clients. Even my sister—and trust me, she's harder to please than a picky child at dinnertime—can't stop singing your praises. You should go for it!"

Her excitement starts to make me excited. "It's still only an idea. I have a lot of work to do before I can start legitimately looking for clients. But at least this time, when I put my heart and soul into something, I don't have to worry about it being taken away."

"*Exactly.*" Eden gets up from her chair and slides onto my lap, her arms coming to rest around my shoulders. "I'm behind you on this, one hundred percent. You're a smart, clever, dedicated man, and I know you're going to do great things."

"Wait, what did you say? Can you repeat that?"

"OMG. Did Mr. Fun Time make another joke?"

36

CARTER

Ring-ring. Reluctantly, I draw away from her sinful lips and pull out my phone.

"It *better* be important," Eden jokes, not even bothering to move.

It's Bradley calling.

I swipe right. "Hey, man, what's up?"

"I need you to come in this morning," he says without even bothering with a greeting. "The board is meeting with their decision, and they want you to be there."

"What time?"

"One hour."

Shit. Earlier than expected. That doesn't give me much time, but I'm not about to say no. "All right, I'll be there."

When I end the call, Eden looks at me with wide eyes. "Is everything okay?"

"Yeah. Bradley says the board is meeting this morning about his case against Huxley, and they want me to be there."

"Holy crap, that's huge. I didn't realize it was happening so fast. You should get ready then, there isn't much time."

A Bossy Roommate

"Wait for me, and I'll drive you in."

She slides off my lap, and I hurry up to shower and change. By the time I'm done, she's packed up the rest of the smoothie to take with her to work.

WHILE WE DRIVE, Eden calls her sister. Last night, we had not only discussed calling Auntie to "fess up," but also discussed the matter of calling Diane to inform her that Eden won't be returning to Maine. Eden's worried she'll be mad, especially since she hadn't spilled the beans about our relationship. Eden has insisted she'll handle the conversation solo, but observed that starting with an invitation to the wedding—just like I had with Auntie—is a great strategy. At one point, Eden puts the phone on speaker for me to eavesdrop.

"...and that's why I decided I'm not coming back to Maine. I probably wouldn't have even if the six months were up, to be honest," she tells her sister. "I love it here. I'm thriving here."

"Wait, what? Did you just say that you're getting married to Mr. Bancroft? *The* Mr. Carter Bancroft? Your boss, as in the man who's helping me turn our family business around?" Her sister's voice comes over the speaker, while incessant ringing of phones persists in the background.

"Yeah...the very same."

"Good for you. Congratulations! With a man like Mr. Bancroft, I would have moved to New York within a day. No questions asked. Of *course* you're not coming back. You'd be crazy to. I'm itching to know the whole story, and how and when he proposed, but now's not a good time. The phones won't stop ringing. Before I go, let me tell you, I'm so proud of you!"

"Wait, what—you are?"

"Even now, everything you've done in such a brief period of time, picking up after such a devastating setback, moving to a whole other state, and opening your heart again takes more guts than I've ever had. Eden, I've always been proud of you."

"You told me I'm always running away from my problems."

"Well, weren't you?"

"Not really. Okay, I was! But that's not the point. The point is—"

"I'll do better," Diane interrupts her. "I'm with you, sis. I know I've been hard on you in the past... It's not because I don't think you can make your own decisions, it's because I love you and I want the best for you. I always have." Her sister falls silent. "I apologize if I didn't express that clearly enough, but I firmly believe that you deserve nothing but the best."

Eden takes a deep breath, and I notice the tension in her body starting to fade.

There's more background noise.

"Thanks to Mr. Bancroft's help, our business is flourishing. It's thriving! Seriously, he's a *genius*. All the articles about him? Absolutely true. I can't even be upset at you for not telling me earlier that you two are a thing!"

Proudly smiling eyes meet mine, and then she refocuses on the call. "I'm sorry about that."

"Yeah, yeah, yeah. Gotta go. Love you, sis. I'll see y'all at the wedding! Say hi to the lucky groom!"

"Well," I turn to her after she ends the call, "that went better than expected, didn't it?"

"It sure did." Eden squeezes my hand and looks out of the window, a radiant smile adorning her face, illuminating the world. Her hum fills the air with a lovely melody.

It's strange taking the route that had been part of my mornings up until a few days ago. Especially with Eden by my side. It makes me think of those last few days when we were working like mad to fix all the problems. I miss working with her. She was a good assistant, and I know she's going to do wonderful things, not only at Legacy but wherever her career takes her in the future, namely—Bancroft Consulting.

Right before we enter the building, I slide my hand back into hers.

She beams at me and squeezes it, the significance of the act not lost. Hand in hand, we walk through the lobby, greeting a new receptionist as we go. She gives us a warm smile and greeting.

The office is already buzzing when we step off the elevator. No doubt, everyone has heard about the upcoming board meeting and is busy swapping rumors and gossip. Truth is, that's one thing I definitely won't miss about working in that office. Heads turn to watch as we walk by, and I can hear the murmuring. It dawns on me that Eden has likely been dealing with that bullshit since I left. How she hasn't snapped at someone is a testament to how strong and positive my woman truly is.

We ignore them, our hands still firmly clasped together as we walk to her office.

My old office.

Bradley is already there, waiting for us, typing away on his tablet as he fires off his morning texts. When he sees me, his face splits into a grin. He gets up and pats me on the back. "Good to see you, man," he says. "Are you ready for this?"

"As ready as I'll ever be."

"Do you need me to prepare anything for the meeting?" Eden asks him, putting her stuff down at her desk.

"Not this time," Bradley says. "It's just us and the board. You should be good to go about your normal duties, though you should connect with Gretchen. She has some...updates...you might be interested in."

Eden smiles, her eyes briefly darting to mine. "Thank you."

"Great." Bradley turns to me. "Let's do this, bro."

We leave Eden to her work and head to the conference room. Everything seems different now, is different. I'm not nervous. Meetings with the board rarely get to me, however, I'm apprehensive. I don't know what to think or expect. The last time I'd seen them, they'd accused me of mismanagement and had brought up my fake marriage. They hadn't cared about my defense then, which only makes me curious as to what they're going to say now that they have the full story.

Bradley and I are the last to arrive. The first thing I notice is that

Huxley is nowhere to be found. His chair is vacant. I take the same seat I did the last time.

"Carter, it's good to see you again," Bernie says once we're settled. "I take it you know why we're here?"

"Actually, why don't you tell me?" I suggest. I bear no ill will toward Bernie. He had demonstrated his support for Eden by ensuring she retained her position. Although he hadn't been able to convince the remaining board members to keep me on, he wields enough influence to have facilitated the internal investigation and prompt today's meeting. Sensing his hesitation, I confront the board head-on, "During our last conversation, the board made their stance on me and my dedicated efforts abundantly clear. It seems that a few errors, for which neither my team nor I were responsible, and my preference for privacy were deemed more significant than my years of loyal service. Consequently, the board decided to terminate my employment."

The board members avert their gazes in response.

"Yes, yes, we did," Bernie agrees on their behalf. "But that was before we had the full story." He takes a deep breath, briefly glancing at his compatriots, not that any of them want to meet his or my eye. "Bradley has brought to my attention evidence that Huxley was the one who was talking to Ecclestone Construction behind our backs."

There it is. The puzzle piece that completes the riddle.

"We were able to verify these meetings, there's no room for doubt," Bernie continues, "as well as recover conversations from our office messaging system that provide undeniable proof of his directive in changing orders and sabotaging projects across multiple accounts."

I sit perfectly still, letting the information wash over me. I know most of it already thanks to Bradley, and I appreciate that Bernie doesn't try to water things down.

"I'm glad to hear it," I say after he pauses for a moment.

Somehow, it seems funny to me that the man who was blatantly out to get me ended up being responsible for the things that I was fired for.

"I am aware that letting you go was a mistake," Bernie emphasizes, casting a deliberate gaze around the board members before returning his focus to me. "Once everything was explained, and we had it all in black and white, I knew we needed to rectify this at all costs. You're an amazing asset to the team, and we'd like to have you back."

"What about Huxley?"

"Huxley is no longer with the company."

"Did you find out what Ecclestone offered him in exchange for selling us out?"

Bernie purses his lips so tight it looks like he's swallowed a lemon. "Several million dollars," he says. "At least, that's what it was at first. As time went on, it seemed that Huxley got greedy, and started asking for more. He wasn't interested in having fellow board members. I believe his goal was to disband the board and be the only one in charge, with all the benefits, money, and power that went with it."

As much as I despise Huxley, I have to admit he went to greater lengths than I anticipated. I'd never have believed him capable of such a move. An absolutely stupid one to be sure. He had completely overestimated himself—but it was audacious and ballsy enough that it might have worked.

"Where's he now?" I ask.

"Huxley has been told it would be in his best interest to retire," Bernie says. "He figured that was a preferable option rather than facing the consequences."

What? It also means he won't be held accountable for his actions, which leaves a bitter taste in my mouth. Goddammit. Clearly, a public scandal of that magnitude would have a negative impact on Legacy's reputation and brand image—by quietly dismissing him, the board is aiming to restore external and internal cohesion and focus on moving forward. Still, Huxley was able to walk away, living a life of leisure on a beach somewhere? It's something I strongly object to. I was fired for something I didn't do, yet the man responsible was given a slap on the wrist.

Bullshit. I sure hope the board had at least negotiated a settlement, which involves an appropriate financial compensation.

It's not my place to ask.

Nor to act.

Yet.

There are alternative, let's say "less conventional" methods to drive a point home without resorting to legal measures. One such approach could entail a carefully orchestrated scenario that will lead to the loss of financial means, *and* respect, *and* influence—all as a form of just desserts. I'm a firm believer in ensuring any repercussions perfectly reflect the severity of the individual's actions.

"This means there is now an opening on the board, and we'd like to give it to you, along with Huxley's position. You'd be a partner in Legacy Builders," Bernie continues, smiling now. "We've heard the full story about your aunt and your unwavering dedication to your family, and it's precisely the kind of person we're looking for." He reaches for a pen and scribbles something on a piece of paper. He hands it to me.

Every single person directs their gaze toward me.

I sit in silence, taking a quick glance at the salary I'd be earning per year. The number is damn high. A lot higher than I expected.

When I don't show the desired reaction, Bernie starts talking about additional compensations I'd receive in the form of bonuses, a profit-sharing agreement, and a range of other perks, such as extended vacation days. I'm barely listening at this point. Not needing the job puts me in the best negotiating position I could possibly be in. A couple months ago, I would've jumped at the opportunity. It was everything I had ever wanted and everything I had worked toward.

However, I don't want it anymore.

The board has shown their true colors to me—both good and bad. Even now, giving me the title of "partner" and Huxley's old job somehow seems more like a consolation prize, a way to placate me while still saving face. They don't want me back because they value me, they want me back so no one else will get me. And, I suspect, part of it is also to silently stick it to Huxley. I bet he's livid that I'm being offered his place.

I think about my own idea. Opening a construction consulting business fills me with more excitement than the thought of returning to Legacy Builders.

I look up at Bernie. "Thanks, but I'm going to have to pass."

Bernie's eyes go wide. "I'm sorry, what did you say?"

"I don't want the position."

"Carter, I know you were probably hurt that—"

"Bernie." I cut him off. "I appreciate my name being cleared, but I'm going to have to pass."

In the depths of my heart, I can't help but feel a tinge of regret toward Bernie, the man who couldn't prevent my unjust dismissal but had played a crucial role in uncovering the truth. Bernie has proven himself to be a true ally and friend. Despite the tempting offer, my decision is resolute—I have to move on, leaving behind the shadows of that boardroom.

"If anything, Bradley Everhart should have the job," I say, motioning to my friend, whose eyes light up. "We have the same experience, and he has proven his expertise over the last few days. He's the one you want on your board."

Bernie sits there, not looking happy, but not entirely surprised either. He's a smart man and he probably suspected that I wouldn't be coming back.

No one says anything.

After a few seconds of stunned silence, I ask, "Are we done here?"

Bernie nods. I don't wait for an answer. I don't need one. My mind is made up, had been when Eden had given me her support this morning. Shaking hands with Bernie and patting Bradley on the shoulder, I get up and leave.

I feel lighter than I have in years. A calmness washes over me, and I know I've done the right thing. The door is officially closed on my time at Legacy Builders, and there's so much more on the horizon to look forward to.

EDEN IS TYPING AWAY at her computer when I walk into the lobby. "Hey, that was fast," she says with a smile. "How'd it go?"

I lean down and kiss her, cradling her face. When I pull away, she looks dazed, and her smile grows.

"Everything's great," I say, stroking her cheek. "I'll be back later to take you to dinner."

"Oh, okay. Wait, what happened in the meeting?"

"They offered to make me partner."

She gasps. "They did?"

"I turned them down."

Eden pulls away and looks at me as if she thinks she hasn't heard me correctly. "Wait, seriously?"

"Absolutely." I lean on her desk, a smile playing on my lips.

She can't contain her excitement and hurries around her desk to pull me into a hug. "Well, I'll be darned! I'm so proud of you."

"You see, I'm not just a pretty face around here."

Laughing, she draws away, then gives me one more kiss.

"Babe, well, guess what? I've made a decision, too—I'm quitting! Yep, I stayed here just to clear your name. But the truth is, I can't imagine being here without you. So, here's the plan: I want to be your assistant at your new place, if you'll have me...I mean, if you say *please*."

I don't need to think twice. "Well, Eden, with an offer like that, how could I refuse?" I lean in and grumble, "*Pretty please* with sugar on top. Be my new assistant, baby. Deal?"

"So glad you asked! Fantastic idea! How could anybody resist such a sweet request? And to make it even better, I'll go all professional and give Bradley my two weeks' notice. World domination it is, *boss*. Let's roll!"

"Sounds like a good plan." I kiss the tip of her nose. "Don't work too hard. I'll pick you up after work, and we'll go somewhere to celebrate."

"What about that little bistro where we took Auntie for lunch?" she asks. "The Sweet Spot? I've been dying to go back."

"Sounds like a plan. The Sweet Spot it is. I could definitely use a dessert."

. . .

Minutes later, I step out of Legacy for the last time and take a deep breath.

For the first time in years, I see endless possibilities stretched out before me. Though I often looked down on New York from my office, being here feels much better. I stand on my apartment's rooftop, gazing at all the skyscrapers and the buildings below. None of them bear my name, yet that fact holds no significance. Maybe someday, one of them will. I found my calling when I decided to act as an adviser. My future can be everything I want it to be.

Life had thrown Eden into my arms, and I have no intention of ever letting her go.

With her by my side, anything is possible.

37

EDEN
SIX MONTHS LATER

Our marriage takes place in the dreamy Château de Chantilly in France, about thirty miles north of Paris. It's as if the sun has painted the dreamscape! We find ourselves at an ancient castle, surrounded by a meticulously cultivated French garden, and the air is thick with the sweet scent of roses and the tune of singing birds. We can practically hear "Here Comes the Bride" chirping in the air.

And there's Auntie, right at the front, beaming with enough pride and joy to power the whole of France (and maybe even Belgium next door). Standing with her is Hattie, her confidante, making everybody laugh by quipping, "Well, let us hope these three terrors don't get up to too much mischief while I'm gallivanting around France—they're probably already hatching a plot to seize control of my apartment."

"Oh Hattie," Auntie says with a mischievous twinkle in her eye, "if your cats pull off a plot to seize your apartment, you'll have to start charging them rent!"

Diane, *my* confidante, shares a knowing glance that suggests she remembers the day I had sprinted down the aisle, *sans* groom. We silently celebrate the fact that this time, my journey to the altar will be —fingers crossed—refreshingly uninterrupted.

A Bossy Roommate

And let's not forget our entourage—Gretchen, Jaylin, Lexi, Bradley, and even Mr. Bernie—all dressed to the nines, showing support like there's no tomorrow.

Just as I feel the warmth of Carter's touch and the confident, loud growl of his voice rumbling, "*I do*," I stir from my slumber, feeling a stir in my belly, my heart still intoxicated by my beautiful dream.

I waddle to the bathroom as fast as my legs can carry me.

Normally, Carter wakes me up when it's time for work, however, this morning, our baby has decided moving around in my belly is an easier way to get me out of bed.

How could I have known that one decision would lead to me getting everything I'd ever wanted? I had come to New York City with no money in my bank account, a broken heart, and a car that was hanging on by a windshield wiper. Now, I have a dream apartment, a wonderful husband, and in five months, our baby girl will be in our arms.

I find Carter in the gym, running on the treadmill like he does every morning. Standing in the doorway, I can't help but smile as I watch him run.

He has his earbuds in and is already on a call. "Does that clear up any confusion?" he's asking. "Feel free to share the report with your partners. If they need more clarification, I'd be happy to set up a conference call and go over my thoughts. Thanks, Mr. Humphries."

I'm not sure what the client said, however, judging by the pleased expression on Carter's face, it was positive. He ends the call and hops off the treadmill. When he sees me standing there, he takes out his earbuds. "Hey, good morning, baby. How long have you been standing there?"

"Not long. Just admiring the view."

Carter has been working from home ever since he'd turned down Legacy's offer. Which means he's somehow even more buff than when we'd met. Often, he'll take breaks by doing some lifting or running, and the results are *impossible* to ignore.

"Can't blame you," he teases. He picks up his towel and wipes his face as he draws closer. When he tries to give me a kiss, I wiggle away. "Carter! Ew, no, you're all sweaty!"

"Hey. Get back here. You don't want to give me a *little* hug?"

He starts to chase me through the apartment with open arms, trying and eventually pulling me into a hug. "*Carter, nooooo!*" I tease, laughing. "Now you got your sweat all over me."

"Well, I always wanted a workout buddy."

"You did not!"

"Too bad. Guess you're officially my 'sweatmate' now." Carter kisses my neck. "Shower with me?"

"Do you even have to ask?"

He leads me down the hall, his hand tightly clutching mine. It's still unbelievable how everything has changed, not just in my life but between Carter and me. When we had first got together, he'd barely had time for anything but work. He'd been settled into this neat routine he had carved for himself and was too stubborn to let anyone interrupt it. Now, it's the opposite. Now, he's the one starting over, the one branching out, taking risks to prove himself.

It's enough to make me chuckle to myself.

"What's so funny?" he asks, pausing in the bedroom to step out of his sneakers.

"I'm just remembering what it was like when I first came to New York, how I didn't know a soul and was trying to make my own way. And now, here we are—"

"Dum. Dum. Dum. The tables have turned," Carter says. "I hadn't thought of it that way, but you're right. It is crazy. And, in a few more months, we'll both be starting something new."

He reaches down to lay his hands on my round belly. The baby moves excitedly. She always does as soon as he touches my stomach, like she knows her dad is close. I smile and lay my hands over his.

"I know. I still can't believe it," I confess.

Carter draws me close, reaching out to lay his hand on my cheek. "Well, believe it, Mrs. Bancroft. Every single day I'm like, 'Whoa, I'm on this insane rollercoaster with this wild and drop-dead gorgeous chick.'"

"Looks like you've got front-row seats to the adventure of a lifetime!" I lean in to kiss him. When we draw back, I give him a smoldering look. "Now, how about that shower?"

We strip down and slip into the large shower together. A few verses into my rendition of the small-town girl's tale in "Don't Stop Believin'" by Journey, Carter starts humming along with me (his adorable off-key version), before he pulls me close. Sporting the cutest smirk, he kisses me under the spray of the hot water and runs his hands down my hips, which Carter is always excited about. The moment I felt even slightly self-conscious about my changing body, he was right there to smooth away all my fears.

Along with physical changes, the emotional ones are a damn rollercoaster. One afternoon I cried because our mail was late, and then laughed at how bewildered Carter was, only to cry again that I was making him confused with my craziness. Another time, me and the girls went out to our usual lunch place, and I had the sudden craving for something sweet and started crying because they were out of those amazing NYC cronuts. As if it wasn't simple enough to waddle those five extra minutes to the next bakery (Gretchen still won't let me live that one down, though she did make the heroic trek for me, bless her heart). And no, I never spilled the beans that I had my suspicions about her being in cahoots with Huxley. I've got to keep a tiny shred of pride intact, after all.

Speaking of work: I love having Carter work from home and me assisting him. No more late nights or coming and going at separate times. He's already transformed the guest suite into a nursery, which was a project he was adamant about undertaking on his own.

I've never really had an eye for that sort of thing, and he was so excited about it that I let him handle the arrangements. He'd picked everything, from the colors of the walls and carpet to what furniture and decorations to use. Ever the pro, he had gone through tons of samples and mockups before deciding. He kept saying he wanted it to be right for his little girl, and it made my heart explode.

Before heading out, I go to the guest suite and stand in the doorway.

No matter how different it looks now, I can still see myself there, sitting on that bed, worried and nervous about sharing a space with my jerky boss. I'd had no idea what was in store for me, what amazing changes awaited.

It all seems like centuries ago.

38

EDEN

His handsome smiling face hovers above mine, tears in his eyes as the nurse places our daughter on my chest.

I barely remember the labor—that's what I try to tell myself. At a certain point, your body goes into autopilot, and you lose focus of everything.

"I don't care, just give me *something*!" I hissed between contractions. They gave me a shot of painkillers. Thank God for that. By the time my doctor came in, I'd already started pushing.

Our daughter was delivered safely, and that's all that matters.

"Baby, she's beautiful." Carter kisses my sweaty forehead and reaches out to lay his hand on our baby's back.

She's gorgeous, even with her scrunched up, annoyed expression. Like she's pissed we've interrupted her sleep. Actually, she looks exactly like Carter when she does that, and it makes me laugh through my happy tears. When I tell Carter my observation, he laughs out so loud I think the whole hospital hears him.

"That's my girl," he rumbles, looking at her, prouder than a bean stick.

After we're both cleaned up and settled in our recovery room, Carter pulls a chair over and sits as close as he can.

"Do you want to hold her?" I ask.

He nods, his eyes wide like a deer in the headlights. It's so rare for him to be out of his element that my heart, which is already a puddle of goo, melts even more. I put the baby in his arms, showing him how to properly support her head.

Seeing them together takes my breath away.

If I hadn't witnessed it for myself, I would have had a hard time believing the man sitting there making cooing noises at our baby is the same grouchy man I met at that ice cream shop nearly a year ago. The same man who'd sworn up and down he'd never have kids and yet, had been ecstatic when he'd learned I was pregnant.

"You can relax, babe," I say with a chuckle, reaching out to rub his shoulder. "She's not made of glass. You aren't going to break her."

"She's so little," he comments, looking at me with those big brown eyes of his. "I've never seen something so tiny before."

"That's because you have massive arms," I say, affectionately squeezing his muscles.

He gives me a kiss, then looks back at our daughter. "I never realized how much love you can have for someone you just met."

"I know exactly what you mean." My smile is permanent by this point, and I lean back against my pillows. I love that little girl more than I've loved anything. The moment my eyes landed on her it was like something clicked.

"It's like all the puzzle pieces of my life have fallen into place," he says, "and I know I'll do anything to keep her happy, safe, and loved."

That.

The door to my room opens and my sister comes in first, followed quickly by Hattie and Eleanor.

"Hey, sis," Diane says, coming over to my side and smoothing my hair back. She leans closer so she can look down at her niece. "She's *so* beautiful. She reminds me so much of you, Eden," she says, with tears in her eyes. "Wow, the resemblance is uncanny."

"Really? I think she looks exactly like her father," I say. "You should have seen her scrunched up face when the doctor held her up."

"Let me guess," Aunt Eleanor pipes up. "She looked pissed at the world. That runs in *our* family," she says proudly. "I remember the doctor holding you up, Cartie, and I asked if babies always looked that mad."

Everyone laughs and the low rumbling of our closest loved ones makes me unbelievably happy. My sister holds our baby close to her chest, humming a lullaby she used to sing to me when I was little. Eleanor stands by her side, her arm around her shoulders as they gaze at the baby together. I have the mental image of Carter and me, gray-haired and smiling, doing the same thing one day.

When the baby is nestled in Eleanor's arms, she asks, "What's her name?"

"Her name is Ellie," Carter says.

"You named my great-niece after me?" Aunt Eleanor looks at us with tears in her eyes.

"That, my dears, is the most impeccable choice, in my humble opinion," Hattie says.

"Oh, so I see you and Carter have realized that greatness should be passed down through generations," Eleanor says, beaming. "I must have left quite an impression on you, *mes chéris*. Let the legacy of greatness continue!"

After everybody has shared their love and congratulations and told us how much they want to stay with us to help with the baby—to coo over and spoil her—the four file out to give us time to bond. I'm exhausted. I can feel my eyelids drooping as Carter takes Ellie in his arms again.

"Rest, babe," he urges, leaning back in his seat. "I've got her. You don't need to worry about anything."

Reaching over, I squeeze his hand. "I know I don't. Not with you around."

Settling into my bed, I let the urge to sleep overtake me, and when I close my eyes, the last thing I see is Carter pressing a soft kiss to our daughter's head.

EPILOGUE: CARTER

I used to think people were full of shit when they talked about being on their feet twenty-four-seven after having a newborn. I really want to give past me a swift kick in the balls, because that level of alertness is no damn joke.

Ellie's quiet most of the time. But when she's hungry, oh, boy, does that little girl have some pipes on her. We have a sassy queen on our hands, that much is sure—and I couldn't love her more.

Even though my business has taken off in the last couple of months, I've put everything on hold for paternity leave. There's no way I'm going to juggle phone calls in between feedings and diaper changes. And, truth be told, I have no inclination for juggling of *any* kind. Unless it's for my little one's entertainment. All I want to do is be there with my girls.

Aunt Eleanor had stayed with us for a few days after Ellie was born, and by the time she next surprises us with her presence, our daughter is three months old, and we've gotten into a routine.

Bancroft Consulting is growing faster than I'd anticipated. Once word got around that I was on my own, it seemed like every client I'd

Epilogue: Carter

ever had had come out of the woodwork, wanting my expertise on their projects. I find myself glad to represent them.

Harbor View Developments were my first major clients. Once they heard that Huxley had "retired" and I'd left, they were concerned about their account. During a phone call, Bradley had organically let it slip that I was starting my own business, and they'd called me that same day, wanting to hire me. So had other clients.

Bradley had a challenging time keeping a straight face when he delivered the news. He was amused by the entire thing. So was Bernie.

The rest of the board? Not so much.

Harbor View had opened many doors. In fact, things have been going so well that I have a couple of realtors on standby for when I'm ready to look for office space. Of course, Eden and I enjoy working from home, and we're more than happy to take our daughter with us wherever we go. At least until she's old enough to attend preschool.

I've never appreciated Hattie more than over the last few weeks when she'll show up at our door, offering to watch the baby while we catch up on sleep or go out to dinner for a date.

Eden is already referring to her as Auntie Hattie, and not just for Ellie's sake.

On the day Aunt Eleanor's surprise flight touches down, Eden has a doctor's appointment. I've just put Ellie in her basinet in the living room when the front door opens, and Auntie makes her grand entrance.

"Cartie! *Mon amour*," she says, arms wide for a hug. However, when I go in, she completely bypasses me and goes straight to the baby. "Where is she? Where is *mon trésor*?"

Without missing a beat, she gathers the baby into her arms and cuddles "her treasure" close. Ellie coos, kicking her feet as the faux fur from my aunt's coat tickles her arms.

In the hallway, I see Hattie dragging all of my aunt's belongings toward her apartment, where Aunt Eleanor will be staying during her visit. "Here, Hattie, let me help you with that," I say, quickly stepping forward.

Epilogue: Carter

"Oh, Eleanor, my dear! One should be tending to one's own belongings!" Hattie chimes to her best friend, even as I swoop in to help.

Eleanor waves her off, too focused on the baby to care.

After I help Hattie take everything inside, the two of us can't help but smile at the scene in front of us. My aunt has made herself comfortable on the sofa, rocking Ellie in her arms. "I knew it!" she exclaims, whipping off her sunglasses that Ellie has been grabbing for and using them to point accusingly at me. "I told you so, didn't I, Hattie?"

"Neither of us possesses the gift of telepathy, you know, love," Hattie says, sitting next to her on the couch with a heavy sigh. "You do tend to make quite a *few* statements, my dear, so I'm afraid you're going to have to narrow it down just a tad."

I sit in the armchair across from them. "What did you say, Auntie?"

"That Eden was pregnant." She has a smug look on her face. "I *knew* it."

"You couldn't have known it then because *we* didn't even know it then."

"Oh, come on, Cartie, we talked about this. You don't have to sugarcoat things on my account. I knew Eden was pregnant the first time I met her."

Hattie and I exchange glances. I have to hide a grin behind my hand and so does Hattie.

"Pardon. Will someone tell me what is so funny?" Auntie asks, annoyed at being left out of the joke.

The front door opens before I can answer, and Eden comes home. "Auntie! Hello!" she exclaims excitedly. "I'm so glad you're here. When did you..." She looks between me and Hattie. Neither of us have stopped grinning. "What's going on here?"

Aunt Eleanor throws up her hand. "Who knows?" she says, bouncing Ellie in her arms. "These two started grinning for no reason."

Eden comes closer, and I pull her next to me, gently rubbing her back. "We're laughing because Aunt Eleanor was just saying that she knew you were pregnant when she visited for the weekend."

Epilogue: Carter

Eden bursts out laughing, and it sends me and Hattie into a giggle fit.

Auntie is not impressed. "Pardon? I want to know what's so hilarious."

"It appears your calculations may be a tad off, my dear." Hattie patiently explains it all like a pro, sorting out the tangle of dates and months that connect her surprise visit to the day of Ellie's birth.

"Oopsie-daisy!" Aunt Eleanor eventually says. "Well, you know, it seems my math skills took a vacation while the stork decided to pay a visit. Forget counting the months, let's instead celebrate this bundle of cuteness!"

That's when Ellie starts crying.

"Duty calls," I announce. Kissing Eden on the forehead to give her a few more moments of rest, I pull away, happy to let her sit there a little longer while I take care of our daughter.

Eleanor hands the baby to me while shaking her head in disbelief that she's crying.

As soon as I lean over her, she stops and smiles up at me, that beautiful sunshine smile I had witnessed on her mother's face a moment ago.

"Come on, little lady," I say, scooping her into my arms. "Let's go see Mommy."

After a while, Hattie politely excuses herself, realizing that her feline companions are also longing for nourishment. Once we all wish her a nice evening, Aunt Eleanor sits next to Eden, who cradles Ellie in her arms as she sways gently and sings to her. Auntie joins in with her, seamlessly blending with Eden's voice and the melody.

I watch them, captivated.

This is one of those moments I will never forget. Having my three special ladies here together is my very own happiness jackpot—past, present, and future merged into a single moment of unforgettable bliss.

Once Ellie is old enough to travel, I want to take her and Eden to France again.

"Cartie," Aunt Eleanor says, turning to look at me.

I slide my arm around her. "Yes, Auntie."

Epilogue: Carter

She reaches up and pinches my cheek, which she hasn't done since I was small. "Seeing you with Eden and Ellie is beautiful. And her name is perfect. Have I mentioned what a brilliant decision it was? Oh, I have? Well, brace yourself for a rerun of my wisdom. Eleanor has such beauty and elegance attached to it."

"It really does."

My aunt nods. "She's going to be just like her aunt. Pretty, witty, beautiful!"

"Nobody is like you."

She looks down at the baby. "See, little one? You'll be just like me. Lucky you."

That's when a knock sounds at the front door.

It's here, a special delivery I'd had made. I excuse myself.

Only a few moments later, I stand on a ladder in the foyer area, carefully hanging the big, framed photo on the wall. With satisfaction, I step back to admire the finished display in the center of our photo wall.

"Eden, Auntie. You can come now."

Eden and my aunt rush into our foyer, their eyes instantly locking onto the new photo hanging on the wall. They burst into laughter, unable to contain their amusement.

"Well, well, well! What do we have here?" Auntie asks in disbelief, putting on her glasses.

"Carter!" Eden laughs, Ellie in her arms. "You actually did it!"

"Oh! *Mon Dieu*! Am I seeing this correctly?" my aunt exclaims, blinking, eyes huge as saucers behind her thick glasses, her jaw still wide open in sheer disbelief. "Cartie! That photo is priceless! It's the *perfect* addition to our little gallery of family memories."

We stand there, gazing at the photo.

It's the one that captures the unforgettable moment when I accidentally stepped on Eden's bridal dress. It'll be one of the first things we and guests will see when they enter, setting a joyful tone. We'll continue to chuckle at the comical mishap forever preserved in that frame.

Epilogue: Carter

"It's a reminder that life's imperfect moments have a way of drawing us closer together," Eden says.

"And a testament to embracing the humorous side of life." My aunt turns to me, a twinkle in her eye. "I guess there's still hope for you. Turns out, you're funny too!"

The End

Thank you for reading my novel. If you enjoyed "A Bossy Roommate," you will LOVE "Faking It with the Billionaire Next Door" from my *Kiss a Billionaire* series. All books in the series are standalones.

I've included a sneak peek on the following pages, so sit back, relax, and enjoy a little taste of what's to come.

FAKING IT WITH THE BILLIONAIRE NEXT DOOR SNEAK PEEK

Miles:
The plan was simple:
Find a suitable girl, move her in for a few months, and pick up my inheritance.
Who's more perfect than my boring next-door neighbor?

Rose:
I have three problems.
#1 I'm stuck in the elevator.
#2 I'm soaking wet from the rain.
#3 HE got in before the doors closed.

Miles Humphries.
My neighbor. The one I HATE.
Arrogant. Cocky. Infuriatingly hot. The biggest jerk I've ever met.
I live next to him on the 17th floor–
and he lives to annoy me.

Imagine my jaw drop when my mortal enemy asks me to be his fake fiancée.

And move in with him.

Together, with my cat.

Complete insanity, right?

Wrong.

Because I agreed.

Excerpt:

Okay, fuck! That did *not* help.

As I stared into her eyes, the massive brown beauties widened in shock. Before I could register what she was going to do, she'd slapped me. Fucking slapped me! Right across my left cheek. *What the hell?* It stung like a motherfucker. I rubbed my face, thinking—strangely enough—about how hot her temper was. I frowned down at her. *God damn.*

"I am *not* a prostitute, you asshole!" She was shouting at me now.

I wanted to laugh. It was so ridiculous it was hilarious. "What? No, I didn't—"

"Get the *fuck* out, Miles!"

The baggy sweater she was wearing hung low across those perfect tits. They bounced as she aggressively pointed at the door. She had on her yoga pants again. Of course, I'd enjoyed the view of her tight ass as I followed her in the apartment. Now, though, I observed the skin across her cleavage growing red. I couldn't help but stand and watch the color of her smooth skin change, crawling up her breasts and along her chest. What did her naked breasts look like?

Whoa there. Maybe not the best time.

I shook myself out of a daze *and* the sudden arousal I felt—and looked back at her fuming face.

"Out!" she repeated, her arm still pointing, her tits still bouncing.

Her tantrum was distracting, because she was so small and petite, and her tits trembled beautifully. Her nipples were puckered, pressing eagerly into the soft material of her sweater, and pointing right at me. Who knew it'd be so sexy when a small woman acted tough?

Trying to rectify the situation, I shook my head, and said calmly, "I didn't mean it like that, geez. Chill, woman. I wouldn't expect anything physical from you. Well, unless *you* want to get physical, that is."

Maybe I shouldn't have said the last part.

Her arm dropped. Her facial expression was priceless. I knew she'd blow her top any second. The redness had spread up her neck and reached her cheeks, which I had to admit, looked pretty fucking cute.

She took in a shaky breath to calm herself, before beginning her rant. "You've insulted me, you... you prick."

"Prick?" I arched a brow in question.

"Yeah. I'm not the kind of woman you want. You already know that. And I *certainly* don't want a man like you. You already know that, too. So, why don't you go and proposition one of your chicks? Huh? I'm sure they'd *only* be thrilled!"

Of course, I'd already considered that.

It would've *definitely* been easier.

But the problem was I needed somebody who appeared responsible. And believable. She was the perfect candidate. Let's face it, she was the *only* candidate.

Dad would buy her as my fiancée, for sure.

Because the good thing here was, Rose wasn't only responsible, she had good traits, too.

She was smart, well educated, maybe even classy. She had a high-level job in marketing, if I wasn't mistaken, so she wasn't a stranger to our family's lifestyle. There wouldn't be a problem with her accompanying me to events and being able to participate in conversations. Her proximity was also perfect, because she already lived here, and I wouldn't have to move in another woman—this was one of the best parts of all.

I wanted to avoid any kind of emotional mess as much as possible.

This needed to be a clean and smooth operation.

In. Out. Done.

However, now she was getting rather annoying with her shrieking. Where did the Ice Queen go? Things were escalating really, really quickly. *For fuck's sake, calm down. I've only asked you a simple question. Fiery was good and hot—better than lifeless, frigid and dry for sure—but don't fucking burn me.*

"Relax. Look, if I ask any of *my chicks*," I shrugged, keeping my voice down, "they'll just get their hopes up, and I don't need *that* bullshit in my life."

Silence.

"You think love and romance are bullshit?" She crossed her arms, arching a brow, clearly annoyed by my response.

"Yeah, I do. I need somebody who knows I'm not going to marry her."

Rose gave me a narrow-eyed look, with her mouth hanging half-open. "Are you serious?" She seemed insulted again. "And you thought I'd be *totally* fine going along with your ruse, only to be fake-dumped at the end of it?"

"Yeah," I said in exasperation.

What was so unclear about it? I couldn't understand this woman. Did she *not* get that I only needed her to fucking *pretend*?

She stared at me with a blank expression.

Then it hit me. "Oh, I get it," I said. "You're *jealous*." I stepped back and nodded, having figured her out.

"I am *not*," she shrieked, her pitch rising even higher.

"Yeah," I said, smirking. "You are."

"Jealous of what?!"

"You hear those girls having the time of their lives in *my* bed while you lay here all alone in *your* bed, and that gets to you."

Her mouth dropped open completely this time. "That's *insane*. I don't give a *shit* about your sexcapades!"

I moved closer to her, so close I could almost feel her pokey nipples against my chest. But I made a point not to get *too* close that I accidentally touched her. I lowered my voice. "Maybe, if you weren't such a rude cold shrew, you could get laid once in a while. I mean, by the looks of it,"

I circled my finger around her, letting her know I was talking about her tantrum, "you haven't had a dick in you for a *very* long time."

Rose fumed.

If death stares could result in injury, I'd have two black eyes.

And no dick.

The color in her cheeks grew more inflamed as she stared at me in bewilderment. "Are you *fucking* kidding me right now?"

Okay, enough was enough. She'd dropped another f-bomb.

We were getting nowhere.

Judging by the current trend, there was no way to win this.

Had I really overstepped? Not really. Well, maybe.

Clearly, I'd pissed her off, and she needed to calm down—without me in her space. I didn't have the energy, nor the will to deal with anymore of this high-pitched shit. I had to protect my eardrums. I had my own stresses to take care of. I had important matters on my plate. Billion-fucking-dollar matters to be precise.

Especially given that she'd now shot down the only plan I had so far.

Besides, I didn't want to risk another slap.

And, I wanted to keep my dick.

With a deep breath, I attempted a somewhat peaceful goodbye. "You know what, don't say anything now. Calm down, calm your tits, calm your lady bits, and think about it. You know where to find me." I pivoted on my heel and headed out the door.

She followed, and before she slammed it shut behind me, she hissed, "I don't need to think about *anything*. The answer is *no*! *Never*! *Ever*! Not even over my dead body!"

End of the sneak peek.

Grab Faking It with the Billionaire Next Door on Amazon.

THE CEO ENEMY SNEAK PEEK

I just made the worst mistake of my life.
I kissed my horrible neighbor.
Okay, maybe it was more like a tipsy slip-up.
But let's clarify one thing: he definitely did NOT kiss me back.

And thank goodness for that, because he's everything I despise.
Grumpy.
Arrogant.
The neighbor from hell.

But wait, it gets worse.
He's not just any neighbor—he's a cutthroat hotel tycoon, now a major shareholder in my little hotel.
And guess who's stuck working side by side?

To make matters worse, he has this absurd notion he can buy me out.

As if his towering 6-foot-2 frame, those piercing green eyes, and his annoyingly cute winks could sway me.

Fat chance, buddy. My "No dating CEOs" policy is rock-solid.

I'm immune to the best kiss I've ever had.
I will not—I repeat, will not—succumb to his ability to render me breathless with every (dirty) word.
And handing over my panties when he asks? Not happening (again).

And as for falling for NYC's wealthiest and most off-limits bachelor? Yeah, right. Like that's ever going to... Oh, crap.

Excerpt:

I knock on the door. "Hello?"

I know someone is home because I can hear the TV news. There's some movement, but it doesn't seem like they're coming to answer.

After a few seconds, I knock again, only louder this time.

"Hello? Anyone home? I need help!" I knock repeatedly. The door opens a second later. "Hi, there, sorry to bother y—*whoa.*"

I can't believe I said that out loud, but I'm not even a little embarrassed about it.

He towers over me. *The* hottest man I've ever seen in my damn life.

This man is *at least* six foot one, rippling muscles, thick dark hair, chiseled jaw (under that thick weekend stubble), bright-green eyes piercing into my soul...and not a damn stitch of clothing on. Yeah. He's standing there completely naked. And here I am thinking that me in my small-ish pink towel, wearing nothing underneath, is weird. My eyes keep straying south—they have a mind of their own. I can't help but catch more than just a glimpse of the view below the horizon.

Yep. There's his dick.

Believe me, I'm as surprised as anyone else here. Even in its "relaxed" state, it's long and thick. Or is he half-hard? Because the size is quite impressive. Easily eight inches. Maybe nine. I'm staring...and disbelieving...and staring...until I realize what I'm doing and quickly avert my gaze back to his face.

My new neighbor looks alarmed, mad even, as if he's rushed to the door without bothering to dress.

His plump lips turn down in a frown as he stares at my face and the thick yogurt mask I slathered on this morning.

"What is it? What's wrong?" he demands, eyes narrowed.

Crap. Why am I here again?

Right, I'm locked out. "Um, sorry to bother you, but, um, I locked myself out of my apartment," I say, gesturing toward my door and the blueberry pancakes I ordered. As I speak, I realize how difficult it is to have a regular conversation when you've just caught an eyeful of all *that*.

"Well," he huffs, "unless you slipped a spare key under my door when I wasn't looking, then I'm not sure how I can help you." He arches an angry-looking brow.

"Er...do you maybe want to put clothes on?"

"I'd rather close the door if you don't actually need help," he grumbles, already in the process of swinging it shut.

"Wait! Please don't! I really do need your help."

I manage to keep my gaze trained on his, mind still reeling. He's a stranger who's incredibly pissed off that I'm bothering him. I better be quick. Also, my pancakes are getting cold, so I really need to get back inside my place.

"So, Ms. Lockout Queen, do you need me to call the super or something?" he asks, scrutinizing me the whole time.

What a jerk. "No, thanks." *Mr. Grumpy King*, I think, but I don't say it. "Actually, our balconies are right next to each other. I was wondering if you would let me in so I could climb over."

"No."

I blink a few times. "I'm sorry?"

"I said no."

"It will only take a second." A glop of yogurt starts to slowly slide down my forehead. Oh no, not now, please not now! I silently plead with it to stick to my eyebrow. *He won't let me in if I start dripping yogurt everywhere.*

"It doesn't matter."

All right. I understand that I barged into this grump's morning while he was obviously indisposed, and he has every right to be annoyed that this random chick yelled that she needed help, then ogled his man-berries. That's on me for panicking and not keeping my eyes firmly locked on his face. However, he doesn't have to be an absolute *chump-head* about it. Lottie had understated this guy's irritability. I crown him the Emperor Extraordinaire of Grumps, the undisputed grumpiness monarch.

"Look, I'm sorry we started off on the wrong foot," I say, trying to take the high road, while casually flicking at my eyebrow, ensuring the gooey disaster stays put. I'm not going to get anywhere with this guy if he's pissed off at me. I gesture to his nakedness and then to my towel. "Clearly, neither of us had our 'social batteries' charged for this early-morning rendezvous. But I promise, it really will only take a second for me to hop over to my place. Then I'll leave you alone."

He gives me a stern look. "Climbing between balconies is reckless and unsafe."

"I'll be fine."

"And if you're not? I'm not going to be held responsible if something happens to you."

"Fine," I say, attempting to keep the exasperation from my tone. "If I promise not to sue you if I get hurt, then will you let me in?"

He studies me for a moment, and it's hard to get a read on him. His expression holds nothing but annoyance, though I'm hopeful I've gotten through to him, considering he hasn't slammed the door in my face yet. I offer him a bright smile.

There's a moment's pause before he mutters something under his breath and steps to the side. "Fine. Come in."

Thank God! I want to do a little happy dance, but well, I'm trying not to lose my towel.

Before entering his apartment, I grab my food delivery and give my towel an extra little tuck for good measure. As soon as I take that first step inside, *plop* goes the yogurt—not this again, and *OMG*—I catch it just in time. Then, discreetly as possible, I wipe it on my towel. I don't think he noticed.

Crisis averted... for now. I'm in!

The place looks minimalistic. Sleek. Somehow bachelor-esque with all the black furniture and monochrome artwork. I spot a black helmet. He rides a motorcycle? Hot!

At once, I realize he was exercising. I notice his treadmill and weights near the balcony, and there's a pile of workout clothes on the floor. He must have been on his way to the shower when I knocked. I should have known he works out. With that body, it's safe to say he's not the "lounge around all day" type.

"Just a second," he mutters, storming down the hall, and that's when I catch a glimpse of his other side, and oh, boy, it's just as appealing as the first. I'm pretty sure I could bounce a quarter off his ass if I had the chance.

Awkwardly, I stay put, switching my weight from one foot to the other, playing with the paper bag in my hands. He returns wearing a simple pair of black boxer briefs. They cover his assets, but honestly, the outline still makes quite the statement.

"The balcony is this way." He motions with his inked arm for me to follow him.

Dear God, his back is rippling with muscles, something I missed when checking him out below the waist. How does someone get that well defined? I don't have the energy for exercise—unbelievable, I know.

I tear my gaze away to focus. When did I become so easily distracted by a man? True, it's been a while since I've had any action, but I didn't think it had been long enough for my knees to just go all wobbly in the presence of a tall, chiseled, tattooed, but let's not forget, rather chilly... let's be clear: masterpiece of grouchiness.

Once we step outside, reality slaps me in the face, and I wince. Crap. The balconies are a little farther apart than I originally thought. Not ridiculously far, only a couple of feet. The distance is still manageable. However, it does make this whole thing a tad riskier. Setting my bag of pancakes down, I move to the edge to get a closer look, trying to figure out what my best move might be.

"We're really high up," my neighbor says. "You know what, I'm going to call the super."

"Nonono, absolutely not necessary. I got this. Easy-peasy. Just...stay there in case I slip or something."

"I thought you said you could handle this?" He sounds even more irritated than before.

I glance back at him to find he hasn't followed me out onto the balcony. He stands in the doorway, tattooed arms crossed, that frown still etched in place. Geez, doesn't this guy have any other facial expressions?

"I can," I tell him. "Doesn't mean I'm immune to the effects of gravity. It might be easier if you come out and spot me. Just in case."

He shakes his head, a protest clearly on his tongue. When he notices that I'm already maneuvering my right foot over the railing, he quietly steps out and moves closer to me. "I got you."

The weight in his voice gives me a warm feeling. My heart flutters as he draws near. Deep down, I know that if anything were to happen, he would have my back. At least in this crazy endeavor. With those muscles, he'd definitely be ready to snap me back up!

But let's be real here. I can already sense it. This is shaping up to be the most awkward moment of my life.

As I carefully maneuver my other leg over the railing, I try to keep my breathing even and focus on *him*, the grim culmination in front of me, in an attempt to avoid looking down. I stand on the other side of the railing, gripping the metal so tight my knuckles turn white.

"Talk to me," my neighbor says.

At the sound of his deep, but surprisingly calming voice, I take a slow breath. "Okay..."

"Now, come back. Careful there. Don't think about the height."

Instantly, I have the urge to look down, and I have to fight it. "Easier said than done."

"Hey, look at me."

I lift my gaze to meet his green eyes. I have never seen eyes with such an enchanting shade reminiscent of lush pine trees, and it takes my thoughts away from my precarious situation. I could easily lose myself in the depths of them...

"You got this," he says. "Slowly. No need to rush."

Nodding, I take another deep breath, tearing my gaze away from the most distracting male specimen I've ever encountered. I figure it will be *hard* to pay attention to what I'm doing if I'm ogling him. Rotating, I face my balcony, and I'm slapped with a gust of wind that nearly sends me flying. The shriek that escapes is foreign to me, practically enough to make me backtrack and say, "Screw it." The last thing I want to do is go *splat*, almost naked, on a Manhattan sidewalk.

No. Thank. You.

"Whoa there," he says, grabbing me like his life depends on it. "Come back. Now."

I can't suppress a surprised squeak, my heart fluttering at the unexpected closeness. "Whoa, buddy, I barely know you," I tease.

But after a moment's pause, with his strong arms enveloping me from behind, I think I'm good.

I can't stop now.

I'm almost there.

It'll be way easier to follow through instead of turning back at this point. Cautiously, I stick my foot out until I feel the ledge. I find it easily and, in one smooth movement, I step over and grab my railing. Dear God, if anybody were to look up, they'd be treated to a firsthand view of what not to wear on a balcony.

Phewwww.

My adrenaline is through the roof. I'm proud of myself as I straddle the railing. Almost there.

Ufff. Thank goodness.

When I glance back at my neighbor, he still has that serious expression he's been sporting since he opened the door. But I notice his shoulders slump and some of the tension leaves his body.

"See?" I say with a grin, lifting my other leg over. "Ha! Piece of cake.

Told ya!" I shrug, waving it off like I've been doing this all day, every day. "Call me Lockout Queen by day, and Balcony Spider-Woman by night," I joke.

I'm too focused on my triumph to notice that my towel has become loose. The next thing I know, I'm standing on my balcony all right, with my towel on the floor and *everything* on display for a complete stranger.

Yes.

I'm talking tits and delicate lady bits, officially making their debut. A balcony drop and a towel flop! Way to keep things interesting, life.

Seriously, though: piece of cake, *my ass*.

My neighbor's eyebrows shoot up.

For the first time since we've met, that surly exterior cracks.

End of the excerpt.

The CEO Enemy is a scorching hot grumpy-sunshine, rivals-to-lovers, fake relationship, workplace romance. It is a complete standalone. Definitely for adult readers only. "The CEO Enemy" is available on Amazon.

ALSO BY JOLIE DAY

Faking It in NYC Series

A steamy hot pretend-relationship series. Grumpy, moody, and licking-lips hot CEOs meet the sassy, sunshiny goddess. Do you love the fake relationship trope? Yes? Then you'll love this romance series. *All novels can be read as single books.*

One Bossy Date

From fake date to fake fiancée to fake pregnancy. All in one night. Who's the guy? My grumpy boss.

(Zoe and Anders)

Real Fake Husband

He's my childhood bully. I didn't plan to see him again, let alone marry him. But his grandmother had other plans: She left us a significant inheritance. The catch? We have to tie the knot and live in her tiny NYC apartment. For a month. With just one bed.

(Josie and Callum)

The CEO Enemy

I just made the worst mistake of my life.

I kissed my horrible neighbor.

Okay, maybe it was more like a tipsy slip-up.

But let's clarify one thing: he definitely did NOT kiss me back.

(Jess and Sean)

A Bossy Roommate

That one-night stand with my boss? Total mistake.

I should have swiftly escaped, but no, not me—I moved in with him instead.

(Eden and Carter)

~

Kiss a Billionaire Series

In this steamy-hot series, alpha billionaires working in the same company will catch your eye and drive you wild. Just some good old fashioned romance, comedy goodness, and sexy fun. *All novels can be read as single books.*

Crushing on my Billionaire Best Friend

She's my best friend. Of course, I'd never think about touching Laney. Not today. Not tomorrow. Not ever. Then she moves into my penthouse.

(Laney and Oliver)

Faking It with the Billionaire Next Door

He's my next-door neighbor. My mortal enemy. Cocky. Infuriatingly hot. The biggest jerk I've ever met. Imagine my jaw drop when he asks me to be his fake fiancée. Imagine his jaw drop when I agree.

(Rose and Miles)

Charming My Broody Billionaire Boss

He's the devil himself: Damon Copeland (he practically carries a pitchfork). He's the top dog at my father's company and my brother's best friend. Oh, and someone I *accidentally* slept with.

(Aria and Damon)

Assistant to the Billionaire CEO

I was madly in love with my brother's best friend.

Until he broke my heart. Now he's my new boss: Ace Windsor. Tall. Difficult.

Insanely gorgeous. And insanely strict. Never run in the hallway. Never loiter. Never be late. Luckily, I'm Miss Punctuality. Until I'm running late.

(Stella and Ace)

Blind Date with the Billionaire Doc

First, Dr. Jerk ghosted me.

Now, I'm pregnant, and he's the daddy.

Skip ahead 9 months, and surprise! Guess who's delivering our baby?

(Lizzie and Dillan)

∽

Oh Billionaires! Series

The plots are set in New York City—the Big Apple (I hope you're ready for a juicy bite). If you love a man in a business suit during the day and biker gear by night, this series is for you. *All novels can be read as single books.*

Billionaire BOSS: Secret Baby

I hate him—the man who'd taken my v-card. Now, I'm supposed to work with him–*for* him. What's worse, he doesn't even recognize me! What if he finds out that I have a son...his son?

SOLD: Highest Bidder

I bought her at an auction. My best friend's sister.

Billionaire Baby DADDY

OMG...I'm pregnant with a billionaire's baby!

Billionaire CEO: Fake Girlfriend

He's my worst enemy. He's about to acquire my family business. But, he's got a solution for me: My company in exchange for an *arrangement*. He needs a fake girlfriend, and I fit the bill. Fine, I'll pose as his girlfriend. Problem is–What if I don't want to stop pretending?

BOSS: The Wolf

You ever wake up completely naked next to your boss? Alpha AF Joel Embry isn't exactly Prince Charming. In fact, they call him The Wolf. A sharp suit by day—a tight T-shirt and jeans roaring the streets by night. Get in line for the hottest night of your live.

CONNECT WITH JOLIE DAY

From a sexy bad-boy hero and laugh-out-loud moments to the happily-ever-after. If you stay up way too late reading sizzling hot romance novels, you've come to the right place.

Jolie Day writes contemporary romance and romantic comedies. She has a soft spot for writing about the swoon-worthy man who wears a business suit during the day and revs up his biker gear at night. He's got a quick wit, a devil-may-care attitude, and he'd go to the ends of the earth to win her heart. He's like a knight in shining armor—except instead of a horse, he's got a Ducati.

Ready for new releases?
Subscribers to Jolie Day's mailing list will be the first to know when a new book hits the shelves. You'll also enjoy delightful surprises and exclusive opportunities to read (or listen to) new releases before anybody else:
www.joliedayauthor.com/newsletter

Read More from Jolie Day on
Jolie Day's Website:
www.joliedayauthor.com

Printed in Great Britain
by Amazon